Alice Peterson's first book, *A Will to Win* – now republished as *Another Alice* – is her personal story of her tennis days (she was one of the top 10 juniors in the country), followed by her fight to beat rheumatoid arthritis. Since then she has written six novels, including *Monday to Friday Man*, the dog-walking romantic comedy that knocked *Fifty Shades of Grey* off the top of the eBook chart. She lives in west London with her Lucas Terrier, Mr Darcy.

Also by Alice Peterson

Another Alice

M'Coben, Place of Ghosts

Letters From My Sister

Monday to Friday Man

Ten Years On

By My Side

One Step Closer to You

The Things We Do For Love

YOU, ME
AND
HIM

ALICE PETERSON

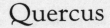

First published in Great Britain in 2007 by Black Swan
Published in ebook in 2012 by Quercus
This paperback version published in 2016 by

Quercus Editions Ltd
Carmelite House
50 Victoria Embankment
London EC4Y 0DZ

An Hachette UK company

A CIP catalogue record for this book is available
from the British Library

PB ISBN 978 1 78648 061 3
EBOOK ISBN 978 1 78206 323 0

10 9 8 7 6 5 4 3 2 1

Typeset by Jouve (UK), Milton Keynes

Printed and bound in Great Britain by Clays Ltd, St Ives plc

To Elaine and Sue

1

My legs and feet shiver in the draught. The noise sounds distant to begin with and then I realise it's right in my ear. 'GET UP!'

It can't be the morning?

Finn and I were bickering again last night. He hadn't bothered to refill the filter jug and, on top of that, he'd left a teabag in the sink. 'You only have to stretch an arm out to put it into the bin,' I had demonstrated, holding the little stained and wrinkled bag in my hand. 'Look! Pop! In it goes.' I am becoming an old fishwife and I'm only thirty-one.

'Are teabags the only topic of our conversation now?'

'Only if you don't put them in the bin.'

'Why are you so crotchety? Is it that time of the month?'

'Shut up.' I didn't tell Finn I am three days late. 'Anyway, what's for supper? I'm starving.' Finn and I have made a decision that he cooks once a week, on a Saturday.

'I'll cook us some steaks, won't take long,' he'd said, voice as light as a breeze.

'And chips?' I have been craving potatoes recently. Maybe I *am* pregnant?

Finn would love to have another baby. He is close to his twin brother Ed, and would love George, our six-year-old son, to have a playmate. I would be happy to stop with one. I'm an only child and have a close bond to my parents. It is true to say that Clarky, my oldest friend from home, was my surrogate brother. Without him, I would have been lonely.

A small hand tugs at my cotton nightshirt again. 'My brain won't let me sleep anymore,' George says.

Finn gets out of bed boasting that he can survive on the same amount of sleep as Margaret Thatcher. 'Wake up!' George bellows in my ear again.

'Don't shout.'

'We might be getting old but we're not deaf,' Finn adds.

I yawn. 'That's something to look forward to.'

Finn is stretching out his arms, circling his shoulders and cracking his knuckles into place like he does every morning. He then starts to sing the familiar lyrics to Matt Bianco's song 'Get Out of Your Lazy Bed'.

George joins in, somewhat flat.

I sit up and rub my eyes. I have a weird feeling in my stomach. I was having the strangest dream that I was marrying Clarky in a hot air balloon. I am terrified of heights and Finn of all people was officiating, dressed in a long dark robe and white collar, and finding the whole event inappropriately funny. He was roaring with laughter in between the vows. I smile to myself, remembering that when Finn and I announced our engagement Clarky wrote all the lovely things that everyone else writes in a congratulations card, but then, in tiny, almost illegible writing at the bottom, he wrote, 'Remember, there are three of us in this marriage'.

I pick up the clock, trying to shake the dream out of my head: 7.19.

Finn ties the cord of his dressing gown into a clumsy loop around his waist and then briefly kisses me on the cheek.

'Stop sexing her, Dad.' George crosses his arms and waits impatiently.

Finn and I look at each other in disbelief before both laughing. Where did he get that one from? School is like the lucky dip. You don't know what expressions they'll come home with.

'Mum's cross because I said the word sex,' George says.

'Well, I reckon we should go make her one of our finest cooked Sunday breakfasts,' Finn suggests, and they leave the bedroom like two happy children, George clinging on to Finn's dressing-gown cord and pretending his father's a horse. 'Giddy-up, Dad!'

Sunday morning is officially my lie-in morning. Finn and George like to spend Sundays together doing their 'boy' things. This is another resolution Finn and I made six months ago. He needs to spend more time with his son. They cook breakfast and then Finn takes him to the car-boot sale. They love George at the car-boot because he spends all his pocket money within minutes, 'bargain-hunting', as he calls it. He's called the Whizz Kid by all the car owners. Last time George came home with a mustard yellow-coloured teapot in the shape of a house. 'Look, Mum, look!' I'd opened the lid and it was full of cobwebs, with a few squashed flies lying on the bottom. 'It was only ten pence,' George informed me as he shoved it back into its flimsy white plastic bag and then placed it on his bed-room floor, alongside all the other junk he'd bought from weeks before.

I would like more time to paint at the weekends. Mum tells me that when I was a child I was easy to look after because all I wanted to do was sit at my little white table with its glossy tablecloth and paint pictures of stars, people, our dogs, thatched cottages, the horses in the field, anything I set my eyes on.

I have turned George's old nursery, that used to be div-ided from our bathroom by white sliding doors, into my art studio. I have a narrow glass desk with my silver lap-top on it for graphic design work. Above it is a small shelf with art and design books, a photograph of Tatiana – Tiana for short, my oldest school friend – in a leather frame, and beside the frame is a large green frog which holds a ten-pence coin in its mouth. Mr Frog promises good fortune in business apparently. I have to kiss him each morning and take the coin out of his mouth at night to allow him to rest. It's a ritual Tiana taught me and which she practises religiously. I often forget.

On the wall is a year planner that I designed, decorated with pretty silver shells. Each day is plotted out with neat boxes representing the meetings I have to go to. But the thing I love most is the old wooden case filled with tubes of oil paints. My studio is like a therapy box. If I had to sum up our home in one word it would be 'clutter', but this room is my own private ordered world where I don't allow even Finn and George to enter. When I sit down in front of my easel I escape into my picture.

I lie back and open my paperback. '**Unputdownable**' and '**Compelling**' is written in bold type on the back of the jacket, which makes me smile. It's been by my bedside for three weeks and I have reached page fifteen.

'Morning, Rocky,' I hear George say. Rocky is our wire-haired sausage dog. 'Can't reach, Dad.' Our kitchen is designed for tall people with high cupboards that George needs to climb on to a chair and then stand on tiptoe to reach. Pots and pans hang on a rail above the cooker. A few minutes later . . . 'Dad, what do I do now?'

'Stand back – careful!' We don't let him anywhere near the hot stove. 'They need more stirring. Remember, not too runny.'

'They're ready, Dad.'

'No, they're not.' I can envisage Finn showing George the sloppy egg mixture as it drips off the wooden spoon.

'Can I put the eggs on the plates now?'

'They aren't READY.' Finn's sunny tone is already beginning to lose its edge. 'Listen.'

A split second later: 'Are they ready now?'

'George! Don't let Rocky lick the butter, get him off the table.' I don't feel so hungry now. Rocky yaps.

'Butter the toast, that's your job.' Finn pops four pieces in the slots and pushes the lever down. The timer starts to tick.

Twenty seconds later: 'Don't force the thingy . . .'

'It's done. Look!'

'Only on one side. Put it . . .'

'Done!'

'. . . back in.'

'Mum won't notice.' I can hear George dropping the knife on to the floor and picking it up again.

'That's enough butter. Remember what I told you about cholesterol?'

'Boring.'

'Too much fat clogs up our heart.' Finn is a cardiologist.

'Boring.' George starts to hum loudly.

'You've only buttered one . . . oh, it doesn't matter.' I can picture Finn's frustrated expression. 'Careful,' he says. 'Whoops! Rocky can have that bit.' Rocky is as fat as a pork pie because his diet consists of all the food that misses George's plate or mouth.

'I'm a good cook, aren't I, Dad?'

'Gordon Ramsay would be proud. OK, Mum likes marmalade on her toast.'

'She likes Marmite and marmalade. I love Mum.'

'So do I. George, it's all over your fingers!' Finn is now laughing wearily. 'What are we going to do with you, Mrs Bourbon?' George is called Mrs Bourbon because those are his favourite biscuits; Finn is Mrs Jammie Dodger.

'I want a brother, Dad. Mrs Jammie D, how many spoons of coffee?'

'Three, dear. STOP!'

'When will I get one? Everyone at school has one.'

'Don't press the plunger down!' There is now despair in Finn's tone. 'Soon,' he answers George's question. 'Sugar . . . bacon's burning . . . Trying to do too many things at once, aren't we, Mrs Bourbon?'

'I'd like a brother, don't like girls.'

'You'll like them when you're older.'

'Why?'

'You just will.'

'Why?'

'Because a life without girls is like . . . a life without biscuits.'

'Without biscuits?' George gasps incredulously. 'I wouldn't like that.'

I enjoy listening to their conversations. I can hear a frying pan being chucked into the sink, the hot grease spitting in the cold water, smoke rising. I can smell grease, bacon fat and eggs. I feel sick. I am going to be sick. I rush into the bathroom and kneel down by the loo, hand held over my stomach. What did I eat last night? Did Finn cook the steaks properly? I can't be pregnant, can I?

Glasses and mugs slide across the tray as George attempts to carry it upstairs to the bedroom. I run back into the bedroom and take my position on the bed, placing a pillow behind my back and trying to look like a queen. The door handle is being turned, the tray rattles again with everything on it. 'Careful, George,' Finn warns.

'Queen Josie! Wheels on meals.' Rocky follows him, scuttling behind. Rocky's legs are about an inch long. He's often mistaken for a large rat. George informs me I need to buy him a tartan coat to keep him warm in the winter.

'How delicious,' I act out, licking my dry lips when he puts the tray on to my lap. George's stripy pyjamas are stained with orange juice and Marmite. 'But I can't eat all of this, you must have some.' George shakes his head adamantly. 'I'm the Queen's maid,' he states proudly.

Finn takes his plate of eggs and returns to his side of the bed.

George sits in between us. I pick out one of Rocky's wiry hairs that sits crookedly on top of my toast. 'Mmm,' I murmur with pretend pleasure. 'Delicious!' To wash the taste out of my mouth I take a sip of coffee. It's as dark as liquorice and most of the coffee grains are still in it. 'Did you bring the paper up?' I ask Finn, almost choking.

'I'll get it,' says George, springing up like a rabbit and leaving a trail of sticky toast crumbs behind him.

When he is out of earshot, 'Want some?' I offer Finn.

He shakes his head and I cram it into his mouth. We start to laugh. 'Eat it!'

'Josie!' Finn shakes his head. 'I'm feeling a bit sick, actually.'

'Really?' I'm smiling.

'Thanks for the sympathy.'

'Those steaks must have been off.' Relief floods through me. Of course there is a simple explanation.

'I don't feel like taking George to the car-boot . . .'

'No way! You're going. I'm meeting Tiana.'

'*Prickman?*' Finn loves saying her surname. Tiana would like to meet someone just to rid herself of it.

'Come on, Finn, eat.' We both look at the messy plate and then try not to laugh as we give a large piece of toast to Rocky instead. 'By the way, I liked the bit about a life without girls being like a life without biscuits.'

'What's a life without men?'

'A life without men is a . . .' I purse my mouth, thinking '. . . life without weather.'

'Great,' he says flatly.

'Think about it. We'd have nothing to talk about if we

couldn't discuss the weather, would we? Makes life far more interesting.'

George crashes through the door with the newspaper and all the supplements fall out and scatter across the wooden floor.

After breakfast Finn takes the tray downstairs.

'Mum!' I hear George shout. 'Look!'

I rush into his bathroom. What's he done this time? He's wearing Finn's snorkel and flippers and is pretending to dive for treasure. His toy soldiers bob up and down in the water with him.

Another normal morning in the Greenwood household.

Normal to us, that is.

2

I think you can always judge a day by the supermarket trolley you choose.

I am late.

I fetch my trolley. When I picked George up from school this afternoon his thin arms were covered in black smudges. Ms Miles, his teacher, had met me at the school gates, saying in a deliberately loud voice that George had stolen her fountain pen in class and flicked ink all over himself and her new skirt. 'I've given him a detention,' she'd stated, the other mothers staring, 'and four black clouds.' If the children are good they get gold stars on the 'happy side' of a chart. If naughty, they get black clouds on the 'sad side'.

I'd smiled, so relieved that it was nothing to do with bullying. 'Mrs Greenwood,' she had said with a scowl. I could almost see fire flaring through her nostrils. 'This kind of behaviour must be taken seriously.'

George runs ahead of me now. 'No dramas. You can have one toy or sweet, that's the deal,' I warn him.

It's been nearly a week now . . . It could be stress? The run-up to Christmas is always stressful. I overheard one of the school-run mums saying that she hadn't made the Christmas cake yet. Last year she'd forgotten to put the brandy in. The best part, she'd claimed with a bark of laughter. Where's George gone? I look around frantically. Then I hear the curtain of the passport booth being pulled back.

'George! Come here!'

It could be that I'm anxious about the new headmaster at George's school. He starts next January. I fret about his teachers, too. If they don't understand him and his behaviour, it makes life impossible. Everyone is talking about the sudden resignation of Mrs Liddell. She had a nervous breakdown.

I am never late.

I have a *hectic* job. I'm not complaining as I love my work, but it can be demanding at times. I work for a design agency called Gem Communications and my boss is called Ruby Gold, a high-powered, pinstripe-suit-wearer who uses so much face powder that by the evening it has cracked like a clay mask above her top lip. Ruby exudes charm in a voice as smooth as caramel, but I am aware that I only have to put one foot wrong to be looking for another job. I can see her now in her executive leather chair, shiny blonde hair tucked neatly behind diamond-studded ears, telling me that Ruby Gold expects: 'One hundred and ten per cent *at all times.*' She has just employed a young South African girl called Natalie. We used to work in Ruby's home, on the top floor of her spacious minimalist house, but as the company is expanding we need more than one room so we have moved into a modern office block in Hammersmith. If Ruby knew I was pregnant . . . I can't think about it.

I am *always* on time. My period strikes as faithfully as Big Ben. I get out my list. 'I love you if you buy me some tobacco, Jammie D's and gin,' Finn wrote on our kitchen blackboard this morning. I want to try to be prepared for Christmas this year. He and I are having all the family in London: my parents, Finn's mother and her boyfriend, and of course Finn's granny, so I need to be super-organised like the other mums and make my cake and Christmas pudding a month before. I can remember my mother making a cake every year and the best part was always when she gave me her leather handbag to rummage through and find some five-pence coins to add to the fruit mixture. Her handbag had exciting hiding places for lipsticks and powder compacts, and she always had lots of parking change in the zip compartment of her wallet. Carefully, I'd cover the silver coins in foil whilst saying a prayer that they would all land in my bowl.

'I want three pounds, Mum.' George pokes his head out of the booth and sticks his tongue out at me.

'I want never gets. OUT, George.'

'Please?' He continues to pull the pale blue curtain back and forth, scratching the fabric against the rail. Then he sits on the stool and starts pressing the control buttons haphazardly.

I try to manoeuvre the trolley. 'If you don't get out now there'll be no Slush Puppy.' Finn gave me a book entitled, *If You Behave, So Will Your Child*. The author, her cheery face beaming from the jacket, tells me that I must not use blackmail or bribery in order to make my child behave; I am no better than a child myself if I adopt these methods.

George races past me into the fruit and vegetable aisle.

I push my trolley and it moves like a crab. I have to make a decision. Do I turn round and get another one or do I persevere?

George is now out of sight.

I am never late.

I remember that half-witted conversation I'd had with the receptionist at my GP's surgery a month ago, just before staying with my parents for the weekend. 'I'm afraid we have no appointments today, Mrs Greenwood. Please try again tomorrow morning at eight-thirty.'

Obediently I had, only to listen to the engaged tone, over and over again, like a funeral march in my ears. When I'd finally got through at 9.10: 'I'm afraid the doctor's full up for this morning. If you ring at . . .'

'But I'm leaving today. Can't he fit me in? I've been try- ing constantly for the past forty minutes.'

'The surgery has been *exceptionally* busy this morning.'

'All I need is a prescription signed,' I'd argued reasonably.

'If you call at two-thirty he might be able to fit you in this afternoon.'

'There's no one else I can see this morning?'

Some tapping on a keyboard. 'The computer says all booked up. Lots of flu bugs around this time of year.'

'This is a ridiculous system!'

She'd bristled. 'Any comments you have, you can place them in the comments box.'

I start to smile, remembering that night at my parents'. Mum, Dad and George had all gone to bed. Finn and I had stayed up talking on the window seat in the kitchen. It's my favourite place in my parents' home, somewhere I feel safe. I'd stretched my legs out across his knees and picked up the nearest glossy magazine. Finn swiped it away from my hands. 'Hey! I was reading that.'

'How to make the most out of your greenhouse,' he'd read out to me, and then shut it immediately. 'Oh come off it, J, we don't even have one.' I'd shrugged my shoulders. 'We'll get one when we move to the country and I'll grow cherry tomatoes.' Finn has always been a city boy; he says he feels lost and confused in front of green spaces and trees.

He'd unzipped my black boots slowly, gently stroking my calves. I was wearing black diamond-patterned tights. He started to massage my feet, raising an eyebrow at me. 'Carry on,' I'd insisted, leaning back.

With his hand moving up the inside of my right leg, we

heard a door shut upstairs and both drew in our breath and looked at each other like teenagers again. I put a finger to my mouth. We'd listened to the sound of my father's footsteps coming along the creaky corridor. I knew they were Dad's because they are heavier and more deliberate than Mum's. My skirt was inching up my thighs; Finn's hands were touching my hipbone now and pulling at my tights. I'd wriggled and arched my back to allow him to peel them off. We heard footsteps again. 'Will you remember to turn off the lights when you come up?' Dad had called down the stairs.

'What's so funny, Mum?' Now George is tugging my coat.

'Will do,' Finn had called back, throwing my tights to the floor with exaggerated abandon.

I laugh out loud, remembering.

'Mum! What's so funny?'

'Nothing. Can you grab some milk with the green top and some of your cheese straw things?'

I remember repositioning myself so that I was sitting facing Finn. I was unbuckling his belt; the leather slipped through the loops of his jeans and on to the floor. I lifted my arms and he'd pulled my jumper over my head. 'The tights were getting lonely,' he whispered. He'd looked at my bra then, a slightly faded off-white number that needed replacing. 'I think you could have dressed up a little more for me. This has to come off . . .'

16

George rushes back to me with no milk. Instead he shoves a CD excitedly in my face – *Best of Kylie*. He's also struggling to hold a Snickers bar, packet of crisps and sherbert dip.

I shake my head. 'That's four things. I said one.'

He throws them into the trolley. 'I want them all!'

I take out the Snickers and Kylie. Although I love Kylie . . . maybe I can keep her? No, I say to myself. George grabs the CD from me and puts it back into the trolley. 'No,' I say, trying to keep my voice low and calm. A man walks past. 'Children are so spoilt these days,' I hear him mutter.

'NO, GEORGE.'

He starts to cry. Anyone would think I had run over Rocky and then reversed to make sure the damage was done. Some more looks askance and murmurs of disapproval.

'*Start as you mean to go on. If your child starts creating merry hell because they want sweets, don't give in to them,*' the cheery woman had advised.

George starts to cry violently now, tears streaming down his face like a sudden rainstorm. 'I want the Kylie CD. It has the "Locomotion" song.'

'All right, we'll keep Kylie, but that means no sweets.'

'But I want the sherbert dip!'

A woman turns round to stare. George and I halt traffic around us like a car crash. 'I won't eat them all in one go,' he insists with big pleading eyes. 'MUM, I WANT THEM ALL!'

I'm beginning to feel sick. It's the smell of coffee. 'OK, fine, keep them.' His tears dry instantly and his smile returns as if it has been quickly painted on again with one rushed sweep of the brush.

I continue pushing the trolley. 'My dad likes Jammie Dodgers,' George tells one of the shop assistants when we reach the biscuit section. He grabs about five packets and another five fall to the floor. I apologise before yanking him up by the arm and ordering him to take one handle of the trolley. With each breath, I am inhaling the smell of coffee beans and the doughy white warm bread that is coming out of the ovens. I shut my eyes. 'Mum!' Our trolley crashes into the sweets section. Pick 'n' mix. George's hand dives into each box greedily.

'Is she all right?' I hear someone muttering.

I can't go through it again. I can see George dismantling the cot, his small hands pressing against the bars, screaming as if I have put him into a cage. A prison. I haven't given birth to a baby, I have a trapped animal that wants to make my life hell. I love George now, but then . . .

Sometimes I couldn't even look at him.

Unscrewing the bars.

I can hear sweets being thrown into the trolley. George is like an abstract figure to me now. I try to tell him to stop, but no words come out.

Opening windows. Trying to jump out of them.

Emulsion paint all over the new carpet.

I can't do it again. I won't. I have a life to lead. A good life!
I can't go back to those days.

'Your child is making a terrible mess,' a shopper observes.
'Can't you control him?'

Radiators being ripped off the wall; curtains being torn
and pulled. Handbrake lifted. Accident. Being locked out of
the car.

Calling the police.

'There's no discipline these days.'

I lean against the trolley. My head is pounding. 'I'm
going to be sick.'

'Someone, call for help!'

'Mummy! I'm sorry, Mum. I'll put my sweets back.'
George is scrabbling around on the floor.

I can hear voices but can't register faces.

My breathing is quickening. I feel hot. Dizzy. Sweat on
my forehead.

George crawling; breaking everything in the house.

Finn and me arguing.

Sleepless nights.

Burning his hand on the fire.

Accident and Emergency.

Anti-depressant tablets.

Being told I'm not a good mother.

Thinking I am a terrible one.

Living in a faded red dressing gown.

End of my career.

End of my life.

I gulp hard. There is a hand on my shoulder. A balding man with a large badge on his white shirt hands me a glass of water which I take gratefully. 'Would you like to sit down?' he asks. 'There's a bench over there, behind the check-out.'

I swallow the water in one go. It's like Popeye's spinach. I have to know. I straighten up. 'Thank you,' I say, 'very much, but I'm fine.' I hand back the glass.

'You take care,' he says.

George runs alongside me. He starts to pull something else that we don't need off the shelf. 'No more trouble or I'll tell your father,' I threaten sternly. '*Try not to bring your partner into the argument; it's always best to deal with the crisis on one's own to gain your child's respect.*' 'I'll tell Finn and he'll stop you from using the computer for a week.' George pauses as he thinks about all those games of Hangman he'll miss out on. I head for the pharmacy, an air of purpose to my stride at last.

I pick up a pregnancy-testing kit. I decide to buy three.

My trolley tries to meander in a completely different direction as I attempt to steer it safely to the car. I bend down to try to straighten the wheel as it is now totally skew-whiff. I hear a car horn honking ferociously and, without thinking, let go of the trolley. 'GEORGE!' I scream, seeing him inches in front of the red bonnet. The driver winds down his window furiously. 'For God's sake, woman! Can't you control your son?'

'I'm sorry, OK?' I say, tears stinging my eyes like nettles. My trolley is now in the middle of the lane too, blocking the driver's exit. 'George, come here!' He runs back to me so quickly that one of his shoes scuffs the tarmac and he trips and falls. His knee is grazed and bleeding. I rush over to him as he starts to cry.

'Jesus Christ!' the man yells.

I help my son up and dust the dirt from his knee. I find a handkerchief from my bag to mop up the blood.

'It's not my fault,' he insists, tears running down his cheeks. 'It stings, Mum.'

'Come on, woman. I don't have all day.'

Other shoppers pushing their trolleys past stop and stare. 'Stop shouting,' I tell the red-faced driver, 'and stop calling me "woman".'

I can't control my own son. I will never be able to. I can't even control my trolley! I keep a firm grip on George and tell him not to leave my side; for the first time that day he obeys me.

'You must never, *ever* cross the road without looking,' I tell him when we arrive home. He wouldn't listen to me in the car. Hands held tightly over his ears, he'd hummed so loudly that I could hardly hear myself speak. 'You stop. You look right.' I do the actions. 'You look left. You look right again, and *then* you decide if it's safe. I was only cross because I was scared. I love you too much to see you hurt.'

I hold his knee still and manage to get a plaster on the cut and even a quick kiss before he wriggles out of the chair.

He runs up to his bedroom, slams the door and turns his music on loudly. I follow minutes later and find him curled up in a ball on his bed, sucking his thumb, a corner of his pale blue cot blanket poked in his nose. Long-suffering Rocky is fighting to breathe against his chest, his big eyes almost popping out with the pressure of being squished into this awkward position by his master. George is breathing heavily, trying to inhale the comforting smell of the blanket. He calls it 'Baby' because it has travelled everywhere with him since he was born. He even takes it to school, hiding it in his PE bag. I remember the panic we'd once had after leaving it behind. I'd been pushing George in his buggy in the supermarket and nothing I said could make the absence of Baby less painful. Then he had fallen quiet. We were in the checkout queue and he'd grabbed a lady's jersey skirt, the exact same pale blue as Baby, taken the hem and pressed it to his nose, his eyes shut, the pain instantly taken away.

I walk to my bedroom, clutching the pregnancy kits with clammy hands. I have to know before Finn comes home. *Finding out you are pregnant can be a joyous moment for you and your partner*, I read on the back of the pregnancy kit box.

I take the test and pray.

The line turns blue.

I take the test again. Best out of three.

Another blue line.

I sit down at my desk and write an email to Emma, my ADHD friend. I met her through a website support group for ADHD mums and dads. George was diagnosed with Attention Deficit Hyperactivity Disorder when he was five, nearly six, years old. Emma has a seventeen-year-old boy called Nat with ADHD. She's so proud because he's just become an apprentice at British Gas.

Fingers trembling against the keys, I tap, '*Emma, if I have another child, what are the chances he or she could have ADHD? Am terrified. Have just found out I'm pregnant. Gene is stronger in boys, isn't it?*'

I pick up the phone, too restless to wait for a reply. I key in a mobile number. Pick up. 'Thank God you're there,' I say.

'What's wrong?'

'Are you free?'

'What, now?'

'Yes.'

'No, I'm about to go to rehearsals.'

'Oh, don't worry.' I can feel tears coming on.

'What's wrong?'

'Everything. George nearly got run over today.'

'Is he all right?'

'He's in his room.'

'There's something else, isn't there?'

'I'm pregnant.'

'I'll be round in a minute.'

'But your rehearsals . . .'

'Doesn't matter,' he cuts in.

'Thanks, Clarky.' Already I feel relieved. 'I don't know what I'd do without you.'

A message appears in my inbox from Emma. *'Josie, congratulations first, although can see it's terrifying prospect too. The condition is two point five times more common among boys than girls. There's always a possibility, but try not to worry. Easier said than done, I know . . .'*

I go back into my bedroom and lie face down against the pillow. Sometimes I wish I could rewind time and go back to those carefree days. If I had a magic carpet I would fly back to that world with no responsibilities. No fear. No George. The world of smoky pepperoni pizzas and warm beer; lazy days by the river and drinking coffee in rundown cafes.

When it was just Finn and me.

And Clarky.

3

I met Finn when I was eighteen and living in Cambridge. I thought it was going to be another ordinary day at the restaurant, washing the glasses, laying the tables, renewing the flowers, refilling the olive oil bottles, writing the specials on the board. I was too busy to think about meeting anyone, my face flushed from the hot ovens in the kitchen and my feet sore from racing around while I tried to remember what everyone had ordered. Look and you never find. Don't look and they walk through the door.

I was living with Clarky, my old neighbour from home. Growing up, he was like the brother I'd never had. After me, Mum couldn't have more children so instead she'd decided to have dogs. She'd bought an Alsatian called Molly and a mongrel called Tinker who was a mixture, we thought, of Bassett hound and Jack Russell. Tinker had a strong chest and sturdy front legs. She took *us* for walks.

Clarky's real name was Justin Clarke, but I called him Clarky. He'd always been popular at school; not in an

obvious way, he was just different from all the other children. The other boys loved football and sport – which he
liked, too – but Clarky was also a brilliant musician. He
started playing the violin when he was four. 'I only began
to talk properly when I was four,' I'd told him.

'Yes, but I wasn't really serious at four,' he'd explained
dismissively, with a little wrinkle of his nose, 'I only started
playing seriously when I was seven.'

His father, short and severe with a dark beard, had
taught him every day for at least two hours. He looked like
the type who'd own a long wooden ruler which he'd rap
against your knuckles if you weren't behaving. When I was
younger I didn't like going round to Clarky's for tea because
I'd be told off if I didn't sit upright in my chair. I didn't dare
lean my elbows on the table either. Clarky's dad played the
flute and his mother was an opera singer, so it wasn't sur-
prising that they wanted their son to follow in their exalted
musical footsteps. My parents' jobs hadn't seemed nearly
so interesting. Mum had looked after me full-time when I
was very young, but when I was at primary school she'd
started to run a Bed and Breakfast. Before she married, she
was secretary to an eccentric scientist who had worked in
a shed at the bottom of his garden. My father was a solici-
tor. He looked important in his dark suit and polished
shoes but, growing up, I hadn't seen much of him. He'd
commute into London and stay with his sister during
the week, only to return grumpy and tired on a Friday

evening. By Sunday he was full of laughter and fun, back to himself, either in the garden or sitting at the kitchen table making things out of wood. That was his passion. He'd made me a tree house where as a teenager I'd sit for hours, painting and drawing. On Sunday evening he had to go back to the 'big smoke' as he called it. 'London leaves you grey by the end of the week,' he'd admitted.

Clarky had been a mini-celebrity at school. His name was often read out during assembly. One day the head-mistress, wearing her usual plum-coloured dress, beamed with pride, saying we must all congratulate Justin for being accepted into the Junior Royal Academy of Music. Each Saturday after that he'd travel by train to London wearing sensible trousers, a white shirt buttoned so high at the collar it looked like it was choking him, and a round-necked patterned jumper. He always carried a dark brown leather case that held his sheet music. I used to love the smell of that leather case. I would press it against my nose. 'Josie, you're mad!' he'd say, trying to claw it back from my fingers.

'What do you want to be when you grow up?' I once asked him.

'I want to go to Cambridge, like my grandfather, and read music. You?'

'I want to be an artist, like . . . Michelangelo! Or Leon-ardo da Vinci, that wouldn't be so bad.'

'He invented flying.'

'Yes, I want to be like him.'

Clarky had the unfortunate label 'teacher's pet', but miraculously this hadn't annoyed the other boys because he wasn't big-headed about his success. I think he'd been embarrassed by the attention. The others were in awe of him, though, just as I was. I would watch him staring out of the window during a maths class, in his own world. I used to long to know what he was thinking. Whatever it was, I'd imagined it to be mysterious and interesting compared to my own dizzy thoughts about what was going to happen in the next episode of *Dallas*. Clarky had pale grey eyes, a neat thin nose, and a mop of curly fair hair that went all fluffy when it was washed. 'He's like an angelic choirboy,' Mum used to say, 'and he always helps me with the washing-up.'

He wasn't perfect, though. When he was ten he went through a weird phase of not talking to me in class. We caught the big coach to school together, but he wouldn't sit next to me on the lurid red-and-purple-patterned seats. He'd sit at the back with all the other boys instead, so I sat next to Tatiana Prickman who was pale-skinned with bright blue eyes, and appeared homesick from the moment she stepped on. She was slight with long blonde hair caught limply at the sides of her head with plastic green hairclips. My hair was in a pudding-bowl cut. I have never forgiven Mum for that look, but she told me it was the most practical style to maintain. Tatiana was a gymnastics freak.

She could bend and twist her body into any shape and would fly across the gym mats in a slick combination of somersaults, bends, flips and cartwheels, while the rest of the class did handstands and forward rolls. We didn't talk much on the school bus. Her arms were always firmly crossed as if she were guarding herself from any intrusion into her world.

I couldn't understand why Clarky didn't like me at school when we'd have such fun at the weekends. We'd watch Mum's Bed and Breakfast guests from between the banisters at the top of the stairs. There was a Japanese man who patiently taught us origami. There was a rich American couple who couldn't get the hang of our old-fashioned loo chain. Clarky and I would listen to them pulling it and then holding it down without letting go. We'd giggle as we watched Mum and Dad take it in turns to stand outside the door telling them to, 'Release! Let go!'

'Embarrassing to have to serve them eggs sunny-side up now,' Dad had laughed as he skipped downstairs, loose change rattling in his trouser pockets.

Dad called us 'Justin 'n' Josie'. 'You're like two peas in a pod,' he'd say. 'I almost think of him as my own son now. Might send his parents a bill for his food.'

'Why don't you talk to me at school?' I'd confronted Clarky one Sunday afternoon when we were singing and dancing in our sitting room. I was dressed up as Madonna with black lace gloves that I'd pinched from Mum's drawers and an old pink suede miniskirt. Clarky was Freddie Mercury, dressed in one of my dad's Hawaiian shirts. He looked nothing like him.

'I do talk to you,' he'd lied, jumping up and down on the sofa with an old white and navy Slazenger tennis racket held in front of him as a fake guitar.

'No, you don't.' I stumbled in Mum's knee-high black boots.

'I certainly do.'

'You don't.' I placed one hand on my hip. 'One day, Clarky, I might not be around, then you'll be sorry.'

He'd laughed. 'Where will you be?'

'Just . . . gone.' I lifted my chin high and with a dramatic sniff turned away from him.

'Dead?'

'No, stupid, I mean I might play with someone else.'

Clarky stopped jumping. 'None of the boys talk to the girls at school,' he had reasoned. 'It's the way it is. It's not because I don't like you.'

'Show me then,' I'd said.

There was a definitive moment when I decided I would love Justin Clarke for ever. I was terrified as I stepped on to the coach one morning wearing a strange orthodontic helmet with thick black elastic bands and wires looped through hooks at the front of my teeth.

I took my place next to Tatiana, knowing she wouldn't say anything, but even she had looked shocked, putting a hand over her mouth and asking loudly, 'Blimey, does it hurt?'

I'd turned to her in surprise. 'Kills,' I'd replied, enjoying the sympathy. 'I have to wear it at night too.'

We were sitting in the front seat, level with the driver, Terry, who looked like he ate too many doughnuts.

'Did you see Josie?' I heard one of the boys saying, followed by roars of laughter. I stared ahead. One of them was walking back down the middle of the bus; my heartbeat quickened. Then he stuck his pimpled face right in front of me. It was Kevin, the leader of the pack. 'Can you kiss with that thing? Wanna give it a try?' More laughter from the back. 'Are you a virgin?' he'd continued. Terry ordered the boy to return to his seat immediately, but Kevin ignored him.

I hesitated. 'Of course I'm not!' I finally replied, sure my voice had a lisp.

'She's not a virgin!' he shouted down the bus.

'Shut up, Kevin,' Tatiana shouted back. 'Crawl back into your dirty hole.' I turned to her with amazement, almost envy.

'What did you say, *Prickman*?'

'She said, shut up and push off,' I told him with renewed confidence.

'SIT DOWN!' yelled Terry, one eye on us, the other on the road. The coach swerved, tyres screeching against the tarmac. I heard more footsteps. Kevin grabbed one of the straps on my head and gave it a sharp yank.

'Kevin, leave Josie alone.' I turned round and there he was. Justin. My hero. Through the wires, I smiled at him and he smiled back. I was glowing inside. It was true love. But there was something equally pressing on my mind. 'What's a virgin?' I whispered to Tatiana when the boys sat back down.

'Someone who hasn't had sex, stupid. You know, kissing a boy and all that stuff. Justin wants to kiss you,' she'd added with a sharp dig in my stomach from her bony elbow.

'No, he doesn't!' But I had felt an excited kick inside me, a punch of pure happiness.

'I can tell you all about sex,' she'd informed me before pulling a horrified face. 'I saw my parents doing it.'

I gained another lifelong friend that day in Tatiana Prickman. She told me she'd always been quiet and self-contained because other people thought she was weird. 'Do you have an invisible friend?' she once asked me. I said yes, his name was Casper and he wore a green velvet cap. 'He's your guardian angel,' she'd confirmed. 'What's your star sign?'

'I don't know.'

'I'm a Capricorn, a mountain goat. And, by the way, call me Tiana.'

Tiana taught me a game that would help me calculate just how much Justin Clarke loved Josie Mason. It worked out at 12 per cent. 'It's a stupid game,' she'd assured me afterwards. 'He definitely likes you.'

But she'd been wrong. We never went out together. Instead he went out with Rosie, a quiet mousy girl. I was consumed with jealousy when they shared a desk together, passed secret notes or exchanged coy glances.

'Why don't you fancy me?' I'd asked him once.

'You're like my sister . . . ugh!' So I went out with Kevin instead. It turned out his attention had been for a reason.

I had a rich uncle in Cambridge who had given Clarky and me his home to 'housesit' during our gap year. He had bought a three-month round-the-world air ticket. We watered the purple pansies in his window boxes, forwarded his mail, made sure the house didn't get dusty and smell like a nursing home, and in return stayed there rent-free. He lived on a long residential road that ran into the city.

We needed to earn some money before we bought tickets ourselves to travel across Europe. I wanted to go to Barcelona, Madrid and Paris; Clarky wanted to go to Venice. He was working in the shop at the Fitzwilliam Museum, taken on for the run-up to Christmas. His main job was stacking cards on the shelves and working the till.

I found work in a baking hot Italian restaurant called Momo's. It was on a street running off King's Parade, opposite King's College. Momo's was small and rundown, I was sure there were mice, and the walls were more like cave stone with small crystals visible inside them. It was romantic at night, lit by white candles stuck into dark green bottles with great wedges of wax spilling over the sides. The food was simple, flavoured with lots of garlic and chilli. There was constant noise from the students huddled around the tables. Momo looked like a giant bear with his dark hair and bushy eyebrows.

'Josie!' he roared across the room one day.

'Yes?'

'What's wrong with this table?'

He was standing in front of a wooden table laid for four. Knives and forks were in the correct places. Olive oil bottle refilled. The menu was wedged into a loaf of crusty bread in the middle of the table.

'I can't see anything wrong.'

'Look again,' came the gruff response.

Another of the waiters, Mikey, came to the table and examined it carefully.

'Take a look at the coasters,' Momo commanded, his breathing fiercer than usual.

Momo had just been to Italy and had returned with new coasters depicting Italian scenes. The Ponte Vecchio graced this table, as did the gondolas of Venice.

'The leaning tower of Pisa is upside down!' he said, gesticulating vehemently. 'Don't laugh.'

'There, it's tilting the correct way now.' Mikey winked at me. He was a year older, had worked at Momo's for six months and liked to look out for me.

'Very good.' Momo nodded his head, tension gone, before he started to inspect the other tables. 'By the way,' he said, 'I'm having a meeting any minute. Some student wants to rent downstairs for his music.'

'His music?' I was interested. 'What do you mean?'

He shook his head stubbornly as if to say, don't ask questions, wait and see.

A group of students piled through the door. I was in the kitchen operating the cappuccino machine. It loved to break down just before the lunch rush.

Chairs were scraped back. I peered through the crack in the door and saw one of the boys who'd just entered taking a wooden chair, turning it round and sitting on it back-to-front. He was wearing a dark hooded top with jeans and trainers. I wanted to see his face. Take your hood off, come on, what have you got to hide? And it was as if he heard me because he did, before briefly turning around as if aware of someone watching him. Momentarily I edged back from the door before leaning close to it again. He had dark brown hair with a shock of peroxide blond falling across his forehead. He was wearing dark jeans that showed off the top of a pair of checked boxer shorts and a patch of bare skin. He waved one arm expressively, saying that Momo's was perfect for what he had in mind.

Through eavesdropping, I established that these students were in their second year and all thought that Cambridge's nightlife needed a serious boost. The man in the hooded top was called Finn. 'There's only one disco in this town,' he complained, 'and not even a good one at that. I don't think we'd have any trouble pulling a crowd in here, Momo.' His voice was authoritative; his manner persuasive. He circled the Pisa coaster with his fingers before tossing it into the air like a pancake. I wanted to warn him to put it down. 'Keep still, boy, and give me that,' Momo demanded.

Finn started to tap his foot under the table instead. They wanted a venue with a liquor licence, he explained. They had their own decks, just needed to hire someone for the door, to take the money and the coats. They wanted the club to operate once a week, on a Thursday night. Entry to be three pounds for the Cambridge students, five for anyone else.

Momo took them downstairs. It was a dingy, dark-walled space; at a pinch you could fit in about one hundred and twenty people. Cobwebs hung from the ceilings and the room smelled musty, but it had definite potential. The idea excited me; every Thursday lots of students coming in here, grabbing a pizza and something to drink and then going downstairs to dance.

*

'Mikey, one lasagne, one pizza with mozzarella and tomato, one pizza with anchovies and olives.' I gave him the order while fetching drinks from behind the bar at the back of the restaurant, just in front of the kitchen. I could now see all the students properly. There were two boys, one of them black with dreadlocks. His name was Christian but they called him Christo for short; his profile was handsome and strong. He looked as if he played hard gruelling tennis matches on clay courts every day. Finn was taller but more fragile in physique. He looked as if he dipped in and out of exercise, like flicking in between television channels. A stylish blonde girl dressed in black sat next to him. She was pretty in a polished way; the kind of woman who would pout perfectly even on a passport photograph. I wondered if she had lent Finn her peroxide. She was called Dominique.

Momo beckoned me over. 'A bottle of red,' he said, 'and four glasses.' Finn looked at me, his eyes narrowing as if he had seen my face before and was trying to put a name to it. There was a small faded scar beside his left eye. I wanted to ask him how he'd got it. 'Well, go on, Josie,' Momo ordered impatiently, looking at me and then Finn.

I returned with the glasses and opened the bottle of wine in front of them. Christo took a sip to taste. 'Not bad,' he grunted, without a thank-you. 'Now, names for the club?'

'So pretentious,' I muttered under my breath as I walked away, knocking a menu off the table.

'Sorry, what was that?' Finn called out.

I picked up the menu and continued walking.

'Waitress girl! What did you just say?'

I stopped and turned, catching my breath. 'Think we're pretentious?' he asked. His eyes flickered with delight that he had caught me out. I was drawn to those brown eyes. I felt there was a whole story behind them.

As he rolled up his sleeves, waiting for a response, his eyes locked on to mine. He was wearing an old leather plaited bracelet around his wrist. The overall look was scruffy but thought-out.

'Come on, Finn,' Dominique said, touching his arm. He shrugged her off.

'What's your name?' he demanded.

'Josie.' He was not going to intimidate me.

'That's a nice name.'

'We've got business to do,' Momo reminded him, telling me with the wave of his hand to scarper.

'So what do you think our club should be called?' Finn called loudly after me. '*Josie?*'

There were groans around the table. 'Come on, Finn,' they all said.

'It's music to get down to. Break into a *sweat.*' He was still teasing me with those dark eyes and I could feel the redness creeping up my neck.

Everyone was staring at me now, even Momo.

I cleared my throat. 'Something like, Dare to Dance? You know, it's "Care to Dance?" but . . .'

'No, don't like it,' Finn pounced.

'Lame,' Christo agreed.

'Born to Dance?' I knew it was bad the moment it came out of my mouth. 'Dance to Death?' That was even worse.

There was stifled laughter.

Christo looked frustrated. 'Leave her alone, she doesn't have a clue.'

'Well, I don't hear you coming up with anything better.'

Christo looked up at me in surprise, caught in the headlights unprotected.

'It's not exactly impressive to come to a business meeting without even knowing what you're going to call your club, is it?' I continued, enjoying myself now.

'She has a point.' Finn tilted his head to one side. He looked as if he were just about to smile but didn't quite do it, as if someone had pressed Pause just in time.

I walked back into the kitchen, proud of my own courage in standing up to second-year students, and briefly looked over my shoulder once more. Finn was still watching me. I pushed through the swing doors and leant against the sink, hands tightly gripping the enamel basin, head bowed. 'Fuck, what was all that about?' I muttered under my breath, turning on the cold tap and splashing my face with water.

I met Clarky in the evening at one of our favourite pubs on the bridge near the river. It was a relief to be back in familiar company where I understood each gesture and look and it did not matter what came out of my mouth. 'I'm not a *bad* dancer,' he answered my question. 'Why?' He was circling the rim of his glass with one finger.

I told him about the students in the restaurant. 'And this guy, Finn, asked me what I would call it and . . .'

'You fancy him, don't you?'

'He's in his second year,' I said, ignoring the question.

'So?'

'He's a medic.'

'You know what he's reading too?' Clarky leaned closer towards me.

'Well, only because I overheard him talking to Momo. Stop looking at me like that, Justin Clarke.' I started to fiddle with the beer mat.

'Josie, you're looking great at the moment. Any man in his right mind would be mad to turn you down.' He picked up his drink and took a gulp quickly.

'You think?' I was fishing for another compliment.

'I mean it.' He looked gratefully at my flat shoes. 'But don't wear high heels, makes me feel insignificant.'

By the age of twelve I was five foot nine and still growing, with what seemed to me abnormally large feet. 'I had to go to a specialist shoe shop,' Mum would remind me. 'Honestly, darling,' she'd say, holding my face between her hands, 'you are going to be lovely and tall so stop hunching those shoulders and be proud of your height.'

'You are going to have such straight teeth.'

'You are going to be beautiful.'

I was always 'going' to be something. Thankfully I had stopped growing by now at just under six foot. Clarky was five foot ten – 'and a half' he liked to point out. My teeth were straighter. My feet were in proportion to my height at size nine. It was as if I had finally stopped stretching and all the bits were falling into place. I had long dark hair that was healthy and thick with a natural curl. When I was working I coiled it into a ponytail and stuck a hairpin or pen through the middle to make sure it didn't get in the way, but long strands always strayed and fell across my eyes. They were large and grey-blue, the colour of the sky before a storm broke, my father always told me.

'You've lost weight too,' Clarky observed before asking me if I wanted another drink. He walked to the bar with a confident stride. He also had changed since being in Cambridge. The patterned jumpers, stiff starched shirts and all the strict formalities imposed upon him were things of the past now. I had finally got over my phase of thinking I was in love with him when I was just sixteen. The closer we became, the stranger it would have been to go out with each other. A best friend was much better, I'd decided. I loved talking to him and getting the male perspective. I would never trade that friendship for a love that could go wrong. Love was fragile. Friendship was for life.

When he returned with drinks I asked him if there was anyone he liked.

'Possibly,' he told me. 'Sandy. Might ask her out.' He started to tell me about her, but all I could think about was Finn. I wasn't sure what he had started, but I had this longing to see him again, as if we had unfinished business.

I knew there was a reason I'd chosen to work at Momo's, I decided. Tiana would tell me it was all part of my destiny and I was beginning to agree.

4

Finally the buzzer rings. I open the front door. Justin is carrying his violin and a canvas bag holding music books. 'I'm sorry you had to miss rehearsals,' I say.

'It doesn't matter.' We walk into the kitchen. Rocky's food is still on the table, along with the old blue flower-patterned breakfast plates with toast and jam on them and a couple of dirty mugs in the sink. I start to wash up manically. 'This place looks like a Tracy Emin creation! I ought to stick a label on it, send it off to the Tate and at least make some money out of our mess.'

Clarky steers me away from the sink. He takes off his cord jacket and hangs it neatly on the back of a chair. I sit down and then jump up again, asking if he wants a drink. 'Thirsty? Hungry?' I open the fridge and pinch a cold roast potato from the bowl. 'These are so good. I love the crunchy bits. Want one?'

'Cold potatoes? No, thanks. Sit down, will you?'

'I'll put the kettle on. GEORGE! Turn Kylie down! Sorry, won't be a minute.' I go upstairs.

I find George in his bedroom, lying face down on the floor building a farmhouse with a windmill out of Lego. He's so absorbed in it, 'hyper-focusing' is what it's called, that he doesn't notice me coming into the room to adjust the volume of Kylie's duet with Jason Donovan.

Finally I sit down with Clarky. 'Finn will be happy,' I start shakily. 'It's all he wants. His patience was running out. "You're getting on, Josie," he always says. I'm only thirty-one,' I add.

'Hardly the best way to persuade you,' Clarky says.

I imitate Finn's voice. '"If we're going to have a bigger family, shouldn't we be doing it now, while we're young enough to stand the sleepless nights?"'

'Do you want another baby?'

'I never ruled out having another, but it terrifies me.' I rub my forehead hard.

Clarky shuffles his chair forward. 'What scares you?'

'Everything!' I lower my voice. 'I'm just about coping with George now. Getting to grips with our routine. I love my work, and I'm happy! When the baby comes I'll be right back at square one.'

'What does Finn say about that?'

'He says it'll be all right because George is at school. Well, Finn leaves the house at the crack of dawn, goes to work and comes home after all the chaos is over. He doesn't understand.'

I tell Clarky about the 'baby' argument we had when I threw an egg at Finn.

'At school?' I had screeched. 'Ah, at school, is he? And I am constantly on the alert, Finn, waiting for the phone to ring and Ms bloody Miles to tell me George has forgotten his games kit or broken one of the computers . . .' I was holding an egg box and something exploded inside me. I hurled an egg across the kitchen. It smashed against a wooden door, the yolk seeping into the cracks. Finn had stared at me and then at the broken egg, his eyes wide with bewilderment.

Clarky smiles. 'Promise never to come near me with a box?' He leans back, away from me. 'Did you eat scrambled for supper?'

I laugh wearily. 'I was mad, OK? Oh, God, I can't . . .' I don't want to say it too loudly.

'Have another child like George?' he finishes for me quietly. He places a mug of tea in front of me. 'I've put some sugar in it.'

'What if it's another boy?'

'Is ADHD hereditary?'

'Yes. We think Finn's mother has it although it's never been diagnosed.'

'Does he know you're pregnant?' Clarky starts to circle the rim of his hot mug carefully. He does one full circle and then stops and changes direction. I've always told him he has artist's fingers.

'No, only you know.'

'Look, you really need to talk to him about it, not me.'

I press my lips together. 'I wish I could. Sometimes he doesn't want to listen.'

Clarky frowns and twitches his nose. 'Finn needs to know that the pregnancy is great news, but at the same time, you are going to need a lot of support. He can't keep his head in the clouds.'

I nod appreciatively.

'If I were Finn,' he continues, taking his hand away from the mug and gently touching mine, 'I'd want to know how you were feeling.'

I remember my dream.

'What?' he asks intently.

'I had a dream about us the other night.'

'Sounds interesting. And?'

'You and I got married in a hot air balloon.'

He laughs. 'Sounds like a nightmare.'

I lean my elbows against the table again, hands pressed against my forehead. 'No, this is. But then I think of George who'd love a brother or sister. I never ruled out having another baby. Maybe it will be a girl.'

'Would that make all the difference?'

I start to chew one of my already bitten thumbnails. 'What's wrong with me? Some people dream of having children and here I am, terrified.'

'No one else knows what it's like bringing up George. We

can try to understand, but you're the one who has to deal with it.'

'I wish Finn saw it that way. Why can't he see it like you do?'

'Do you want this child at all?'

'What?'

'It's your decision, Josie.'

I feel uncomfortable. 'I don't think he'd ever forgive me. It would ruin our marriage. I couldn't.'

'But if he loves you?'

'This is our child. I couldn't.' I open the fridge and eat another cold potato.

'Sorry, J, all I want is for you to be happy. Your health, your sanity, comes above everything else. I remember you struggling with George in the early days, pretending you were OK and getting little support from anyone. You've got to do what *you* think is right.'

I turn to him. 'You know me better than anybody, sometimes better than Finn.'

He smiles. 'I've had years of practice.'

In that split second I think of Clarky and me as eighteen-year-olds.

'Josie? What are you thinking?'

'Relationships: they're not easy.'

He nods. 'Look how scared I am to commit to anything. No steady girlfriend, no children. Who the hell am I to talk?'

I close the fridge and hand him a bottle of beer. 'I think you're clever,' I say with a dry laugh.

The front door opens. 'He's early,' I whisper. It's 6.30.

Finn drops his case on the floor by the sofa and slings his jacket over the banister. 'Hi, honey, I'm home!' he calls, like he does every evening. He strides into the kitchen. 'For once I didn't have any bleeps, I finished my clinic and . . . oh, Justin.' He stops talking momentarily. 'How are you?' he adds awkwardly.

'Very well, thank you,' Clarky replies with a formal nod.

'Good day then?' I ask on autopilot.

'Yep. I did six angiograms without any major hiccups and a patient even thanked me.' Finn cocks his head, waiting for a reaction.

'Is that rare, to be thanked?' Clarky asks.

'Yes. Waiters and cab drivers get tipped, even if the service is lousy. All *we* hear are patients moaning about the NHS. One time, this man came into my office and actually tipped over my desk, can you believe it?' Finn laughs. 'He started to say, "In my country, we don't have these ridiculous waiting times." So I said to him, "Well, go back to your sodding country then."'

I've heard this story many times. Eventually Clarky says, 'Good for you.'

Finn was hoping for a more responsive audience. 'Sorry, was I interrupting something? It was *awfully* quiet in here before I turned up.' He pulls a face. 'I'm famished! Didn't even manage a sandwich in the canteen today.'

Clarky scrapes his chair back. 'I ought to be going.'

'What about your beer?'

'Another night,' he says. 'I have a date.'

'Who's it this time?' Finn enquires.

'Miranda.' Said in a tone that invites no further questions.
'Bye, Finn. Good to see you.' Clarky's voice has increased in volume and boldness.

I walk him to the front door. 'Have a good date,' Finn calls out. 'With *Miranda*.'

I open the front door. Clarky grabs my wrist. 'Call me tomorrow, promise?'

'Promise.'

Finn opens the fridge and eats a cold roast potato. 'God, these are good. How was Justin then?'

'Great.'

'You two were so serious, like little spinsters.'

'Finn, I have something to tell you . . .'

'Why does Clarky date such shallow, dizzy girls? That last one . . . Christ, what was her name? Anyway, she was the pits.' The last time we had all gone out to a new Japanese restaurant round the corner, Clarky had brought his latest date, Samantha, a pretty blonde who did nothing but whisper to him in a baby voice and ask him to feed her because she couldn't use chopsticks. Finn eventually lost his cool and told her that if she had something to say, why not share it with everyone?

'He's a bright, good-looking-ish guy. I don't get it.'

'He hasn't met "the one" yet. When he does, I reckon

he'll be so bowled over that he won't know what's hit him. Anyway, I need to talk to you.'

'You are never going to meet the "perfect" girl.' Finn opens the beer bottle and takes a swig.

'You're never going to meet the perfect man either.'

He raises an eyebrow. 'But I come close.'

'Ish. Finn, I've got something to . . .'

'It's like he's too scared of meeting the right person so he only goes out with airheads who won't challenge him. He needs to take the bull by the horns, you know? He also needs to stop hanging around here. He should meet Alessia. My God, now she is close to perfect.'

Alessia de Silva is a Senior House Officer at the hospital. I haven't met her yet, and from the way Finn describes her I'm not sure I want to. Not only is she the sexiest woman on this earth but I am also told that she is 'seriously clever'. Finn likes to tell me she works 'under him'.

'Finn?'

'If you sit and wait for this perfect angel, you are going to be disappointed. There are always compromises.'

You are too right, I think. I'm not entirely sure, however, what compromises Finn has made for me.

He takes off his tie and it falls to the ground. He loosens the buttons of his shirt. He circles his neck. I put his tie on the kitchen table. Next he kicks off his shoes and swings his feet on to the table. 'Are you like this at work?' I ask.

'Ah, that's good, I've been rushing round that hospital

all day. The lift decided to break down today. I like Justin, but . . .'

'FINN!' I start once more.

'. . . the ice should have melted by now. I still think he loves you and can't move on . . .'

I rush up to him and cover his lips with the palm of my hand. 'For one second, don't talk. You are just like George. I have some news.' I speak slowly and clearly.

'News? Let go.' I release my hand. 'What kind of news?'

'Think of something you really want.'

'You got promoted?' I shake my head. 'Won a premium bond? A gallery accepted your work?'

'No. Something *you* want.'

'I want what you want. Your happiness makes mine complete,' he fools around. Then he starts to get it. 'You're not . . . are you?'

'I took the test today.'

'Josie!' He lowers his legs to stand and then wraps his arms around me. 'I can't believe it! That's amazing. You're not joking?'

'It's real.' I think about what Clarky said. 'There's no going back.'

'This is the best news. How many weeks?'

'About six.'

'This is the point when I scoop you up into my arms and . . .' He attempts to pick me up.

'I'm too heavy.' I can't help laughing. 'Too many potatoes.'

He kisses me. 'I'm so happy,' he exclaims. 'Are you OK about this?'

'Yes.' I bite my lip. 'And no. I had a panic attack at Sainsbury's. What if I have another child with ADHD?'

Finn takes my hand hurriedly and we sit down on the stools. 'You've got to stop worrying about this. I've seen the research at the hospital. You can have one child with ADHD and four children without. There's no certainty. It's a risk, but there's always a risk. Everyone worries about whether they are going to have a healthy child or not.'

'If it's a girl, there's less chance she'll have it, isn't there?'

'No, not necessarily. Girls are not so externalised with their symptoms when they are young. They can have ADHD but not be diagnosed until adulthood. And if we do have a boy, it doesn't automatically mean we'll have another George.'

'I love George.' I feel so guilty for talking about him like this.

'I know. Look, the ADHD will probably always be with him, but, as hard as this stage is now, people affected as he is can lead independent lives. Look at Emma, the mum you met on the internet, and her son the British Gas boy. These children are often talented and bright, with high IQs, they just need to find something they're really good at. Great figures like Winston Churchill and Oscar Wilde are believed to have had ADHD.'

'And Einstein,' I add. George has a monkey in his bedroom which he's named after him.

'I don't believe there could be two boys like George, do you?' Finn suggests.

'Why not? Give them both to me, I love a challenge.'

'This is great news. We are going to have another baby.' He talks as if he can hardly believe it. 'How did it happen? I thought you were taking precautions?'

'I missed a couple of days. We were at my parents',' I tell him. 'Come on, Finn, am I that forgettable?' I hit his arm playfully and stand up.

He slides off the stool and grabs me by my waist, pulling me towards him. 'Come here. I remember.'

We hear George slide down the banisters. I squeeze my eyes shut. He's going to hurt himself one of these days. 'We're going to have another one of those,' I whisper to Finn, prodding him helplessly on the shoulder. The phone rings and George snatches it up.

'It'll be great,' Finn assures me with a kiss. 'We're going to be just fine. One day at a time.'

'Dad's sexing Mum right now.'

I bite my lip hard and look at Finn. We both burst out laughing. 'Who is it?' we call out to George.

'All right, Granny Greenwood.'

I press my face against Finn's shoulder. 'Why did it have to be Granny, of all people?'

'Can Daddy fix your tea trolley? OK, Granny. I'll ask him. 'Bye.'

5

It was a rainy afternoon. The restaurant was quiet except for Finn who was sitting at one of the corner tables. He appeared at ease in his own company. I had been to the cinema only once on my own, when I was seventeen. Three people were in the auditorium, one of which was an old lady with wispy grey hair eating a banana from a mouldy brown paper bag. I'd looked around me uncomfortably and then fast-forwarded my life in a panicked second. Would that be me in years to come?

Back to Finn. He hadn't shaved and he looked tired, as if sleep were his enemy. 'We're calling the club Mirror Ball,' he said when I asked for his order.

'That's quite catchy.' I was drumming a biro against my pad; he was tapping the menu against the table.

He raised an eyebrow. 'Look at that. You and me are making sweet music together.'

I continued to stare at him, pen poised. Tiana had advised me to play it ice cool.

'Sorry. I'll have a pepperoni and cheese pizza and a black coffee, please.' When I walked back to the bar I could have sworn he was watching me.

I gave the order to Mikey and then sat down at the bar, picked up a paper napkin and pulled free the pen that was holding my hair in a ponytail. I started to sketch a picture of two figures dancing. I gave the girl an exotic feather in her hair and fantastic legs, long and slim. I loosely drew an open-collared shirt for the man with one of his arms around the woman's tiny waist; I arched her back seductively. I sketched a mirror ball above them.

'Josie!' Mikey called from the kitchen. Finn looked over at me. I heard plates smashing against the floor. 'Momo's going to take this off my wages,' Mikey said with a frown as we both picked up the broken china. We heard the door open and shut and a group of students piling in. 'You go.' He winked. 'Thanks for your help.'

Finn was standing at the bar. 'Can I have another black coffee, two sugars? By the way, who did this?' He was holding up the napkin.

'I did.'

'Quite the artist, aren't you, waitress girl?'

Arrogant shit. I tried to retrieve it. He sat back down in his chair. 'Give it to me!' I snatched air. Finally I managed to grab his hand and attempted to pull the napkin free, but he wouldn't let go. He leant back and waved it in front of me. When I tried to reach it again he was too quick, swapping the napkin to the other hand and then back again. I gave up. He placed it inside the top of his jeans.

'Cut it out, you two,' Mikey ordered, walking past us. 'Momo will be back in a minute. Finn, your pizza's ready.' He plonked it on the table.

Finn and I exchanged looks, bonded by being told off.

He sat with his hands behind his head and looked down at the napkin. 'I promise you my hands will stay here. Come and get it.'

'No, thanks, you can keep it.' I turned away with a wide smile and walked back to the bar.

A couple of students walked in holding files and library books and sat down at the corner table. One of the girls blew on to her hands to warm them up. 'Don't look now,' she whispered, followed by a huge sigh because the other instantly turned to gaze at Finn. Frustrated and destined to invisibility, Mikey took their orders. I touched him on the shoulder. 'You OK? It's only a few broken plates.'

He nodded distractedly. 'Josie?'

'Mmm?' I said, pouring coffee.

'Do you fancy going for a drink after work?'

'Sure,' I said, still looking at Finn.

'He's an idiot, leave him to it.'

Finn walked up to the bar and sat down on one of the stools, leaning towards me. I slid the cup of coffee over to him and then bent down to find the sugar sachets.

'Great view,' I heard. I tried to pretend I wasn't thrilled by the comment.

'Are you going to buy that coffee, Finn, or are you just going to hang around Josie all afternoon?' Mikey asked, slamming ice into Diet Cokes.

'I think I'll do both, particularly the latter.'

Mikey stomped off. 'I didn't know you could draw,' Finn said with that smile that was about to happen.

I crossed my arms. 'I was doodling. I know I'm no Picasso.'

He raised his hands defensively. 'I'm sorry. Other people's talent frightens me so much I turn into an immature monster.'

That wasn't what I'd expected. He smiled properly. 'Seriously, I really like it. That kind of image would make a great flier for the club. Would you . . . I mean, I don't suppose you'd consider helping me design them?'

'I'll think about it.' Tiana would be so proud.

'How about this evening? We could meet and work on them?'

'Tricky. Not sure I'm free.'

He shook the slim pink packet of sugar between his fingers and I watched him closely as he tore it open with his teeth and then poured it into the coffee.

Another group of students piled in and sat down. Finn followed me as I walked over to their table with my pad and pen. 'What can I get you?'

'Hot chocolate,' said one.

'Cappuccino.'

'Make that two. Ooh, I might have the chocolate fudge cake too.'

They were gawping at Finn. 'Come on, what do you say? Will you help?' he persevered. 'I'll do anything in return.'

I raised an eyebrow. '*Anything?*'

'Anything,' he repeated, running a hand through his hair.

'Are you mad?' one of the girls exclaimed. 'Take him up on it!'

'Or if you don't, I will,' another said.

Then Dominique walked in. She was wearing skinny blue jeans which wrinkled under the knees because they were so tight, a pink mohair jumper and beige cowboy boots. 'Finny!'

Finny?

'I've been looking for you everywhere. Didn't you get my message?'

He shook his head.

She tugged at his arm proprietorially. 'What are you doing here?' She eyed me suspiciously. 'Come on, lectures start in a minute.'

There were disappointed sighs around the students' table. The show was over.

Finn grabbed his leather jacket from the back of his chair. Then he was ripping a piece of paper out of one of his books.

'What are you doing now?' Dominique asked impatiently.

'Hang on.'

She blew a large pink perfect bubble right in front of me. 'I'll be outside.' She slammed the door.

A piece of paper was thrust into my hand. '*Meet me outside Kings, under the arch at seven. PLEASE*,' I read.

Finn and I were sitting together in the college library. The air was static with concentrated energy. Before meeting Finn, I'd had to call Clarky. He'd mentioned buying some food to make a curry tonight. 'Is it a date?' he'd asked.

'No, I'm just helping him design a flier for the club.'

'Ah, that's what he calls it. I'm going out with Sandra anyway.'

'Oh.' I'd been worried about letting him down and he was going out anyway. 'I thought her name was Sandy?'

'Sandy. Sandra. Much the same.'

'Great, have a nice time.'

'I will.'

As I was about to leave, Mikey had asked me where I'd like to go for our drink. I had to make up a quick excuse that I'd forgotten it was my dancing class tonight.

We sat by the window. Finn wanted to be 'someplace quiet'. I told him we had two options: we could try to find an image from a dance or film book which I could scan on to the computer; or I could draw him something. 'Draw me exactly what you drew on that napkin,' he insisted, moving closer. He was almost childlike in his enthusiasm, settling in to watch me as if waiting for his favourite movie to begin while he clutched a box of buttered popcorn.

As I drew, I could feel a tension between us, something I'd never felt before. Up until now I'd had lots of kisses but only one serious boyfriend, Jonathan. We went out during our A levels. I can remember the floor was sticky with beer as we danced to George Michael's 'Careless Whisper' and shared our first kiss. Jonathan had bouncy brown curls and an easy open smile, but he didn't exactly make my pulse race. One night we had rented a movie and were sitting alone in the dark. He wanted to go 'all the way'. I was more interested in unwrapping Quality Street. 'Everyone else is getting past second and third base,' he'd complained.

'It's not a rounders match,' I replied, watching him reluctantly return his attention to Steve Martin and wondering what was wrong with me? Why didn't I want to do it? 'Perhaps you just don't want to do it with *him*,' Tiana had reassuringly explained.

'Damn,' I whispered. I'd given my lady too large a head so carefully had to rub out my mistake, blowing on the paper gently. Finn lowered his head too; our lips were only inches apart. 'What have you done?' Normally I wouldn't have liked anyone sitting so close to me while I drew. 'Her head's too big,' he commented. I could feel his breath on my cheek.

'I know. Don't back-seat draw.'

He laughed. 'Have you been to New York?'

'No. Why?'

'Just wondered. I started going there in the holidays with my twin brother, that's when I started to collect records.'

'You have a twin?'

'Ed. We're nothing like each other.'

'Is he good-looking?' I started to laugh at my own joke.

'Very. That's the one and only thing we do have in common.'

Damn. Why did he have an answer for everything?

'Actually that's not quite true. We have good looks and music in common.'

'You sound close.'

'Yeah, we are. There's no competition between us which is great. The last thing he'd want to be is a doctor and I'd never go into acting. I think he's deluded. There's no money in it.'

I laughed. 'Unless you're successful like Robert Redford; he's my pin-up.'

'You've got a nice laugh. Sexy, like you've got a sore throat. Is it natural or do you put it on?'

'It's natural, thank you. Now, how about that?' Finn leant in much closer than he needed to, our arms touching. 'She's more in proportion now.'

'That's better,' he agreed, but his eyes weren't on the drawing.

'Shh,' said one of the readers.

'Do you want to go somewhere else?'

'Where?' I looked out of the window. It was raining heavily.

'My room? Don't worry, it's not far. Then we can make all the noise we want,' he suggested with that raise of the eyebrow.

Finn gallantly held his file over my head as we ran across the gravelled path. Already I felt protected by his height. He must have been six foot three. It was rare that a man was taller than me. I followed him into an old dark building. Students' names were painted on a wooden board at the foot of the stairs.

He opened the door. 'Well, this is my space.' He led me into a sitting room with pale walls and an old wooden floor. 'Easier to do it here don't you think?' he suggested as he opened the door to his bedroom. He pointed to a desk under an arched window that was covered in books and papers. 'My bedder hasn't been in, sorry about the mess.' He started to stack books into piles. They formed two tall towers.

'I could do this at home.'

'No, no, better if we do it together.'

He pulled his jumper off in one swift go and then put on some Aretha Franklin. 'I love old vinyl, there's nothing better than that crackling sound just before the music starts. You know what I mean?'

I nodded.

'Are you into music?' He gently placed the needle on the vinyl.

I loved Madonna, Kylie and Fleetwood Mac. 'Love it, all kinds,' I added quickly.

I took out my drawing and started again. We talked. I learnt that he rowed every morning at 6.30 but was often late and got told off. He wasn't sporty like Christo but liked to keep fit. He was restless if he didn't take exercise. He lived off adrenalin and lack of sleep.

'Or it could be all that coffee. Why do you drink so much?'

'Because it's bad for me. How about you, Josie? What do you love?'

'Lots of things.'

'Like?'

'Art. Ever since I was a child, all I've wanted to do is paint. I wasn't interested in toys. My father built me a tree house and I used to hang out there all the time, painting. It was my escape.'

'From what?'

'From the norm. I think we all need an escape. I created my own little private world. Everyone should do it, have a secret obsession.'

'You're right. My escape is music.'

'Exactly.'

'Where do your parents live?'

'Dorset. It's beautiful there.'

'Isn't it boring? I've always lived in London – find Cambridge way too quiet.'

'I don't find it boring.'

'This is looking great,' Finn said, referring to my picture. 'You're lucky to have such talent, to know what you want to do.'

'But you do too, don't you?'

'Yes, I want to be a doctor, more than anything. I wish the academic work wasn't so dry though. There's so much stuff you have to cram into your brain, then when I don't think any more can physically go in they give me another ten-foot-long reading list.' He made a fist and tapped the side of his head, as if it were hollow. 'Still, I've got to learn it.'

I watched him lighting a cigarette and noticed his hands were shaking. I wanted to put mine over them to try and calm him down. 'You don't mind, do you?'

'No, go for it.'

'I smoke like Pat Butcher. Want one?'

I shook my head. 'Just don't wear the earrings, OK?'

There was that flash of a smile. 'What bad habits do you have, Josie?'

'Going back to strangers' rooms?'

'I'm not a stranger.' He was standing behind me now. Flustered, I stood up and turned to him with the drawing, bringing us back to more comfortable ground.

'I like it.' He took the piece of paper out of my hand. 'Have you thought about what you'd like in return?'

There was a loud knock on the door and it immediately swung open. It was Christo. I couldn't decide whether I was relieved or disappointed. Finn and me, it was going too fast, in a direction I hadn't prepared myself for yet. 'All right, mate. Oh, hi . . .' Christo had forgotten my name.

'Josie,' Finn said, his voice back to normal. 'Look, she's going to draw our fliers for the club.'

'Wicked! Wow, thanks, Josie.' He looked sheepish. 'Sorry about the other day. I was rude.'

'That's OK. All we need to do is find a cheap printer and get however many copies you need,' I said. 'Right, I'd better go.'

'Dominique is looking for you, by the way, she's in the bar,' Christo mentioned.

Finn came to the door with me. 'Can I walk you home?'

'No, it's not far.'

'It's no trouble.'

'I'm fine.'

'Thanks for all your help. Are you warm enough? Take one of my coats or . . . here, take this.'

Christo stood back in amazement. 'What have you done to him? He's never this chivalrous.'

Finn was holding out his hooded top. 'Thanks.' It was cold. It had been one of those days when it started off bright and crisp in the morning, so I hadn't bothered to wear a coat. He lifted the hood over my hair and brushed a wayward strand away from my eyes. 'It suits you.'

My uncle's house was cold. I wore Finn's top in bed that night and the night after, until the smell of it became so familiar it was like having him lying next to me.

6

I start to run a bath.

Finn is reading George a bedtime story.

'I'm bored, Dad,' I hear him say. 'Can you tell me about the America circus again?'

Finn was five when his family moved to Connecticut. His father ran an IT consultancy and took the business to America.

Finn shuts the book. 'Once a year a horse show would come to our neighbourhood. They put up this large circus-like tent and me and Uncle Ed would climb up on to these wooden boxes with the neighbourhood kids. It was a long way up, almost as high as the clouds. We wanted to reach the top so we could slide down the top of the tent. I don't think it was safe but it was great fun.'

'Like sliding off the roof of the house, Dad?'

'Don't get ideas, George. This one time, when I managed to reach the top, I started my descent and then my shoe got caught. It ripped the canvas and I fell through the hole.'

George laughs outrageously. 'Did it hurt?'

'Yes, I cut my face. Look at my scar, it's still there.'

I can imagine George touching the scar like he always does.

'I landed on a large pile of horse manure.' Finn laughs. 'My friend Mick . . .'

'The skinhead!' he shouts.

'Calm down, George. Yes, the skinhead. Mick and Uncle Ed rescued me.'

'When am I going to have a brother? If I'm good, can I have one for Christmas?'

I turn off the bath water and listen to Finn's response.

'I'm sure Santa will give you one, maybe not for Christmas . . .'

'Why not then?'

'Because that might be too soon to make one.'

'Why? How long does it take?'

'No more questions, George.'

Our son's thoughts are scattered haphazardly in his mind like hundreds and thousands. That's how I think of it anyhow. 'How long?'

'Wait and see.'

'How do you make them?'

'Time to switch off.'

'Can I make the baby?'

'No.'

'I'd make a boy just like me!'

Finn needs rescuing so I open the door and walk along the narrow trail in George's room that isn't covered in Lego or soldiers or plastic bags with car-boot junk in them.

'Lights out.'

'My brain isn't tired, Mum.' I take hold of George's restless legs and he pushes them against my hands. I call his legs 'lucky legs' because they are so thin they are lucky not to snap. They are smooth as marble and each toe is perfect. 'Mum!' He giggles, legs wriggling under his *Thomas the Tank Engine* duvet cover. 'Stop it!' Rocky looks put out as he finds another spot on the bed.

'I want another story.'

'No more. It's a big day tomorrow.'

'What's happening tomorrow?' Finn asks.

'It's his Nativity play.'

'Oh, yes, of course.'

'Tell Dad what you're going to be.'

'I'm a shepherd and I play the triangle,' George says, trying to impress him.

'And what exactly is happening when you hit the triangle?' Finn asks.

'The Kings are arriving. You'll be watching, won't you, Dad?'

'I can't promise, George, but I reckon you'll be the best shepherd.'

He shifts position and holds on to Baby tightly. He has lots of toys under his pillow too, including his monkey

Einstein which he refuses to move, however much I argue that it must be uncomfortable.

'I want your eyelashes,' I tell him, wrapping my arms around him in his warm flannelette pyjamas and smothering him in kisses. 'You're my best boy.' I now know what Mum meant when she used to say to me, 'I could eat you up.' George *is* beautiful with his bushy brown hair the colour of a shiny conker, his father's brown eyes, the light that falls on his cheekbones and those long dark eyelashes that curl perfectly like the shape of a half-moon.

'I could eat you up.'

'With tomato ketchup?'

'Lots.'

'And chips,' Finn adds. He presses a pretend button on George's head. 'There, brain is switched off.'

'Thank you.'

We shut the door quietly and walk into our bedroom. 'Can't we tell him?'

'No. We're going to wait three months, in case something goes wrong, like last time.' I test the temperature of the bathwater.

'I want to see his face when we tell him,' Finn continues. 'I think this could be the making of George. It'll be a great distraction, not all of his attention will be on us, and more importantly not all the attention will be *on him*. I think a baby will bring us a sense of normality. Life can be too intense with George, you know what I mean?' Finn's words are rushed.

'Yes, I do, sort of, but we're not saying anything, not yet.' I sit on the corner of the bath and start to undress. 'If we do, I'll have questions for the next eight months and it'll drive me insane.'

Finn kisses me hard on the lips with a frustrated groan. 'It's just so tempting to say something. I want to tell Ed. Can I at least tell him?'

'But he'll tell your mum by mistake; he's like that. He gets so enthusiastic about things.'

Finn starts to unbutton his shirt. 'I hate keeping things from him.'

'It won't be for long. For now it's between you and me . . . and Clarky.' I throw all the clothes on to our double bed.

'Clarky knows?'

'Yes.' I take a towel, wrapping it tightly around my bare body.

'You told him before me?' A darkness spreads across Finn's face, that familiar flicker of distrust in his eyes.

'The other night, when he was here.' I open the mirrored cupboard, one hand keeping the towel in place. I start to hum as I get out some cotton wool.

'You should have told me first.'

'I wasn't expecting to see him, he just turned up and I had to tell someone.' I am cleansing my face with toner, anything not to face my husband while telling that lie.

'You couldn't wait until I got home, what, five minutes later?'

I stop what I'm doing, acknowledging defeat. He's right. 'I'm sorry Finn, I should have waited.'

'I'm not going to let anything spoil this news, especially him.' He sits on the edge of the bath.

'I'm nervous, Finn, about having another child.'

'Don't be.'

'I can't do it all on my own.'

'I'll be here for you.' His words sound flimsy.

'After George . . .'

'Can't we just enjoy the news for a while? Let's have the baby first. There's every chance we'll have a healthy child.' He laughs coldly. I can tell he's still thinking about me talking to Clarky first. The resentment is clear in his eyes.

'What?'

'It's just you and him . . . I don't get your relationship. How would you feel if I had a girl friend I told everything to, before you?'

I'd hate it.

'If you'd known her for years, I'd understand. I'd be *extremely* wary if it was somebody like, er, Alessia,' I finish, trying to sound casual.

He throws his head back in a gesture that tells me I deserve some competition. 'Alessia even has great tits, not that I've seen them,' he says when I throw the flannel at him.

'You and Clarky . . .' he continues. 'He was obsessed with you when we were at Cambridge. Those dramatic violin performances late into the night. He was trying to play me out of your life.'

I tie my hair back in a band.

'Yet you didn't even sleep together when you went travelling?'

'No, we've been over this. It's boring.'

'A hotel room's a lonely place,' Finn probes. 'Come on, six months and not one fling?'

'No.'

'Have you ever been in love with him?'

'I thought I was in love with him when I was about twelve. He was the only one who stuck up for me when I had to wear my ugly head brace at school.' I step into the water and Finn and his questions join me. I lie back, resting my head against his chest. 'Tell me about your day?'

'So you never loved him?'

'No!'

He picks up a handful of water and soaks it into my hair. I shut my eyes, feeling the water trickle down my back. He takes the shampoo bottle and squeezes a little into the palm of his hand. I begin to relax.

'One last question,' he says, 'and this is important.'

'What?'

'I hope he was pleased about the baby?'

'Uh-huh. He thought it was great news.' I make ripples

of water with my fingers. 'Are Alessia's tits as good as mine?'

'It's a close contest.'

I turn and splash water into his face. He grabs my wrists to stop me. We're both laughing. 'Yours are better, OK! I have no eyes for anyone except my beautiful wife.'

'Yuk. Quit while you're ahead.' I take his damp face in my wet hands and kiss him.

He pulls away quickly.

'Finn!' I implore. 'What now?'

'Hypothetically, let's say you did sleep with him . . .'

'OK.'

'So you did?' Finn jumps in.

'No, you said hypothetically.'

'Right. We weren't married; we weren't even going out. But the thing about Clarky is . . .' Finn struggles for the right words. 'I could cope with you sleeping with anyone but him. Does that make sense?'

'Finn, you know I love you. You trust me, don't you?'

He nods. 'When Mum and Dad were going through their divorce, I remember my father saying it wasn't so much what Mum had done, it was all those filthy lies. She made him feel so humiliated and worthless.'

'I'd never, ever, do that to you.'

'I know. I'm sorry. It's the last time I'll ask you, but can we cut a deal?'

'Go on.'

74

'You promise to tell me any news about us *first*. Me, not him.'

Finn is fast asleep.

I'm panicking because I know I'm going to be tired tomorrow. It's two o'clock in the morning, I have to be up by 6.30. I need to sleep.

Forget it. I get up and tiptoe downstairs. I sit and drink a cup of herbal tea, staring at the strawberry magnets on our fridge. Under one of them is the picture George drew of the tarantula he saw at London Zoo. He'd made Finn hold it. There are passport pictures of us all: George sticking his tongue out, Finn wearing his cap backwards.

A sleepy George walks into the kitchen, clutching his Harrods teddy bear that Uncle Ed gave him. He climbs on to the stool next to mine.

'Why aren't you in bed?' I say.

'Why aren't you?' he answers simply.

'Good point, but you need your beauty sleep.' I ruffle his hair.

'So do you,' he says with a giggle.

'Another good point.'

'My brain won't let me sleep, Mum. I hate it when I can't sleep. I hate the dark. I bet everyone in my class is asleep. Am I handicapped, Mum?'

'Where did you hear that word?'

'Jason said I was. What's a spasmo?'

We had trouble with Jason last term. He bullies George, but, 'Stay away from him,' is all the teachers suggest.

'I'm stupid, aren't I? I can never finish my homework.'

'Now, you listen to me. There are things you can't do as easily as others, but you are not stupid.'

George nods.

'You're special.'

'I don't want to be special. I want to be like everyone else.'

I take his hand and we walk back upstairs. I tuck him up in bed.

'You promise to tell me if Jason says anything like that again?' He nods.

'You must never lie, George,' I had once said when I knew he'd stolen a ten-pound note from my purse to buy some Lego.

'Why?' he'd asked so innocently.

'Because lies hurt the ones you love. Makes it hard for them to trust you again.'

But this is the truth, I think as I kiss him goodnight. A single lie will multiply.

If only I had told the truth right from the beginning.

7

'That's not yours,' Clarky noticed. He followed me, watching as I unchained my bicycle. I was about to meet up with Finn and Christo to distribute fliers all around Cambridge. It was raining and windy so I was wearing the hooded top Finn had given me. We hadn't spoken about my returning it; it was tacitly understood by both of us that I'd keep it.

'It's Finn's.'

'He's lending you his clothes now?'

'Only this. Right, gotta go.'

'You'd jump off a multi-storey building if he asked you to,' Clarky said. 'You're mad.'

'Madly in lust. It does strange things to you.'

Finn, Christo and I cycled all over Cambridge distributing hundreds of fliers. Cambridge was bike city; I can still hear the constant ticking of the bicycle wheels going over the cobbled streets.

We split up, the boys going into each college and pinning fliers to every possible noticeboard as well as taping them to the black iron railings that lined the streets. I went to book and clothes shops, cafes and bars, where I knew students hung out. I took some to the market stalls that sold Cambridge memorabilia, old records, books and nightshirts that flapped in the wind.

In the evening Finn and I met up in a small cafe down one of the alleyways off Kings Parade. It was in the basement of a larger building with rainbow-coloured painted walls. My legs and bottom were aching from all the exercise.

'I hope this isn't a big waste of time,' Finn said.

'It'll be fine.'

He was playing with a matchbox. '*Fine?* Who wants fine? What if no one turns up?' He reached into his pocket for a crumpled pack of cigarettes. 'You'll be there, won't you?' He inhaled deeply, the action accentuating the hollows in his cheeks. Then he stubbed the cigarette out as quickly as he had lit up. It was the first time I'd seen him look vulnerable and it suited him almost as much as his confidence. 'Didn't want it anyway.' His hands were shaking and this time I did put mine over his and held them there. 'You're going to be fantastic, and of course I'll be there.'

'I couldn't have done this without you, Josie.' Christo joined us then and we withdrew our hands immediately. It was like someone above was watching us. The moment we became close, we were warned away from each other.

It was Thursday morning, the day of Finn's club opening. I pushed the bedcovers off me quickly, grabbed my towel and hoped I bagged the bathroom first. The door was closed. I turned the doorknob. 'You nearly finished in there?' I was jogging on the spot. It was cold standing in the corridor.

'Hang on,' said Clarky. The door opened. 'What's up with you?'

'It's a beautiful day.'

He rolled his eyes. 'Right. Another day of stacking Christmas cards on shelves. Yippee. My father would be so proud.' He put his thumbs up and walked past me.

Clarky's parents, in particular his father, were furious that their son had wanted to take a gap year. Their generation hadn't had gap years; they got on with it. Before we'd come to Cambridge I'd told Clarky to stand up for himself, tell his dad that he wanted to go travelling, see more of the world than the Dorset Downs.

'I told him,' Clarky said, standing on my parents' doorstep later that day, his hair dripping from the rain. I'd ushered him inside and into the warm kitchen.

'What did he say?'

'That he was disappointed in me.'

I'd slammed the mug against the table. 'How dare he say that! I'm sorry, Clarky, I know he's your dad but he's such a fucking control freak. I am going over there right now to tell him what I think of him.'

I grabbed my coat from the back of the door and felt a hand fall on my shoulder. 'Don't. It won't help.'

'But you can't let him get away with it.'

Both his hands on my shoulders now, he'd looked me straight in the eye. 'I'm not. I'm going to Cambridge with you.'

Clarky and I had stayed up talking late into that night. We were outside on the terrace. It was a summer's evening and the sky was clear and scattered with stars. 'I'm going to miss this place,' I'd said. 'Nothing will ever be the same once we leave home, it's the end of an era.'

'I can't wait for the next stage.' Clarky smiled. 'Dad said he hadn't taught me music just so I could "arse" around Europe with you.'

'Charming.'

'I've never heard my father say the word "arse".' We both laughed then. 'To us,' Clarky said as we held up our shot glasses of neat vodka. 'To you and me, our friendship, and last but not least, to *arsing around*.'

'What are you doing tonight?' he asked as I walked in my towelling dressing gown down the creaky corridor back to my bedroom.

'It's the first night of Finn's club.' I shut the bedroom door.

A few seconds later I grabbed a towel to cover myself. 'Clarky! Knock before you barge in.'

'I've seen you naked before.' There was almost a smile on his face.

'When we were about five in the paddling pool, that's different.'

'You're spending a lot of time with Finn,' he said, almost as an accusation. 'I thought he had a girlfriend.'

He was dampening my mood. 'Maybe he has, we're not doing anything wrong. Just having fun, that's all.' I looked into his face and couldn't help adding, 'You should try it.' I closed the door on him.

'Believe me, I know how men think,' he called.

I knew he was still waiting outside, brooding. 'By the way,' I opened the door just wide enough to pass him a large handful of leftover fliers, 'can you circulate these round the museum? Tell people it starts tonight. Thanks.'

It was the end of the day and I had just finished laying out the tables for supper and was hanging up my apron at the back of the kitchen when I heard, 'Josie!' Oh, God, what hadn't I done? I stepped out into the main part of the restaurant. 'Yes, Momo?'

'Come here,' he instructed, and I followed him to a table in the corner. 'What do you see?'

I went straight to the coasters to make sure they weren't

upside down. Everything was in place. 'I can't see anything wrong, Momo.'

'Nor can I.' He patted my shoulder with one large hand. 'Well done.' He dug into his apron pocket and handed me my wages in a brown envelope. There was always a message written on the back of the envelope. The last had been, 'Please tie your hair back so it doesn't get into the soup.' But this time it said, 'Thank you, Josie, you're a good worker.'

I cycled home high on his praise and full of anticipation for the night ahead.

I ran a bath and turned on some Madonna. Before getting dressed something made me walk into Clarky's room. It was dark, the floral curtains still drawn. His music stand stood in the corner by the window and lots of sheets were scattered across the floor. The black violin case was on the bed, along with the old leather bag which held his music and books, now worn and frayed at the edges. I still loved its smell.

'What are you doing?'

I turned round, my face caked with a mask that looked like a compost heap. I was dressed only in knickers and my black bra. 'Clarky!'

He blinked.

'What are you doing?' I screeched.

'What are *you* doing, more like?'

He was wearing a dark jacket, a white shirt underneath it and jeans that I hadn't seen before, held up by a dark brown leather belt. He looked different.

'Are you snooping?'

'No, I thought I heard a bat. They like old houses.'

'A bat? You're crazy, J.'

I tried to cover myself, wrapping bare arms around me. 'What are you doing all dressed up?'

'I'm coming with you,' he declared. 'I want to meet Finn and see what all the fuss is about.'

Mikey was standing outside the door, taking the money. For the opening night he was wearing a red spotted tie and had cut his long hair. 'Wow, Josie, you get in for free,' he said when we reached the top of the queue. I was wearing a black sequined top with jeans and heels. 'Your friend has to pay, though.'

'Oh, Mikey,' I said, hitting his arm. 'Go on, let him in.'

'All right then.' He stamped the backs of our hands with the mirror-ball logo before we were pushed forward by impatient people standing in the queue behind us.

I spotted Finn behind his decks. He was wearing head-phones, a grey T-shirt and jeans, and the blond streak that fell across his eyes had now been dyed a dark red. He had a twelve-inch in one hand, cigarette in the other. There must have been about eighty people squashed into the room. A girl approached him with a request.

'I imagine that's him?' Clarky enquired, leaning closer to me. 'I'm not sure about the hair. What's this music?'

'Don't know,' I answered distractedly.

'Isn't there a bar here?'

'You have to go upstairs.'

Clarky looked around the dark space. It smelled of joints and sweat.

'Who's that guy in the miniskirt?' he whispered, followed by, 'Why does that bloke have a shepherd's crook? Weird!' He shot a convert sideways glance at the man next to us who looked like a forty-five-year-old trainspotter.

Women surrounded Finn. 'You've got competition,' Clarky murmured. A busty blonde started to jig in front of him. She was wearing large silver hoop earrings that bobbed up and down as she danced. She pulled him towards her. 'Are you OK?' he asked me over his shoulder.

'You carry on,' I told him.

I made my way over to Finn, pushing through the crowd. 'Hi!' I said, an octave too high. 'How's it going?'

'Josie! Great!' he shouted above the music. 'I can't believe it, so many people!'

'I know! I told you it'd be great. Hi, Christo.'

He waved.

'This is my twin, Ed,' Finn said proudly. Ed shook my hand. 'Hello! Thought I'd pay my brother a surprise visit, see what he was up to. This is fantastic.' He looked around the dark room. 'I hear you designed the fliers? They're great!' He was tall, just like Finn, but there was an ease and openness about him that Finn didn't have. I could picture him acting in a Walt Disney movie.

Finn got pulled to one side with another request. I saw him flirting with the girl. What was I thinking? He wasn't interested in me.

Clarky and I danced. He clasped his hands around my waist and pulled me close. Was Finn watching?

'You're good, Clarky,' I shouted above the music.

'I am?'

'Yes!'

'Josie?'

'Yep?' I could see Finn coming towards us.

'Forget about him.'

'What?' He was behind Clarky now.

'FORGET . . . ABOUT . . . HIM.'

The music faded and Clarky's words echoed around us. The room seemed to go silent; there was laughter. Then a new track came on, helping to evaporate the tension.

'Clarky!' I whispered. 'You don't even know him.' Why was he behaving like this? He couldn't have feelings for me, could he? He was my best friend. I thought we both knew we didn't cross that line. 'He's nice, OK?'

'Finn Greenwood,' he introduced himself, shaking Clarky's hand. 'I'm guessing I'm the "him" she should forget about?'

'I'm getting a drink of water,' Clarky mumbled.

Finn led me to the edge of the dark room. I leant against the wall. He stood in front, arms flanking me on both sides so I was trapped. 'You see, the thing is, I can't forget about you,' he said. My heart was thumping. 'That's not your boyfriend, is it?'

'No. I'm just sharing a house with him, we're going travelling together in Europe later.' I stopped talking, fed up with tiptoeing around the issue. There were all these smooth chat-up lines and near-kisses but . . . 'Is Dominique *your* girlfriend?'

'No.'

I couldn't hide my smile.

Finn grabbed my hand and led me upstairs. We walked outside. 'It's too noisy in there,' he said. He held a strand of my hair and twisted it slowly in his fingers. Was he finally going to kiss me? Just as his mouth came towards mine . . . 'What are you going to wear?'

He distracted me. 'What am I going to wear when?' I looked at him and he raised an eyebrow.

'On our first date this Saturday, seven-thirty, I'll be picking you up.'

'A see-through lace black dress?' Not that I owned one.

'With what underwear?' He was almost smiling again. 'I mean, if the dress is see-through you've got to consider the underwear.'

'Wait and see,' I said, feeling utterly out of my depth. My ears were still ringing from the loud music.

Finn scribbled my address on the back of his hand. 'Better go, Christo needs me.' He walked back into the restaurant.

'Do you know where it is?' I called after him. 'It's a blue door and next to . . .' I was standing at the top of the stairs.

Finn stopped abruptly and turned to me. 'Don't make it too easy. I'll find you.'

8

I'm sitting in our open-plan office, staring at the computer screen with an image of a passport on it, the stamps of various countries and the words in bold, **Explore a World of Opportunity**. I'm designing a poster for a language school and have to submit at least three different concepts for them to choose from.

I finally drifted off to sleep at four last night. I need to get a grip on reality. What is the point of my saying anything now? All I'd be doing is hurting Finn and why would I want to do that? If I have lied about Clarky and me, then what else have I lied about? That's what he'd think. He would never trust me again. Imagine how awkward it would be, let alone difficult for Clarky and me to have any kind of friendship afterwards. Each touch of the hand, hug, kiss on the cheek, would be misinterpreted because Finn would be looking for a reason to distrust us. He'd turn me into his mother.

I don't think he would ever forgive me.

I'm not going to let one night jeopardise my marriage. It's in the past and that's where it should firmly stay.

Tiana won't tell Finn. So that only leaves Clarky, and I know he won't say anything.

What's the time now? I have to get to George's school by 3.30. Normally our neighbour Rose Billingham picks him up for me the three days of the week that I work. George calls her Mrs B. She dog-sits Rocky and looks after George as if he were one of her own grandchildren. She makes working life possible for me, but more importantly she is one of the few people who understand George. 'I won't stand no messing around,' she always says. George has a great respect for her.

I shall never forget the first time we met. It was when Finn and I had just moved to Shepherds Bush a year ago. When he became a registrar his basic salary increased and we finally took the plunge and bought our first home together, a three-bedroomed terraced house. Finn and I had loved it the moment we stepped through the front door. The sitting room had glass doors opening on to the sunroom, and a kitchen with a stylish slate floor and Moroccan tiles over the walls. It had a great feeling of space and light. While we were still in the process of unpacking boxes and deciding what paint samples to go for, there had been a knock on the door. I saw a shock of white hair, partly covered by a green hood with fur edging. 'Hello, Rose Billingham. I live next door.' Rose is Irish. She walked straight in, carrying a large orange earthenware dish. 'Thought you'd like a lasagne.' She placed it on the stove with such an air of authority anyone would have thought it was her home.

I thanked her profusely before offering her a cup of tea. 'Not that Earl Grey stuff. Builders' tea, please.' She took off her parka to reveal a tight-fitting white shirt with frills down the front, a pair of black pinstripe trousers and shiny red boots with a wedge heel. I took all that in before studying her face which was strongly lined and framed by long white hair with the odd streak of dull blonde. The two didn't add up somehow. But she had the most incredible blue eyes that shone like bright stars in a dark sky. George had been instantly transfixed. 'Wow! Look at your hair! Your parents must be really old.'

Finn abruptly stopped working when he saw Rose. 'Now, you must be the man of the house,' she said, winking at him. 'Rose Billingham.'

His eyes came to life as he took in the figure in front of him. 'Finn.' He stared back at her.

'Look at the pair of you, as tall as the skies. What do you do, Finn?'

'I'm a doctor.'

'Oh.' She'd blushed and glanced at her tea, clearly impressed. 'Are you a GP?'

'No, I'm just a registrar.'

'Just a registrar? That sounds very impressive to me. What do you specialise in?'

'Cardiology.'

'Hearts. I bet you've broken a few,' she said with a wink and he winked back. Rose relaxed into the sofa finally. 'My husband Michael used to be a volunteer for a heart charity – for young sufferers, you know. He visited so many hospitals, studying the latest technology for fighting heart attacks. Ironic that he died of one, really,' she said sadly. 'I have to watch my cholesterol, can't eat macaroni cheese anymore.'

The office phone rings.

'Gem Communications,' Natalie says in her slow South African accent that could lull you to sleep. I like Natalie. She is young and her manner as gentle as a lamb, but there is a steely determination beneath. I've learnt that she loves roller-blading in Hyde Park and *ER* is her favourite hospital drama. Her face is pale and clear, accentuating almond-shaped eyes, and she has neat bobbed hair. She wears a silver necklace with a heart-shaped pearl pendant. She told me her mother gave it to her as a leaving present. Occasionally I notice her touching the pendant, deep in thought, as if talking to her mother secretly.

'It's Finn,' she says.

I stop spinning the cards in my Rolodex and pick up. 'I'm not going to make George's play,' he says hurriedly.

I'm disappointed, but at least I have a backup plan. 'Don't worry, Tiana's coming.'

'Great. Say good luck, will you? I'm sorry, darling.' He hangs up abruptly.

I look at my watch. 'Shit, I need to go.'

The phone rings again. 'Go now, before Ruby gets back,' Natalie urges.

I collect my bag, throw an empty sandwich box into the bin and do a quick tidy of the desk. Just then Ruby walks awkwardly into the office in the tightest grey skirt I have ever seen. It has an enormous metre-long slit up the right-hand side. Her boobs are trying to burst out of her tight white shirt, the buttons on the brink of popping. 'Are you going?' She looks at her watch, gold bracelet jangling.

'It's my son's school play, need to dash.' 'Dash' is a word Ruby frequently uses.

'I didn't see it in the diary.' She sits down and starts to tap on her computer keyboard with manicured nails. 'Off you go then, have fun.' She smiles, but there is tightness around her lips. The smile doesn't reach her eyes.

'Thanks, I'll make the time up.'

'Josie, it's Christmas! But next year we are going to have to pull out *all* the stops. That means you too, Natalie.' She chuckles. 'I'm going to need one hundred and ten per cent from you both, at all times.' Natalie is already hiding behind her large Evian bottle. The phone rings. 'Gem Communications, Ruby Gold speaking . . . Oh, Steve, hi! Uh-huh . . .' She's nodding vigorously. 'Uh-huh.'

I look at the door.

'You get the pun? Gem and Ruby, that's right!' She laughs as she swings herself round in her chair and I swear I hear the material of her skirt tearing.

I exit rapidly. What is she going to say when I tell her I'm pregnant? I think for what must be the hundredth time that day as I jog along the blue-carpeted corridor and towards the lifts.

'Slow down, Josie!' calls Diana, the receptionist. 'You'll have a heart attack!'

'Husband's a cardiologist. He can sort that one out.'

Lights are dimmed in the school hall. I'm waiting for Tiana. She's George's godmother. Tiana's free in the days because she's just given up her recruitment job in the City, fed up with the long hours and not meeting anyone. 'Something strange happened,' she'd started explaining to Finn and me over supper one night, about a month ago. 'This photograph of me shaking hands with my boss . . . the one taken last year when I won the award for recruiting the most people in the calendar year . . . well, it fell off the shelf and the frame smashed into pieces.'

Finn had braced himself. 'You're giving up work because you knocked over a photograph frame?'

'But I didn't! That's the whole point.'

'Prickman, you're doing so well at work. You'd be mad to give it up for a premonition.'

Beneath Tiana's smile she had looked hurt that she

wasn't being taken seriously. 'I know, in here,' she tapped her heart, 'that it's the right thing to do. I believe something is telling me to leave this job. I'll find something better, you watch me. It's time I used my languages.' Tiana is fluent in Spanish and Italian.

Now the music teacher, Mrs Luty, is playing Christmas carols on the piano, looking deadly serious. She has a long thin nose and large front teeth that seem to protrude even more when she concentrates. Although only in her forties, she has silvery-grey hair.

How I wish Finn could be here. He would be laughing, and once Finn starts, I can't stop. During the last parents' evening we both got the giggles and he was squeezing my knee so hard, trying to control them. That's what I love about Finn. He wants George to fit in, but when it comes down to it, he doesn't take any of this stuff *too* seriously, whereas other parents have already signed up their children to stage school.

Parents start to fill up the rows of seats and get out their flashy digital cameras. I hear quick footsteps. Tiana rushes in with carrier bags swinging off her arms. 'Blimey,' she says, putting a sweaty hand on my shoulder. 'I didn't think being a lady of leisure was this exhausting!' She plonks herself down next to me and fans her face with the programme left on her wooden chair. She slides her small feet out of her heels and I can see they have left a deep indentation across the foot. I first began to notice just how pretty

Tiana was when she turned sixteen. Her hair was swept off her face and her skin had become acne-free after taking herbal concoctions and using skin creams. Mum thought she was as beautiful as an exotic bird with her naturally fair hair and crystal-blue eyes. 'I'm Capricorn, a sun sign with Scorpio rising,' she had once explained earnestly.

'What does that mean?'

'The eyes talk.'

She's much shorter than me, with delicate hands and feet, and I've always been envious of her nose. It's still a little girl's nose.

'Aw, that's better.' Her cheeks look red from the cold winter air. She's wearing a bright pink suede coat over white jeans, with a fur scarf clipped together with a sparkling green brooch.

'What have you bought?' I peek into one of the bags.

'These jeans.' They're tight and white. 'I didn't have time to take them off.' Tiana's life always resembles speed dating. 'Here, look, I bought this peacock feather to go in my hair.'

'Ooh,' I sigh over the prettiness of it, holding it up to my face. 'I want one.'

'Portobello. Bargain, only a fiver,' she says with a nudge. 'I've got a date tonight with Ben . . . wait for it . . . Shuttlecock.'

'Prickman? Shuttlecock?' I shrug my shoulders. 'Not much in it really, is there?' We both laugh.

'Anyway I'm not going to marry the guy, am I?'

I raise an eyebrow. 'Why not? You'll marry someone in the end so why not take off with Mr Shuttlecock?'

Mrs Luty finally stops playing and the red velvet curtain is drawn. Voices become muffled until there is complete silence. I'm nervous. 'He'll be great,' Tiana whispers.

The back of the stage is painted navy with silver stars and the hills of Bethlehem. Mary sits at the front, behind the hay barrels, looking angelic with her blue hood and long fair hair. Angels with silver-glitter tiaras and white feathered wings surround her. Mothers and fathers cluck proudly.

A group of shepherds emerges from the wings. I squint because I can't see George. 'There he is!' Tiana calls out. He's huddled at the back wearing one of Finn's old striped shirts and clutching a woolly lamb in one hand. 'George, stop picking your nose,' I immediately mutter under my breath.

'*Then in a cattle shed in a manger lay the King. The angels sang for him.*' The angels start to flutter their wings and do peculiar dances. One girl's wings fall off and she starts to cry. I can hear George laughing. A teacher rushes on to the stage to put her back together again.

'*The shepherds came to where the baby lay.*' George's group of shepherds shuffles across the stage holding crooks, some playing tambourines. My son decides it's a good idea to overtake them. The blue-and-white tea towel slips from the top of his head and is now lopsided. By mistake he knocks off a white napkin that was sitting on one of the other shepherd's heads. The boy pats his fair hair self-consciously. I am sinking lower into my seat. I can't watch.

'Can I play now?' George calls out loudly in the middle of their song. I am almost on the floor with embarrassment. 'What's he doing?' I whisper loudly, one eye shut.

'Hi, Mum!' I hear. Please, God, what have you got against me? Did I do something appalling in my last life?

'Mumdog!' George continues. The other children stare back at him. 'Where's my dad?'

'Has to be centre of attention, that boy,' Jason's mother tells the one sitting next to her. 'What's a stupid Mumdog, anyway?'

'God-mum spelt backwards,' Tiana tells her with a tap on the shoulder, 'but don't worry, we wouldn't expect you to get it.'

A smile spreads across my face. 'Well said.'

'*Now I lay me down to sleep, angels watching over me, my Lord,*' they all continue to sing, shaking their tambourines.

'Can I play now?' George shouts, triangle at the ready.

This is worse than childbirth. He pings the triangle with all his strength, and laughs. A teacher places a firm hand on his shoulder to remind him where he is. He looks at the audience, at her hand and at the audience again, and says, 'Nothing to do with me!' Everyone starts to laugh as George is hauled behind the curtain.

He reappears when the Three Kings arrive decked in gold crowns and brightly coloured cloaks that trail across the floor. *'We bring gifts of gold, frankincense and myrrh . . .'* they sing, each holding an old shoebox. George hits his triangle and everyone applauds. I look around in astonishment. 'Are they clapping George?'

'Yes! He's jazzing it up. Otherwise,' she leans in closer, 'it'd be rather boring.'

I begin to relax and drop my shoulders. All the children line up and George steps forward, in front of all the rest. He bows. The audience continues to clap and now I join in. George is pretending to be Superman, flexing his muscles. 'He should be on the stage,' says one of the fathers to me.

I'm astounded by the sudden turnaround. 'Thank you.'

'D'you know what my mother said to me the other day?' Tiana asks.

'What?' I'm still watching my son fooling around. Where does he get it from? I wonder what Finn was like at his age?

'She told me that unless I get a move on, she'll be too old to be a proactive granny.' She laughs lightly, but then her voice lowers. 'The thing is, I would love to meet someone and this is all great fun,' she says, gesturing to the stage, 'but I can't imagine being a mum, I don't know how you do it. What is it, J? What have I just said?'

'I'm pregnant,' I tell her.

*

98

'You'll never guess what I heard today, Mrs Bourbon,' Finn says to George.

'What, Mrs Jammie Dodger?' George starts to kick his legs up and down under the duvet.

'Well . . .' Finn stands with one hand under his chin, right leg cocked, 'I heard that someone called George Greenwood stole the show.'

'Oh, my giddy aunt!' More snorts of laughter and wriggling under the duvet.

'Mrs Bourbon,' I start, but they shake their heads at me.

'She needs to stick to her day job, doesn't she, dear?' Mrs Jammie Dodger says regretfully to Mrs Bourbon.

'Fine.' I kiss George goodnight once more. 'I'll leave you to it.'

'Why weren't you watching, Mrs Jammie D?'

'Funny you should ask, dear. I developed a nasty wart on the end of my nose and my purple rinse didn't turn out so good. I didn't want to embarrass you, Mrs Bourbon. Now tell me, will you be receiving an Oscar for your supporting role performance? I hear you're up against George Clooney. It's going to be a close contest.'

I love it when I hear them laughing. It feels like the warm sun shining against my face.

9

'He's early!' I mouthed at Clarky when the doorbell rang.

'You've got a ladder in your tights,' he observed from behind me.

'They're new, I can't have.' I looked down. 'Oh, shit, that's a rip off! Can you let him in?' I raced back into my bedroom and peeled the tights off me at galloping speed, my fingers agitated and clumsy. I could hear Justin and Finn talking woodenly. I decided to fling on a pair of jeans instead and a black top. I grabbed the necklace I had carefully selected for the evening from my dressing table. 'Come on, J,' called Clarky.

'Coming!'

'Where's the black see-through lace dress?' Finn asked. Clarky decided to leave at this point.

I pulled a face. 'It died, sadly. It's been worn to death.' I stood protectively by the door. I wasn't sure what Finn would make of the house. It was old and the floorboards creaked beneath worn kelims. My uncle collected chipped china and there were cracked plates and teapots everywhere, along with other strange objects littered around the house – like a kitchen clock in the shape of baked beans on toast and a peculiar ashtray in the shape of a lobster with big claws staring out at me. My bedroom contained a single bed fit for a spinster.

It wasn't exactly cool, although I was growing to like it.

Finn looked amused, with that flicker of a smile passing over his face again. 'D'you want me to put that on for you?' he asked, the line between his lips curling upwards, something I have always found unbelievably sexy. I had forgotten I was still carrying the pale green necklace. 'Oh, right, yes, thanks.' He took it from my hand and stood close behind me. The narrow space between us felt electric. Could he feel it or was it just me? He smelled nice. I couldn't describe the smell, just that it was a man's. 'Men smell of old shoes and leather, mixed with a bit of sweat,' Mum had told me when I was fifteen.

I'd wrinkled my nose. 'I thought they smelled of aftershave?'

'No, your father doesn't wear that awful synthetic stuff. It's much more subtle than that. People are drawn to one another by their smells, like a magnetic force. I could quite happily nestle into your father's armpits.'

'Mum!' I'd cringed, shaking my head in disgust at the image. Now, a rather inane grin spread across my face.

Finn lifted my long hair away from the nape of my neck. I held it up for him. His touch tickled. As he moved away I said, 'So,' with great effort, then couldn't think what to say next.

He looked at me as if I were an object he had just created and put the finishing touches to. He touched the necklace gently. 'You look great.'

I turned around swiftly so he couldn't see me smiling like a schoolgirl who had just received a golden star.

'Where did you grow up?' I asked Finn. We were sitting at a low wooden table in a smoky, dimly lit bar, drinking beer. The place was heaving with students. I wanted to cut through the crowds with a knife, make it just Finn and me.

'London. I had a pretty freestyle teenagehood, was left to my own devices half the time.'

He seemed to examine me all the time; I felt more in control at Momo's when I was on my own territory. I was sure he could hear my pulse beating, see the heat which crept up my neck and flowed into my cheeks.

I asked him what he'd done in his gap year.

'Broke into warehouses with Christo. We cleaned them up, somehow managed to get electricity from the street-light and used it to power all the lights and our sound system. We had a great time. There were a lot of drugs, clubs, and, er, women.'

I felt innocent when I was with him. I was still a virgin, but at least I knew what it meant now. He lifted his glass, looking thoughtful. 'You know, it was probably the best year of my life.'

'You're only twenty,' I pointed out. 'It's hardly time for *This Is Your Life* just yet.'

His eyes met mine as he laughed. 'I know, but don't waste yours serving pizzas and coffee to pretentious students.'

And meeting you, I was thinking. Even Momo had noticed my daydreaming recently and asked me if it was anything to do with the music man. 'I was young once too, you know,' he'd said, before showing me one of the coasters, which had a loose thread hanging off it.

'I'm leaving after Christmas.' An awkward silence fell between us.

'So . . .' we both started.

'Sorry, you go first.'

'No, you go,' I insisted. Finn asked me what I was going to do after my gap year. First dates are always like an interview, finding out who you are and what you do. I told him I had a place at Reading, reading Typography.

'Typing?'

'No! It's the art of type, letterforms, you know, the history of how letters came to be.'

'I thought you wanted to be an artist?'

'Well, yes, I do, but very few people actually make a living out of being an artist.' This was an argument I'd had with my parents. Even as I said it now, I felt cross that I'd let myself be talked out of doing what I loved. Mum had advised me to do something more practical. Dad, whose own passion had always been sculpting, agreed. 'I want to be a graphic designer but I'll keep up my painting,' I vowed. 'What's it like at Cambridge?'

Finn pressed his lips together. 'Different.'

'In a good or a bad way?'

'Both. I felt out of my depth to begin with. Thirty-two hours a week of lectures and tutorials and then all those reading lists I was telling you about. I got OK grades at school, but this place is competitive.' He started to shake his head. 'Most students claim they don't work, but secretly they're working their butts off.'

'Do you pretend?'

'No. It's a challenge and I'm proud I'm taking it. I never thought I'd get here.' His tone hardened. 'I mean, I don't have a parent or relation who went to one of the colleges, I didn't go to a private school. Everyone asks, "Did you go anywhere?" when you first arrive.' He leant in closer. '"A school in Berkshire" means you went to Eton. Daft not to say so because you can spot an Etonian's accent from Australia. "Chin up, old boy,"' he imitated. 'They have accents like cut-glass.'

'Does it matter where you went?'

He shrugged his shoulders. 'Not to me. I don't play sport. I'm not a rugger-bugger. You can spot *them* a mile off too.'

'Are you always this defensive?'

'I don't like punting,' he continued, oblivious. 'I'm not going to take you punting, OK?'

'I don't want to go,' I claimed.

'Come off it. That's what you people do.'

'*You people?*'

He shrugged his shoulders.

'I don't want to go punting with you,' I told him. 'There wouldn't be enough room in the boat for you and the giant chip on your shoulder.'

He raised his glass to mine in surprise. 'Hear, hear.' He smiled. 'Bravo! You speak your mind, don't you?'

'When it needs to be spoken.' Finn looked around the crowded room. Bodies pressed together at the bar in a huddle of noise and smoke. 'Shall we go?'

'Already?'

'It's pretty smoky in here and my contacts are hurting.' He moved closer to me. 'Think I need to take them out and put my specs on.'

I stared at him as he rubbed one of his eyes. He could tell I was watching him because he looked up at me with a broad smile. 'Not quite so rock 'n' roll as you thought, am I?'

'You cut up frogs' legs! Ugh.' We were walking in the direction of my house, but neither one of us had mentioned what we were going to do next.

'We have to cut up bodies too. If we're to learn how the heart works, we've got to see the real thing, haven't we?'

I nodded. 'Why medicine?'

'Do you want me to say that I've always wanted to heal the sick?'

'Only if you mean it.'

'Well, I do. Call me sentimental, but that's exactly what I want to do.'

'Well, why didn't you say so in the first place?'

We walked on, our hands gently brushing together in the cold night air.

'Are you going to invite me in properly?' he suggested, leaning one hand against the wallpaper in the hall that was positively medieval, like stepping into the Dark Ages. Green ivy in between a trellis pattern, its leaves sprouting stiffly over the grid-like lines.

'Do you want a coffee or something?'

'The something sounds more interesting.' Violin music filled the house. 'Who's that?'

'Clarky.'

'I've always thought the violin was a bit screechy, like fingernails running down a blackboard.'

'Not if it's played well,' shouted Clarky crossly as we walked past the sitting room and into the kitchen. Finn sat down at the table that was covered with a glossy tablecloth with large red and yellow tulips on it. 'I think Clarky must be getting to the part where someone is murdered,' he guessed, putting his hands over his ears and then faking his own death, hand beating frenziedly against his chest.

'Stop it,' I laughed.

'This place is great. Who owns it?' All my earlier fears were being realised. He was staring at the baked-bean clock.

'My uncle.'

'Can I smoke? This is cool,' he said, picking up the lobster-shaped ashtray. He shook it in front of me, claws extended too close to my face. I pushed it away with a giggle. He started to roll a cigarette.

'Got anything we can spice up our coffee with? This place must have a cellar.' We walked down the cold dark stairs and into a musty room that smelled of rich red wine and old paint. Finn and I stumbled around in the dark, groping the walls for any sign of a light switch. 'This place is a health hazard!' he complained. 'I could have opened my club here.' Finally I found the switch behind the door and a soft glow warmed the room. Bottles lay in wooden racks shrouded in cobwebs. There was also an old larder fridge in one corner of the room which looked as if it had been out of action for years.

I bent down to examine the labels on the bottles.

Finn crouched down to join me. His closeness made me jump. 'Want to play five questions?' he asked.

'OK.' We sat down and I tucked my knees under my chin. I could feel the dust on the floor and in the air.

'Have you really got a see-through lace dress?'

'What do you think?'

'Shame,' he replied.

'That was a waste of a question.'

'It doesn't count.'

'Yes, it does.' I hit his arm and he hit me back.

'That was a warm-up.'

'I'm waiting.'

'I've gone blank now, I'm still thinking about you in a lace dress. Do you have brothers? Sisters?'

'Only child.'

'Parents still together?'

'Yes.'

'Lucky you. What's your favourite food?'

'Pecan pie. Yours?'

'Lemon meringue. OK, next question . . .'

'That's three,' I reminded him. 'And they're slightly boring so far, I have to say.'

'Right, got to make the next two seriously more interesting then.' He stroked his chin thoughtfully. 'What's the story between you and Clarky?'

'Story? We're friends.'

'Friends,' Finn repeated. 'Only he acted strange when I picked you up earlier. I don't think he likes me. And then the other night, at the club, he was all over you.'

'We were dancing.'

'Mmm. And then telling you to forget about me?'

'He can be overprotective, that's all.' I was worried about Clarky, though. He had been behaving strangely around me lately and was hardly encouraging about Finn. When

I'd asked him about it he'd simply said, 'If you like him, go for it. It's your life.'

'I didn't think boys and girls could be just friends?'

' 'Course they can. It's a different shade of love, isn't it?'

'Shade? What, like red love is passion, blue platonic?' He wasn't taking me seriously.

'Only one more question.' I shifted into a new position and adjusted my hair.

'Are you nervous?'

My 'No!' came out in a high-pitched voice as Finn moved in to kiss me. I shuddered, moving jerkily away like a startled rabbit. His kiss landed on the middle of my left cheek. 'Oh, God, I'm sorry.' I started to laugh. 'I *am* nervous.' I brushed the dust off my jeans.

'Why are you nervous?'

I held his gaze. 'I think you know.'

We moved closer to each other then, knees touching. A surge of electricity shot right through me. If he could have measured my pulse then it would have been off the scale.

'My turn,' I whispered. 'Will you just kiss me otherwise I'll go mad and . . .' His lips were pressed against mine. Our kiss was soft to begin with, but then it became intense. I shut my eyes, lost in his touch. One hand was cupped around the back of my neck, the weight of it telling me this wasn't a dream.

10

I open the oven to check on the turkey, and steam rushes
to my face. The turkey smells of congealed fat and the Brus-
sels sprouts smell of George's socks. 'Are you all right?' my
mother asks, standing over the stove heating up the bread
sauce. I feel like nothing on earth, I want to say. 'Fine,' I
tell her.

My father is helping Finn lay the long oak table with our
best silver which we were given as a wedding present; I
bought dark red candles for each end of the table, white
linen napkins and gold-and-silver crackers. George is
upstairs playing with the toys we put into his stocking.
Last night he left a glass of sherry and an oat biscuit outside his bedroom for Santa, along with his Pokémon cards.
I believed in Father Christmas until I was ten. Finn stopped
believing when he was four. 'I heard Mum and Dad arguing,' he'd told me, rolling his eyes, 'my bedroom door
was flung open and the entire contents of the stocking
was thrown in.'

'Why don't you have a rest after lunch?' Mum suggests. I want some of her energy. The only things that give away her age are her lined hands, fingertips roughened from gardening, and I sometimes catch her out squinting because she will not wear her glasses except in bed when she reads.

My father, on the other hand, looks his age, with deep frown lines from the years spent commuting into London. His grey hair is thinning and wispy and his skin fragile, like thin tracing paper, showing a cluster of tiny red veins in each cheek. Today he's dressed in a pink shirt with sparkling cufflinks that Mum gave him, and looks every inch the gentleman. I'm proud of my parents.

Finn rubs his hands together eagerly, 'Now, what can I do next?' I've never seen him so proactive in the kitchen. Since the news of my pregnancy he has been walking on air. He doesn't even mind talking to his mother, Gwen, on the telephone.

But before I have time to tell him to make the gravy the doorbell rings and he strides across the kitchen floor to the intercom. My father refills his glass with gin, neat this time.

Finn lets them in.

'What on earth is Richard carrying?' Dad asks. Richard is Gwen's boyfriend.

'No idea.' I take a deep breath and adjust the sequinned scarf in my hair.

'Happy Christmas!' My mother-in-law sweeps into the room, clutching a bottle of champagne. She kisses her son and I can see Finn wiping the sugary-pink lipstick off his cheek. We hug, but it's a quick flittering contact. She leans her cheek towards me and slightly puckers her lips to kiss, but she does it too quickly to make proper contact, brushing her lips against me like a feather instead.

We're all staring at a gigantic white furry creature that has a pink tongue drooping out of its mouth at an odd angle. 'For George, we thought he'd like him,' says balding Richard.

'Thank you, Richard,' I say faintly.

'Call me Dicky,' he insists with a wink. He's wearing a suit and a spotted pink-and-silver bow tie. 'And how is Finn's lovely good lady wife?'

Not so good after being called that. 'Very well.'

'We would have wrapped him but one gets so busy. Before you know it . . . whoosh!' says Gwen, sweeping one arm out in her habitual gesture. 'Time flies by.'

I once asked Finn how she'd found the time to give birth. For the first time ever, he didn't have an answer.

Finn places, let's call it the dog, stomach first on the ironing board, its great big paws almost touching the floor. Everyone's standing in the open-plan kitchen, getting in each other's way. My father is the only person who's tactfully retreated to the end of the sitting room. Dicky pulls a pack of cigarettes from his trouser pocket.

'Put them away,' Gwen barks, thank goodness, 'and do something useful.' Her boyfriend looks more like a spaniel every time I see him.

She touches my top. 'These maternity-type clothes are very much the fashion aren't they?'

'It's not maternity,' I correct her quickly. 'You look well, Gwen.'

'I wish! Dicky and I were comparing notes on old age in the car. My crow's feet virtually touch my ears, and look at these bags! I'm seriously considering plastic surgery. Might even get my boobs done while he's at it.' She nudges them both upwards.

Finn hands her a glass of champagne. 'Age gracefully, Mum, please.'

'Nothing wrong with a bit of nip and tuck.'

'Why not have your head looked at while you're about it too, Gwen?' my father mutters sotto voce, raising his glass to her in a courtly gesture.

A car horn is hooting outside.

Granny shuffles through the door then, her skinny legs fragile as a spider's. Gwen glances at her son in alarm. 'I didn't know *she* was coming.'

'If we can't all be in the same room for a couple of hours on Christmas Day then it's pretty sad,' he tells her. '*I wouldn't say I have a family,*' Finn told me once when we were at Cambridge, '*I'd describe us more as a loose relationship of people.*' I squeeze his hand.

'Why's that ridiculous man here?' Granny tries to whisper, but everyone hears. I kiss her soft powdery cheek. Her grey hair is immaculately brushed with little strands curling about her ears and she's wearing a smart navy outfit. Granny always wears blue. Her late husband, Bobby, used to work on a cruise ship. 'Did you go to church?' She waves her stick at Dicky.

'I go to church once a year on Christmas Day, just for insurance.' He puffs his chest out like a crow.

'How's the work going?' my father asks him.

'Funny you should mention it, Phil.' I can't look at Dad as I know we'll both get the giggles. 'I met a couple in London who want me to redesign their kitchen, real City slickers, you know.' Dicky has an unfortunate front tooth that moves when he talks. 'I told them today it's all about smooth marble surfaces and units painted a uniform colour, to give it the minimalist look. "*Voilà!* It's a no-brainer," I said.'

'*Absolument*,' Dad replies gravely.

Finn touches my shoulder for solidarity before he hands Granny her glass of brandy and ginger and leads her to the tall comfy chair that's angled precisely towards the large flat-screen television.

Dicky continues, 'So the next stage was . . .'

'Why are you orange?' Granny interrupts. 'Where have you been? Ibiza?'

I try not to laugh. Dicky does have faint lines around his eyes where the sunbed goggles have been.

Next Ed arrives with his new girlfriend. 'Granny, this is Zoe.'

She eyes them cautiously. 'You're late. Stopped for a bit of nooky, did you?'

'Granny!' we all say together.

My father laughs. He likes Granny. She delves into her handbag to find her old silver cigarette case. 'I need a twig.'

Soon glasses are being refilled, crisps and nuts are being heaped into serving bowls. Finn is laughing about some new voice-over Ed has just landed for a soap powder. Ed is still an actor. He's had a few minor roles in soap operas and hospital dramas but hasn't made his name yet. 'When are you going to get a proper job?' Gwen always asks him.

I take some salted nuts over to Granny. I try hard not to inhale cigarette smoke, but she pulls me down on to the sofa next to her. 'Where's my favourite great-grandson?' she asks.

'Upstairs. He's tired, didn't sleep at all last night.'

'Good. I've brought you something.' Has Granny bought me a present this year? A piece of vintage jewellery, perhaps? With one shaky hand she gives me a newspaper cutting. 'Thought it was rather interesting,' she says. 'The experts say ADHD doesn't exist.'

Lunch is finally over and we are all watching the Queen's Speech. I can hear George jumping down the stairs. He never walks; he runs. He reaches the bottom and skids across the floor. George never lands; he crashes.

Gwen offers one side of her face to him and I watch her wipe it afterwards, the way I used to with an 'Ugh!' when either Mum or Dad kissed me. Her first grandchild and she can hardly bear to look at him. Granny pats the seat next to her. George ignores the signal and starts to tell everyone in great detail about the school nativity play. Already I can see glazed expressions. It's like a long-winded joke being recalled and then heavy disappointment because no one really gets it.

'Bravo,' Granny kindly says.

'Wow, look at all the presents!' He starts to shake them. 'Are they all for me?'

We decide now is a good time to open them and wrapping paper gets torn off with enthusiasm.

'Thanks for the cheque, Mum,' Finn says.

For the first time she looks sheepish. 'I know money's unimaginative but . . .'

'It's great,' he says graciously.

'I love my cardi, darling.' She presses it to her chest, but of course doesn't have time actually to try it on.

The telephone rings. 'Who calls on Christmas Day?' shouts Granny. 'It'll be "the lover", won't it?'

It is Clarky. 'Can we talk later? Lots of love,' I mutter quietly, aware of Granny staring at me like a hawk.

'Right.' Finn taps his champagne glass with a teaspoon again. 'I would like to make a toast to Josie.'

Is he going to praise me for my cooking? Thank me for hosting Christmas Day?

'This year, she couldn't have given me a better present.'

A shiver runs down my spine. 'I want to tell them,' he says.

'Finn,' I stare hard at him, 'don't you dare.'

'Josie and I are having a baby.'

Even George is quiet.

'You're what?' Gwen finally asks, straining her neck forward.

'Pregnant. Still early days, but we're thrilled.' He takes my hand and holds it tight.

'Fantastic, Josie!' Ed hugs me.

'Does that mean I have a brother?' George blurts out.

Finn looks expectantly at his mother. He still craves her approval. 'Was it a mistake?' is all she can say.

Mum walks over to me. 'I think it's lovely news.'

Gwen looks horrified, as if she's just been presented with a catastrophic tax bill. 'But I didn't think you wanted more children, Josie?' she says.

Ed looks at her with despair. 'Mum, you can't say things like that.'

'I think it's grand news,' Granny declares.

'I'm getting a brother!' George leaps up and starts to clap and dance. 'When, Mum? I want one now.'

'But what if it's another boy like George?' Gwen gasps. 'How will you cope if you have another child like him?'

'Twaddle! Will you shut up, Gwen?' Granny demands.

Has anyone noticed that I haven't said a word yet?

'What's wrong with me?' George asks, standing still now.

'Nothing.' I pull away from Finn and hug my son tightly, burying my head in his hair. I'm trying not to cry.

'Tell me,' Dicky starts enthusiastically, a sparkle in his eyes and one hand on his hip, 'what's new in sex these days?'

That's it. I'm off. Finn stops me at the banisters. 'Are you all right?'

'Don't even ask.' I walk upstairs.

'Has Mummy gone to have the baby?' George cries out happily.

Finn's family leave promptly.

Why hasn't he come to talk to me yet? Mum and Dad have left too, but Mum spoke to me earlier. 'He shouldn't have announced it like that, but I would have *loved* to have had a second child. Don't lose sight of what is very happy news,' she'd said, hugging me tightly.

I have to talk to Finn before I explode.

'Oh, Josie, I was going to bring you up a cup . . .'

'How dare you tell them!'

Finn starts tidying up the wrapping paper.

I am shaking violently.

'What difference does a couple of weeks make?' he asks, still not looking me in the eye.

'If you don't understand why I am so angry, I don't even know why we're together.'

He huffs. 'That's a bit drastic.'

I walk over to the sofa and hurl a cushion at him. It lands near the fire.

'Bad shot.'

'Why did you do it?'

'OK, I realise it didn't exactly go down the way I'd hoped . . .'

'That's an understatement.'

'I wanted to share our news. I'm happy!' He claps his hands. 'Is that so bad?'

'Yes. I didn't want George to know so soon.'

'Stop using him as an excuse.'

'He's not an excuse, and I knew your mum would react like that. I needed to get it sorted out in my own head first before you started telling everyone how *thrilled* we were.'

'Anyone would think you didn't want this baby.'

'There's a part of me that doesn't.'

'Do you know how that sounds?'

'I'm being honest.'

'There is no evidence to say you'll have another child with ADHD, I've told you that.'

'I don't care about the *evidence!* This is how I feel. I'm the one looking after George, day in, day out. All you do is take him to the car-boot sale.'

'That's unfair. I do my bit.'

'Well, you need to do a whole lot more. It doesn't matter that I might love my work at the moment. I can give all of that up for you and the next baby, like I gave up my job in Paris . . . for you, the almighty Finn!' I bow in mock reverence. 'It's always been about YOU.'

'You gave it up for us. It was bad timing but . . .'

'Bad timing?' I laugh.

'I'm so sorry I forced you to marry me.'

'So am I!'

'Oh, great. Mother's cheque's been ripped up with all the wrapping paper.'

'How very symbolic.'

He frowns. 'I can't talk to you when you're like this.' The telephone rings. He picks it up. 'Justin,' he says abruptly, with a roll of the eyes holding the phone towards me. I snatch it out of his hand. I can't even look at him. Finn takes off his glasses and rubs his eyes.

'Hi, Clarky,' I say, out of breath.

'I wanted today to be special,' I can hear Finn muttering. 'I wanted my family to know how proud I am that we're having another baby.'

I shift irritably. He always comes out with something sentimental to make *me* feel like the baddie.

'Besides, you told Clarky the news before me, what's the difference?'

He walks to the front door and slams it shut behind him.

I am curled up on the sofa. Finn still hasn't come back. I hear steps and feel a small smooth hand on my shoulder. I hadn't even thought of George in his bedroom listening to us howling at one another like wild dogs. I lift my face and he looks into my eyes, one hand still resting on me, the other clutching Baby. In his own way I think he is trying to say he loves me. We look at one another and finally make a connection that I didn't think George was ever capable of making. He's always lost in Legoland or his world of Pokémon cards. As he looks at me my heart swells.

I move my legs and he sits down next to me, resting his head against my shoulder. His eyes look blurred with tears. Stroking his hair, I tell him how sorry I am to have shouted at Dad.

'It's OK, Mummy. I know I'm difficult, I get a bit mental sometimes.' George forgiving me so easily makes me feel even worse. 'You don't want a baby like me.'

'I love you so much,' I tell him.

He nods. 'Do you love Dad?'

I take Baby from him and wrap it around both of us. George huddles in close. 'Yes. You see, when you love someone, that's when it hurts the most.'

11

I had been seeing Finn for four weeks. He was more tender than I had expected; more patient than I could have hoped for. 'And, oh, my God, he is so sexy,' I'd confided to Tiana, still unable to comprehend that he was with me. 'You're a good catch too, Josie,' she'd reminded me, as if I were a fish.

Finn only had to walk into a room and the atmosphere changed, girls instantly flicking their hair and applying gloss to their lips. 'All they want to know is, "Who's your friend?"' Christo would often say in despair because Finn hogged all the limelight.

I couldn't believe that it was my arm around him, that I was the one he kissed goodnight. Girls stared at me, no doubt wondering what I had that they didn't. However, I wasn't ready to sleep with him. 'You make him wait,' Tiana had advised too, 'I jumped into bed with Sean on the second date and it's game over.' I loved her advice; it was entertaining and generous in its honesty. The truth was I was terrified I'd do it wrong and then the spell would be broken. I knew Finn found it difficult because he'd told me; but at the same time I could sense he relished the challenge because I hadn't fallen into bed with him immediately.

I started to go to Finn's club every Thursday after work. I'd dance all night and by the end of the evening have red raw blisters on my feet. He'd often bring his friends into the restaurant. 'Josie, this is Paddy, Adam, Dom, and you know Christo.' Finn liked to untie my short white apron or stick notes into my bra, 'For the sex later,' he'd tell his friends, grinning, and they'd all pound his back in approval.

I was getting to know them all well. Paddy had a gathering every Monday night. He always wore flared jeans and a thick woolly jumper. He played Reggae music, smoked marijuana, and his dad sold watches in India. Adam wanted to be an actor. Finn called him 'the Thesp'. He teased Adam, saying his room was more like an English drawing room. 'I caught him hanging a pheasant from his window,' he'd told me incredulously. Dom was a drifter, living in his own world. He was the one who carried a stick like a shepherd's crook and often wore miniskirts. His father was a fashion designer who lived in Italy. I liked him because he was different, but Christo was my favourite of Finn's friends. One evening at Momo's I was carrying a couple of plates of penne and pesto when I saw a mouse scurrying over the worktop, near the baskets of bread. I shrieked and the plates crashed to the floor and smashed into smithereens. Finn and Christo rushed into the kitchen as if it were an Accident and Emergency ward. 'Mouse,' I managed to falter, as if I'd just been attacked by a great white shark.

'Where? How do we kill it?' Christo had grabbed a large broom and held it in front of him like a weapon.

'Any traps?' Finn looked at me. 'Or glue? Where'd it go?'

I pointed a wobbling finger towards the bread bin. 'Behind there.'

Christo took a few tentative steps. 'Do we get it into a bag and then hit it with a rolling pin or something hard?'

'That's cruel,' Finn said. 'How would you like to be hit on the head with a rolling pin?'

'I'm not a mouse. Josie, what do you think?'

'I don't care, just get rid of it!' I hid behind him.

'Christ, you're a scaredy-cat, Josie.' Finn was shaking his head at me now.

Christo leant in close to me. 'Don't worry, I'm scared of spiders.' We watched Finn as he took a long loaf of bread out of its bag and in one deft motion lured the mouse on to it; it wriggled out of his grasp, whiskers twitching, and Finn had to dive for it again before finally placing it in the bag and running out of the restaurant. 'Couldn't kill it,' he confessed when he returned, looking pale.

'You were scared!' Christo and I laughed at him.

Finn scratched his throat. 'What's the poor little thing ever done to us?'

I'd quizzed Christo on his background and learnt that his father came from Nigeria, his mother from Trinidad. He had always been educated in England. He'd gone to an English boarding school and had hated it. 'It was positively Victorian,' he said, shaking his head. 'I can still remember the feel of those wafer-thin blankets and the cold horrible bathroom. There was no comfort in that school.'

'Christo was put into the reject dorm, too,' Finn added. 'Tell J.'

It was the first time he had shortened my name and I did a double-take before listening to Christo.

'"We're English, we're white, so we won't make any of you prefects,"' he explained. 'That's what they told us straight out. I was chucked into the reject dorm with two Chinese blokes. "You won't ever be promoted to anything," the headmaster told us. Don't feel sorry for me,' Christo insisted, looking my way, 'that kind of thing has made me very self-sufficient. I got into music, it was my escape into another world.'

When I saw Finn and Christo together, it made sense to me why they were such good friends. They both had this sense of not being quite good enough, not fitting easily into Cambridge. Setting up their club was a way to carve out their own territory, do something meaningful to them both.

In between all of this, Finn worked hard. He had two essays to hand in each week, and had to work at least ten to twelve hours a day to get the reading done. 'The first three years are dry, nothing but learning facts and more facts. Physiology, biochemistry, anatomy . . . I can't wait to actually meet some real patients.' Sometimes we'd sit on my bed and I'd test him on what each joint and tendon were called and, more specifically, how to spell them. I'd point to diagrams illustrating kidneys and intestines, liver and gall bladder, and test him on the function of each. I was learning a lot about the fibula and the tibia, the metatarsal joints, and how my blood supply worked. If I cut my finger I'd learn how the body had receptors that picked up the message of pain. There was one time when I got bored with testing him. 'What's this called?' I asked, unbuttoning my top instead and pointing to my collarbone. He kissed it gently. 'Josie, you're distracting me.' All his papers scattered on to the floor.

His discipline was admirable. Sometimes he'd look so tired, his skin washed out, hair dishevelled and cheeks sallow. But there was always a steely determination in his eyes; something he felt he had to prove to himself. It was as if no one had ever believed in Finn and what he could achieve, so he had to make up for it by believing in himself. Underneath his bravado I was discovering someone who was very different from the Finn I had first met.

On a Saturday night we'd see a film or go out for a meal, as long as it wasn't pizza. One Saturday he took me to the local disco because they played my music there, he'd teased. On Sundays I'd join his friends in our favourite greasy spoon and we'd feed our hangovers on scrambled eggs, sausages, orange juice and coffee. At the end of an evening we'd lie on my single bed, our long bodies squashed together like a couple of happy sardines.

I loved everything about him: the smell of his skin, wet and salty after dancing; running a hand through his soft hair. We'd smoke joints in my room, the lobster ashtray becoming a best friend. There had been one time when Clarky was practising his violin next door and Finn and I were listening to a new CD he'd brought round. 'Keep it down. I'm trying to practise,' Clarky had shouted through the wall.

'Why does he play pieces that make you want to slit your wrists?' Finn asked me.

'But he's brilliant. Listen.'

'This is better.' He'd put the headphones on me instead. 'You like Kylie?' I had stopped hiding my music collection under my bed.

'I do. So?'

'So do I. Nice bottom too,' he'd added, grabbing mine instead.

It was all unexpectedly innocent, that's what I loved about it most.

The more time we spent together, the less self-conscious I became, as did Finn. But I was aware of letting my friendship with Clarky suffer. I felt guilty, but at the same time couldn't help it. I didn't want to start thinking about the fact that I had only a few weeks left in Cambridge and then

Finn and I would be in different countries. But I did think about it. All the time.

'I thought we could spend the day together?' Clarky suggested. 'Have some lunch, see a film.'

'I'm sorry, I promised Finn. His granny's coming to Cambridge for the day and . . .'

Clarky looked surprised. 'Hardly a hot date with Granny around.'

'We're taking her out punting.' I smiled, remembering Finn's vow never to take me out on the river. 'It's what she wanted to do,' he had explained, 'and you'll soon learn that what Granny wants, she gets.'

Clarky crossed his arms and clicked his tongue against the roof of his mouth. 'Grannies tend to be the head of the household. If she doesn't like you, well, that's it.'

'Thanks. I wasn't feeling nervous, but now I am.'

'When can I see you then?'

'Finn's working tomorrow night so I'm free.' The moment I'd said it I wanted to take it back.

'Thanks for making me feel second best, J. Thanks a lot.'

'I didn't mean it like that.'

'Have a good time.' He shut the door in my face.

It was a cold day, but the sky was a clear blue and the air was calm. Cambridge was the chilliest town I knew. 'Wear some extra-warm socks,' Finn had told me. I walked down the high street which was heaving with enthusiastic shoppers, fellows in their gowns, students on their bikes. I saw the pub where Clarky and I liked to meet after work. I still felt guilty. I had made him feel like a stand-in when Finn wasn't around. But he also had to stop being snide. Why couldn't he be happy for me?

Heading towards Magdalene Bridge, I spotted Finn standing by the steps leading down to the water. Beside him was a tall, smart-looking woman in a blue woollen coat and matching skirt.

Finn turned round as if he could sense I was close. He waved and told his grandmother who I was.

I held out my hand. 'You're late,' was the first thing she said to me in a voice that sounded as if she had smoked since the day she was born; either that or she was dying of thirst.

She examined me, just as Finn had. 'It's lovely to meet you,' I said.

She huffed, 'You don't know what I'm like yet.'

'Great, let's go,' Finn suggested, taking Granny's arm and leading her down the steps. She was broad-shouldered like him, with a generous chest, but her legs were as thin as twigs, her long and narrow feet planted in elegant blue high-heeled shoes to match her outfit. I wondered how they carried her weight.

Finn led her to a punt and helped her sit down. 'Thank you, darling,' she said, brushing the creases from her skirt once she was carefully positioned at one end. The punt rocked in the murky water. Finn took a striped wooden paddle and his pole. He rolled up his sleeves and stood squarely on the platform at the rear of the punt. 'Here goes. We call this part of town the Backs, Granny,' he said, trying to manoeuvre us out into the middle of the river. 'And it's called that because you can see the backs of all the famous colleges.'

'You're a bit quiet, aren't you?' Granny said to me.

'My father always says, keep silent unless you have something worth saying.'

I noticed the sapphire rock on her finger. 'You're the new piece of fluff in Finn's life, then?' she continued, unabashed.

'Er, yes, I am.' Though 'fluff' was hardly the word I'd have used.

'What happened to that Hatty girl?' She stuck out her chin, waiting for a response.

I looked at Finn.

'She had lovely little legs, but I didn't like her,' Granny continued. She started to twist the ring round her finger. 'She was a gold-digger, that one.'

'You think all women are gold-diggers. Anyway, what was she digging for? I'm a penniless student.'

I laughed in mock disappointment. 'Shucks! I thought you were rich!'

Granny crossed her arms tightly. 'My boy's going to be a successful doctor. You're a waitress, aren't you?' she couldn't resist adding.

'Josie's an artist,' Finn informed her. 'She's got a lot of talent.'

'Ah, thank you,' I said.

'Well, you have, J. So, Granny, I'll tip you out of the punt if you're not careful what you say.'

'Twaddle! He wouldn't dare.'

'Finn will be a fantastic doctor,' I returned the compliment.

'Ah, thanks, J.'

'I bet you're proud of him, Mrs Greenwood.'

She nodded. 'And he's going to row for Cambridge. He's going to be on the box.'

'No chance! Not fit enough, I drink and smoke too much.'

'He's a dreamboat, isn't he? I tell you, he's the spitting image of his father.'

I was enjoying the openness of our conversation. Finn's pole got stuck in the riverbed then and he lost his balance as he tried to retrieve it. 'Come out, you bastard,' he muttered. The punt started to rock from side to side and Granny was clutching on to the edge with both hands, her knuckles white. In the end he let the pole go and we started to paddle back to retrieve it. 'Don't worry, Finn, you're doing great,' I encouraged. A party of children with purple balloons tied on the back of their punt glided past us. A man in a boater and green waistcoat was steering them down the river in a beautiful straight line. They laughed and pointed at us. Granny shooed them away with her hand. I was trying not to laugh at Finn's pained expression; this was his idea of hell. Instead I asked Mrs Greenwood where she lived, how many grandchildren she had and what her husband did.

'He's dead. Passed away on St Valentine's Day, 1992. I cooked him a romantic meal and he expired, just like that. Heart attack.'

I was still trying to find the appropriate response when thankfully Finn stepped in, telling me his grandfather had worked on a luxury liner, organising fabulous cruises. 'Granny always wears blue, the colour he loved her in best. If I'm half as happy with the woman I love as Granny was with Grandpa, well, I'll be a lucky man.'

'My video player has broken down,' she suddenly announced. 'I miss not having a good handyman in the house.'

'What was your husband like?' I asked.

'Bobby was the salt of the earth. He loved ballroom dancing.' Her brown eyes came alive at the memory. 'I have dancing legs, you know.' She lifted her skirt to reveal sheer tights and smooth sculpted legs beneath. Not a hair in sight. 'I'm a freak of nature,' she boasted. 'We loved the movies, always sat right at the back, if you know what I mean?' She was tapping her long nose. 'Now, on to the things that really matter.' She raised one eyebrow. 'What does a girl like you want with my boy?'

'Granny, you can't vet every girlfriend I have like this.'

She chose to ignore him. 'Are you roosting together?'

'Roosting?'

'Sleeping,' Finn filled me in with a wink. 'Granny, it's none of your business. Leave Josie alone.'

I smiled wickedly. 'No, we're not. I've begged and tried every trick in the book, even a black lace see-through dress didn't work on him, but I figure he's got to relent sooner or later.'

Granny allowed herself to smile. 'Hold on to this girl, Finn. I like her!'

'Funnily enough, so do I,' he replied, looking directly at me. 'In fact, I love her, Granny.'

'Love me?' I repeated with a dumb smile. I wanted to walk over to him, but as soon as I put one foot in front of the other the punt started to rock again, this time more violently. 'Watch out!' Granny cried out. 'We'll all fall in and this jacket can only be dry-cleaned.'

We missed a canoeist narrowly. Finn and I were laughing madly now. 'I told you I was no good at this,' he shouted.

'All right, Mrs Greenwood, I'll stay put because I can tell your boy from here that I love him too,' I said. Granny raised an eyebrow, unmistakable amusement in her shiny eyes. 'She loves you. You love her. Everything's dandy. Now, can we get a curry? I'm bored and getting cold.'

'Praise the Lord,' Finn said, turning the punt around.

12

George lies on his bed refusing to get up.

'It's your first day back. You have to go.'

'Leave me alone!' he screams, bashing his head against the pillow.

With all my might I pin down his legs and pull off his stripy blue pyjamas. George covers his crotch. 'You're not allowed to see my bits, Mum.'

'I'm not looking,' I tell him, unbuttoning his pyjama top. 'Hey, how did you get that bruise?' It's on his right arm.

'Football.'

'Promise?'

He nods without hesitation.

I grab a hand and march him to the bathroom. Finn tells me I spoon feed George, but what he doesn't understand is that George *can't* do it. Anyway, the child psychologist told me there was no harm in helping him get dressed. 'There are bigger things to worry about,' she'd said, 'like his education.'

'I won't go to school. Over my dead body!'

'You have no choice,' I tell him.

Ten minutes later I sit on the loo seat watching George splash his face with cold water.

'Have you brushed your teeth?'

'Yes.'

I hold up his brush. 'It's dry.'

George takes it sullenly and then proceeds to squeeze the tube of toothpaste so hard that an enormous dollop lands on his Mickey Mouse brush and half of it falls on to the floor. 'Other children don't need their mummies to brush their teeth for them,' is a conversation Finn and I have had over and over again. In fact, he and I still argue about pretty much every single aspect of George's getting washed and dressed routine, so much so that he now won't take part in it at all.

I bite my thumbnail, trying to hold in the frustration. He *kind of* brushes his teeth before running back into his bedroom where I have laid out his school clothes. He yanks on his shirt and buttons it up incorrectly – nothing lines up. Is Finn right? Should I be doing it for him?

'Brush your hair.' George drags the brush through his hair once before dropping it on to the floor. I pick it up and tell him his hair's still tangled.

'What's he going to do when he's older? Marry a full-time carer?' is another typical Finn argument, each word like a blow to my heart.

'But George CAN'T do it. What part of that don't you understand? If I leave him he won't get dressed and then I miss my meeting. What else can I do?'

This is the only time when Finn looks as lost as me because there is no answer. 'Why don't we swap roles for one week, see how you get on?' I had once suggested.

'Right, gotta run,' he'd said with a flash of the car keys, a brief glance in my direction and rapid steps out of the front door.

George throws the brush on the floor again.

'You do that one more time and no pocket money. Remember your tie.' I go downstairs, telling him he needs to be ready in five minutes. I make myself a strong coffee.

Finn is eating a last mouthful of muesli. 'He'll never learn,' my husband helpfully reminds me. 'Right, I'm off.' He gives me a perfunctory kiss on the forehead.

After slamming the door on Christmas Day, Finn returned just an hour later. I was still with George, curled up on the sofa with Baby over our shoulders.

'Can I join in?' Finn sat down with us and I gave him some of the blanket. He put an arm around me; his hand was purple with cold. 'I'm sorry,' he said, moving in closer, our heads touching. 'I was naïve to think it wouldn't end disastrously. Anything that involves my mother normally does.'

'You deserve better than your mum.'

'I'm sorry,' George copied us.

'Do you think my mother has a single nice bone in her body?'

'She must have, she had you.' His grip on me tightened.

We have tried to patch things up, but he deeply resents the way I feel about this pregnancy. He wants to be excited about it, but says he can't even show that now. And I resent him for barely acknowledging my fears and concerns. He treats them as trivial which makes me realise he never fully understood how I felt when George was growing up. There is a big gap between us and we don't seem to be able to meet anywhere near the middle.

George tears downstairs, no tie on and holding no PE bag. His shirt is hanging out of his trousers and he isn't wearing any socks.

'Upstairs, George, NOW! Get dressed properly,' Finn orders.

'Don't shout.' I take George by the arm.

Finn clamps his briefcase shut. 'ADHD can't always be his excuse not to do anything properly. He's nearly seven years old.'

'Seven?' I laugh at how clueless or in denial Finn is. I tell him that Emma's son, Nat, the British Gas boy, still has to rely on his mother to get him up and out of the front door in the mornings, and he's eighteen. '*I'm exhausted,*' Emma wrote to me. '*Nat was on the internet late last night to a girl and he hadn't ironed his shirt for work Monday morning and kept on saying, "In a minute, Mum, in a minute." I didn't dare go to sleep, thinking he'd leave the iron on . . . the house would burn down . . . then this morning he wouldn't get up so in the end I had to chuck a bowl of freezing cold water on him.'*

'Well done,' I wrote back quickly, *'but isn't it a hassle having to dry all those sheets?'*

'Lose apprenticeship or wet sheets? Tumble dryer is the answer.'

'Get dressed, George.' Again Finn ignores what I've just said.

'I am dressed.' He looks at himself. His trousers and his shirt are on. I know exactly what he's thinking.

'No, you're not.'

'Dad, I am.'

'Do I go to work looking like a scarecrow?'

'I'm not a scarecrow,' says George, lip quivering.

'Where are your socks then?'

'Upstairs.'

'Well, go and get them.'

George runs back upstairs and a few minutes later returns wearing his socks inside out.

'At least he's got them on,' I say to Finn, who still doesn't look satisfied. 'I'll get his tie.'

Finn shakes his head. 'Has he taken his Ritalin?'

'Five minutes ago.' Give the patient their pill; they get better. If only life were that simple.

Finn picks up his house keys and heads towards the front door. 'Have a good day,' I call out as mechanically as

Finn's earlier peck on the forehead. I hate it when he leaves like this. It only takes the everyday grind of getting George ready for school and we're straight back to playing harassed husband and wife, unable to communicate. George is now preparing food for Rocky, heaping great spoonfuls into his bowl with gravy dribbling on to the clean white shirt that I ironed yesterday.

I go upstairs to get him another one. I attempt to hold him still while I put it on, followed by his half-chewed tie. George bangs my coffee mug against the table and some of that goes on his sleeve but I'm not changing this one. 'Won't go to school,' he starts to chant. 'Won't go to school.'

'You're going whether you like it or not.'

'Can we go to the Science Museum?'

'Nope.'

'Can we go to your special clothes shops, Mum, not the toy shops?'

'NO.'

Finally he is dressed. George puts Baby into his PE kit, along with his plimsolls and Aertex shirt. He takes his canvas satchel with homework and textbooks. I frogmarch him to the car and he struggles against me as I try to put on his seatbelt. 'I HATE you,' he screams when I shut the car door. 'Hate you, hate you, HATE YOU.'

I drive. Neither of us says a word. I should enjoy the rare silence, but instead the air feels spiked with tension.

'Mummy?'

'Yes.'

'Can we start the day again, please?'

My shoulders relax as I stop at the traffic lights. I turn to him. 'Yes, I'd like that.'

George smiles. 'And how are you today, Mummy?'

'Very well, thank you, George. How are you?'

'Very well too, thank you. Did you know that Mercury is the closest planet to the sun?'

'I didn't. How interesting.'

'The sun is about four point five billion years old, did you know that? Can we have some music?'

'Yes, go on.' He flicks in between the music stations, unable to settle on any particular one. I blot out the noise, an art at which I have become skilled. Kylie's 'Locomotion' starts to play loudly and the mood changes instantly as we both start to sing. When we stop at a red traffic light I turn the volume down. There's a tall man in a black cloak, with long bushy hair and a wispy beard, twirling around a lamp post, declaring at the top of his voice, 'JESUS IS LOVE! HE HAS COME TO SAVE US.'

He's wearing enormous headphones that are connected to a sound system in a bag slung across one shoulder and crossing his middle.

'JESUS IS HERE!'

We both can't help laughing at this funny sight. 'Where is he?' asks George, leaning out. I try to pull him back in.

'JESUS LOVES YOU.'

'He loves me?'

The man starts to pirouette around the lamp post. 'JESUS IS LOVE! HE'S ALL AROUND US.' His voice is so loud, I'm sure my parents can hear him as far away as Dorset. Someone opens a window from a top-floor flat to see what's going on. George looks to the left and right. 'But I don't see him!' he tells the man.

The light turns green and swiftly I drive on. George turns to wave at the prophet.

As we reach the school gates he's quiet. 'I don't want to go,' he says once more, but this time his voice is calmer and I know it's not going to lead to an argument.

'Why do you hate it so much?' I ask gently, dreading the answer. He's being bullied.

'I haven't got any friends,' he replies and stares ahead, tapping his hands restlessly against one another. The gesture reminds me of Finn when he's overdosed on caffeine.

I park the car and unbuckle George's seatbelt. 'You're my friend,' I tell him.

'You're my best friend, Mum,' he says back.

There are lots of mothers at the gate kissing their children goodbye. I watch George run across the playground. His *Thomas the Tank Engine* lunchbox snaps open and out fall his rubber cheese and ham sandwiches, wrapped in clingfilm, along with an apple and fromage frais yoghurt. Everyone laughs and jeers as he kneels down to pick it up off the ground. 'George is a loser,' one of the other boys calls. I want to rush over and help him put his lunchbox back together again, but know that would only encourage the other children to tease him more. George picks himself up off the ground and walks through the main school door. He doesn't turn round to see if I'm still there.

I turn on the engine and drive away.

'*Dear Emma,*' I write at work before Ruby arrives at the office, '*just taken George to school. OH, I feel blue. He tells me he has no friends. A part of me dies when he says that. Does Nat have friends now? Tell me it gets better . . .*'

'Oh, God,' she writes back. '*I remember those first days at school. I used to feel like a bad lion letting my cub go out into the wild, unprotected. Nat has made friends, he tells me he's "grown up a lot" and is better able to keep them now. George is a sweet boy. I'm sure it'll get better.*'

I hope she's right. Another message comes on to the screen.

'*PS Nat even made sausage rolls on his own with no prompting. Made a real mess, but I never would have believed it in a million zillion years. Keep the faith.*'

13

I park the car behind a shiny white van with a big blue disabled badge on the back and a luminous yellow sticker
which reads, 'IF YOU PARK IN MY SPACE WOULD YOU
LIKE MY DISABILITY TOO?'

There is a great buzz of noise outside the iron school
gates.

I suck a peppermint. Next to me is a mother with long
chestnut-coloured hair, the colour of autumn, that almost
reaches her waist. She's wearing a blue velvet jacket with a
patchwork skirt and heavy black lace-up boots. There's a
strong smell of garlic. What did I eat for lunch? I panic,
subtly trying to smell my breath.

'Sorry,' she says, hand over mouth, 'I've been making a
chilli sauce. I'm a cook.'

I could almost fit a napkin ring around her waist. She
clearly doesn't lick the wooden spoon. 'Josie Greenwood.'

She holds out one hand. Virtually every slim finger is
covered with rings with large aqua- or amber-coloured

stones. 'Agatha, but call me Aggie. *Murder on the Orient Express* was my father's favourite novel.'

I smile. 'What year is your boy in?'

'Two.'

'Mine too.'

'It's his first day. I moved to this area after my divorce.'

'I'm sorry.'

'About the area or the divorce?' She laughs. I like her already.

'The divorce.'

'God, no, I'm much better off without the sod.'

I laugh. 'The area's not so bad, there's a park with tennis courts and a playground. My son and I go for runs in the morning, but avoid the Uxbridge Road.'

'What's your little monster called?'

'George. Yours?'

'Eliot. I call him El. I wanted to call him Holmes, but my husband said he'd get teased at school. He was probably right,' she adds tight-lipped. 'About the only thing he *was* right about, though. I hear the old head had a breakdown and they had to get someone else in quick?'

'Mr Phipps. I haven't met him yet.'

The bell rings and children start to file out. Most of the girls carry pale blue and pink rucksacks, the boys carry black and red ones. Some boys kick a ball across the playground, others just walk straight to the gates and their mums. They're given a quick hug – George tells me it's not cool to hug your mum for too long now.

'Come on, El,' Agatha starts muttering. 'First days are always a bloody nightmare, aren't they?'

'General rule of thumb is, you know you're in trouble if a teacher comes out before your child. It means they have something bad to report,' I inform her.

Another crowd of boys walks out of the main entrance, but George is not amongst them. I feel like I am playing a game of Monopoly at school. If he comes out on his own, I've passed Go and can collect my £200. If he's with a teacher I haven't passed Go, I don't collect my money and we both go to jail.

Soon Agatha and I are the only two mums remaining outside the gate. It is eerily quiet.

'How many children do you have?' I ask.

'Oh, there he is!' we both exclaim at the same time. George is pushing a young boy in a wheelchair across the grey tarmac. Ms Miles follows closely behind. She's wearing a dull jacket with a dark skirt that matches the colour of her hair and general personality. Her hair is curled and looks waxy and stiff like a wig. 'I don't like this teacher,' I whisper to Agatha. 'She's been at the school for years and hates George.'

'Not so fast, George,' Ms Miles screeches at him. 'It's not a sports car.'

'Hi, Mum!' He lets go of one of the handles and waves.

'Looks like El's made a friend,' says Agatha. I want to ask her why Eliot is in a wheelchair, but now isn't the right time.

'Is everything all right, Miss Miles?' My heart is beating fast.

She smiles twitchily. '*Ms Miles*, please, and no, I'm afraid not. We had an "incident" in the creative writing class. Plagiarism.'

'It wasn't my fault!' George blurts out. 'Mum, we were asked to write 'bout what we did at Christmas and I said we'd visited my great-granny by the canal and I heard her fart.'

Eliot's shoulders start to heave up and down in the chair and he lets out a snort.

'George isn't lying,' I tell Ms Miles. I have passed Go! We're safe until the next round.

'I'm not lying,' repeats George. 'Eliot copied me! He said that his granny farted too!'

Eliot now sits quietly in his wheelchair which is largely covered by stickers of Bart Simpson. He has a knot of curly red hair, a splattering of freckles over his cheeks and nose, and he wears black-rimmed glasses, just like his mother's, except his are round and Agatha's are more oblong-shaped.

'El, why didn't you write something about that jungle puzzle we finished?' Aggie suggests.

'Boring!' George says with a laugh like a hyena. 'Dad gave me a scooter.'

Eliot hits his wheelchair in a rage. 'I don't have a dad.'

Ms Miles demands an apology from George.

I encourage him with a stern nod. I had been thinking more along the lines that a scooter would be no good for Eliot because he's in a wheelchair. So, in fact, double-whammy.

'Sorry. What's for tea, Mum?'

Ms Miles turns to Agatha and me. 'It's Eliot's first day. He was nervous, that's understandable.'

'I was nervous,' Eliot says as sweetly as an angel, but I am sure I can see a smirk behind those large hazel eyes.

'I think you owe my son an apology too,' I say.

'George shouldn't have given Eliot his work,' Ms Miles responds curtly.

'Wasn't he sitting in the front of the classroom? Couldn't you see what was going on?'

She purses her lips. 'Mrs Greenwood, I am a professional. Make sure it doesn't happen again, both of you. Is that understood?'

'Bitch,' George says as she walks away.

'George!' I gasp as if ice-cold water has been tipped over my head. 'Where did you hear that word?'

Eliot's shoulders are moving up and down again.

Aggie starts to push him towards the white van. 'Ms Miles is strict, isn't she?' She digs into a large leather satchel bag to find her car keys.

'She shouldn't be a teacher. I don't think she even *likes* children. Do you need a hand?' I say.

'No, we're pros at this.' She opens the boot of the van and presses a button on her keypad. A ramp automatically comes into place with tracks for the wheels of the chair. George stands watching, mesmerised.

She pushes Eliot into the back of the van and shuts the door.

' 'Bye, Eliot!'

George presses his face against the glass and starts to pull faces. I grab the arm of his dark green v-neck jumper and wrestle him away from the van. Aggie watches, wondering why I can't control my son. I can see it in her eyes. Eliot puts both fingers up at me. I blink and look again. 'Bugger off,' he mouths now, hitting his wheelchair triumphantly with a wicked smile and a lick of his lips.

'George!' I shout above the noise in the car. 'Turn it down. What's wrong with Eliot?'

'What?' he shouts back.

I reach to adjust the volume switch. 'Why's he in a wheelchair?'

'His legs don't work properly,' my son states simply. 'Is it the same thing as my head not working properly, Mum? My head's too busy all the time, isn't it? Are Eliot's legs lazy all the time?'

Finn is on call today, but should be home by now. It's past eleven. I'm in my pyjamas, tucked up in our large double bed. A soft glow warms the white room. With the money Finn's mother gave us for Christmas (Gwen had to write out another cheque) I bought a new glass lamp base for our bedroom and a white pleated shade. The only colour in our bedroom comes from the orange, yellow and pale blue flowers on the curtains and a bright pink stool near my dressing table. I am talking to Tiana on the telephone.

'How did the date go with Mr Shuttlecock by the way? Sorry, that was ages ago and I never asked.' Clearly not that well otherwise I would have heard about it.

'Another frog. He had rather bad, let's say, "hygiene issues".'

'Oh,' I say, more disappointed than her.

'Has Clarky met anyone?'

'No.'

There's a sigh of relief. This piece of news is as comforting to Tiana as hot sticky pudding because it means that she's not alone in her quest to find the perfect soulmate. 'The thing is, he's still hung up on you, isn't he?'

'Oh, come off it.'

'The whole country knows it, except you, although I think you do know really. How's Finn been since announcing the baby's arrival to the whole world? I love that man, but God, he can be difficult, can't he?'

'He's now convinced I don't want the baby. It's like his pride is hurt because I don't want *his* child, and that's not true.'

I hear a key in the lock. 'He's back.'

'You go. Talk to you later.'

Finn takes the stairs two at a time. I hear him going into George's bedroom first. Finally, he puts his case down and lies on the bed next to me, kicking his shoes off.

'You're late,' I say.

'I had a quick drink with Christo. Last orders.'

'You didn't ring, that's all.'

'Do I have to call all the time outlining my movements?'

'Finn, what's got into you?'

'Where do I start? Sometimes I wonder why I do this job.'

'Because you're good at it?'

'I saw a young girl who's been snorting cocaine like there's no tomorrow.'

'How does that affect the heart?'

'It tightens the arteries; they can go into spasm. If it's short-term use it's normally fairly temporary, but in this case . . . oh, God. I lost one patient in cardiac arrest today and had to tell the mother. She was only twenty-fucking-two.'

I touch his shoulder and start to rub it gently. 'I'm sorry.'

'Hey, it's the job. That's what I'm paid a shitty amount to do. Tell relatives that we couldn't save their loved ones.' He looks at me, his eyes tired and flat.

'I'm sure you did . . .'

'We should have been able to save her.'

'You're a doctor, not God. I'm sure you did everything in your power to help that girl.'

He shakes his head with miserable frustration. 'J, I know you're trying to help, but you have no idea what it's like.'

'No, I don't,' I admit. 'I can only imagine.' I reach out to try and touch him, but he flinches. His mind is far away. He's still with that twenty-two-year-old. 'How was your day?' he asks absently.

I tell him about the first day back at school and meeting Eliot and Aggie. 'I'm tired and it's only day one.'

'Are you saying all this to make me feel guilty about you being pregnant?'

'What?'

'You're trying to tell me again that another baby is the last thing you need.'

'No, I'm not,' I say slowly. 'You're twisting my words.' I turn off the light and turn away from him, pulling the duvet closely around me. 'I'm going to sleep.'

We lie next to each other, but there's an ever-widening chasm between us.

14

It was approaching Christmas and the end of term for the students. I was sitting at the kitchen table watching Clarky chop an onion. 'I can't wait to go home, J. I like Cambridge, but I'm bored to death by my job and I miss my music.' He was making up for my silence by rambling. 'If I have to stack one more box of flipping cards . . .'

'If I have to serve one more pizza,' I muttered distractedly.

'Are you all right?'

'Fine.'

'You're not thinking about . . .' Clarky shifted from one foot to the other, 'you know who?'

'You'd like him if you got to know him.' I wasn't sure why I was defending him.

'Hmm,' he said without conviction. 'Maybe.'

'I need to call Mum,' I lied. 'Back in a minute.' I knew he was watching me as I walked out of the room.

*

I shut my bedroom door and stared at the telephone, willing it to ring. Finn hadn't been in touch. How could someone's feelings change overnight? Was he bored because I hadn't slept with him? I hated myself for being so dependent on another person's actions. I would stare at the restaurant door, willing him to walk in. My feet felt sluggish; my heart wasn't in anything. The idea of food made me feel ill as I placed it in front of other people. The last message Momo had written on my pay packet was, 'Men aren't worth it.'

I'd miss Momo, his bushy moustache and volcanic temper. It was impossible to imagine not seeing Finn again, though. This couldn't be it? The last time I'd turned up to his club he was like the evil twin. 'Suppose you're going to ask me why I haven't been around?' he'd said, immediately on the defensive.

I'd been shocked by his abruptness. 'No, I'm here to have a good time, thanks.' He was looking at me, but he was absent, his eyes blurred with drink. 'It's all a load of bollocks,' he started to say.

'What?'

'This.' As if that were explanation enough.

'What are you talking about?'

'You wouldn't understand,' he'd said sternly, jaw clenched. Everything about him was unforgiving.

'I can't if you won't tell me. What's going on?'

'Don't worry about it.' He'd wiped the beer froth from

the corner of his mouth. He looked grubby, like he hadn't slept for a week, stubble on his chin, hair needing a wash. His breath stank of cigarettes and alcohol.

'Finn, can we talk?'

'Now's not a good time.' Three girls came tottering up to his booth. 'What can I do for you lovely ladies?'

'When you stop behaving like an idiot, let me know.' I walked away, expecting him to come after me and apologise profusely, but he didn't. 'What's wrong with Finn?' I asked when I bumped into Christo at the top of the stairs, putting my hand on his arm. 'He's in one of his moods,' was the enigmatic reply.

'Meaning?'

'Meaning, let him be until he cools down. It's family stuff.'

Walking home I told myself over and over again that he wasn't worth it. 'You're going anyway . . . thinks he's God's gift . . . arsehole . . . you can do better.' Yet I'd known then, as I do now, that even if I could, I didn't want to.

'What's wrong?' Clarky asked when I walked through the front door. I could see he was about to go out, then I remembered he had a date with one of the girls he worked with in the shop.

'Nothing. You scrub up well, Clarky.' I'd straightened his shirt collar, trying hard not to cry, but my lip was quivering, chin wobbling.

'Do you want me to stay with you?'

'I'll be fine, promise. Finn's being a shit, that's all,' I conceded, unable to keep anything a secret from him.

Next thing I knew Clarky was on the phone running off a list of excuses to his date. 'Feeling sick . . . it came on suddenly . . . make it another night . . . sorry.'

'You didn't have to do that.' I leant my elbows on the table. 'That's lame.'

'I don't care. Come on, what's he done?' He sat down next to me and listened. 'No one should treat you like that, Josie,' he said, taking me into his arms. 'Not even Finn.'

I shut the front door and Clarky ran after me, flinging it open again. 'Where are you going? Supper's ready, I've even made our favourite custard cream.'

'I've got to see him.'

'J, let it be.' He took my hand possessively, trying to draw me back in. 'He's not worth it.'

'You don't know him like I do. You don't see everything I see.'

Clarky coughed. 'I hope not.'

'He *is* worth it.'

'Is he?'

'If you met someone, had the best time with her . . . and then nothing, no explanation, wouldn't you want to find out *why*?'

He let go of my hand, as if finally setting me free. 'Right,' he said, stepping away from me. 'Go.'

'I'm going to miss your supper.' My stomach was so knotted with nerves I knew I couldn't eat anyway.

'Oh, for God's sake, J, just go.'

'Clarky, what's wrong?'

'Stupid onions.' He wiped one eye. 'Mum says I should cut the root off, but I always forget.'

I blew him a quick kiss before I ran out into the cold night air.

15

It's the weekend. George survived the first week of term without a detention. As a reward, I allowed him to stay up for an extra half an hour on Friday night.

I am furious with Finn. He's playing golf this weekend. 'It's tradition,' he had argued. 'I thought you knew it was this weekend?'

'Oh, I should have known! Did you tell me via sign language or was it telepathy?'

'It's the Sperm Bank Cup, J.' It's called the Sperm Bank because every year one of the boys has to buy a trophy for the winner. When it came to Finn's turn, having left himself no time to buy one, the only thing he could find was a trophy in the shape of a sperm.

'I wrote it on the blackboard, George must have wiped it off.' I knew he was lying then.

My precious Sunday, my one day off, has now been flushed down the plughole. I haven't painted for weeks. All my plans to try and build up a portfolio aren't happening. I hate it when I don't get any time to paint. 'Go,' I snapped at him then. 'Have a great time, but next weekend you're on duty.'

'I'm working next weekend. On call. Mmm, this is delicious.'

'Fine.' I started to clear the dinner plates.

'Hey, I haven't finished!'

'Who's going to take George to the car-boot?'

'You?' He looked guilty because he couldn't say it to my face.

I dropped the plates in the sink. Water slopped on to the floor.

'You take me for granted. And don't you dare tell me I'm hormonal!' I shouted halfway up the stairs.

He has gone to a golf club in Berkshire. I didn't hear him leave this morning.

Thankfully I have signed George up for some weekend tennis coaching and the course starts today. It's for six to ten year olds, every Saturday morning.

He runs into the kitchen dressed in purple shorts, a bright orange T-shirt, his knee-high grey school socks which show off his knobbly knees, stripy sweat bands over his wrists, and finally his purple swimming goggles. 'Where's Dad?' he asks.

'He's at the Sperm Bank,' I say without thinking.

'What's the sperm bank?'

'He's playing golf and you're not . . .' I look at him again to make sure, '. . . going to a fancy-dress party.'

I march him back upstairs. 'But, Mum, I want to look cool.'

I walk into his bedroom as if I am walking on stepping-stones to avoid the mess. When I open the wardrobe the door hits a pile of junk. I take out a blue tracksuit and white aertex shirt. 'Do you want to look different from everyone else?'

'No.'

'Put these on then.' I try to take the goggles off him.

'Bitch!' he yells, hitting my arm hard.

'What did you just say?'

'Bitch,' he repeats.

This is when I need Finn. 'Where did you hear that word?'

'Eliot.'

'Don't you EVER say that word again. It's horrible and it hurts me. Have you washed properly?'

'Yes.'

I go into his bathroom. George has dropped his towel into the bath. I fish around in the sink to retrieve his tooth-brush and the soap which is a buttery mess now, congealed and misshapen. I go back into his bedroom, but the track-suit and top are untouched. 'Wear what you like then, George. Downstairs in five minutes for breakfast.'

I turn on the kitchen radio. *'We have become a society of pill-popping addicts, John. Why are children given Ritalin?'* I stop what I'm doing and listen carefully. *'It seems very extreme to give kids pills these days just to keep them quiet.'*

'Is it lazy parenting?'

'Excuse me?' I shout out.

'Yes, John. Parents should teach their children how to behave.'

'Right, it's all my fault then. Wanker.'

'Our generation never had this type of problem. These kids need to stop sitting in front of the computer all day long and take some exercise.'

'OH! That's what we need, is it? George can play tennis, that'll fix it. Tosser!'

'A good diet helps too. Children eat too much junk food. All children wriggle about and have short attention spans, that's normal. Goodness, I was a manic little thing! There's no need to put a label on children like this and drug them. It's a phase they'll grow out of.'

'What? When they're ancient and decrepit? Come and live with us, you'll soon get the picture. Idiot.'

'ADHD – myth or fact. Why don't you call us with your views? But now for some mellow music to put you in the mood for the weekend . . .'

I turn it off.

'Honey or jam, George?'

'Don't mind.'

'Right, jam it is. Cheerios or Shredded Wheat?' I place a glass of orange juice on a coaster in front of his plate.

'Don't mind.' He moves the glass away from its coaster and places it on the edge of the table, where he can reach it with minimum effort.

I hand him both cereal boxes and take Finn's advice, telling him to decide for himself. I move the glass back on to its coaster. George takes the Cheerios box and turns it upside-down, the entire contents falling into the bowl and spilling over on to the table and floor. Like a chess move he pushes the orange juice back to the edge of the table.

He eats about three rushed spoonfuls and then jumps up, knocking over the glass. It's plastic because this happens all the time. He runs over to the television and turns it on. He tells me he wants us to take Rocky to the tennis club. He doesn't understand that pets aren't allowed. I'm wiping the orange juice off the floor as he asks me again and again and again.

I drive us to the gym in silence.

'Mummy, can we start the day again, please?'

Shoulders drop. 'Yes, I'd like that. How are you?'

'Very good, thank you, Mum. How are you?'

As George is talking I say a prayer that he will behave during the tennis lesson.

I liken trying to find a hobby that suits him to the dating game. It all starts off well and then we get that ominous telephone call two weeks later from the coach, saying, 'I'm sorry, it's just not working out.' I have to break the news to George and when I see his face trying so hard not to crumple in front of me, we go and get Baby and sit together on the sofa for a minute, both of us wrapped in the warmth of the blanket. As I hear his rapid breathing against my chest, I say gently, 'I'm sure it's not you, Georgie, don't take it personally.' He then flings the blanket off and says, 'It's all right, Mum. I don't care.' And he's on to the next date. We've tried non-contact rugby, football, even gymnastics.

'*Nat tried Tai Kwon Do, Judo and Karate, but all he did was jump on the other children,*' Emma wrote. '*Have you tried tennis? Nat's quite good at that.*'

I park the car. George pulls impatiently on the door handle, but it's child-locked. 'Listen to the tennis coach, and don't talk to the other children when they're trying to hit the ball.'

He nods.

'Wow! Look over there!'

As he turns I pull his goggles off.

'Mum!' He cradles his head as if in pain.

'Trust me, darling, I'm doing you the world's biggest favour.'

I am on the cross-trainer and can see the tennis courts through the glass walls. Most of the children are wearing tracksuits and Nike or Reebok tops and they all have flash shoes and racquets. The tennis courts are bright blue, the colour of the sea. They make me feel dizzy.

The coach is young with fair hair. He wears a bright red tracksuit with a navy sweatshirt. His name is Paul Lobb. I explained to him that my son is 'a little hyper and gets restless. By the way, great surname,' I added. Finn once told me there was a dermatologist at the hospital called Dr Cream.

Paul seems to be shouting some instruction because they all put down their racquets and start to jog around the two courts. I can't hear anything through the plate glass. I lose my footing as George starts to pull at another boy's T-shirt, pulling it so tight that the boy has to stop running and then George overtakes him. The boy turns round furiously. Paul intervenes. I adjust the pace of the machine but press the wrong button because it starts to accelerate rapidly. The woman next to me gives me a funny look.

The boys gather in a huddled circle to hear Paul's instructions. He's showing them how to bounce the ball up and down on the racquet. George is at the edge, out on a limb. He picks up a ball and hits it with all his strength across the two courts. It lands in the netting. When he catches my eye I wag a furious finger at him. 'BEHAVE,' I mouth, and lose my balance on the machine again.

They start to scatter around the court to try out the exercise. George nudges one of the children who is deep in concentration. Oh, lord, what's he saying? The other boy pelts the ball straight into George's eye and I nearly fall over. 'Oh, shit,' I shout, only to be met with yet more stares.

George is busy trying to buy some crisps even though I said he couldn't. I didn't give him any money so he's thumping the machine instead.

'Freak!' one of the boys on his course mutters as he walks past.

'Can't you try once more?' I beg Paul.

He shakes his head.

'Oh, please! Make him sprint round the courts, anything to burn up his energy.'

'We can refund you for the other five lessons. If you go to the reception desk they'll sort it out for you.'

With a heavy heart I join George who is staring at the spicy Nik-Naks. He gives the machine another whack. 'Come out, you bastard!'

I drive him home. 'Why do you do it, George?'

'What?'

'Behave so badly.' I always make a point of being cross with George's *behaviour*, not with George himself.

'I don't know,' he replies simply. 'My head's busy all the time, Mum.'

If I could make one single wish, it would be to reach inside George's head, take out all the hundreds and thousands of thoughts buzzing in his mind, each vying for attention centre-stage, and put them into a logical sequence. I wish the ADHD would leave my son in peace.

I wish it would leave us all in peace.

Sunday mid-morning and Clarky and I are about to go for a swim at a new centre in Shepherds Bush. It's in a gleaming white building and they have two pools. One is smaller with water as warm as a bath and is well equipped for disabled children; the other is for general swimming. George's school has just started lessons here. However, he has already been banned for two weeks. 'All he wants to do is drown the other children,' the teacher told me.

I walk into the steamy swimming pool area, the tiled flooring hard beneath my feet. A lifeguard, wearing a yellow T-shirt and shorts, sits on a tall chair looking bored. I see Clarky watching George dive bomb into the turquoise pool at full-speed, almost colliding with a young girl in a Speedo swimming cap and goggles. The spotty youth stirs himself into action, climbing down from the chair and crouching at the side of the pool. 'Watch where you're going,' he calls to George. 'Who's supervising you?'

'I'm with him,' Clarky says. The lifeguard nods. I walk down the shallow steps. 'There's Mum,' shouts George. I feel his arm wrap itself around my leg. He clings on so tightly that I nearly sink underneath the water. Next I am marking his handstands out of ten.

'Six, your legs weren't straight,' I tell him.

'Oh, Mum.' He plunges into the water again.

'How about me?' Clarky dives in.

'Rubbish!' George and I laugh together. George doggy-paddles to the other side of the pool.

'We haven't spoken for ages,' Clarky says to me. 'Well, it feels like that, with Christmas being in the way, which incidentally was awful. "What have you got to show for your life?" was all Mum and Dad could ask. They might as well have said straight out what a huge disappointment I am to them because I'm only a music teacher.'

I tell him briefly about our Christmas and Finn breaking the news about the baby without telling me. 'He was also put out that I'd told you about the pregnancy before him. He asked me again and again if we'd ever . . .' I stop.

'What?'

'Oh,' I wave dismissively, 'nothing.'

'He asked you what?'

'If there'd ever been anything between us.'

'You've never told him about that night, have you?'

I lean against the edge of the pool and circle my feet. 'No.'

'Why not? Doesn't he deserve to know?'

'Can't some things be private? We were eighteen. It was between you and me. It was a long time ago. Let it be.'

There's an awkward silence. I start to shiver and say I'm going to swim a length to warm up but his arm pulls me back. 'I wish we'd talked about it,' he says quietly. 'Why didn't we?'

'I don't know. We were immature back then, I guess, a bit embarrassed, but there's no point now.' I attempt to swim again but his arm grips mine even more tightly.

'I was in love with you.'

'In love with me?' Unnerved I pull my arm away from

him. 'Clarky! Don't say that! I'm not talking about this. Besides, it's disloyal to Finn.'

'Disloyal? You weren't even with him then.'

'That's not the point. It's weird talking about it now.'

'I *was* in love with you.'

'Well, you had a very strange way of showing it. I seem to remember you did everything in your power to avoid me for the next three months. I started to think that it had been a complete figment of my imagination.'

'You didn't exactly come forward either. I woke up and you'd gone. I knew you'd thought it was a mistake, I didn't want to hear you say you still loved Finn.'

I shake my head, almost smiling. 'I can't believe we're talking about this now, in a pool.'

'Nor can I.'

I look towards the seating area and see Aggie through the glass window, drinking a cup of coffee. She's wearing a thick cream scarf with pom-pom edging. I didn't know Eliot went swimming. I look around to see where George is. He's about to jump into the water, fingers clamped over his nose. I wave to Aggie. 'We should be able to laugh about it now. No big deal. It was one night, that's all.'

'Right. Who's that?'

'Aggie. She has a son in George's class.'

Eliot is pushed into the pool area, a team of professionals surrounding him. There's a tall man wearing a pair of black swimming trunks and a white T-shirt. He must be the teacher. He has well-muscled arms, and a whistle on a piece of cord hangs around his neck. George waves at his friend and Eliot does the royal wave back before being pushed towards the much more luxurious heated pool.

Clarky turns to me again. 'I should have told you how I felt.'

'Well, it's a bit too late for us to "chat" now,' I say. 'Twelve years too late to be precise.'

George swims over to us.

'Let's not talk about it again, OK? It's unfair on Finn.' Just mentioning it makes me feel guilty, as if I have betrayed him this very moment.

'I won't say another word.'

'About what, Daddog?' George asks.

Clarky swims off in a fast front crawl. George looks at me.

'Nothing, sweetheart. Boring stuff.'

'Oh. There's Eliot!'

Different kinds of coloured floats are being attached to Eliot's spindly body. The small pool is divided into two sections by a red-and-blue barrier. I introduce myself to the teacher, explaining that El and George are school friends. 'Can my son watch for a minute?' I ask.

But already George has jumped into the other pool. 'It's like having a bath, Mum!' he shouts. 'It's hot.'

'George, out! I'm sorry.'

'Frédéric,' the man introduces himself in heavily accented English. 'And this is my assistant.' He signals to a young woman wearing a navy costume. 'Your son can join in, I am very happy if Eliot is?' They lift him carefully on to a white plastic chair.

'Are you all right, Eliot?' Frédéric asks. '*Bien*. Are you ready to go?'

Eliot assumes his kingly position on the throne as he is propelled into the air and lifted over the water. The assistant turns a wheel and the chair is gradually lowered into the pool. George watches, fascinated. He jumps up and down in keen anticipation, waiting for Eliot's toes to hit the water. Why can't *he* sit on the chair? I know that's what he's thinking.

George is splashing El already. I pull a worried face.

'That's good,' Frédéric is saying, holding Eliot carefully in the water, 'splash your friend back. *C'est important* . . . it is important being comfortable in the water. It is the first thing I teach children, not to have any fear.'

George certainly has no fear. I remember even as a toddler he used to jump trustingly straight into the pool. More importantly, he floated afterwards. 'Come on, kick those arms, Eliot, get your friend really wet,' Frédéric encourages. Eliot has little strength in his arms but he is trying so hard, his face getting redder and redder, almost matching the colour of his hair.

'Come on!' shouts George. 'Harder!'

He has now dived under the barrier and is on his back, slicing his arms and legs through the water.

I notice Frédéric watching him. 'He has good body position,' he tells me.

'He does?' Is he talking about George?

'Yes, he is naturally flat, buoyant in the water, with long straight legs. Could you take over with Eliot for a minute?' he asks the assistant. 'That's right, Eliot, push those arms.'

Frédéric walks across to the other side of the pool. 'George, could you come here?' He's not listening. 'George,' he repeats, 'can you do this?' He pushes his own feet away from the wall and glides across the pool on his back.

George sort of does it. He pushes off in a burst of energy then loses momentum. 'You need to do it more slowly, it's all about control,' Frédéric tells him. 'Once more, please.'

George does a handstand instead.

'He finds it difficult to concentrate,' I inform the coach. 'He has ADHD and . . .'

But Frédéric stops me, uninterested. 'I teach many like him before. For each child there is an obstacle. Many are scared even to put their face in the water. I had one child, Peter, it take weeks to make him trust it. He even hated having a bath. He felt, what is the word . . .' He clicks his fingers.

'Scared?' I suggest.

'No, claustrophobic. I told the mother to sprinkle water,' he mimes it, 'over his head during bathtime, which she did. I also ask her what her son's favourite toy is. She say Nemo from *Finding Nemo*, so I buy lots of little Nemo and make Peter dive to get. That was the answer.' He looks over at George who is playing with Eliot again. 'If you look hard enough, there is always an answer.'

At the end of Eliot's lesson Frédéric claps. 'Well done, Eliot, and thank you, George. You come again and I teach you to swim like a professional? You are good.' He pats George on the back. My son is being praised and you can see it in his smile.

He kisses me on the lips. I feel the warmth of a naked body next to mine. His hand feels hot against my skin.

'I'm sorry,' he says. 'Really sorry. Are you awake?'

I open my eyes as he brushes the hair away from my neck and kisses my skin, the touch of his lips soft. 'Christo gave me a lecture right the way around the course, telling me what an arsehole I am.'

'What's the time?'

'Midnight. Were you asleep?'

'Yes.'

'I thought you were awake.'

'Right,' I say doubtfully.

'OK, I woke you up, but it's to say something *very* important.'

'I'm listening.'

'I'm really sorry for taking you for granted, and I do know how lucky I am to have you.' I turn to face him in the dark. 'I rehearsed that line all evening,' he says with a smile, 'but I mean it, every word.'

'You *can* be an arsehole, and you're *very* lucky to have me, but thank you for telling me.'

He traces the outline of my cheek. 'I don't know why you put up with me when you could have had anyone you wanted.'

'The trouble is, I don't want anyone else.' I hold him close to me; his hands are inside my nightshirt, touching the curve of my stomach.

'I'm going to try harder, J . . .'

We start to kiss, the intensity of his touch taking me back to the first time we made love. Finn holds me tight, our legs locked together perfectly. I rest my head back, my hair falling over my shoulders, Finn's hands firm around the base of my spine, fingertips digging into my skin. I feel light again, his touch letting me escape from reality into a dreamy blue existence where everything is OK. Finn and I are in love. We are happy.

16

I walked past the porter's lodge, under the arch, adrenalin kicking in. I went to the bar. No sign of Finn. He had to be here. I hammered on the door and he opened it readily. 'No need to shout,' he said, walking across the sitting room and back into his bedroom.

'No need to shout?' I belted out even louder.

His room was a mess. Papers strewn across his desk, ashtrays full of cigarette stubs, curtains tightly shut, bed not made. 'What has happened to you?' He hadn't shaved and looked as if he hadn't changed clothes either for about a week. I started to pace the room and stopped when I saw the lipstick mark on his pillow. I felt sick. 'Have you slept with someone else?'

'Someone else? *We* haven't even slept together yet,' Finn pointed out. 'Let's not get into that boring relationship stuff anyway.' His eyes were as hard as stone.

Bags and books were strewn on the floor, and a dark brown trunk. 'What's this?'

'I'm busy packing. I'm leaving Cambridge, I'm not cut out for this shit.' He indicated his desk with its small spidery lamp shining across a heap of papers. I sat down on his bed, hoping this was a bad dream.

'You can't leave.'

'Christ, you're naïve sometimes,' he commented with a patronising laugh. 'I guess it's the age difference.'

It was the first time he had used that against me. 'What – two years? Besides, it's not me acting like a two-year-old right now, is it?'

He laughed cynically. 'Cambridge isn't what it's cracked up to be. Most people are only here to fill their address books anyway.'

'That's not true.'

'Isn't it?'

'No, you've got great friends and your club.' Still he said nothing. 'So, you're going to quit, just like that?'

He started to roll a cigarette. 'Yep, just like that.' I walked over to him and pushed the tobacco away. To my surprise he didn't fight to get it back as I leant across the desk to open a window. 'I want to know what's going on.' I chucked the ash and stubs into a bin along with some empty bottles.

He took a deep breath. 'Well, my excuse for a mother has walked out on my father, again, and he's a mess. I'm leaving Cambridge. That's about the sum of it.'

'I'm sorry . . . about your dad, your family.'

He frowned heavily. 'Family? That's a joke. I don't have a family, more a loose relationship of people. Dad's in hospital, drugged on anti-depressants. I can't just stay here, my nose in a book. It's not real. My father needs me.'

'Right. So you think you're helping your dad out by just giving up, drinking and smoking yourself into depression too?'

'He needs me,' Finn stated flatly again.

I knelt down in front of him. 'But what do *you* need? You want to be a doctor. You can't throw it all away. I can imagine what you're going through . . .'

'You've got no idea,' he interrupted. 'You have a cosy little family life.'

I couldn't argue with that.

'I've had enough of the work anyway. It's years of training before I even make any money and I don't have a trust fund I can dip into. I'm not good enough, I'd only disappoint myself.'

I stood up and moved away from him. 'Will you listen to yourself? You think you've got it so tough. Poor Finn, the whole world's against him. Here you are, in one of the best universities in the country, with so much ahead of you, and all you can do is feel sorry for yourself. I'm sorry about, your parents splitting up, but it happens to a lot of people. OK, not me, but don't talk to me as if I know nothing about life. The only thing I've been naïve about was believing you were a nice guy. Leave, then! Smoke, take more drugs.

Drink yourself into oblivion. Your father will applaud your decision.'

He was silent.

'Why couldn't you tell me about your dad before? And then you go and sleep with someone else! Nice touch.'

'Well, what do you expect? I was tired of waiting for you.'

'You are a shit. Clarky was right.'

'Like the violin man's objective!'

'I'm leaving in a few days, I'll probably never see you again, and you weren't even going to come and say goodbye?' I turned away from him. I needed to get out. ''Bye Finn.' I walked out of his bedroom and out of the front door. 'Have a nice life,' I called out behind me. The tears were flooding down my face now. His chair scraped back and before I knew it he was out in the corridor, grabbing my arm. 'Oh, God, I'm sorry, don't go. Please.'

I wrenched my arm free.

A door opened. 'Could you keep the noise down?' Finn's neighbour asked. He was so introverted he couldn't look either of us in the eye. He was a 'natsci' which Finn told me was a student of natural sciences. 'I'm trying to work.' He shuffled back inside his room.

'I'm sorry, so sorry,' Finn repeated as if stuck on the words. 'I don't know what I was thinking.' He held my face between his hands. 'I need *you*.'

He led me back inside. Before I had time to say anything his face was pressed against mine and we crashed back against the door.

'Ow, Finn!'

'You are the last person I wanted to hurt.' He took my hand and guided me back into his bedroom.

He was kissing me urgently now and I kissed him back. How could he have so much power over me? There wasn't a single part of me that wanted him to stop. 'I've wanted to do this since I first met you.' He moved to my neck and then back to my face and our lips met in exactly the right place. It felt incredible. 'Will you stay with me tonight?'

'I'll stay.' He lifted me into his arms and I wrapped my legs around his waist. Any sense left me. This was my last chance to be with Finn, and whatever happened I wanted him to be the first person. 'Haven't . . . done . . . this . . . before.'

'I know,' he said gently.

He lowered me on to the bed and started to unbutton my top, quickly and efficiently. He undid my bra in one simple swift movement. I grappled to unbuckle his belt. His jeans and my top were added to the heap on the floor. 'We can stop at any time. I don't want to force you if . . .' His breathing was jagged.

'Shut up, Finn, I want to.'

He pinned my naked arms to the bed and kissed me again. We couldn't stop; it was like a drug between us.

17

This morning I remembered to kiss the frog that sits in my studio. I have an important meeting.

It's week sixteen of my pregnancy, the week I should officially be telling Ruby I'm pregnant. My initial twelve-week scan was fine. I'm starting to show a little, but because I am tall I can disguise it easily. During the scan I was told that if my baby were male, the female reproductive organs would have degenerated by now. I have to wait for the next scan to find out the sex. It's only four weeks but that feels like a lifetime to me.

I'm staring at my computer. George is my screensaver. He's sitting on Rowan, my mum's Shetland pony, who is the worst-tempered thing ever, but George somehow manages to control him. He bites Finn and me. Finn calls him 'the little shit'.

'One moment, please,' Natalie says. 'Ruby – Martin Collins from Caviar Travel on the line.'

The boss shakes her head theatrically, bracelets jangling. Her perfume is overpowering today.

'I'm afraid she's in a meeting. Can I take a message?'

'Now, Josie, team talk,' Ruby says in a hushed tone, sitting poised behind her desk.

'Right, yes, *shoot*.' Another word popular with Ruby.

'We need to nail this client. If they want us to do their company literature and design their new logo, that's big money.' Her eyes sparkle with greed. 'I know it's not the most dynamic job we could do,' she says, hunching her shoulders and frowning, 'but it's serious bread and butter money.' She smiles again and I'm sure she's had her pearl-white teeth cosmetically whitened. 'Do you think you're up to heading the meeting this afternoon?'

'Absolutely,' I reply. 'I'm looking forward to it.'

She makes the sound that comes after a games show contestant has answered the question correctly. 'That's my girl! The competition will be steep but I'm sure they'll go for your pitch if you play it right. Remember all my tips?'

'Quick flexible responses . . .'

'Uh-huh.'

'. . . fresh thinking and innovation.'

'Bingo.'

'Thank you for giving me the responsibility.' I feel like I should be saluting, 'Rule Britannia' playing in the background.

'You're more than ready, Josie. We need to get to a stage where we don't have to pitch. It's time-consuming and we are effectively giving away our best ideas for free. I want clients to come to *us*, Gem Communications. We are going to be the *Titanic* of the design world.'

I don't want to point out that the *Titanic* sank.

'But,' she swivels round in her chair, winking at Natalie and me, 'it's just the way the industry works so for now we have to work with it. You'll get there soon, Natalie, being in the exciting position of heading a meeting.'

'I think I am ready,' Natalie says, which annoys me. 'I feel confident I could do it now.'

The phone rings again. I gather up my work to take to the meeting in a portfolio bag: sketches, presentation boards, colour run-outs and examples of previous work I've done for the company.

'Gem Communications.' Natalie looks puzzled. 'Sorry, who's calling? Miss Miles.' My face freezes over like ice. 'Oh, sorry, Ms Miles. One moment.'

Pain shoots down my arms and through my finger-tips. I'm not here. But it's too late. Ruby is watching me closely. The button on my telephone is flashing red like a warning sign. Perhaps George has had a terrible accident? I pick up the phone immediately. 'Ms Miles, how can I help?' I smile reassuringly at Ruby who is pretending not to be interested as she taps on her keyboard with scarlet fingernails.

'You need to pick up George, now,' his teacher informs me.

'I'm sorry?'

'He flushed one of the boys' hoods down the toilet during playtime. I will not tolerate this behaviour.'

'Could we talk about this calmly and rationally after school? I shall be picking him up at three-thirty.'

'I don't think you heard me, Mrs Greenwood. I have suspended George for the rest of the day, and from now on you will have to pick him up at lunchtime too. George's behaviour is too disruptive, we do not have the staff to monitor him every second of the day. We have the other children in the school to consider, all two hundred of them.'

'Very well, thank you. Goodbye.' I try not to slam the phone down.

'There isn't a problem, is there?' Ruby asks.

'No, all fine.'

'Set to razzle-dazzle them?'

'All set.' She examines my outfit. I'm wearing pale pink tweed trousers but the top button is undone and covered by a thick black belt. 'Er, still carrying the excesses of Christmas,' I titter.

'I must say, you do look a little on the large side . . .'

'Right, I'm off.'

'But the meeting's not for another hour,' she says, her voice razor-sharp with mistrust.

I laugh nervously. 'The ladies' room. Back in a weenie sec.' Am I becoming a clone of Ruby?

I sit on the loo and punch in Clarky's number. Why is Mrs B on holiday? I really need her. No answer from Clarky. WHERE IS HE?

I ring Gwen. 'Darling, I would love to look after George . . .'

'That's wonderful!'

'No! Sorry, sweetie, you know I'd love to, but I simply don't have the time. I'm having my hair coloured and then Dicky and I are thinking of going to see that new film with Jude Law . . .'

'But can't you see the film another time?' I ask desperately.

'No, it's only on for another day or so. By the way, I never got round to sending you a thank you card for Christmas. Isn't it awful the way time flies and . . .'

'Then . . . whoosh! You haven't had the time. 'Bye, Gwen,' I finish for her. I pity Finn for having her as a mother.

I ring Tiana but she's not answering her mobile. I leave a message before trying Granny. 'I'm not having that little nipper in my home, not today. I've got the gasman here. Dreadful pong in the house.'

I try Clarky again. No answer. I hear a door open and high heels clicking across the floor. They walk into the cubicle next to mine. I bend down to see if they are Ruby's heels. Pointy black ones with little bows on the end. Shit, they are. I sit rigid, trying to hold my breath, knees tightly pressed against one another, feet dangling off the floor. She's pulling lots of loo roll out of its holder. I bet she's placing it around the seat so her bare skin avoids touching it. Her bracelet jangles as she flushes the loo. She turns on the tap and scrubs her hands for what seems like ages. Then there's a spraying noise. She can't be spraying on yet more perfume? 'She smells like the entire cosmetics department in Boots,' Finn once told me. The door finally swings shut.

I call my husband in a desperate final attempt. 'If I pick George up from school now, can I bring him into the hospital?'

'Oh, God, what's he done? Why are you whispering?'

'I'm hiding from Ruby. George flushed a boy's hood down the loo.'

'What?'

'He flushed a hood down the loo.'

'He's done WHAT?'

'I have to get to this meeting. I can't take George with me. Can you have him?'

'I've got procedures all afternoon. Angiograms and echo scans. George can't hang around in the hospital, you've got to be joking.'

'Does this sound like a joke?' I ask in a strangled voice.

'The school can't expect you to pick him up now. I could

murder George, why did he do it? Ring them and say you can't collect him, you've got a meeting.'

'Why don't you? A male voice might have more effect.'

'My bleep's gone.' And the line goes dead.

I ring Clarky and he finally answers. My heart jumps for joy. 'No, sorry, J. I've got to get to work.'

'Please, please, please. I'll do *anything* if you can help me out just this once?'

'No,' he says, surprisingly firmly. 'You can't always rely on me, Josie.'

You're the only one I can rely on, I think to myself as I turn my phone off. There's no other option. I have to go and collect George.

George and I enter the building through rotating glass doors, but he stops dead when he's a foot inside, gazing dreamily at the spiral staircase, the glass-walled offices with people working on their computers, the silver lifts with all their buttons. Everything is slick and polished and waiting to be explored. New places are like treasure chests to my son.

When we make it to the front desk, the receptionist is on the telephone. She's got mousy-coloured hair that's cut into a sharp fringe and streaked with blonde. 'I know. I said to him that unless he was prepared to make more of an effort . . .' I stand waiting. When she puts down the phone she starts typing. I find myself coughing loudly.

'Sorry, who are you?' She's still not looking at me.

'Josie Greenwood, Gem Communications. I have a meeting with Mr Allen.' I smile politely.

'Right, take a seat. Sorry, what did you say your name was?' she asks again, picking up the telephone.

'Greenwood.'

'Can you spell that?'

'Green and then wood.'

'And where are you from again?'

'Planet Zog,' I find myself saying.

My son giggles.

'Can you spell that?'

Is she for real?

Finally she looks at us. 'Is he with you?' George flicks an elastic band at her, but luckily it misses. Where he got it from I don't know. 'Stop it,' I tell him firmly. 'Behave or you go back to school at once.'

'But you've got a meeting. You can't take me.'

Damn it, he's right. 'I'm sorry. Can we start again? I'm from Gem Communications. I did ring Mr Allen to warn him I'd be bringing my son.'

The receptionist rolls her eyes. 'Mr Allen, Mrs Greenwood from Gem Communications is here to see you. She's got her son with her.'

George has seen the fish tank. 'Wow, Mum, look at the fish! Look, this one's all on his own, the others don't like him. I'll be your friend, I'm going to call you Gary.'

My skin is burning with anxiety as I manage to make him sit down. There is silence for a second until George starts to spin his black leather chair round and round. 'GEORGE! Sit still,' I demand, grabbing the chair to try to make it stop. I hear a snap and a crunch. One of the springs must have broken.

The receptionist stares at us icily. 'Look, why don't you build this?' I suggest to him. 'I've got your digger here. See if you can make it before my meeting ends.' Thank God he starts to get out the coloured Lego pieces.

Mr Allen, the Marketing Manager, comes to reception before I've had time to check that my designs are in order. He's young, good-looking, dressed in jeans, trendy trainers and a smart white shirt that has been immaculately ironed and pressed. I shake hands with him. He's wearing a gold watch which contrasts with the dark hair that sprouts from his wrist to either side of the strap. I apologise once more for bringing my son into work. 'Call me Neil, please. Yes, don't worry, a bit unconventional, but hey, we'll let it pass just this once,' he says with a wink. 'Debbie, could you watch Mrs Greenwood's son? Thanks.'

Oh, lord. Oh, lord. I might as well have told her she was a silly cow. I'm scared that she'll drown George in the fish tank.

'No problem, I love kids,' she says sweetly, blushing in front of Neil.

I look at her sideways and she smiles.

'We'll be in the room opposite.' We walk through the

glass door and I shake hands with the Head of Communications, then the Publications Manager, and they've also
brought in the copywriter. I feel unusually nervous as I
open my portfolio and lay out my work on the long table in
front of me, Gem Communications incorporated on to the
top of every sheet, together with the logo of a sparkling
ruby. I start my presentation.

'What we strive to do at Gem Communications is to
help established or new organisations define, create and
evolve their brand communications across different media.
Design serves a purpose: to communicate clearly, engag-
ingly and above all distinctively. I love impact, contrast,
colour, texture, but all of it has to be there for a reason – to
express you and your objectives as a company.' Neil nods
appreciatively. 'I've experimented with a couple of designs
and concepts. First, if you want to go down the more
traditional route, I've done a design in serif type. The background is in a timeless navy.' I pin the logo to a large
display board.

'I quite like that,' comments Neil, turning to the others.
From the corner of my eye I glimpse George running past
the door. I have an awful feeling I saw a fish in his hand.

'However, if you wanted to go down the more contem-
porary route, reflected by a fresh colour palette, then I
thought the logo could be in a cool blue rather than navy
and in sans serif type.' I show the two together to illustrate
the contrast.

'I'm not sure about the cool blue, it's cold,' Neil starts to say. 'I don't think it stands out enough. Shorter lifespan too.'

'I have done a sample of colours.' I hear a shriek. 'If you could excuse me, for one second?' I suggest as they are looking at the designs.

I shut the door gently behind me before bolting down the corridor. 'What are you doing? George!' He's sitting on the floor with a striped fish in his hands. He is trying to stroke it. 'Look at it, Mum. Isn't it sweet?'

'George, it's a fish!'

'He's called Gary. He has a name.' The fish is slithering around in his hand.

'Where's Debbie gone?'

'She said she wanted a ciggy or something.'

'Put Gary back, NOW!'

'The other fishes were picking on him, Mum. Pinching all his food.'

I lunge forward to try and get hold of the fish but it is so slippery that I cannot grip it properly. 'Back in the tank, now! He needs water. You'll kill him.'

'I don't want to kill him . . .'

I return to the meeting room. 'We're not sure either option really *talks* to us . . .' Neil starts.

George is now pressed up against the glass door. 'Where's the loo?' he mouths desperately. He's holding his crotch.

'Excuse me, Josie?' Neil is staring at me.

'I'm sorry, I missed that point. Could you just run that by me again?' I say desperately.

'We were saying, we weren't convinced either option really stood out enough,' Neil repeats. 'We want something more dynamic? Eye-catching?'

I can see George's pained face pressed against the glass. He's hopping up and down in agony.

'OK. Let's consider the third option,' I say, panicking like mad, 'which I think you're going to like. This will set you apart . . .'

'MUM! I NEED THE LOO!'

Everyone in the meeting room turns round and looks at George. I put down my design. 'I'm so sorry, please excuse me.'

'Fine.' Neil folds his arms tightly.

I run out of the room and grab George, leading him down the corridor. I am going to kill my son.

I'm driving George back to school ready to tell the head-master exactly what I think of this lunchtime punishment. I've probably just lost Ruby a client; I might have lost my job, and all because of Ms Miles. 'We'll get back to you,' Neil had said with a smile, showing me promptly to a door with a great big EXIT sign over it.

'Why did you try and flush Jason's hooded top down the loo?'

'He made me.'

'You could have said no.'

'He said if I did it, I could play football in his team.'

'And then?'

'He said it was a joke or something. Ms Miles hates me. She calls me stupid.'

Right, that's it.

I knock loudly on the headmaster's door, but don't wait for a response. A thin man with fair hair sits behind a desk. 'Er, hello,' he says, 'can I help?' His office is small and tidy, each shelf completely filled with books.

'Josie Greenwood. This is my son George whom apparently I have to collect every lunchtime now because you can't cope.' I sit down and cross my arms. 'George, sit down.'

'Don't want to.'

'I mucked up THE MOST important meeting today because . . .'

'Mrs Greenwood, I have no idea what you're talking about.'

'You run the school, don't you?' I begin to tell him about the hood incident.

He holds up one thin hand like a human traffic indicator. He looks too insubstantial to run a fleapit, let alone a school. 'I would like to talk to your son about this.'

George tells him. It seems they know each other quite well already.

'I see. And do you think your behaviour was acceptable?'

190

'It wasn't my fault, Mr Phipps.'

'Why?'

'He made me do it.'

'So, if I tell you to jump out of the window in my office, will you?'

'George would jump off a skyscraper . . .' I start, but Mr Phipps signals me to stop again. 'Go on then, jump.'

George starts to jog up and down on the spot in preparation. 'I want to be a fireman when I grow up,' he says. That's the first I've heard of it. He starts to run but Mr Phipps puts out a surprisingly strong arm to halt him.

'If you jump, you'll hurt yourself. Consider the question before acting on it.'

'He can't,' I cut in. 'It's a classic symptom of ADHD.'

'George, why don't you go to the computer room, play some games until your mother and I come and get you?'

'I can play Hangman!' He sprints out of the office.

Mr Phipps turns to me. 'I know George has ADHD. I see he's on Action Plus and has been seen by an educational psychologist in the classroom.'

Action Plus is when the school contacts outside agencies such as educational psychologists, behavioural specialists, occupational and speech therapists, to assess a particular child in order to determine if they need a statement of special educational needs. Typically George behaved like an angel when they brought an observer into the lesson to monitor him so they didn't feel it necessary to assess him further, but the school had told me they'd continue to keep 'a close eye on him'.

'One of my friends' brothers had ADHD,' Mr Phipps continues. 'Still has it. He has learnt to control his behaviour, and I'm sure it's possible for George to do so too, but he needs to be shown how. He's a bright boy. There are ways the school can help; practical things like making sure his desk faces a blank wall so there's as little distraction as possible.'

My anger starts to subside. 'And teachers need to tap him when they want his attention, not shout like Ms Miles does.'

'I agree with you that this lunchtime punishment is too disruptive. Also, I see George is behind on his reading and spelling. His handwriting is pretty poor too . . .'

I sigh with frustration. 'We've been waiting well over a year for an occupational therapist to get him splints.'

'I would like to give him a few extra lessons after school, if it's all right by you?'

I smile. At last my son seems to have an ally at school and at least one tiny part of my day is being salvaged. 'That's more than all right. Extra lessons would be great, thank you.'

'Why is he watching television?' is the first thing Finn calls out to me when he arrives home. He drops his case on the floor and starts to undo his tie. 'I hope you gave George serious time-out, Josie? Don't you realise your mother and I have more important things to do than pick you up from school, George?' Finn is looking for the television remote. He slips a hand down the side of the sofa. No luck. 'George, I'm talking to you.'

His eyes are glued to the screen.

'Finn, it's been dealt with, OK?' I take off my plastic apron featuring a picture of a barmaid with a huge cleavage. Granny gave it to Finn for Christmas.

'He shouldn't be allowed to watch anything tonight. He won't learn what's right or wrong that way.'

'Finn, will you . . .'

'Shouldn't he be doing his homework?'

'I'm trying to watch *Star Trek*, Dad. This is the good part.'

Finn strides across the room and turns the television off, tripping on a piece of Lego in the process and twisting his ankle. 'Oh, fuck!'

'Finn!' I shout.

'Mum! You said I could watch this if I was good.' George starts to cry.

'That's my whole point. You haven't been good today, have you?'

'But Mum said . . .'

'How would you like it if someone flushed Baby down the loo? It is not acceptable behaviour. Do you understand?'

'Finn, stop shouting,' I demand. George runs past us both and upstairs to his bedroom, slamming the door.

'Fuck, fuck, FUCK!' shouts George.

I shake my head. 'Great. Now he knows the word fuck. We need to be consistent, Finn. It doesn't help, you storming in here, undoing all the good work I've done. He doesn't know what he's done wrong now.'

'We don't set enough boundaries. It's your fault he does these things again and again . . .'

'You bastard!' I exhale furiously.

The phone rings and I pick up. 'Hi, Nicholas.' It's Finn's father. 'We're fine, thanks.'

'FUCK YOU!' George shouts from upstairs followed by another slam of the door.

'That noise?' I say when Nicholas asks, appalled by my son's language and ashamed by the example we set. 'It's the television.'

Finn's lying on the sofa, hitting his face repeatedly with a cushion. 'He's right here.' I cover the mouthpiece. 'Take it,' I snap. I can smell the mince burning. I hurl the phone at him.

'Josie!' He sits up. 'Hi, Dad. Yeah, we're fine. It's the television, I've just turned it off. Work's good. Busy . . . George is fine . . . Josie's great.'

Aren't grown-ups full of bullshit?

'Can you hang on a minute, Dad?' He opens the front door. 'Josie!' I hear him call down the street. 'Come back!'

But I'm a long way away.

With each step I take all I can hear is, 'It's your fault, your fault.' How is it possible that one man can make me the happiest woman alive one moment and the most miserable the next?

18

'Where are you going with that bin?' I stretched myself across Finn's bed.

'It's the same as a "do not disturb" sign.' He shoved it outside the door.

'Do you put your bin out a lot?'

'All the time.' He started to laugh.

I threw a pillow at him. 'You're so arrogant!'

'But beneath it I'm a crumbling mess.'

'The bedder could do with giving this room a clean,' I suggested.

'Well, mine is old and has congestive cardiac failure.'

I turned to him. 'In fact, why on earth should you have some poor man on his last legs cleaning up your rubbish?'

'Fair enough, but I don't let him. I give him a Jammie Dodger and we have a chat and a cup of tea.' Finn circled the room with a hand. 'Hence the delightful mess.'

'You should clean it yourself. Do you put your bin out all the time?' I couldn't help asking again.

'Why? Are you jealous?'

I readjusted my position. Finn took my hand and rubbed each fingertip in turn gently. 'Yes.' I lifted my face to his and we kissed. Now that we had slept together I felt even closer to him. Why had I been frightened about my first time? With Finn it already felt familiar. 'I wish we'd met at a different time,' he started to say. 'Things could have been a whole lot different. You're eighteen, and I act like a twelve year old.'

I feared where this was leading. Deep down I knew he was right. What was the point in starting a serious relationship when I was about to leave? It still hurt, though.

'I think it's better to be honest, don't you?'

'Yes, and no,' I added. He was slipping away from me already.

'I don't regret anything, Josie.'

'Thanks.' I turned over on to my back.

'All I'm trying to say, pretty inarticulately, is how much I've loved being with you.' Already it was in the past tense, and I hated it. 'But we're too young to be tied down. You're going off travelling and . . .' he paused for effect, '. . . I'll be here, *studying*.'

I turned on to my side to face him. 'You're not leaving then?'

'I'd be mad to give it up. I am in a good position and I do want to be a doctor. I need to start growing up, not constantly finding excuses to do the easy thing and run.' He twisted a strand of my hair in his fingers and tucked it behind my ear. 'Thanks for coming over last night and giving me some home truths. How did you become so wise so young?'

'I don't know.' I was still thinking about not being with him. 'I wish you'd told me about your dad.'

'I'm sorry. It was like I was rebelling against any kind of relationship, thinking they were all doomed like my parents'.' Finn cleared his throat. 'Tell me where you're travelling? Imagine this,' he touched my bare stomach and outlined a rough shape, 'is a map of Europe.' I reached for his hand and guided him to different places using the tip of his finger.

'So what happened with your parents?' I asked. We were still in bed, sitting up, the duvet wrapped around us both, eating bacon and mayonnaise sandwiches. Finn grabbed a pillow and rested his back against it.

'It's a long story,' he warned me.

'We have all day in bed, don't we?'

'If that's the case,' he smiled, discarding the food and leaning across to kiss me, 'we could be doing something much more interesting.' His hand was inside my T-shirt.

'Finn, behave! I'm being serious, I want to know,' I said, though I made no attempt to move his hand.

'OK. My father, Nicholas, lives for success, money and work. When he was in his teens his father used to beat him with a wooden spoon, literally, saying, "You have to work hard to provide for your family otherwise you are worth nothing." '

'That's pretty extreme.'

'Dad's father was a piano tuner, spent all his time away from home tuning the damn things, but didn't make any money. He was terrified my father would turn out to be poor like him. Dad won this scholarship to a private school but they couldn't even afford to pay for his school meals. My father's biggest fear in life has been not being able to provide for Ed and me. And Mum, of course.'

'What does he do?'

'He set up his own IT consultancy company and took the business to America when I was five. We lived in Connecticut. Mum hated it. It was in the middle of nowhere; she was lonely. I don't think she even liked looking after Ed and me. That generation often had children because they thought they should, not because they wanted to. She certainly didn't want us.'

'But that's terrible! I can't imagine having a child and not being interested in him or her, loving them more than anything in the world.'

He laughed ironically. 'Well, the only person Mum cares about is herself.' His voice started to tremble, the hurt coming from deep within, a place I wanted to reach. 'My dad got back late from work one day and by then she'd attacked the booze cabinet and was shouting about how miserable she was in this "godforsaken place".'

'Did you hear all of this?'

'It was hard not to. Dad kept on saying, "Gwen dear, let's not discuss this in front of the children." He couldn't see the problem. He was the provider, why couldn't she be the stay-at-home mum?'

'So what happened this time?'

'She's left him, for good. She's done it before, for the same man . . . Richard. I was fifteen then.' He let out a deep breath. 'I was walking down the corridor when this man strolls past me wearing my father's purple dressing gown. He says, "Do you have any shampoo?"'

'No way. Where was your dad anyway?'

'On a business trip. I confronted them both of course.'

'What did you say?'

'"What are you doing on my father's side of the bed?"' Finn said it with such clarity, as if he could see his adulterous mother right in front of him. '"Who is he, Mum?" I asked. "Oh," she says, "this is Dicky. He's a member of my bridge club."

'She said it with no hint of apology. It was as if she felt she'd suffered enough in her marriage, why shouldn't she have some fun now? I never said anything to Dad.'

'What about Ed?'

'I didn't tell him either. It's strange, we're twins but I've always felt like the older brother, like I've needed to protect him. He's much nicer than me.' Finn laughed. 'He never says a bad word about anyone, not even Mum. Ed soon found out, though. I was sixteen and we were about to go to Dorset for the weekend. Mum came into my bedroom while Ed and I were packing and said, "I've got something to tell you both. I don't love your father anymore and I won't be coming to Dorset." '

'She walked out on you? I don't know how she could do that. How?'

'Don't know. Ed cried. I couldn't show what I felt, I just stared at her.'

'But then she went back to your dad?'

'Mum's as restless as a butterfly. Dad thinks she's got Attention Deficit Disorder. She goes back to him, he forgives her, and then she leaves him again. Oh, Granny hates her for that, calls her "Gwen the Gold-Digger". The thing is, Dad still loves her.'

'Is that it now, for good? I mean, how much can your father take?'

'I hope so.' Finn was shaking his head. 'I called Mum and told her I was going to give up Cambridge, that I was worried about him. "Go to the doctor's," she said, "take some happy pills and get on with it." '

'Finn, I'm so sorry. How's Ed taking it?'

'OK. He's busy doing some drama course in London. He has the nice bit of Mum in him, the flightiness. If it tears him up inside, well, he hides it. But I can't forgive her and I could never forgive someone who did that to me. You have a good time before you get married, go out, get laid . . . Sorry,' he quickly said to me, 'you know what I mean. Just don't get married if you're not prepared to stay faithful.'

I considered this. 'OK, but what if you still loved that person with all your heart and they were truly sorry? If it was just the one time and it was a terrible mistake? Could you forgive them then?'

'No. You get only one chance. What?'

'I'm surprised, that's all.'

'You see people like my parents and you realise you have the choice of being like them, because that's all you know, or being positively the other way. I know which I want to be. What about your parents?'

'The only drama might be Dad putting one of his maroon socks into the white wash.'

'I crave boring.' Finn laughed. 'Mum probably had all these romantic fantasies about being married. Dad was her first love. She expected excitement, not a man who worked every minute of the day.' He opened a plastic box with a chocolate brownie in it and offered me a bite. 'Important lesson, Josie Greenwood!'

'What's that?' I took a large one.

'Don't marry the first person you sleep with.' He smiled sheepishly at me.

'But I was hoping we could set a date?'

'You wouldn't cheat on someone when you were married, would you?'

'I wouldn't cheat on someone when I was dating,' I said, 'but you have no problem with that.' I got out of bed but felt a strong arm pull me back. 'Let go!' I said, trying to wriggle free.

'It meant nothing.' I escaped his grip but he leant over me, both arms imprisoning my body.

'So why did you do it? You're coming over all sanctimonious now but . . .'

'I felt so guilty, J, that's why I couldn't even talk to you at the club. I was angry with myself, not you.' He kissed one of my cheeks. 'It was stupid.' He kissed the other. 'I regretted it the moment it happened.'

'Was it Dominique?'

'Yes.' I tried to move but he clamped his hands round my arms. 'I swear it was nothing. With you, it's different.'

I rolled my eyes.

'Christ, Josie, I've never felt like this.'

I put a hand over his mouth and he kissed my palm. I wanted to absorb every feature on his face. His light brown eyes, soft hair, the shadow that fell across his cheekbone, his small neat ears, the scar to the left of his eye, each contour and shift of expression, the way a smile lit his face as if someone were about to tell him the most exciting story. His hands that were always so busy drumming on coffee tables, playing a record, lighting a cigarette, touching me. I wanted to take him with me.

'You're amazing,' he said.

'Carry on.'

'Beautiful . . . smart . . . strong.'

We both sat up now. I held my arms around my knees, cold at the thought that this was all about to end. Was I ever going to see him again?

He handed me an empty matchbox. 'Your going away present,' he said.

'Oh, you shouldn't have. A whole matchbox.'

'Open it.'

I slid open the drawer. Inside he had written, 'I love you.'

I held his face in my hands. 'I love you too.'

'What do we do now?' he said. 'Write to each other?' There was a glimmer of hope in that. 'Maybe we can make this work?'

19

'Clarky, I know she's with you,' Finn says on the answer machine. He pauses. 'Ask her to come home. Please, Josie. I'm sorry.'

The phone rings again. It clicks into answer-machine mode. 'Hi, Justin, it's Kelly.'

'What's she like?' I ask when she's finished leaving a longwinded message about meeting up.

'OK.'

'What does she do?'

'Er, marketing or something.'

'You were clearly paying attention. Is she pretty?'

'She's all right.'

'Clarky, make the most of this time. How I'd love to be single again. Want to swap roles?'

'And be Finn's wife? No, thanks.'

I kiss him on the cheek. 'I should go. Why are you always so together, Clarky?'

'Hardly,' he mutters.

I look around the kitchen which is painted a pale blue. Nothing out of place, the latest gadget on every surface. This time it's a very high-tech wine-bottle opener although Clarky doesn't drink wine. I put on my coat. 'I don't think I've ever seen you blue. I mean, *really blue.*'

'I've had my moments.' He looks at me. 'Maybe it's plain sailing because there's nothing in my boat that I care enough about to make it rock? You and Finn, you're living, even if it is stormy at times. I'm just drifting, not sure what matters to me.'

I take his hand firmly and kiss it. 'You are my rock, Justin Clarke.' He shifts awkwardly from one foot to the other. 'Thanks for tonight. I wish Finn understood me as well as you do.'

'Let me walk you.'

'No, it's not far.'

Clarky hands me an umbrella. 'Here, take this.'

I am about to leave when he says, 'Can I ask you a simple question, Josie?'

I nod. 'As long as it is.'

'Do you still love Finn?'

I run down the floodlit street as fast as I can, avoiding the puddles. There are plenty of people still out, newsagents still open, restaurants lit by candlelight. Do you still love Finn? I had laughed out loud. 'You call that simple!'

'Yes. If you love someone there shouldn't be any hesitation, should there?'

'Why did you have to run to Clarky?' Finn asks me when I return. I found George asleep in his school uniform; he hadn't let his father undress him.

'You made me so angry, I can't speak to you when you're like that.'

'But don't you understand that running to Clarky every time we have a problem doesn't make it go away?'

I let out a strangled cry. 'Well, don't you get it that I wouldn't need to if you weren't so pig-headed all the time? You haven't asked me about my meeting, about George's headmaster. All you do is shout and criticise the moment you come home. You don't listen to me!'

'And, let me guess,' Finn says in defeated tones, 'Clarky does?'

We both sit down on the edge of the bed. 'I'm sorry,' he mumbles. 'I know I fly off the handle sometimes.'

'I hate us fighting.'

'How was the meeting?'

'Do you love me, Finn?'

'What?' He looks as if I've asked him something impossible.

'*If you love someone there shouldn't be any hesitation, should there?*'

'We say it to George all the time, without even thinking,' I go on. 'Do you love me?'

'Of course I do,' he finally says.

20

'Can we go to the Science Museum?'

'No! Stand still, George.' I am trying to put on the fifth tie I've bought him in a year.

'Emma, does Nat lose ties? They're either chewed to death or they disappear into the vortex. How does this happen? How?'

'Ha! The chewing tie syndrome. Nat used to chew and suck his like a stick of rock. Only buy the cheap ones now.'

The doorbell rings. Mrs B bustles inside, wearing her parka with the fur lining. I hug her tightly. 'I'm glad you're back.'

'It's good to be home. I missed my bed, the fireplace and my home-made celery soup. Funny the things you miss, isn't it?'

'Mum's having a baby, Mrs B. When's it ready? It's taking ages.' George picks up his cold fruit drink. 'Ugh!' He starts hitting his forehead. 'Brain freeze.'

'You're pregnant?' She looks at George to see if he's joking.

I cannot miss the flash of horror on her face, as if a sharp pebble has just hit her, but she manages to compose herself quickly, forcing her features into a smile. 'Congratulations. How many weeks?' she asks.

'Sixteen. I'll tell you all about it later. Right, George, where's your homework?'

'I don't want to go to school.'

'Why not?' Mrs B asks. 'I strayed off once, must have been about four at the time, and the police found me at the local infants' school. All I wanted to do was learn like my sister.'

George's eyes are not focusing on Mrs B anymore, his mind moving on to something else as he turns away from her. I call it the ticking clock; his face starts turning away from somebody in a clockwise, or anticlockwise direction, depending on what it is distracting him. This time it's Rocky pattering into the kitchen. Yet Mrs B boldly carries on. 'I didn't like it that she was learning all these new and exciting things and leaving me behind. I hated staying at home.'

'I haven't got any friends.'

'You've got Eliot,' I say.

'He doesn't count.'

'Why not?'

'He's in a wheelchair, Mrs B,' George explains. 'He doesn't play football or anything. We play together, but that's because he hasn't got any real friends either. He doesn't have proper legs.'

'That doesn't mean he can't be your friend, George,' she argues firmly.

'He's called "Ginger" at school. His hair is the colour of a carrot!' He starts to snort with laughter.

'You need to respect Eliot for who he is, now don't you? Red hair can be very attractive.'

'Paul's having a party at McDonald's with Ronald the Clown and everything, but I'm not invited,' George goes on matter-of-factly. 'Eliot isn't invited either.'

'Well, that's because we're doing something else,' I improvise.

'Can I have a party, Mum? It's my birthday soon.' He starts to hum again. This is absurd. George says he has no friends and in the next breath he wants a party. Finn and I had planned to take him to the cinema, but if he wants a party . . .

'Your shoes aren't on properly.' I watch Mrs B take them off effortlessly. The battered leather is squashed down like a flat tyre around the heels because he can never be bothered to untie the laces first. 'Now, let's do this right,' she mutters as he lifts his foot obediently towards her. She slots one back on to his foot and pulls the laces tightly towards her. 'There we go, don't want you falling over now and knocking that pretty head.' She ruffles his hair like a favourite pet and he looks at her with fascination, his brown eyes opened wide. 'You see, the slipper fits Cinderella.' I notice we all smile at that. 'And Cinderella can have a party if she goes to school.'

*

'I had a call from Neil,' Ruby says the moment I walk into the office carrying a hot cup of tea. My heartbeat quickens.

'Why did you take your son to the goddamn meeting?'

Is that the flicker of a smile on Natalie's face? 'I'm sorry but I had no choice, there was an emergency at school.'

Already her eyes have glazed over. Children aren't real to Ruby. They are mere inconveniences. 'I'm running a business. I am a professional, I thought you were ready for the responsibility?'

'I am.'

'Can you promise to give me one hundred and ten per cent over the next year? That's all I need to know. Natalie's on board, aren't you, Natalie?'

'Yes, definitely. One hundred and ten per cent.'

'I promise I'll do my absolute best.' How am I going to tell her I'm pregnant now? I know she can't sack me but she'll start giving me the mundane jobs just because. She'll think baby-free Natalie is a safer bet.

'I'm sorry I lost the client, Ruby.'

Natalie is by the window cutting some card with a scalpel. I can tell from her expression she is enjoying this. She thinks she's going to take over my job. No way. 'But I won't let you down again, Ruby.'

'Well,' she spins round in her chair, 'the funny thing is, I spoke to Neil – and Gem Communications won the pitch!'

'We have? I don't believe it!'

'Shit,' Natalie says, holding up a cut finger. She finds the first-aid box which we keep at the top of the cupboard, above the filing system.

'I had to do a lot of sweet-talking, mind. This can't happen again, Josie. There's only so much I can do to save your pretty arse. I said I employed only the most talented designers, and . . . well, he has rather a soft spot for me.'

There's a knock on the door. It's Diana, who controls the switchboard and generally looks after the entire office block. 'Ms Gold?'

'Yes? What is it? I'm busy. I'm about to get my nails done.'

'Sorry. Does anyone in here have a black Audi, registration number CR8 TV?'

'That would be me,' Ruby answers proudly, clicking her tongue against the roof of her mouth. 'Brand-new that baby. CR8 TV, get it, girls?' She's nodding vigorously, waiting for our explosive reaction.

I look blank. Natalie says nothing.

'Um . . . anyway,' Diana tries to go on.

'CR8 TV. Come on, Josie.' Ruby hits her hand against the desk. 'You must get it?'

'Oh,' I force myself to laugh. 'Creative . . . CR8 TV . . . yes, wow, you personalised it. Clever.'

She chuckles. 'Well, I thought so.'

'I'm afraid it's just been clamped,' Diana finishes, trying hard not to show a hint of satisfaction.

Ruby tries to rush out of the door, but she can't run in her tight skirt. 'Oh, my God!' she cries down the corridor. 'Someone, stop the bastards! Stop them!'

We all remain poised, trying hard not to make a squeak until it is safe to do so. One . . . two . . . three . . . Then Diana and I burst into laughter.

But only seconds later Ruby bolts back into the office. 'Sort it out, will you? I don't have time to dig Josie out of a grave and my car too.' She slams the parking ticket down in front of Natalie who still looks aggrieved that I won the pitch.

Now who's smiling?

21

It's my son's birthday tomorrow and here I am, the perfect mother, walking down a busy London street, my skirt swishing in the breeze and carrying a dozen Bob the Builder helium balloons. How very Sarah Jessica Parker, I tell myself.

'Wait, don't cross the road!' I pull George back and six of the balloons hit me in the forehead and obscure my vision. As I lean towards the 'wait' button, another gust of wind catches the entire cluster and they proceed to hit me under the chin and then pelt me in the forehead. An old lady wearing a raspberry-coloured beret presses the button instead with a frail wobbling finger.

'I wanted to do it!' George stamps his foot on the pavement. The green man starts flashing.

'Next time you can do it, OK?'

'No.' He starts to cry.

'We've got to go.' I pull at his arm. 'Come on.'

'No!' he screams. The light goes back to red and the tears

stop. George stands, poised and ready to press the button, back in control.

We walk back to the car. I struggle to find the keys as I clutch the balloons tightly.

'Come on, Mum. Snail.'

I am getting redder and hotter as we pull over at the cake shop. Can I leave George in the car and quickly pay for the cake? I touch the handle and am about to go without him . . . but the handbrake would be off, George and the car would hurtle down the road . . . chaos and disaster. 'Don't bring them,' I tell him as I unlock the side door.

'But they're *my* balloons.'

'Keep them in the car.' I am going to hyperventilate any minute. Oh, no, I need the loo, I think with despair.

'I want them,' he insists, struggling to get out with all twelve of them in tow.

I have to weigh up the time it will take to argue with him against the time it will take simply to allow him to bring the balloons. 'You can take just these ones, OK?' We cross the road, a trio of balloons bobbing furiously in the air behind us, ready to strike like cobras.

The shop smells of chocolate and icing sugar. There's a long queue. I tap my foot restlessly against the floor, trying to control my bladder at the same time. I keep an eye on the car, its hazard lights flashing. 'Greenwood,' I say in a breathless voice when it's finally my turn, 'I've ordered a chocolate castle.'

She nods and calls out my name to someone in the kitchen. 'Ah, is that your son?' She gestures to George who is standing in the corner of the shop next to a plate of flapjacks and brownies.

I nod back impatiently.

Finally the cake arrives in a nice clean white box. When I thrust a twenty-pound note into her hand she tells me they've run out of change. Can I wait a minute?

A family enter the shop, the bell tinkling as the door swings open. One of the children starts to sing, 'Bob the Builder, Can He Fix It?' An impressed George gives him a balloon, explaining it's his birthday, but then the other child wants one too so they start to fight over it and Bob flies out of the door and high into the sky. George knocks over the flapjacks and treads on a brownie. I have to pay for that too.

Finally I am handed the correct change and George and I return to the car, only to see a man in uniform writing out a ticket and smacking it on to my windscreen. Oh, fuck.

'Not *another* ticket, Josie?'

I had forgotten I'd hidden it in the cutlery drawer. 'Did you put money in the meter?'

'I was picking up the cake, Finn. Don't start.'

'OK, sorry.' But he's still thinking about it, I can tell. 'We need a secretary to pay all our traffic fines. All you had to do was stick money into the meter . . .'

'Well, I failed! You should be congratulating me for managing to get the cake and balloons back in one piece. I'm amazed the only casualty was a parking ticket.' I storm out of the room and plonk myself on the sofa.

Finn pours himself a glass of red wine and follows. He sits down next to me and starts to rub my back. Every inch of my body stiffens. 'I'll deal with it,' he says.

'I can, don't worry.'

'No, I will.'

'So now we're arguing about who is going to pay for it?'

'I hope people turn up for this party after all the trouble you've gone to.'

'They will.'

He's not convinced, which irritates me even more. 'Anyway, Clarky's coming . . .'

'Of course he is.'

I ignore his tone. 'And Tiana, Mrs B, Mum and Eliot.'

'The one in the wheelchair?' Finn flicks absent-mindedly through the television guide.

'Yep. No reply from your mum or Dicky, though. Probably too busy.'

'I did ask her. I'll call again.'

'Don't bother. You need to write in George's card. I bought him a funny space card. He loves his planets at the moment,' I inform him.

'I know he loves planets,' Finn says back, equally acid.

'I've wrapped up the bicycle. I bought him a course of piano lessons too.'

'Piano?'

'Maybe we're going down the wrong track with sport. George might be musical. Clarky says . . .'

'Clarky this, Clarky that . . .'

I put my hands over my ears. 'How about you suggesting something then?' I walk away.

'I'm happy to give the piano a go. My grandfather was good. Oh, look, there's a good thriller on tonight. Hey, where are you going?'

'Upstairs. I need to lie down.'

I sit down on my bed with my old portfolio which I keep on the top shelf in my studio. I wipe off the dust and unzip the edge. There's an abstract oil painting of a silver jug next to a bowl of apples and grapes, painted in shades of grey, blue and pink. It was one of the A level pieces on my still life course. I smile, remembering when a tall father in a tweed coat offered to pay my teacher Mr Dowsky two hundred pounds for it at the end of term exhibition. I was dreaming of all the things I could have bought with the money but . . . 'It's not for sale,' Mr Dowsky said firmly.

There's a picture of my mother in the garden, a green-and-gold scarf around her hair and wearing a thick cream jumper and jeans with a mud stain on them. That was for a 'work in progress' piece. Lots of students did factory workers or men drilling holes in roads. I look at the next one. It's a pencil sketch of Finn when we were just married and still living in my multi-coloured apartment with the orange-painted kitchen. I pick up the photograph from my bedside table of Finn and me on our wedding day. We married quickly. We didn't want a big fuss and all the trimmings, just a small church wedding with our closest friends and family. Supper had been honey-roasted sausages and mash followed by sticky toffee pudding. We'd danced into the early hours of the morning.

Soon after, when I still had dreams of having my own exhibition, I'd signed up for an art course in London. It was on a Thursday and if it was sunny the teacher took us out across London. We'd sketch parks, rivers, bridges, markets, interesting buildings or landmarks like the Houses of Parliament.

One of the terms was spent on life drawing.

'I'm not posing nude for you,' Finn had said when I'd begged him to come into the college and be a model.

'Darling, you'd knock 'em dead.'

'You can have a private view, take it or leave it.'

'Spoilsport . . . but I like the idea of having you all to myself.'

We were in our bedroom on a Sunday morning and he was sitting by the window, the sun streaming in against one side of his face. I watched him as he stared out into the outside world. 'Be quick, you know I can't be still for long,' he'd said.

Finn is beautiful in a kind of damaged way. One moment he looks as if he is in a room filled with adoring fans; the next he is alone and vulnerable, as if someone has told him his life will amount to nothing.

I'd picked up my pad and flipped it to a clean page, starting to draw the outline of his face. 'Keep still! And no covering up.'

'Who else is on this course?' he'd asked. 'Can't one of the men model for you?'

'They're all women.'

'What's the standard like?'

'Good. One of them is a graphic designer. Then there's Sally who paints nothing but angels.' He'd laughed at that. 'Each painting is exactly the same, these funny mountains and skies with little angels dotted about in clashing colours. I don't think our teacher knows what to say. Hold it right there.'

There was a little crease at the corner of his mouth as he tried hard not to smile.

Finn is easy to draw, with his strong jaw line, wide mouth, the small scar at the corner of one eye that gives character to his face, and the hair that flicks across his forehead. I don't need to look at him. I can draw him from memory.

'You are beautiful,' I told him again, sketching the long sweep of one arm which was draped across a knee.

'What's your dream, J?'

'My dream?' I tilted my head sideways, giving the impression that I had never thought about it before. 'I'd love to move out of this cramped apartment, live in a large Victorian house with a studio on the top floor where I would paint all day. And make a very good living out of it, of course.'

'Of course.'

'I'd have my own exhibitions. A Josie Greenwood painting would go for thousands at Sotheby's.'

'Millions, you mean.'

'Exactly. I'd be the hottest property in London. I'd have a wonderful husband . . .'

'You have that already.'

'And we'd have a son called George and fly kites on Sunday afternoons.'

'I didn't know you'd thought of names already?'

'Haven't you?'

'What if it's a girl?'

'It's a boy.' I tapped my stomach as if to tell the baby not to let me down. 'And I'll do a bit of acting on the side when I'm needed for the odd Robert Redford film and no one else will do. How about you? What's your dream?' I asked in a fake American accent.

'To be a great doctor, and to be happy.' He must have felt my surprise because he'd turned to me.

'Finn!'

'I might pretend to be all complicated, but that's all I want. To be happy.'

'It's not finished,' I protested when he looked at the picture and then pushed it away. I felt the heat of the sun on my face, his mouth grazed my cheek and I closed my eyes as we kissed.

'Josie?'

'Um?'

'Josie?' I feel a tug on my arm and open my eyes. Finn is standing over me. 'What are you doing? Oh, that's the picture you drew of me.' He picks it up. 'It's not bad.'

I gather the papers back into their portfolio. 'I thought you were watching the film.'

'It's boring. I was just wondering . . .'

'Yes?'

'What's for supper?'

I sink back against the bed.

When Finn and I were first married we used to have a 'date' night. Every Tuesday we'd take it in turns to arrange something and keep it a surprise. I used to love those evenings. It made the day at work pass quickly. Finn once took me to the Ritz. I'll never forget the smart-suited man at the reception desk saying he couldn't go inside looking like that. He had forgotten to do up the zip on his trousers and his Union Jack boxers were on display. I'd never laughed so much. We sometimes went to a show and would hop on to a rickshaw and be scared stiff that we were about to hit a bus as we were driven across the West End by a furiously fast-peddling driver. On one of my nights I'd taken him to Wembley to see Prince, which he'd loved. Sometimes we'd get hopelessly drunk and then decide it was a great idea to do a bit of karaoke at the nearest bar. But most of the time we'd go to the local Thai restaurant where we'd met again after five years.

We don't do that anymore. Why don't we make an effort? Too tired? Do we use George as an excuse? Or work's a good one. Or have we let ourselves become bored with one another?

'Josie?' Finn says again. 'Supper?'

I feel resentful that everything becomes so mundane. 'Have a look in the fridge,' is all I can say, 'and let me know.'

22

'Happy Birthday to me!' George shouts on his new bicycle, the pedals turning furiously. Finn and I watch him. His monkey, Einstein, is dressed up in a leather jacket and helmet and sits between the handlebars, about to fall off. 'Don't go far!' we both shout together. Finn starts running to catch him up. 'Turn around!' he calls. 'GEORGE!'

Mrs B and Clarky help me put up Happy Birthday banners and balloons. We cover the table in a bright blue cloth and load it with cucumber sandwiches, crisps, chocolate fingers, Mrs B's mini-Scotch eggs and sausage rolls. 'I wish Finn could be here today,' she sighs then turns to Clarky. 'Still, never mind.'

Clarky has told me he's terrified of Rose. 'Those blue eyes look as if they can see right through you, like an X-ray.'

'Not working at the moment, Justin?' she asks, lips pursed tightly.

'It goes like that, Rose. Sometimes I have a lot of concerts and . . .'

'Right,' she cuts him off.

'Anyway, I wouldn't miss my godson's birthday.'

'I forget you're his godfather.'

'What's her problem?' Clarky asks when she's out of earshot.

I know. The only man she has ever trusted is her husband, Michael. 'I've never been able to have a close male friend,' Mrs B once told me. 'I once knew a lovely man called Timothy, but I discovered, much to my chagrin, he'd always held a torch for me. He became quite aggressive in the end, very unpleasant.'

George is sprawled on the floor playing with his Lego in the new bright red hooded top that Grandfather Nicholas, and Angela, the new woman in his life, sent him all the way from America. Wrapped in pink tissue and placed in the hood was a white crystal. 'Why's she given me a stone?' George had asked, giving it a shake in case a secret bank note fell out of it.

I met Angela for the first time when we went out for lunch with her and Nicholas last year. She was wearing a long purple dress. We'd already learnt that she was a leading expert in 'life training', running her own enterprise from home.

'Drugs give you cancer!' she had gasped when we told her George was on Ritalin. She proposed some healing instead. Back at home she laid him down on the ground, saying she was going to take him back to his birth to start the healing process.

Of course, George couldn't keep still. 'Birth is extremely traumatic,' she was telling him, 'a rude awakening after being cosseted in Mummy's tummy . . .'

'What's she saying?' George sat up and she pushed him back down again like a puppet.

'Relax. Close your eyes.'

'What's that weird smell?'

'Incense.'

'Mum, she's a weirdo.'

'I'm going to take you back to your birth, George.'

'Nothing's happening,' he'd said eventually, sitting up again. 'I'm bored out of my brain.'

Finn likes Angela because she makes his dad happy. When I met Nicholas for the first time at our wedding, he was painfully quiet, standing five feet away from everyone else, head bowed. I couldn't relate this awkward shy person to Finn. After Gwen had left him the second time he became a recluse, Finn told me.

Clare, the entertainer, arrives early with a large brown suitcase bulging with party equipment and a guitar. She tells me that when the children arrive she'll gather them in a circle to sing 'Happy Birthday'.

Half an hour later George is running up and down the stairs waiting for his classmates to arrive. He sticks his hands to the wall and pretends he can climb.

Mum and I smile awkwardly at Clare. How long is she going to sit and wait? She picks up her cup of tea. 'Let me get you another?' I take the cup before she has time to answer.

My mobile rings. 'How's it going?' Finn asks.

'It's not,' I whisper loudly.

'What?'

'No one's turned up yet.'

'Shit. Where's George?'

'Around. What do I do if no one turns up?'

Finn draws in breath. 'They will, they've got to. Don't panic. I'll call later.'

'Where is everyone?' George asks, coming up to me. Mum decides to hand him her present. It's a black plastic case with a red cross on it. George unclips the fastener. Inside are a play stethoscope, thermometer, gauze mask, roll of bandages, plastic blue cap, green apron, and finally a personalised badge saying Dr George Greenwood.

'I think you'd make a smashing doctor just like your father, a real hero,' Mrs B says. Clarky pulls a face behind her back.

I hear some footsteps outside and my heart lifts. 'Hello! Come in.' It's Mrs Heaven clutching the hand of her daughter, Imogen, who wears a stripy blue dress with a pink ribbon tied around her waist. 'Am I early? I thought I had the wrong house.' She starts to laugh, followed by a pert, 'Where is everyone?'

'They'll get here soon,' I echo back cheerfully. 'Oh, here's Tiana.' I introduce them. 'What a fabulous surname,' Tiana says.

'Thank you. My maiden name was Bliss.'

'Is that for me?' George is looking at the present Imogen holds while staring down at her shiny patent shoes. He grabs it from her feeble grasp and starts to rip off the paper.

'What do you say, George?' I urge.

'Thank you.'

When her mother has gone Imogen shuffles towards a beanbag and sits down. We wait another ten minutes and still no one else arrives.

'Do you want me to sing to these two?' Clare suggests diffidently.

Finally the doorbell rings and I open it, praying. 'Is it someone's birthday?' the postman enquires, handing us a large parcel.

George promptly forgets Imogen's offering of a puzzle. 'Wow!' he says, planting a cowboy hat on his head. It falls off, but he's lost interest in it already. George needs presents that demand his attention, like model aeroplanes he can build.

We start to sing 'Happy Birthday'. Clare is playing the guitar and singing as loudly as she can; Clarky, Mum, Tiana, Mrs B and I are belting it out too. 'I want my mum,' Imogen says at the end of the song.

I hear a car engine being turned off. I don't wait until the doorbell rings. 'Hello, sorry we're late,' Aggie calls from the window of her shiny white van. She opens the back door, presses a button and the ramp slots into place. Eliot glides effortlessly to the pavement in his wheelchair.

'Hi, Eliot.'

'I'm an outlaw,' he says with delight. His hair is swept back and tucked behind his large pink ears. He's wearing a muddy orange-coloured scarf and an old dusty jacket with silver studs down the arm. On his bottom half are combat trousers with rips across the knees and he carries a long-bow on his lap. He must be Robin Hood.

'One of the tyres got a puncture. Eliot was furious,' exclaims Aggie, shaking her head. 'He's been longing to come to this party, hasn't stopped talking about it and who is going to be here.'

Aggie takes one side of the chair; I am about to take the other when Clarky joins us. 'Here, let me help.'

Aggie looks up. 'Oh, hello, again,' she says. 'We met at the pool, didn't we?'

'Yes.'

There seems to be an overly long pause.

'Hurry up, will you?' Eliot demands with a wave of his hand. 'I haven't got all day.'

Tiana takes my side.

'It's Agatha, isn't it?' Clarky asks.

'Yes, but everyone calls me Aggie. Justin, right?'

'Yes, but everyone calls me Clarky.' They both start to laugh.

Tiana raises an eyebrow at me before she and Clarky summon all their strength to lift Eliot over the steps. I need to build a ramp. Eliot is fast becoming George's only friend at school so I think I should do as much as I can to maintain this.

George insists on taking over once his friend is inside. He pushes Eliot to the table, knocking over Imogen's present, the puzzle's box massacred under the wheels. Already he has forgotten that no one else has bothered to turn up. At least there is one advantage to having ADHD. He is unable to dwell for long on one particular thought, instead sailing on to the next obliviously. I wish I could do the same.

'Mind out, Mrs B!' George and the chair hurtle towards her and she jumps out of the way, clutching her bright pink plastic hairclip. Wisps of white hair fall loose around her face.

The next hour is the most painful of all. Eliot and George start having a food fight, the chocolate castle pasted on to their cheeks and noses like face paints. Clarky suggests he plays Imogen a tune on the guitar and starts to strum 'Bright Eyes' from *Watership Down*. She starts to cry.

'Try something more upbeat, can't you?' I insist.

George now has a whole wing of the chocolate castle topped with a red marzipan flag in his hands and I can see he is about to smack it down slap-bang on the middle of Eliot's head. I gasp with horror and am about to break it up when Aggie pulls my arm back. 'What are they going to do if they don't throw food at each other?' She shrugs her shoulders. 'It's only cake.'

'It cost almost twenty quid,' I tell her, rubbing my fore-head, 'and a parking ticket. Eliot is covered in it.'

'Well, thank God for the washing machine.' She laughs and then pops a sausage roll – well, just the pastry – in her mouth in one neat go. She doesn't seem to notice that George and Eliot have eaten the juicy sausage part and cast aside the flaking pastry.

'I want to be like you.'

'Like me?' She looks at me incredulously. 'Why?'

'You let things fly over your head.'

'I think you try too hard sometimes. You watch George all the time, like you know something's about to go wrong.'

'But if I don't watch, he's about to take a flying jump out the window or . . .'

'If George hurts himself, hasn't he learnt a valuable les-son? Eliot says he has ADHD, although he doesn't have a clue what that is. Sorry if this sounds silly, but aren't all children hyper?'

This question usually makes me want to kick people in the teeth. However, Aggie is a new friend so I practise self-restraint. 'There are normal children who play up from time to time and then there's George. I swear on my life it's not a made-up condition. It's a chemical imbalance in the brain that affects the parts controlling concentration, attention and impulsivity.'

'So he acts without thinking, like running across a busy road?'

'Exactly. George finds it impossible to filter all the messages his brain receives so he's constantly being distracted.'

'El says he takes a pill at lunchtime?'

'Ritalin. It's a central nervous system stimulant.'

'Fuck, he's on an amphetamine?'

'Yes, and believe me, it's the hardest thing giving your child a drug, but without it he'd never get *anything* done.'

Aggie nods thoughtfully. 'So how was he diagnosed?'

'We were about to leave for school, but George had forgotten his PE bag. I told him to go and get it . . .'

'I can't,' he said. 'There's something up there.'

'Upstairs, now.'

'There are fumes.'

I laughed nervously. 'Don't be silly.'

'There are fumes coming from the radiator, they've burnt my Lego.'

'George, I was in your room five minutes ago, it was fine.'

'Can't you smell the burning?' His arms were violently shaking; his forehead covered with sweat. Scared, I picked up the phone to talk to Finn.

'Tell the GP it's an emergency. I'm on my way home, now.'

George was shaking as if he had a terrible fever. 'What's wrong with him?' I whispered down the phone.

'I don't know, but everything's going to be fine.'

'Sit with me, George.' I wrapped us both in Baby. 'Daddy's coming.'

'There are chemicals on my hands.' He was hitting my arms. 'Get them off me!'

I rocked him, telling him everything was going to be fine while I had a sinking feeling that this was only the beginning.

'Shit. Then what happened?' Aggie asks.

'He was seen by a leading child psychologist and diagnosed with ADHD. There isn't a formal test as such, diagnosis is widely based on behavioural and psychological questionnaires that parents fill in.'

'Sod it. Must have been awful.'

'Yes, but right from the start I knew something was wrong. "He is irritable baby," his Indian health visitor used to say. She always wore red lipgloss which stuck to her two front teeth.' Aggie laughs at this. 'At playgroup he sat in the corner doing his own thing.'

'Eliot says sharks only eat you if you annoy them,' George calls out. 'Is that true, Mum?'

'They might eat you if they think you're a turtle,' Eliot adds.

They go back to their food fight. 'I feel bad. Here I am complaining about George when you have El.'

'He has Muscular Dystrophy,' she says. 'His muscles don't work properly. It's a rare genetic disorder in which muscles degenerate to such a point that, well, they can't function anymore. Eliot used to be able to walk, he used to be able to swim, but now . . .' Her eyes are watering.

I touch her arm. 'I'm sorry. Life's not fair sometimes, is it?'

'Josie, shall we save our woeful tales for another day? We're supposed to be at a birthday party.' She picks up the rabbit puppet Clarky gave George who for some weird reason has called it Mr Muki.

'Who gave this to him?'

'Clarky.'

'Now, that's much more interesting.' Her eyes widen. 'How do you know him?'

'We grew up together.'

'Talk about dishy too.'

'Dishy?'

'Fuck, yes.' She slaps a hand over her mouth again, as if telling it off.

I smile. 'I'm not questioning whether or not Clarky is dishy, I'm questioning the word itself.'

'He looks artistic, like a writer or a musician. You know, one of those attractive but elusive types?'

'Possibly.'

'Did you ever go out?'

'Not really.'

'What does that mean?'

'No.'

'Is he single?'

'Yes, think so. There was some girl called Kelly on the scene, but he didn't seem that keen.'

'Can you set me up with him? You see, I don't get out that much,' she confides, 'what with, well, you know . . .' She glances at Eliot. 'So I need all the help I can get.'

'Who are you talking about?' Tiana joins us.

'Clarky.' Aggie nods eagerly. 'I think he's dishy.'

'Why don't you ask him out?' Tiana suggests.

'I'm not sure I can, can I?'

Tiana grabs a handful of crisps. 'Why not?' we both say at the same time.

'Clarky won't bite! My new year's resolution was to meet five new people this year,' Tiana continues, crunching, 'and already I've smashed that target.'

Clarky puts the guitar down by the fireplace and walks towards us, but not before mouthing a 'sorry' in my direction and then throwing a mini-sausage at George who howls with laughter and throws one back at twice the speed.

'There's no chance Imogen was born sunny-side up,' he says.

Aggie coils her long auburn hair into a bun and lets it loose again. 'What do you do, Clarky?'

'I play the violin.'

She looks at me in triumph. 'Can you make a living out of that?'

I laugh at her directness.

'Er, that's a good question. Well, I'm available for birthdays, christenings, ruby wedding anniversaries, weddings – you name it. Let's face it, for money I'll do anything.'

Everyone has left. Clarky helped Aggie carry Eliot down the steps and then she offered him a lift home. The funny thing is, I had expected him to stay.

''Bye. Happy Birthday, George,' they all shouted out of the windows before the white van raced off into the distance.

As Mum left, she tried to comfort me, telling me that today was a success because George, in his own way, had enjoyed it.

Now he is lying on our bed with a wet Mr Muki laid out on a damp towel across one of the pillows, his pyjamas are on inside out and he still has chocolate crumbs in his hair. It doesn't matter. I need to take a leaf out of Aggie's book.

I walk downstairs, ignore the washing-up and make myself a cup of camomile tea. I wonder if Aggie will ask Clarky out? Would he go for someone like her? She is tall like me. His last official girlfriend was called Annabel. She was just over five foot and wore little pumps and neat pleated skirts. She looked like a sparrow hanging off his arm. 'All she wants to do is settle down and bake scones,' Clarky told me when they broke up two months later. Justin normally goes for quiet girls, whereas Aggie's the type to speak her mind. I like her, though, very much. Maybe someone like Aggie is exactly what he needs? Clarky's great with George, too, so he wouldn't have a problem with Eliot. I laugh at myself. Already I am playing Happy Families. Switch off. I shut my eyes and press an imaginary button on my head.

The front door opens. 'Mum!' I hear George screaming. 'MUM!'

Finn comes into the room and throws his briefcase down. 'What's that burning smell? Where's George?'

I run upstairs.

'What's that smell?' Finn runs after me.

'George, are you OK?' I call.

'Muki's on fire!' I fling open the bedroom door. The puppet is lying across the bedside table lamp, burning to death.

'He was cold after his bath, I wanted to warm him up,' George says, teeth chattering with fear.

I grab him but he's piping hot. 'Shit!' I shout, withdrawing my hand. Finn takes him instead and runs to the bathroom where he throws the rabbit into some cold water. I unplug the lamp immediately.

'Is Mr Muki dead?' George starts to cry. 'It's not my fault, Dad. I wanted to keep him warm.'

'George, quiet,' Finn says sharply.

'Have I killed him?' He's sobbing now.

Finn lays Mr Muki on the towel and starts to make the

sound of an ambulance siren. 'What the hell are you doing?' I ask him.

'Mr Muki has been brought into Accident and Emergency. He needs open-heart surgery. Stand back.'

'Is he going to be all right, Dad?'

'Shh. I need absolute silence. Keep back.' Finn listens to Mr Muki's heartbeat and does pretend cardiac arrest treatment. After a couple of minutes: 'That was a narrow escape,' he informs us seriously.

'Is he alive, Dad?'

'He's pulled through . . .'

'He's alive!'

'. . . but if that's ever done again, Mr Muki won't make it next time. Do you understand, George? You cannot put anything on lights.'

He nods.

'Do you understand?' Finn repeats firmly.

'I understand. Thank you, Dad.' George hugs him tightly.

'Go to bed, OK. I'll come and say goodnight in a minute.' George jumps up and cradles Mr Muki in his arms. The rabbit's fur is burnt and his eyes charred as black as coal.

What was Aggie talking about? I only have to turn my back for a second and the house will burn down. I'm crying now. My back hurts; my hand hurts. I'm so tired.

'Hey.' Finn kneels down by the bed.

'It's my fault.'

'Let me take a look at that hand.' He walks into the

239

bathroom and returns with a cold flannel. He presses it against my lobster-coloured skin, the coldness stinging against the heat.

'Will I live, Doctor?'

'It's touch and go.'

'I shouldn't have fallen asleep, but children's parties are exhausting.'

'Even if no one turns up?' We both laugh helplessly.

I shift over so he can lie down with me and we're quiet for a couple of minutes until Finn says, 'We've got the twenty-week scan tomorrow, haven't we?'

'Mmm,' I murmur. 'You'll be there, won't you?'

'Yes.'

'What would have happened if you hadn't come back?'

'Don't think about it. It's OK now, that's all that counts.'

We haven't hugged for a long time. I try to imagine not having Finn in my life. I hold on even tighter.

'Although,' he starts again, 'that damn rabbit could have burnt our house down. Imagine having to tell the insurance people. Who gave him that scary puppet anyway?'

'Clarky.'

'Clarky,' he repeats slowly. 'I should have guessed.'

23

I was staring at my computer screen waiting for my boss to deign to come into the office. He was the laziest genius I knew.

After Cambridge and travelling with Clarky, I had gained my degree in typography and was now a PA, working for a leading London designer, David Hamilton. His offices were along Westbourne Grove, the seedier side near Bayswater. David was a wildly contradictory character: temperamental, brilliant, flamboyant, frustrating, creative and infuriating. I hadn't realised quite how successful and well known he was in the industry until I started working for him. He was heralded as one of the most important designers of the 1980s. For my interview I had dressed in a long polka-dot skirt that Mum had insisted was the thing to wear. I felt I would have stood more of a chance of getting a trendy media job if I'd been wearing suspenders and a black leather jacket.

'*Alice in Wonderland* was my favourite book as a child.'

David winked at me when he told me I'd got the job. There was a frisson of chemistry between us. I abandoned the skirt after that.

He loved to stroll into the office around midday, wearing dark jeans, black cowboy boots and a white shirt that showed off a few stray dark hairs on his chest. Sometimes a tall long-legged model would strut behind him, mascara smudged around her eyes, looking like she had just crawled out of his bed. He was constantly hungover and clutching a Styrofoam cup of strong coffee in one hand, a bacon sandwich in the other. 'What have you got in your in-tray, Josie?' he'd ask, perching on the corner of my desk and flicking the plastic lid off his takeaway coffee.

'Josie, wake him up and get his arse into the office, OK?' was a typical morning call from a client.

'I'll try him again,' I'd say, feeling more like the nagging wife as I picked up the phone.

'People who start the day early are very boring, Josie,' was David's justification.

'That sounds more like an excuse to stay in bed.'

'Do you really want to work for a boring person?' I knew he was smiling then.

'No. I wouldn't mind a social life, though.'

Still no sign of my boss. I picked up the phone. How long could he get away with this? I punched in a number. 'Are we still meeting tonight?' I asked Alex. He'd been my boyfriend since my final year at Reading: ambitious, clean-living (he liked to 'detox' once a month), and being positively nice was a hobby with him.

'I've got a mountain of work to get through.' He worked for a bank in London. 'What time's the concert?'

'Seven-thirty. If it's difficult we can meet afterwards.'

'I'll try my very hardest, pumpkin.'

I put the phone down and started tapping my desk with a rubber-ended pencil. It was time for a caffeine fix. I walked outside, into the hustle and bustle of London traffic and people. I needed a new job, one where I was doing the designing; I wanted to use my degree. I had loved my job to begin with, but now I was ready for more responsibility. I crossed the zebra crossing and a tall man walked past me, striding in the opposite direction. I turned round. There was something about his face, the way he walked, that click of the heel against the pavement. It couldn't have been, could it? I stood motionless in the middle of the road until a car beeped at me and I was forced to move on.

I headed for Starbucks and bought a latte. I sat on a stool near the window and gazed out on to the busy London street. For the past month I hadn't been able to get Finn out of my mind. I'd lie awake at night and wonder what he was doing now. Had he finished his medicine degree? Had he met anyone else? Was he married? Happy?

He was relentlessly in my thoughts; I'd even been dreaming about him. It was always the same dream, where his hand held mine but his touch was so light. I was terrified of losing it again. I'd wake up feeling this closeness to him, a layer of warmth wrapped around my body. As I rolled over, wanting to rest my head against his chest and hear the reassuring beat of his heart, instead I'd hear, 'Morning, precious.' And there was Alex, propped up against the bed-head reading the newspaper. 'You were restless in the night,' he'd say. 'Things on your mind, pumpkin?'

After I left Cambridge Finn and I had kept in touch to begin with, but our calls became less and less frequent until they fizzled out altogether. There were many moments when I felt so angry with him, angry that he had left me *wanting*. I'd close my eyes when I kissed other men and imagine they were Finn. What was wrong with me? Why didn't I feel anything anymore? I threw myself into my work instead. Painting was my therapy. When I'd met Alex in my final year, I tried to make myself believe I could love him.

I had been with Tiana one evening recently at her flat in Pimlico, sitting cross-legged on the floor, eating fish and chips. Tiana's flat was the size of a shoebox, but so inviting that I never wanted to leave. Her bedroom was fit for a princess to sleep in – dark red silk bedspread, ornate silver mirror, crystal chandelier with fake diamond and pearl drops. 'I work in a cut-throat world,' she'd say, 'so when I come home I want to be surrounded by prettiness.'

'Shall I contact Finn?' I asked her, dipping a chip into mayonnaise.

'Definitely. Why don't you try his college?' she suggested. 'They'd at least forward post to him. Go on, I'd like to meet him.'

I had thought about this already, but allowed myself to think of all the reasons not to, the main one being fear. Perhaps I had been thinking about him because Alex was getting too serious about me and my mother was getting way too serious about *him*. He'd told her she had the most beautiful garden he had ever seen. 'When is that delightful young man coming for lunch again?' she'd asked recently. 'I'd love to show him my new herb pots.'

I looked at my watch. Nearly midday. David still wouldn't have arrived in the office so I had time to order another latte. He'd better not be too late because I couldn't stay tonight. It was Clarky's concert.

Now Clarky was a person I couldn't talk to about Finn. Everything about him shut down and switched off if I tried. The only thing he'd once said to me, shortly after we'd returned from Europe, was that I had to stop looking back on Finn through rose-tinted glasses. It had been lust, that was all. 'Don't worry about it, J, we all make mistakes.'

His words cut right through me. 'Meaning?'

'We think we're in love but . . .'

'Are you still talking about Finn and me?'

He'd laughed at my question. 'Who else? You were just stupid and starry-eyed, let it be.'

Let it be.

Clarky was another story altogether and one that wasn't so easy to piece together.

We had climbed to the top of the Eiffel Tower, strolled along the Champs-Elysées, exhausted every museum in Madrid, gone on long bicycle rides in Barcelona. I'd painted on the beach while Clarky sat absorbed in a paperback. He'd made me go to a few operas in exchange for accompanying me to art galleries. He'd helped me get Finn out of my mind. Or so I always maintained. 'You're thinking about him, aren't you?' Clarky had asked one day when we were in Paris.

'No.'

'For most men it's out of sight, out of mind.'

'I'm not thinking about him, OK?'

'Fine. Good.' He wrapped an arm around me. 'Because we're in one of the most romantic cities in the world, let's not waste our time dwelling on thoughts of Finn. We're going to meet a lot more people at university and it would be foolish to feel tied to anyone while we're only nineteen. It'll get easier, I promise.'

The fact that we were seeing and experiencing so many different things certainly helped too. Clarky and I became even closer; I hadn't thought it possible to know someone as well as I knew him.

'Don't do that!' He'd been standing at the sink at the time, after brushing his teeth, spitting water out like a dead fish. 'Ugh! Stop it!' I cried.

'Josie, do you realise you click your tongue against the roof of your mouth?' he said one day, watching me as I drew on the beach.

'I don't.'

'Yes, you do. And you do this when you're writing.' He was biting his lip, chin stuck out, pretending to write against the table.

'I don't!'

'Sorry, you do.'

'Well, this is you playing the violin.' I'd given myself a double chin and pressed my lips tightly shut as I played the imaginary instrument.

'I get so swept away in the music that I forget what I look like.'

'And you do this with your nose when you're in a mood.' I'd touched the end of mine and given it a tug.

'I get that from my father. It's a control thing.'

Then there was that one night when we were in Venice. It was our last destination before we went home for the summer.

We'd been eating out, couples surrounding us on every table. Hands were being held, people were kissing at every opportunity, street vendors were selling dark red roses from champagne buckets, men ushering them over with a click of their fingers, ready to hand their girls a single symbolic stem. Meals were followed by romantic evening strolls in the square or late-night trips on gondolas, being serenaded on the water. 'I *will* marry you!' I heard from every street corner. If you were single it felt as if your face were being rubbed in it. 'Come back when you're in love,' the skies seemed to hiss at you.

Clarky and I had been walking back to our hotel one evening. My head was spinning from too much red wine. The buildings, the light on the water, candles in the restaurants – everything was lit up with hope and love. I'd felt so happy walking with him. We had a contest as to who could walk in the straightest line.

Outside our hotel room we'd kissed goodnight clumsily on the cheek but then Clarky had knocked on my door five minutes later and staggered in before waiting for me to respond. The weird thing was I had expected him to come back. I was standing naked in front of the cracked bathroom mirror. Giggling, I'd grabbed a skimpy towel from the rail, but it barely covered my bottom. 'I've run out of toothpaste,' he'd said, leaning one hand against the wall. He was still in his jeans and cord shirt. Turning to get him some, I felt a hand on the back of my waist and the towel dropped to the floor as he twisted me back round to face him. 'You've run out of toothpaste!' I'd laughed, pulling his shirt off, drink not allowing me to feel any inhibition.

'And you were actually going to get me some?' He'd kissed me then and his mouth smelled of mint. His arms went around me and I kissed him back; it felt great to be held. He pulled me closer. 'You're beautiful, so beautiful.'

'You're drunk, so drunk.' We'd fallen on to the bed, high on red wine; high on each other.

The morning after I had looked over at Clarky who lay with one arm above his head, his lips slightly parted as if someone were about to sprinkle something magical into his mouth. I could hear his breathing. Quietly I lifted the duvet and found my clothes in the bathroom. I looked in the mirror. Black smudges around my eyes, skin blotched from alcohol and hair that wasn't easy to control at the best of times sticking out all over the place as if I'd suffered a major electric shock. I got dressed and shut the door softly behind me.

I walked to a bar, sat down in a crumpled heap and drank a cup of strong coffee. What had we done? It was sort of nice, I'd decided, twisting a strand of hair nervously around my fingers. It wasn't the same as Finn. Oh, God, how could I put it? Sleeping with Finn had always felt strangely familiar, yet with Clarky our lack of inhibition had surprised me. But Clarky and me? Only the other night we had been sitting watching a movie in my room, eating a takeaway, Justin happily clipping his toenails.

'D'you have to do that in here?' I'd asked. How on earth had we moved from that to passionate sex?

We never talked about that night.

We met later on that day, bumping into one another awkwardly in the hotel reception area.

'Hi!' Clarky had smiled at me overenthusiastically, like a host pretending it was wonderful that their guest was staying on for another month.

'Are you all right?' I asked him.

'Great, but tired. Very tired, in fact.'

'It's only eight o'clock. Do you want a drink? Something to eat?'

'I'm having an early night, need to nurse my hangover,' he replied.

'Are you really all right?'

'Fine. See you in the morning.'

I was staring at him as if he were a ghost. Had I imagined last night?

The summer before we both started university Clarky went out of his way to avoid me. I'd walk into a room and he'd walk out with some excuse; if I was with Tiana all his attention would be directed towards her. I'd felt invisible and acutely aware of the way he was behaving, but he seemed oblivious. Tiana told me men don't confront anything, especially something as tricky as sleeping with a best mate. 'By the time you're both at university things will be back to normal,' she'd promised.

I stared into my coffee. I wasn't in love with Clarky back then, but I was confused by his behaviour. His avoidance had hurt me and I missed him as a friend. I started to wish we'd never done it. It had been a terrible idea, mixing friendship with sex. It was a lethal combination, like business and pleasure. If I could rewind time I'd have been cleverer about it, I thought, as I put my coat on and walked back to the office. Why had I acted like a useless lump of stone whenever he was around me? Why couldn't I tell him that we needed to talk about it, just so we could get back to normal? Lots of people had one-night stands. I'd wanted to laugh about it, feel at ease with him again. Instead our silence about 'that one night' was building it into something deeper and more complicated than it should have been.

When we were at university the time apart and distance between us helped. And things did go back to normal. After about six months we became close again, as if nothing had happened. Only every now and then did we make references to it. When friends commented on how close we were, we were both single and had we ever, 'you know,' Clarky would say quickly, 'Been there, done that,' and I'd laugh, saying in a voice I hardly recognised as my own, 'Blame it on the red wine.' We still hadn't talked about it properly and I doubted now we ever would.

I climbed the steps into the theatre. I could hear footsteps and turned round to see if anyone was behind me. Nothing. I shook my head and walked on. The building was impressive; pale-coloured stone with large imposing pillars. Inside it was lit with a golden chandelier and the seats arranged at the front of the orchestra were a rich red velvet. I took my own seat and flicked through the programme.

The orchestra was already seated. I watched Clarky going through the music with one of the other violinists. She wore a pink flower in her fair hair. They both looked pale-skinned in contrast to the dark lustre of their violins. Clarky looked so earnest, too, dressed in his black trousers and matching waistcoat.

I clapped loudly when the conductor took his place. There was a dramatic pause before the music began; the air static with anticipation. This was not the time to have a tickle in your throat or a coughing fit, which unfortunately had happened to me once, forcing me to make a sharp exit.

I watched the conductor with fascination; the way his shoulder blades writhed with energy, his arms dancing gracefully to the music.

It was halfway through the concert when I noticed the couple sitting directly in front of me, literally unable to keep their hands off one another. She was wearing a backless green dress and had a streak of her hair dyed to match. He was wearing a dark suit. She stroked his cheek with one hand. Honestly, get a room, I thought to myself as I adjusted the position of my seat. Soon the entire audience became aware of them. There were stifled laughs, people nudging one another. I tried to focus on Clarky, but then the couple started to kiss passionately. I didn't know where to look and now they were blocking my view! I turned to my left and then to my right, anything to avoid looking straight ahead.

And then I saw him.

I sat back abruptly in my seat as if I had been slapped hard. What was going on in my imagination? I must be crazy. I gently moved forward in my seat again and turned to glance to the left and behind me. Yes, three rows away. The programme dropped off my knee. I could feel my hand shaking as I reached down to pick it up off the floor. Then I knocked my forehead against the back of one of the kissing couple's chairs. The girl turned round and had the cheek to give me an evil look, as if I were at fault for distracting them from their embarrassing display of affection. I looked over again, terrified that Finn's image would have melted into nothing and the seat would be empty.

But he was still there. I laughed out loud and then had to cough abruptly to disguise it. Isn't there a kind of fear that makes you react like that? When life throws you a different number on the dice, one you never expected to see after all this time and you're laughing at its sheer insanity? I sat up straight and tried to steady my breathing. A door opened to the right and Alex shuffled down the row towards me, raising an eyebrow at the passionate twosome in front.

He gave me a peck on the cheek.

I knew Finn was watching us. I could feel his stare burning into my back.

After the performance Alex and I walked towards the door. 'Josie,' I heard from behind us. My heart was galloping.

'Finn,' I exclaimed before even turning round. 'What a surprise.' He was exactly how I remembered him except that his hair was now all one colour – dark brown. It was as if part of his character were missing.

Alex stood looking at me and then at Finn, cocking his head like a bird. He was waiting to be introduced.

We just stared at one another. Eventually I said, 'Sorry, Alex. This is an old friend of mine, Finn. We haven't seen each other for . . . what? Er, so long . . .'

'Five years,' Finn helped me out.

Alex put an arm around my shoulders. 'What a small world. Shall we get a drink? I should think the two of you would like to catch up.' We walked down the stone steps and into the bar. 'Just nipping to the loo,' Alex told us.

When he was out of earshot we both turned to each other and at precisely the same time said, 'I can't believe it's you.'

'I know. I was meeting a friend in the square and there you were, walking up the steps. I only caught a glimpse of your back, but I remembered you liked the colour red. And, of course, that friend of yours, the violin man. I saw there was a concert tonight.'

'Clarky.'

'Yes, him. What have you been up to? How are you? Where are you living?' Finn's voice was as quick as a fast-flowing stream. It was as if he were aware we had only minutes but wanted to cover everything that had happened in that entire five years while we had the chance.

'It's weird, I've been thinking about you lately and I had this feeling I'd see you. How are you?' I babbled.

'I'm good. You?' He reached out to touch my face and I clamped my hand on to his, not wanting to let it go. It didn't feel strange; it felt normal. 'God, you look great,' he told me. 'Give me your telephone number, quick.'

I scrabbled in my handbag to try to find a pen. I wrote my home number on a business card. Alex returned and Finn gripped my hand when he wasn't looking. I got butter-flies in my stomach from one touch of his fingers.

'It must be extraordinary to see each other after five years?' Alex said cheerily.

'Extraordinary,' Finn repeated.

'Why didn't you two stay in touch?'

'That's a very good question, Alex. I ask myself the same thing every day.' Finn was staring intently at me.

'Right, good stuff. Well, Josie and I have been an item for . . . how long is it now? Over a year.'

An item? How could I be going out with anyone who said 'an *item*'? From the look in Finn's eye I could tell he was thinking the same. 'Clarky!' Alex called out then. Justin had walked into the bar with a few of his musician friends, but made his way over to us. Finn was looking down, as if he wanted to surprise him. Alex thumped his hand appreciatively against Clarky's back. 'Congrats, mate. You were brilliant! Best concert I've ever been to. You'll never guess who we've just bumped into?' He nudged me like a dolly that couldn't speak. 'Finn, isn't it?'

He looked up with a confident smile and held out his hand. 'Hi, Justin, how are you?'

Clarky blinked to make sure. 'Hello,' he said, 'what a surprise.'

'Josie hasn't seen him for five years,' Alex pattered on. 'Now, let's get the drinks in.' He put an arm around my shoulders again. 'Darling, what would you like?'

'Double vodka,' I said without hesitating.

'Make that two,' Finn added.

'Three,' finished Clarky.

24

'AN EXCITING MOMENT FOR BOTH OF YOU,' is written in capital letters. 'Ultrasound scanning gives a woman and her partner the opportunity to see their developing baby for the first time.' I sit in the waiting room. I am bursting for the loo. I have had to drink what seemed like gallons of water before the scan in order to make the image clearer. Think of a very dry spring, or earth so dry it cracks in the heat . . . Sod it. I really need to go.

'Congratulations,' Natalie had said sweetly. 'You must be delighted.'

'You're what!' Ruby screeched again although it was obvious she had heard me first time. Her face was so close to mine that I could see the caked powder on her top lip.

'Pregnant,' I'd said. That was two weeks ago.

From the corner of my eye I could see Natalie working out in her head exactly when I'd be leaving so that she could take on some of my clients. 'I promise you it won't affect my work. I intend to be here right up to when the baby is born, or just a few weeks before,' I'd added, knowing Ruby would take it literally otherwise and expect me to work while I was having contractions.

She'd spun round in her chair a few times to calm herself down. 'And I thought you were putting on weight! Why do you want another sprog?' she couldn't help asking, holding the edge of the leather seat tightly. 'Isn't the one you have enough trouble? Why in God's name do women have children? Career or children? It's such an obvious choice!'

I nodded. 'I understand it's not the best timing, but it's still some months ahead.'

She pressed her lips together, red lipstick smudging her teeth. 'Well, I can't sack you.'

'Sack me?' My eyes opened wide.

'Very strict legislation about that,' she'd said, fingers tapping the desk. 'Besides, Gem Communications needs you. Natalie's only half up to speed.'

'I am fully up to speed and ready for more responsibility,' Natalie had argued.

But Ruby wasn't interested. 'Spit out sprog two and back you come.'

Now I flick nervously through a magazine. 'Are you going to have the baby today, Mum?' George had asked me this morning.

'No,' I'd told him again. 'The baby is only twenty weeks old. A pregnancy lasts nine months.'

'Nine months? That's like a whole lifetime. Eliot says babies come out of your bottom. Do they, Mum?'

'Finn?' I had turned to him with a broad smile. 'You're the doctor, you explain.'

Please God, please may this child be happy and healthy. If you answer this prayer, I will start going to church, I promise. I know I only pray for what I want, like running my own art gallery, which is bad, really bad, so I promise I'll change. I'll start to say prayers for those who aren't as well off, like the bearded man George and I see on the street who shouts 'JESUS IS LOVE', and then there's that man who moves about on a black trolley because he doesn't have any legs. The homeless woman who's always pushing a suitcase aimlessly in the Piccadilly Waterstone's. I'll even say a prayer for Ms Miles. Just please grant me this one wish: let me be a good mother.

'Mrs Greenwood,' calls out the nurse wearing a white-and-red uniform. Her hair is dark and tied back into a ponytail. I could kill Finn. He promised he wouldn't be late.

She holds the door open for me and I walk into the room with its stark white walls and pink curtains.

'Make yourself comfortable,' she says. 'You've got a full bladder?'

'Oh, yes.'

I lie down on the hard couch that is covered in a sheet of

blue paper that looks like wide loo roll. The couch is next to all the scanning equipment and machinery. 'How are you feeling today?' she asks.

'Not bad, thanks. Excited.'

'No one with you?' She sits down next to me.

'Not unless they're invisible,' I trill. She looks at me strangely. 'My husband's running late. He's a doctor,' I explain as I roll up my grey T-shirt and unbutton my trousers.

'Try to relax, drop the shoulders.' She starts to rub a cold gel on to my abdomen before picking up a microphone-like object and moving it back and forth over my stomach. 'Do you work?' she asks.

'Yes.'

'Are you remembering to sit with your feet elevated at the desk? It's a good idea to turn a waste-paper bin upside down.'

'Keeping my feet up. Very important.'

'Do you have other children?'

'A boy.'

'How old is he?'

'Seven.'

'A lovely age, old enough to look after himself now.'

'Yes, absolutely, he's very good.' What a great fictional life I lead.

She's looking carefully at the screen. 'The picture is quite clear,' she says. The baby is too big now to see it as a whole on the screen. 'This is the baby's elbow, there's the foot . . . the toenails are beginning to grow now . . . and there's the shoulder.'

'Look at the spine, it's so perfect,' I say, my face turned sideways to the screen. 'Look, it's yawning!'

She smiles. 'There's the heart, it shows up as grey.'

As I look at the screen I feel overwhelmed with guilt for sometimes wishing this child weren't there. For only thinking about how it is going to affect my life. Now that I see something so real, I realise how lucky I am. Where are you, Finn? I gather up more of the sheet and grip it tightly in my hand. Suddenly I wish my mother were with me. I should have taken her up on her offer to come and stay for a few days. 'I'm sorry,' I say when the nurse hands me a tissue.

'Don't worry. It's natural to cry, Mrs Greenwood.'

'I'm going to have the best baby, aren't I?'

'You are. Now, did you want to know what the sex is?'

I grip the sheet again.

All I have to do is say 'yes'. All she has to do is tell me.

The door swings open. It's Finn.

'Sorry I'm late. I'm the father,' he says breathlessly to the nurse.

'I'm bursting for the loo, Finn,' I say, pushing past him.

'How did it go? Is everything all right?'

'I'll leave your wife to tell you.'

*

I stand in front of the sink and wash my hands with liquid soap. I dry my eyes and reapply my powder. Right, I'm ready. I hold out my hand and it is trembling like jelly.

He is in the waiting room, pacing up and down. When he sees me he stops abruptly by the water cooler. 'Come on.' He pulls at my hand and leads me outside into the car park. 'How did it go? Did you find out the sex?'

'Finn, I wish you'd been with me.'

'I'm so sorry I'm late, J, but Alessia needed . . .'

I put up my hand. 'You were late because of Alessia?'

'There was an emergency. I couldn't leave her on her own. I wanted to be here, I got here as quick as I could.'

'It doesn't matter, it's fine.'

'Is it? Nothing seems fine between us.'

We both stand looking at each other.

'Don't punish me for being late. Please tell me,' he asks more softly now.

'It's a girl!'

'A girl?' His eyes widen. 'We're having a girl?' We both start to jump up and down.

'Thank you, GOD!' I shout out to the sky, wherever He might be.

More people walk through the double doors. 'We're having a girl!' Finn says to them.

I laugh. 'Let's go home, ring our friends and family . . .'

'And I want to call her Emily!' he shouts to their retreating backs.

'OH, FINN! We agreed to call her Gertrude.'

'On my deathbed!'

The automatic doors open and a couple walk through. One of them turns around and looks at us, smiling. Happiness is contagious.

'We're really doing it?' he says. 'We're having another child.' It is as if Finn finally feels complete, the gap in his own family filled. We stand still and he holds my face in his hands and kisses me.

'*Regarder la télé*,' George scribbles in his French homework book. '*Boire quelque chose*.'

'Don't hold the pen so hard,' I tell him again.

He throws it down in a tantrum. 'I'm stupid! I can't do it!'

'You're not stupid. Try again.'

But he's looking at the printed scan now. 'What do you think of your little sister?' Finn asks.

George squints hard as he turns the paper upside down. 'She looks like a crocodile,' he says.

The telephone rings and I pick up. I am longing to talk to Mum. It's Clarky. 'Ahh, so sweet of you to call.' You see, Clarky never forgets.

'What?'

'You remembered I was having my twenty-week scan.'

'How did it go?'

'I'm having a girl.' Oh. He didn't remember.

'That's wonderful news. I'm really happy for you.'

There's something different in his voice. 'Are you OK?'

'Sorry, J, I have to be honest, I'd forgotten about the scan.'

'Oh, it doesn't matter.'

Finn is listening now. 'I was wondering . . . can I have Aggie's telephone number?'

'Sure,' I say, an octave too high. 'You really like her, then?'

'I think she's great.'

'Right, I'll look it up. Hang on.' I hold the phone under my chin as I start to leaf through my address book. 'Here we go.'

Finn asks me what that was all about when I put the phone down. 'Clarky likes Eliot's mother. They met at George's party.' I walk into the kitchen and pour myself a glass of water.

'He wants to sex her?' George asks, flinging open the fridge. He's so quick that I hadn't heard him come into the kitchen. He rips open a carton of milk and the entire contents sloshes on to the wooden floor. A packet of grated Parmesan falls out of the fridge too. It stinks. 'Oh, GEORGE!' Finn shouts.

'Wasn't my fault.' He takes out another pint of milk.

'Well, whose fault was it? The bogeyman's? Clean it up,' Finn demands, wringing out a J-cloth, 'before you start on the other.'

George takes it and half-heartedly cleans the floor at a whirlwind pace. He throws the cloth in the sink, pours himself another glass so full that some of it spills on to the table. He drinks it all in one go, leaving himself with a milky-white moustache. 'Ugh, brain freeze!' And then he runs off again.

'Why don't we invite them both over for supper?' Finn suggests. 'Josie, sit down. I'll do it.'

I position myself on the stool.

Finn bends down and starts to clear up the milky cheese mess on the floor. 'It'd be fun to have a party. We haven't had one for ages and I'd like to meet Aggie.'

I don't know why the dinner party we had with a few of Finn's medic friends, a couple of months ago flashes through my mind as I watch him clear up the mess.

George had come downstairs in his pyjamas. 'Surgeons aren't as clever as doctors, are they?' he'd said conversationally.

'I don't know where you heard that,' Finn laughed.

'You told me.'

'Oh, really?' one of the surgeons asked. He turned expectantly to Finn.

'I didn't say that exactly.'

'Yes, you did,' George corrected him. 'You said all they did was put the bits in and get all the glory.'

Finn had almost disappeared under the table with embarrassment.

'Yes, you should meet her,' I say to him now. 'It's thanks to her that George found this swimming teacher too.'

The lessons are going well. Frédéric says that George is beginning to grasp the breathing technique.

'Let's organise it then. Why don't we invite Tiana and Christo? Or Ed and Zoe? Actually they're away right now. You know what, I think Christo's seeing someone, but he won't tell me; he's being highly secretive about the whole thing.' He hands me the phone. 'Ring Clarky, or I will.'

'Great, would love to,' Clarky says when I ask him. 'Saves me from ringing her up too, thanks.'

I ring Aggie next. 'I'll bring over a pudding. Do you like treacle tart? Thank you, Josie, quick work! I under-estimate you.' I don't tell her it was Finn's idea. 'I like Justin. I mean, *really* like him. Do you think he likes me? What shall I wear?' She starts to think out loud. 'I don't want to be too casual, but at the same time I don't want to look like I've made this massive effort either. Better not wear my tiara, hey? Oh, listen to me. I'm nervous already just thinking about it.'

'He does like you, Aggie, *a lot*,' I encourage her.

'She's a talker,' Finn says when I finally put the phone down. 'Can you see Clarky with her?'

'Possibly, who knows?'

'Does Daddog love Aggie?' George asks, running into the kitchen again.

'Do you want your dad to take you out for a run,' I ask

him, 'burn off that energy?' Before I was this pregnant we used to run before school too, around the park.

'Will they get married?' George continues.

'No,' I say too quickly, followed by a more thoughtful, 'They've only just met, poppet.'

'It was love at first sight for us,' Finn comments.

'Was it?'

'Yes. You fell for me straightaway,' he says with that cocky arrogance.

'OK,' I admit, remembering how Finn made me feel dizzy with love. 'But did you fall for me *the moment* you saw me?'

'Yes,' he states simply.

'Did you?' I must have frowned in disbelief.

'I liked being near you, hearing that laugh, seeing you in that tight little apron. I liked your honesty, the way you didn't say things to impress, you were just yourself. Come on, J. Why do you think I used to hang around Momo's drinking endless tasteless cups of coffee and eating cheap pizzas? I wasn't doing it for him.'

'I made good coffee!'

He shrugs. 'You were always the girl for me, J. I was the luckiest man alive to find you again after five years.'

He kisses me. Finn has just said the sweetest, loveliest thing to me, so why do I feel unsteady, as if something is about to rock our ship, when now of all times we need the water to be calm?

Why am I thinking about Clarky?

25

Alex and I were in the restaurant, but I felt too excited to eat. He ordered some kind of vegetable tartlet for a starter. 'Are you sure you don't want anything, pumpkin?' I watched him picking something from his tooth. I knew I had to say something. Guilt was leaving an oily taste in my mouth. 'Wretched spinach,' he laughed.

'I don't think it's working.'

'I know, it really is stuck.' He was ramming his nail down the side of his tooth.

'No, Alex, I mean us. It's not working.'

'What?'

'I'm so sorry.'

'Right. What do you mean?'

'It's me, not you,' I tried to assure him lamely. He excused himself, suddenly saying he had to nip to the loo.

*

After the meal Alex offered to drive me home even when I had said I could catch a taxi. He insisted. We were driving in silence when my mobile started to ring.

'It's me. I want to see you tonight.'

'I can't talk now. Call me tomorrow.' I hung up, fingers trembling.

Alex turned briefly to me, keeping one hand on the steering wheel. 'That was Finn, wasn't it?'

'Yes.'

'He's the reason, isn't he? Not the spinach-picking?' He laughed weakly.

'Yes.' There was no point in lying.

'Josie, I really like you. Are you sure we can't make a go of things?'

I shook my head. Never in my mind had I been clearer about anything.

The following morning Finn called again, this time at the office. We arranged to meet in the evening. I started to rearrange my desk, a pointless task but I was so jittery I had to do something. 'Stop humming,' one of my colleagues shouted across to me. 'You've been doing it all bloody morning.'

Right, calm down. It's only a date. We might have nothing in common anymore. It could be a disaster.

'David wake up! I have all your flight details for tomorrow. Gatwick, south terminal, two-thirty check-in time.'

My voice had lost that nagging edge. I was too happy to be cross with him.

'You're a star, Josie.'

'David, as much as I love being your nagging wife, I need to talk to you about what I want to do next. I need to use my degree. I've learnt so much from you, but . . .'

He stopped me. 'Josie, you can do anything you want. I'd give you a golden reference. I've been lucky to have you with me for this long.'

I was glowing with pride. 'Thank you. By the way, just because you complimented me doesn't mean I can work late tonight!'

'Hot date?'

'Yes, sizzling!'

We met in a small Thai restaurant. We were both looking at the large white menus, pretending to be absorbed in what to choose for a starter. Finn had put on his glasses to read. 'I'm thinking of having laser treatment,' he said, 'because I hate wearing contacts.'

'They suit you, the glasses.'

'Thanks.'

'The prawns sound nice,' I said blandly, the words on the page blurring into one another. Our menus were shielding us from finding out anything we didn't want to know about each other. Like Finn had a child or I was engaged or had some hideous disease. The menus were swept away then, along with the wine list, leaving our table bare. It was just Finn and me with nothing between us anymore.

Where did we start? 'Five questions,' he suggested, 'to cover the five years we haven't seen each other?' He poured us both another glass of white wine.

'OK. Me first.' *Why did you stop calling?* 'Did you finish your degree?'

'Yes. Thanks to you,' he quickly added. 'Really, I mean it. I went to London after three years at Cambridge. I trained at St Mary's and surrounding hospitals. I went to Chicago for eight weeks, too, and worked in the trauma ward.'

I was gripping my napkin tightly, knees pressed together. 'Was it like *ER*?'

'Kind of. I saw gunshot wounds and terrible car accidents and stabbings. People jumping off buildings.' I was nodding as he spoke, interested, of course, but all I wanted to do was to cut through all the formalities and get right to it. 'Pretty grim but exciting to have the experience,' he went on.

'How did you do in your finals?'

Finn actually blushed. So there was a humble gene in his body. 'You'll think I'm showing off,' he said, running one hand through his hair.

I smiled. 'That depends on how you say it, doesn't it?'

He looked relieved, familiarity beginning to set in. 'You haven't changed, Josie. OK. Well, I got a 2:1 overall at

Cambridge in my pre-clinical degree. It was in biological anthropology, you know, studying genetics, evolution of man and the monkey/ape kingdom.'

'Oh yes,' I nodded, trying to keep a straight face, 'I know all that.'

Finn smiled. 'And then for the next three years at medical school, my MB, BS, medical bachelor, bachelor of surgery,' he described earnestly, 'I passed with As in all my subjects and distinctions in obs and gynae, and medicine. Those exams were hell, though, especially the clinical ones. You have this high-flying consultant dressed in a power suit expecting you to know exactly what is wrong with patient A, a child with asthma, or patient B who has kidney failure. It's terrifying.'

'I can imagine. Well done. You deserve it.' *Have you got a girlfriend?* 'So what stage are you at now?'

'I've just become a senior house officer.'

Are you in love? 'Which means?'

'I spend most of my time on the wards, chasing results for X-rays and bloods,' he explained modestly. I leant forward, cupping one hand under my chin and biting my little finger, desperately trying to focus on what he was saying. 'I get to be in clinic, though, twice a week. It's not as menial as being a house officer. They have to do everything they are told.'

'I bet you didn't like that?' I was playing with my fork now. It slipped on to the floor.

'I forgot you were clumsy. Here, let me get it.'

He bent down to retrieve it from under the table. I fanned my face with the napkin and then inhaled sharply when I felt his hand stroking my leg, touching my ankle-bone. I was wearing red high heels.

He sat up again. 'No, but that's the way it is,' he said with that old flicker of a smile. I was nodding, but I'd forgotten my question.

'Do you mind if I smoke?'

I nearly laughed. So much more grown-up than our smoky student nights. Here we were in a formal restaurant with Finn having to ask if he could light up, and both of us sitting straight at the table when all I wanted to do was let my body melt into his.

'No.'

Finn reached into his shirt pocket to get a packet of cigarettes. Even the way he lit one was sexy. He held it to his mouth and inhaled. I watched the smoke cloud between us. 'What are we doing here, Finn?' Cut to the chase.

He rolled up one of his sleeves. 'I did think about you, a lot. All of the time.'

Already I wanted to hold him. Discover him all over again. But it was too easy for Finn, wasn't it? I wondered if he had ever had to work at a relationship or did girls still flock to him at a click of his fingers? He flicked away some ash, not taking his eyes off me.

'You stopped calling,' I said.

'I wasn't sure it was a good thing, stepping back into the past. I was scared of what I'd find. You with someone else perhaps.'

I leant in closer. I didn't want people to overhear. 'Is that more terrifying than never seeing me again? For Christ's sake, Finn, that's so cowardly. I left you messages when I was abroad.' After that night with Clarky I had wanted to talk to Finn more than anyone else. Clarky and I weren't really talking properly anymore, and don't you always want something familiar when everything else feels so alien?

'Josie, I was too wrapped up in my life, I know that now. What we had at Cambridge, it was a snapshot of happiness, almost too good to be true. I didn't want to tarnish it with disappointment. It wasn't the right time, not with you travelling. But isn't it a sign that we've found each other again now? This is our time.'

'So you're finally ready for me?' I reached across the table for a cigarette.

He looked lost, as if the flow of conversation was going against the current. 'I didn't know you smoked? I would have . . .'

'Finn, there's a lot you don't know about me.' He lit it for me and I inhaled deeply. When we met at Cambridge he had seemed so much older, better travelled in every way. But now, five years on, things were different.

He leaned towards me, trying to touch my hand, but I moved it firmly away from him. However excited I had been about seeing him, I had to do this right. I needed to know he wanted me as much as I wanted him.

'What if I don't want to be hurt again? The easiest thing to do is see you tonight, then we go our separate ways again. No hard feelings.'

I would die a tragic death if he agreed, but I had to risk it.

'I'm not going to do that. I'm not going to let you go again.' The tempo of his voice changed. He had to work harder now. 'Who was that man you were with last night?'

'Alex.'

'I know his name,' he said, his tone as sharp as a blade. 'He's not your type.'

I laughed. 'You don't know what my type is.'

He shook his head crossly. 'You don't go out with someone who says the word *item*. He's too rock-steady for you.'

'But someone like you, someone so elusive that I never see him, is my type?'

'We were teenagers!' he shouts out, and then glances sideways to see if people are listening. They pretend to be absorbed in their food, but I can sense their ears twitching. 'J, I can't turn back time but I can do something now. Please tell me you're not serious about him?'

'It's not that straightforward.'

'When we saw each other last night, you can't tell me there was nothing between us?'

My willpower was weakening.

'If you are serious, I'll fight for you.' His hands clenched into fists. 'It's as simple as that. Tell me you're happy I came back into your life. That's all I need to know.'

Was it me or had the whole room suddenly dissolved into silence until all I could hear was my own breathing?

'I'm happy.'

There was relief in his smile now. 'Shall we stop wasting time and get out of here?' he suggested.

I felt too enclosed by other tables, trapped by other people's conversations. We stubbed out our cigarettes immediately. A few people looked up from their tables, wondering what the sudden urgency was.

'Excuse me,' shouted the waiter. 'Your prawns in blankets, sir! You haven't paid!' Finn slammed a fifty-pound note on to the table. I had to look at it to make sure. 'I'll take this,' he said, picking up the bottle of wine, 'but I'm feeling rich,' he told the waiter. 'I've just met the girl I love again, so keep the change.'

Finn and I climbed the three floors up to my flat. Before I had even opened the door he was kissing me. We were both out of breath, the stairs seeming never-ending and steeper than usual. I was trying to put the key into the lock, but it kept on slipping. 'Finn,' I murmured as he lifted my hair and kissed the back of my neck. I turned to him. He pushed me against the door, my back hitting the letterbox. He was unbuttoning my top. 'Inside,' I said, 'someone will see us.'

He groaned with frustration. 'All right. Open the door.'

'I'm trying! If you'll leave me alone for a minute.'

'I can't leave you alone for a second.'

I could hear him drinking from the bottle of wine. He left it on the dirty cream carpet in the hallway and put both arms around my waist, his mouth pressed against the back of my shoulder. He inhaled deeply, breathing in the smell of my skin.

'Finn.' I hunched my shoulders. His touch was jogging my hand. I was laughing now as I attempted to hold it steady. We were like time bombs primed to go off if we didn't have each other right now.

Only a few steps inside and Finn and I were pulling at each other's clothes like clumsy teenagers again. We weren't trying to impress or seduce; we just wanted each other. He unzipped the back of my black dress, but the zip got caught. With one swift tug it came loose, the material tearing. 'Hope it wasn't expensive,' he said. I tripped on the dress and we both crashed into the table, the light and phone hitting the floor. I reached with one hand to find the switch on the wall, but Finn pulled it away.

'Did you have lots of girls at Cambridge?' I unbuttoned his shirt quickly.

'One . . . or two.'

I pushed him down on to the sofa. 'Did you go out with Dominique?'

'Briefly . . . Said I was too moody.'

'Never! You?' He pulled me down with him on to the white rug. Finn's arms were around my back, unhooking my bra. He kicked his shoes off.

My hand was inside his trousers. 'She . . . never . . . knew . . . where she stood . . . was Alex a good fuck?'

'Was Dominique?'

Our lips were pressed together, our bodies hot. 'Who cares?' he said. 'The only person I want to be with right now is you.'

We made love on the sitting-room floor; we made love in the shower, cleansing our bodies of past loves, until our skin was red and raw and we could feel only each other. We made ourselves some bacon and toast in my tiny orange-painted kitchen at three in the morning, laughing and kissing as both burnt. 'Shit!' Finn plunged the pan into cold water. Nice idea to distract ourselves from each other for a minute but it hadn't worked.

We didn't want to fall asleep. We could hear the sounds of my flat: the tick of the clock, the sudden rush of water in the pipes, the wind rustling through the leaves of a tree outside in anticipation of morning. We lay face-to-face, the light beginning to creep in through my bedroom window like the enemy, reminding us that a new day was about to begin. Finn hadn't changed, his hair still soft and slightly uneven at the back, that small neat scar to the side of his left eye telling its story. In many ways he looked younger than in his grungy student days with the dyed hair and stubble. The only signs of an older Finn were two small frown lines which gave his face more character. If possible, he was even more beautiful. 'What do you do now?' he asked. 'I want to know everything. Are you still painting?'

'Yes, whenever I can.'

'I remember you told me you wanted your own exhibition. You said you'd be the hottest thing in London.'

I laughed. 'How about lukewarm? I'm building up my portfolio. I need to tout myself to all the galleries, that's the hard part.'

'You can do it. I can't see anyone rejecting your work . . . or you. So, what will you be doing in . . .' He leant across me to pick up my old clock in its battered leather case. It was something my grandmother gave me. He turned the face to him. 'Precisely three hours' time?'

'Telling David Hamilton to get off his arse and into the office.'

'Didn't he design the record label for Red? They're one of my favourite groups. He's huge. What do you do for him?'

'Run his life.'

Finn was stroking my hand; he kissed the bruise on my arm, a stamp of his love on me. 'Clarky's not going to be happy.' The change of subject was abrupt, a sting after a caress.

'What do you mean?'

'That I'm back in your life. He doesn't like me.'

'He does.' But I knew that wasn't true.

'Did you ever go out?'

'No.'

'Have you kissed?'

Something was telling me that such a small detail could complicate things in a big way and I didn't want anything to ruin this moment. Clarky had barely acknowledged it so why should I? It was completely unimportant. 'No,' I said.

'I don't know what's worse. Not seeing you for five years but having you mentally stalk me, or Clarky seeing you and not being able to have you. He's in love with you, I'm sure of it. You haven't slept with him?'

'Finn, you've been out of my life for five years, I'm sorry if I haven't remained celibate.'

'So you *have* slept with him?' he insisted.

'No. But, look, what's in the past is in the past. Clarky and I have a lot of history. If you want to see me, you're signed up to him too. Best friends are for life, whether you like it or not.' Finn nodded, thinking about this. I wrapped an arm around his neck. 'So, you need to get on.'

'OK, I'll try. Maybe I'll learn to like the man. I mean, if you like him so much . . .'

I wanted to change the subject. 'How's your father?'

He looked surprised, but touched by the question. 'Divorced. He's living in America now, doing OK, but I hardly see him.'

Finn gently traced the outline of my face; there wasn't a single part of me he left untouched. Every nerve was heightened at the touch of his fingertip. At last, I could feel myself again.

26

'Emma, you won't believe this,' I tap on my computer, adrenalin rushing through my body. 'I went to the supermarket yesterday with George. He wanted a toy which I said he could have providing he behaved, you know the deal . . . But of course he cried and sulked and misbehaved as usual, and when we arrived at the checkout people were staring first at him and then at me. I didn't get into an argument with him, just as the cheery woman in the book advised, and I think this is what people found hard to believe. That I could just ignore a screaming blubbering child and continue to talk calmly instead of a) either smacking him (someone in the queue suggested that); b) giving into him, or c) getting out of the queue double quick with embarrassment. I had people in front of me, behind and to the sides trying to calm George down. I wanted to shout at them to leave him alone, didn't they understand that my boy thrives on attention? They were giving him more fuel to add to the fire. BUT I DIDN'T! Then the girl at the till said that she was sure Mummy would buy him the toy if he stopped crying. I told her to mind her own business (well, not quite as* *rudely but near enough), and that I wasn't going to be blackmailed by my own son. Then, it gets better! The manager came over and virtually begged me to give George the toy. But I stuck to my guns. I told him calmly, while my heart was thumping, that I was dealing with it in my way, and thanked everyone for their kind suggestions but said I was the mum and I knew what was best for my son. It was really horrible, but I knew I had to do it.*

'On the way home I told George that we'd go back to the shop tomorrow, because I needed to buy food for a supper party at the weekend, and if he could get round without crying, then we'd get the toy. I knew I had to do it quickly, strike while the iron was hot! AND DO YOU KNOW WHAT? IT WORKED! Today he was as good as an angel. My head feels light with success. This is better than any business deal; this feels like I have overcome a major stumbling block. For the first time in years I can see light at the end of the tunnel, d'you know what I mean? Wait till I tell Finn. He is going to be so happy. George is so happy too because I'm so pleased with him. This is what happiness is, isn't it?'

27

The salmon is in the oven; I've made a crème brûlée for pudding. George is at Mrs B's. I'm still praising him for being so good. Finn's reaction, however, *infuriated* me. 'I've always said this is what you should do.' He'd looked distracted while he spoke, his mind far away.

'At least give me some credit, Finn, and tell George you're pleased.'

'Sorry. It's great,' he'd said, followed by that annoying perfunctory peck on the forehead. 'Well done, J.' It's never the same being complimented when you feel you've had to squeeze it out of someone.

George had a swimming lesson tonight. Frédéric was teaching him the front-crawl action, kneeling down in the pool and holding George's arms steady as he showed him the movement. However, George's best stroke is backstroke. 'He finds the breathing hard, but on his back, it is much easier,' Frédéric informed me. 'His arms and legs are nice and long, your husband must be tall, *non*?'

The house is quiet. I have time for a bath this evening. I pour myself a small glass of wine. 'It's good for the soul,' I tell my baby girl. 'Now, what's Mummy going to wear this evening?' The midwife tells me I should be communicating as much as possible with my baby now as she can recognise the sound of my voice. 'Talk to her. Sing to her!' she had said theatrically, as if performing a leading role in *The Sound of Music*.

It's strange but I don't feel connected to this baby as I did with George. He used to make it very clear to me that he was around by kicking, hiccupping and punching pretty much all the time. This baby is quiet, to the point where I sometimes panic. The midwife tells me foetal movements are different with each baby and that I shouldn't be unduly worried because some are very active, others much more placid.

I lie in the bath, hair submerged in the water, my glass of wine sitting on the soap dish. My mobile rings so I reach over to pick it up. 'Hi, gorgeous.'

'David, how are you?' I wipe water away from my face.

'Are you in the bath?'

'Yes.' I'm smiling.

'Naked?'

'No, I'm in my dungarees. What do you think?'

'I'm thinking of you naked. Listen, an interesting project came up, I wondered if you were up for it freelance?'

'Yes, tell me.'

'It's for a cosmetics company. They're huge in America, but they want to come to the UK and have asked me to revamp their brand. I need a girl's eye.'

I'm always flattered when David rings me spontaneously like this. 'I'd love to help.'

'Great. What I'll do is send over all the info on email. I won't go into it now, don't want that water to get cold and your beautiful body to turn into a prune.'

I laugh. 'By the way, I'm pregnant.'

'Oh, fuck, *déjà vu.*'

'I should warn you. Only twenty weeks in.'

'It's up to you, Josie. It's a big project so you'll have to tell me if you can fit it in or not. Give me a call.'

Tonight I am going to wear the black wraparound dress which covers my bump and doesn't make me look enormous.

Finn comes home just when I need him to put on my silver necklace with the initial 'J'. David gave it to me when I left his company. It's a fiddly clasp. 'Ow! It's caught in my hair.'

'Sorry,' he mutters. 'There, done.'

I turn to him, knowing something's on his mind. He sits down on the bed. 'I sent this girl home today . . . she had chest pain . . . but I'm not one hundred per cent sure I did the right thing. I mean, she's unlikely to have major coronary heart disease, but I can't get her off my mind. It's impossible always to know and we can't X-ray everyone who comes to the ward . . .' I sit down next to him and put a hand on his shoulder.

'I haven't done anything wrong,' he says firmly.

'I know.'

'It's probably muscular pain.'

'Exactly. I'm sure it'll be fine.' We sit quietly for a moment. 'David called,' I mention. 'He wants me to take on some freelance work. Mum has offered to come and help look after the baby for three weeks or so . . .'

'Three weeks?'

'I really need some help, Finn. I'm not turning her offer down. Anyway, David's work would be good and we need the extra money.'

No response. 'Finn, try not to worry about this girl, I'm sure you did the right thing.'

'Why are you sure? What if she was our daughter? The one you're carrying now?' He always adds nobility to his cause, because he knows that way he can get away with anything.

'You can't ask me that.'

'You'd want me to call, wouldn't you?'

'What do you think about David?'

'I should, shouldn't I?'

287

I hand him the mobile. 'Yes, if it'll set your mind at rest.'

He's walking downstairs. I can hear him on the tele-phone already.

The doorbell rings. It's Clarky. He's wearing jeans with a V-neck black top and a pair of new boots. He's freshly shaven and smells of leather and cologne. I can tell he's washed his fair hair because it's soft, like a child's fluffy toy. I run a hand through it. 'Wow, you've made an effort,' I say.

'Thanks. Something smells delicious. Where's Finn?'

'In the garden, smoking.'

'I thought he'd given up?'

'He smokes when he's stressed.' I roll my eyes.

'You're not getting on?' he whispers with that flicker of hope in his eyes. Or am I imagining it?

'Not great. What's new?'

Finn comes inside. 'Clarky.' They shake hands with wooden cheer. 'Finn,' he says back.

Finn puts an arm around my shoulders and I shove it away, too forcibly because Clarky throws me a strange look. He stinks of cigarettes.

'So,' Finn starts, 'you've got the hots for Aggie?'

'Finn!' But I want to hear what Clarky says.

'She's nice.'

'*Nice?* Boys don't describe girls as *nice*. Is she a looker? Do you fancy her? *Nice* is a bonus. Come on, *Justine.*'

'Back off, Finn,' I warn him. 'Sorry, Clarky.'

He shrugs. 'I don't mind being called Justine if it makes Finn feel like more of a man for saying it.'

'Good answer,' Finn acknowledges awkwardly. 'What can I get you to drink?' The atmosphere always stiffens like beaten egg whites when these two are in the same room. The best thing they could have done was to have had a punch-up when they were both in Cambridge, to get it out of their systems. Now this insecurity and falsehood sits heavy over their relationship.

Clarky asks for a gin and tonic. Finn goes into the kitchen and puts a record on as he gets the drink.

The doorbell rings. 'You'll knock her out!' I tell Clarky as I answer it. And I can't help adding, 'Wish I was Aggie.'

Tiana and Christo arrive together and for a moment it takes me back in time, back to when we were young and single and everything was so innocent and free. Tiana looks happy, her skin glowing.

'It's leaving that job,' she insists, but I'm not convinced. She looks like she is in love. 'My old company is in serious trouble,' she tells us. 'Boss walked out and the place is in complete turmoil, redundancies and everything.'

'No way! So you were right to leave? The photo was some kind of sign?'

'It's just pure coincidence,' Finn argues irritably.

Tiana shakes her head adamantly. 'When are you going

to believe that there are things you can't control or rationalise? There's something bigger and better going on in the universe, something more spiritual.'

'Perhaps. Let's face it, none of us really knows.'

Aggie is fashionably late. She arrives wearing a white fitted shirt and chunky silver necklace over a stunning electric-blue long skirt and black boots. Her auburn hair is half pulled up into a tortoiseshell clip. The effect is messy, but it works. 'Hi,' says Clarky when she walks into the sitting room. Their foreheads bump together as they both try to kiss each other on the cheek. 'Oh, sorry,' they both say at the same time, and then giggle.

'What's this?' Aggie peers at the scan Tiana and Christo are looking at. 'Are you . . . ?' She turns to me.

'Yes.'

She places a ringed hand on my stomach. It's funny the way people think they have an automatic right to touch you. 'Is it kicking yet?' We wait, but nothing happens.

'It's a girl,' Finn adds.

'Well, I think we should make a toast,' Clarky proposes. 'To new friends.' He smiles at Aggie and she smiles back. 'And,' he turns to me, 'to your baby girl, J.'

'She's mine too,' Finn adds, 'as far as I'm aware. It wasn't the Immaculate Conception.' He looks across at Aggie, waiting for her to laugh, but her gaze is fixed firmly on Clarky as they raise their glasses to each other.

*

During the main course Clarky hits his glass with a pudding spoon.

'I didn't realise speeches were on the menu,' Finn says.

'You and J are having a baby, but I've got some news too.'

Tiana leans in closer. 'Come on then, don't keep us in suspense.'

Finn sits back and pretends to look bored.

'I'm going abroad in the autumn,' Clarky announces.

'Abroad?' Aggie blurts out.

'Yes, for work. I've been asked to organise a tour. We'll be travelling to Venice, Rome and Florence. It's what I've wanted to do for years.'

'Italy! Oh, I love Venice, fabulous pasta. Have you been before?'

'Yes.'

'So romantic,' Aggie continues.

'Very.' Clarky briefly looks at me.

'How long will you be going for?' I ask.

'Six months.'

Six months? I want to cry out. *You can't go for that long!* Instead I say, 'Congratulations. That's wonderful, Clarky, amazing.'

'But people can come out and visit me.' He starts to circle the rim of his wine glass slowly. 'I have no ties . . . no children . . . there's nothing to stop me going, is there?'

'Absolutely nothing,' Finn agrees.

*

'Why do people get married these days?' Aggie asks, now a little drunk. The crème brûlée was overcooked. Finn tells me we need hammers, not spoons. 'It's delicious,' Clarky says over him.

'Because you're telling your friends, everyone you love, that you are committed to that person,' Tiana starts.

'You just want to get rid of your surname.' Christo hits her arm affectionately.

'What is it?' Aggie asks.

'Prickman.'

'I used to know a Hellbottom.'

We laugh. Everyone likes Aggie.

'People get hitched because they want to have children,' Clarky says.

'Hitched?' Finn says critically. 'You get married because you love someone, not because you want them to reproduce. Sure, children are a part of it, but it's not the sole reason.'

'But you can love someone without getting married. You can have children without getting married,' Clarky argues back.

'I don't think that's fair on the child,' I say, and Finn looks my way, almost in surprise that I am backing him and not Clarky.

'I wouldn't have a baby with someone who wasn't prepared to marry me,' Tiana asserts. 'A child needs stability.'

'So, if you're not married you're unstable? It's only a piece of paper,' Clarky reasons.

'If you can't commit to marriage then what does it say about your relationship?' Finn asks.

I nod. 'To me it says that if someone better comes along, there's an easy way out.'

'Exactly.' Finn and I smile at one another. It feels great to be on each other's side for once.

'Clarky makes a fair point, though,' Aggie puts in. 'My marriage wasn't stable for me or El, and my divorce was painful and expensive.'

'How long did your marriage last?' I ask.

'Three years, but I'd known him for seven. I knew I'd made the wrong decision the moment I walked up the aisle. It felt like I was walking up this high cliff, and when I reached the sod, all I could see was this terrible drop. Then I saw my parents and it was the thought of the caterers, the party, the expense . . . I couldn't back out. Pathetic, I know.'

'It's not pathetic,' Clarky assures her.

'I was too young,' she admits gratefully. 'You see, he'd asked me a number of times and eventually his sheer perseverance wore me down. But when I started to have problems with El . . . well, he did a runner. A disabled child ruined his image.'

'You clearly married the wrong man,' Finn says.

'Like she doesn't know!' Clarky laughs mockingly.

Finn stares back at him, hard. 'It must have been tough, Aggie, but that doesn't mean marriage isn't valid. I think you have to take a stand in life. You say "I do" in front of your friends . . .'

'And God,' Christo adds. Recently he's been going to church.

Clarky's shaking his head. 'I think it's completely wrong to suggest saying "I do" in church means more than a couple deciding they want to be together but they don't want to do it that way. People who marry are like sheep. Most of them don't even believe in God. All they want is the church, the flowers, the party, the white dress . . . not that they're even virgins. Besides, I read somewhere that most children today are born out of wedlock. You lot are seriously old-fashioned and out of touch.'

'Some traditions are worth hanging on to,' I argue. 'You really don't want to get married?'

'I'm not rushing up the aisle. My parents had a suffocating relationship. You see so many screwed-up marriages these days. I don't want to add to the statistics.'

Finn laughs. 'That's the coward's way out, Justin. "Let's not bother because it never works." What a sad way to look at the world.'

'It's not.'

'I agree with Finn,' Tiana says. 'You have to have a belief system. If you don't, you're a shell.'

'A shell? It's not your mumbo-jumbo talk again, is it?' Clarky jokes.

Tiana tries not to look hurt. 'At least I believe in something and stand firmly by what I value. What do you believe in, Justin? When have you ever truly taken a stand? Or do you run away from all your problems?'

There is a crackle of tension around the table.

'I'd still like to get rid of my surname,' she starts again, attempting to lighten the conversation.

'Again, why lose your surname? Tiana, if you get married cling on to yours, however it sounds. Why lose your identity?' Aggie questions.

'You're not losing your identity!' Finn cries out in despair. 'It's just the way it is! Keeping your own surname is so . . . I don't know . . . so *defensive*, like calling yourself *Ms*.'

'No, it's not, Finn,' Clarky says. He looks as if he's washing a bad taste out of his mouth. 'It's personal choice, that's all,' he continues adamantly. 'It's sensible to use your old name for work too.'

'Sensible? That's romantic,' Finn says with a large dollop of sarcasm.

'You romance Josie, do you, Finn?' Clarky waits for an answer.

'I am romantic.' He looks over at me. I'm feeling distinctly uncomfortable by now. Clarky and Finn will draw their swords before we know it. 'J, aren't I?'

'You can be,' I back him, thinking a few more cups of tea brought to me in bed would go a long way. But he did say that lovely thing to me about love at first sight not so long ago.

'Thanks, darling.'

'Always room for improvement, though.'

'Did you want to keep your surname?' he asks me.

'Doubt she had a choice,' mutters Clarky.

Finn ignores that.

'The switch felt odd to begin with, but I had no longing to keep it.'

'Well, I think you should tread very carefully before you marry because it can have disastrous consequences,' says Aggie. 'Don't marry because you think you have to, or worse still because you're pregnant. I know someone who did that and . . .'

'Can we drop it now?' I begin to clear the plates. 'Coffee, anyone?'

I start to stack the dishwasher when they've all gone. Clarky and Aggie caught a taxi home. Will they kiss in the dark? Will they spend the night together?

'The matchmaking worked,' Finn says. 'They clearly got on.' He scratches the back of his head. 'You're quiet?'

'Did we marry for the right reason?'

'I believe in us,' he says. 'Tiana was so right, you have to have a belief system. Clarky drifts, uses one excuse after another not to commit to anything.'

'I'm not talking about Justin.'

'Christ, if you left me, J, I'd be lost. I'd grow a long beard, drink out of a whisky bottle and live on the streets, shouting "Jesus is LOVE," like that old man you and George see.'

I smile at the idea. 'We were young, though, weren't we?'

'We were old enough to know what we wanted. My parents' marriage was a disaster, just like Clarky's, but . . .'

'You really don't like him, do you?'

'He's all right.'

'The tension was pretty clear tonight.'

'J, he doesn't like *me*.'

There's a long pause before I say, 'If you both dislike each other so much, why did you suggest a dinner party in the first place?'

He laughs with a shake of his head, as if I really should know the answer by now. 'When you told me he liked Aggie, I felt this overwhelming sense of relief because,' he breathes deeply, 'at last it might get him out of our hair, once and for all.' He takes the keys off the hook in the kitchen. 'I'm going to get George.' I watch him walk away from me. The door shuts behind him.

28

'Blimey, he's gorgeous,' Tiana had said to me when she'd first met Finn, followed by a deep nudge to my stomach. 'He was well worth the wait.'

In fact I still spent most of my days waiting until the evening when I could see him. Weekends were a slice of heaven. Forty-eight hours without interruptions. 'When are you coming home?' Mum would ask. 'Your father and I can't remember what you look like. When can we meet this Finn?'

We'd go out to nightclubs with Tiana and Christo, the music and happiness ballooning around us as soon as we entered the dark space. Finn had an old yellow Mini which we called Miss Lemon. The four of us drove around London in it late at night, music on in the background and the lights along the Embankment glittering with life. In the summer we had evening picnics in Hyde Park, each of us bringing a bottle of wine or cans of Pimm's and beer. Tiana and Christo became close, so close that Finn and I wondered if they would get together, but they didn't. They were like two lines that never quite met.

We'd meet on Sunday mornings at our local cafe, clutching mugs of coffee. We talked about books and films and politics and work and friends. The four of us loved to put the world to rights. I'd often ask Clarky if he wanted to join us, but there was always 'something on'. I knew he wasn't exactly thrilled about Finn and me getting back together, but I was too happy to care.

I loved getting to know Christo again. He didn't live in Finn's shadow anymore. He worked for a record company, searching out new talent. He loved his job; you could see it in his face when someone asked what he did. He'd motivate me to circle every exciting job advert I saw. I had even applied for a job in Paris although I didn't expect to get it because they were looking for someone with more experience. On the off chance I did, Finn and I would have to travel to see one another at weekends. This time a long-distance relationship would work.

Christo had also inspired me to carry on painting, saying that having my own exhibition wasn't a ridiculous pipe dream. His encouragement was gentle but genuine. 'All my life I've been told I'm no good. Don't listen to stuff like that, J. Go out there and do it.' Finn had agreed with him and together we'd gone to a few galleries to show them my work, but the truth was I needed a lot more in reserve. If I was really serious, I needed to be painting every spare minute I had. On one occasion I'd been distracted by seeing Finn's back through the window. He was waiting outside for me as I tried to impress the gallery owners.

'You have great talent, but we're not currently taking on new artists. Come back in six months' time and I'll see what's on our books then,' I was told.

'Don't give up,' Finn said afterwards, taking my hand and locking his fingers round mine. I loved him for coming with me. With each day my love for him grew deeper. He was so much a part of my life now, as unchanging as the colour of my eyes.

David called me. 'J, you know that job in Paris? Well, it's yours!'

'What?' I was in my orange kitchen making myself a cup of tea. 'You're kidding?'

'They're going to ring today – pretend I haven't told you. I did some talking to all the right people. It's all yours, darling. Pack your bags.'

I felt this surge of joy, as if I were on a fairground ride, success lifting me high into the sky, followed by the fast downhill plummet; the sinking realisation that I couldn't go.

David was waiting for me to say something. 'Josie? Do you know what this means? There were hundreds of applicants and they want *you*. I have every faith you can do it, so go off and be a beautiful Parisian chick. Oh, and ring me once in a while.'

'I can't.'

'What do you mean, you can't?'

I leant against the counter and shut my eyes.

'You're not staying because of that boyfriend of yours? Tell me you're not? I mean, love is as sweet as honey, but it doesn't last.'

'It's complicated.'

'Only if you let it be. This is Paris, the city of love. You'll have a ball, it'll be fantastic for your career, just think of the . . .'

'David!' I had to stop him. 'I'm pregnant.'

29

I am lying in a white room, on a firm couch, looking at the screen with the nurse. Her dark hair is coiled into a bun and her skirt is as full as a ballgown's.

'Your child is nearly ready to come into this world,' she says.

Finn is now by my side. 'Who's he?' she asks, alarm in her voice.

'He's the father.'

'I'm the father,' he repeats proudly.

She veers back. 'He's not the dad.' She looks scared of Finn.

'Yes, he is.'

'No, he can't be.' There is venom in her voice now. '*This* man is the father.' She turns to the screen and a picture of a man's face flashes in front of us.

'You're lying,' Finn says, but the face continues to flash before us. The image seems to be growing bigger and bigger until I can see his face on every wall. I look up and it's on the ceiling too. Each way I turn he's there.

'Josie? Tell her she's lying.'

I can't. I open my mouth but nothing comes out, just air. The nurse moves closer to us. Now she's dressed in a long black gown and her hair is long and flowing and black too. 'This man isn't the father. Tell him the truth, Josie.' She turns round and points to the screen once more, as if it's a blackboard. '*He's* the father.' She starts to roar with laughter. She is turning into the Wicked Witch of the West.

The face is Clarky's.

I wake up in a sweat, disorientated. I turn, expecting him to be by my side. Instead there's an empty space next to me. Relief sets in. I look at my watch. It's only midnight. I walk into the bathroom and splash my face with cold water. When I look in the mirror I'm shocked. My skin seems to have taken on an unattractive tinge of grey. I pat one cheek. I feel puffy in the face; in fact, puffy all round. No matter how often people say you're pregnant, not fat, it doesn't matter. I was with Tiana today and felt like an elephant next to her. I must be at least twice her size.

I put on my dressing gown and walk slowly downstairs. I find Finn scrunched up on the sofa again, one arm raised above his head just like George sleeps, the television still on, neat gin in a tumbler by his feet. I turn the TV off before trying to wake him. This is becoming a regular ritual. 'Come to bed.'

He half stirs.

'Finn, it's late.' I tap his shoulder, hard this time. 'Wake up!'

He rubs one eye and squints. 'I was watching that.'

'You were fast asleep.'

He yawns and stretches out both arms. I kiss him on the cheek. 'Come to bed with me,' I say more gently. 'I miss you up there.' I kiss him on the lips. Run a hand through his hair.

'Josie,' he says.

'What? Come on, we haven't slept together for ages.' And I don't just mean sex. I like lying next to him in bed. I kiss him again.

'Josie!' He extricates himself from me as if I'm some kind of irritant. 'Stop it.' Next he'll be getting out the female killer spray.

'What's wrong?'

'I'm not in the mood, OK.' He stands up and turns the television on again.

'Fine,' I say sharply. 'I'll take me and my clearly unattractive self upstairs.'

'I didn't mean it like that. If a guy doesn't want to do it, that makes you suddenly unattractive?'

'It would be nice to go to bed together every once in a while, that's all.'

'I'll be up in a minute.'

I know he won't. He'll fall asleep again. 'Don't do me any favours.'

'Josie!'

'Quiet, you'll wake George. Turn the lights off and turn the volume down,' I demand before going back to bed on my own and into the darkness of my dream.

30

'I haven't been with a man since my husband left four years ago, not that he was much of a man,' Aggie reflects as we stand at the school gates. It's a good place to talk, rather like being in a car because there's no escape.

Clarky and Aggie have been dating now for two months.

'You haven't had any other relationship?' I am trying hard not to sound too surprised.

'No. I told myself I had enough on my plate with work, El, moving house. I made myself believe that no one else would want the responsibility of looking after my boy. I built up a pyramid of excuses when the only thing really stopping me was fear.'

'Of being hurt again?'

She nods. 'I know I come across all talkative and full of confidence, but inside, well, I'm scared shitless. How sad, hey?'

'It's not sad. You've been through a lot. Believe me, sometimes I'm scared shitless too.'

'About what?'

I tell Aggie how scared I am of having another child; of how Finn has been working longer hours than usual until at times I feel as if I'm leading a single life. 'And when we are together each conversation is interrupted with, "Don't do that, George," or "Have you brushed your teeth, George?" Christ, I bore even myself to tears!'

Lately I have been thinking about Paris and how my life might have turned out if I'd gone. It's a strange thought, putting myself in another country with a different set of people. Would I still be with Finn? 'When I was a little girl I was convinced I'd be running my own gallery by the time I was twenty-one! Do you ever think about all the things you could have done with your life?'

Aggie laughs hollowly. ' 'Course. I know this sounds morbid, but after I divorced I wrote my own obituary.'

'That *is* morbid.'

'But it makes sense. It's thinking about all the things I want to be recognised for. I always thought I'd own a restaurant by now, Mexican food. I'd have brightly coloured walls with chillies and garlic and peppers painted on them, and the place would always be packed at the weekends with live music, glam people and all that jazz. And what do I do instead? Cook up the odd quiche or lasagne for someone's fridge.'

'Don't be so hard on yourself. You're bringing Eliot up on your own, no mean feat, OK?'

'Thanks. You're happy, though, with Finn? Apart from the long hours and all that?'

I don't tell her that I actually asked myself if I married for the right reason. It had just been a stupid, flash thought and the result of spending too much time on my own. I remember my dream again and seeing Clarky's face.

'We're going through a bit of a rough patch at the moment,' is all I say. 'Make the most of it, OK? It's so nice when you first start going out with someone. You get married and then no snogs. Nothing.'

'Why not? Finn's a fucking Adonis!'

'OK, I'm exaggerating a bit. What's happened to your ex?'

'I only hear from the sod occasionally. His new wife doesn't want him to have anything to do with us and he's too weak to go against her.'

'It sounds like you're better off without him.'

'I don't mind for myself, but what about El? He's grown up without a dad. George doesn't know how lucky he is.'

'I'm sorry, it really . . . stinks.' I can't think of a better word.

'My mother used to tell me I was a bad picker of men, that some people have that quality. But with Clarky, it's different. He's so artistic . . . a good cook. Makes the best curry, you know?'

'I know,' I say, 'he used to make me . . .'

'I can talk to him,' she continues, 'I mean, a man who actually communicates? My ex was like a sodding brick.

Clarky and I love having breakfast in bed at the weekends. He brings me up warm croissants and coffee. And he's wonderful with Eliot. You know, with discipline and trying to talk to him about men's stuff. I know El plays up and can be very naughty . . .'

That's a serious understatement, I think. He should be called Damien.

'I reckon in his own way he's punishing me for getting rid of his dad. He needs a man's influence. Clarky plays cards with him and takes him to the shops and . . . fuck, I'm sorry, Josie, listen to me going on and on when you know him better than me anyway.'

'It's fine,' I assure her. 'It's good to know he's happy too.'

'He talks so much about you. Sometimes I have to tell him to stop or he'll make me jealous. Nothing ever happened between you two, did it?'

'No.' The question breaks the easy flow between us. It isn't the first time she's asked me either.

'You've known him for years. He said you went travelling together?'

'We've always been friends.' I smile but there are tears in her eyes. 'I'm sorry,' she says, trying to find a tissue in her bag. 'For the first time in years I've found a great man and a nice friend who makes standing at the school gates fun, and look at me, I'm a bloody mess.'

'Here.' I hand her one of my tissues.

'Why are *you* crying, Josie?'

'I . . . don't . . . know. I'm pregnant?' That's my answer to any emotional outburst. I am thinking about how hard life has been for Aggie, of George without Finn, of how my life would be without my mother or father, and how much I miss my friend Clarky. The last time we'd spoken I was certain he was in bed with Aggie. I had wanted to talk to him after an argument I'd had with Finn, but Clarky told me I should be talking to my husband about it, not him. He was right, but his assertiveness had made me feel uneasy.

I miss the feeling of a new relationship, the fire, the passion and excitement; my whole body tingling from head to toe with the anticipation of just a kiss. I bite my lip to fight back more tears. Aggie's face crumples in front of me again. 'Look at us!' We start to laugh uncontrollably. 'I think I've fallen in love with him.' She blows her nose loudly. 'He hasn't even had any relationship in the past to haunt me. This one boyfriend I had, way before I married, actually kept a photo of his ex on the bedside table. I kept on hiding it but back she came, like a ghost. I mean, talk about how to make a girlfriend paranoid! Clarky's past is as clean as a whistle. He doesn't seem to have had any girlfriends before me.'

'No,' I reply simply, 'no one serious anyway.'

'We're not very different then. We've both been lonely for too long. But I don't know what it is . . .' She looks straight at me with needle-sharp eyes. 'I keep on thinking, here's this great man, who wants to be with me and take on El. Tell me, surely there has to be a catch?'

31

To my Darling Finn,

The news of your engagement has made me so very happy. I remember liking Josie very much when we went punting. I welcome her into our family with open arms. You are the most important boy in my world and your happiness means everything to me.

I hope Josie will stop working when you get married. She's a big girl, not dainty, but she is very beautiful. She had lovely big blue eyes. Inquisitive. I remember them.

I think she will make a wonderful wife. A good faithful companion to you, Finn. I hope you will be as happy as I was with my dear Bobby. I think about him every day. I think about that beautiful boat of ours, the Blue Banana, and all those lovely cruises and adventures we had. I hope your father pulls himself together and comes to the wedding. I shall have words with him. And I suppose you have to invite Gwen the Gold-Digger.

I know you must be very busy with the marital plans as it's not long now until the big day, and I know how popular you are too, but my garden chair collapsed and I wanted you to come and fix it. When you bring Josie down to lunch, can you bring your toolbox?

Lots of love,

Granny

PS What's with the sudden rush to get married so soon? You haven't got her in trouble, have you? Sit on your digits if you get the urge.

PPS I hope she's bought a dress and that she's going to cover her shoulders in church.

32

I walk downstairs with a large basket of dirty laundry. Finn left today. He's gone to the British Cardiac Society Conference. With Alessia.

'Do you have to go?' I had asked, knowing that of course he did and I was simply trying my luck. I remembered he'd once told me that these conferences were an excuse for doctors to play away. 'Although of course I don't,' he'd added with that familiar smile. Drug companies sponsor the event and the doctors get wined and dined like celebrities for five days.

'You'll miss one of my antenatal classes,' I'd complained. 'You missed the last one too and I felt such a dill not having you there. Honestly, there was everyone else lined up with their birthing partners, huffing and puffing to get on to the crest of the wave. And there was me, a big fat moron on her own.'

'*My* lovely fat moron,' he'd corrected me. 'I love going to this conference, J. I get to learn about all the new procedures and research. There are going to be talks on defibrillators this year.'

'Oh, well, in that case . . .' I'd rolled my eyes. 'Is Alessia going?'

'Think so,' he'd replied.

I put the laundry basket down at the foot of the stairs, exhausted by the exertion already. I look at myself in the mirror and turn away, depressed. It's high time I met Alessia. In my mind she is impossibly beautiful, one of those girls whose entrance into a room demands attention. She's graceful, the kind of girl who'd never lose her keys or trip over the pavement. Yet she can be one of the boys, too, when appropriate. She'd love football and wouldn't ask stupid questions about the sidelines or free kicks, and of course she's clever and funny, the last two qualities not being *essential* but great plus points, like the bonus ball after winning the Lottery.

And now she is on an aeroplane with Finn. My husband. This slim and glamorous vixen who no doubt always wears matching lacy underwear. They are probably ordering their gin and tonics and tucking into their roasted peanuts this very minute while I'm about to tackle his dirty washing.

My blood pressure rises. And I am allowing this. WHY? What can I do? I'm sure she's not that pretty, I think, trying to calm myself down. Finn would never cheat on me while he's away. He'd never cheat on me, full stop. I trust him implicitly. But then I think of the other night, when he made it quite clear he didn't want to hold me or even kiss me. He could barely *look* at me. I stare at my reflection again. I don't want to be pregnant anymore. I hate the extra weight; I hate the swollen currant-bun ankles; I hate the sweat. I'm even developing the beginnings of varicose veins. Is this what Finn sees? No wonder he couldn't wait to hotfoot it to this conference with Alessia. I have another image of sunglasses perched neatly on the top of her head, keeping her long mane of glossy dark hair away from her eyes.

Forget about it. It's purely professional. Get on with your day. Put that washing in the machine.

'Me and machines, we're not a great partnership,' Mrs B says. My washing machine has broken down.

She presses the 'on' button again. 'My husband used to tell me I only had to touch something electrical and it broke down.'

'The machine has got to work.' I crouch down and my knees crack like splintered wood. 'I feel like an old pregnant lady, Mrs B. My pelvis is so sore and I get terrible groin cramps too. *So* glamorous. I haven't been doing my painting, which always makes me feel crotchety, and I'm shouting at Finn like it's all his fault!'

I wipe my forehead and press the 'on' button again but nothing happens. Dead. No flash of life.

I have to wash George's school clothes and games kit. Thankfully I am working from home today, but I have a meeting with Neil tomorrow and this is the only suit that fits me now and it needs to be clean. I press the button and wait. 'That's weird,' I say. 'I don't understand. Everything's switched on at the wall. A fuse hasn't blown?'

'No, all the lights are on.'

I press the power button again, holding my breath. Nothing happens. I have to stop myself from asking Mrs B what she has done to make the thing die. It has never broken down before. 'I haven't got time for this,' I shriek, my voice piercing the walls. 'I've got so much to do!'

Mrs B attempts to calm me down. 'Don't worry, we'll work it out.'

The phone rings and I pick it up quickly. It's Finn, telling me he's just arrived. 'I can't talk now.' I can hear lots of voices in the background.

'What's wrong? Is George OK?'

'He's fine.'

'So what's up?'

'The washing machine isn't working.'

'Oh, God, is that all?'

I slam the phone down. Mrs B fetches me a glass of water. Five seconds later the phone rings again. I snatch it from the receiver. I can feel those X-ray eyes watching me. 'Come on, Josie, you didn't have to hang up. It's not exactly a life-or-death situation, is it? Get someone round to fix it. What else is wrong? You're nowhere near eggs, are you?'

His joke doesn't work this time. 'Fuck off, Finn.'

Mrs B is pretending to be absorbed in studying the buttons on the machine. She's humming loudly. The phone rings again.

'Josie?' It's Clarky. 'Is everything OK?'

'No. The washing machine's broken down.'

'D'you want me to come round?'

'Yes. Can you? Right now?'

'See you in twenty.'

Mrs B looks at me disapprovingly and quickly turns away again.

I put the phone down and it rings immediately. 'Darling, it's Mum. How are you?' My head is throbbing now. 'Have I called at a bad time?'

'Right,' Clarky says firmly. 'Do you have a helpline for this machine?'

I open a drawer and sift through various guarantee forms and pieces of paper that I had forgotten were there. 'Here we go,' I say eventually, clutching a pale yellow piece of paper.

'I'll give them a call.' I feel much better after my cup of tea and thick slice of pecan pie that Clarky brought round as a treat. 'Sometimes Finn makes me feel about this big,' I grumble, showing Clarky a tiny space between my thumb and finger. 'Like the little woman at home stewing in domestic strife.'

'He's always been like that though, hasn't he, J?' He smiles, but there's something distant in his eyes, as if he's tired of talking about Finn, someone he doesn't even like that much.

'I wish he'd take lessons from you on how to be less patronising and arrogant.'

'Thanks,' he says uncomfortably.

I punch in the numbers on the telephone. Then I have to listen to a stream of options before finally getting to number ten which is the customer helpline for machines in trouble. After five minutes and a lot of Handel's *Water Music* in between I am finally connected to a voice. 'What do you mean, you can't come out today?' I stand up and start pacing the floor, a habit I have copied from Finn. 'But it says here on the form I have in front of me,' I scan the page again, 'that you deliver immediate service. I can't wait until tomorrow.'

'What seems to be the problem with the machine?' a bored voice asks. It seems to be enjoying my predicament.

'Probably something very minor. It was working perfectly yesterday.'

'Today is today.'

'I know today is today!' *You imbecile*, I want to add. 'There must be someone who can come over?' Clarky is shaking his head vehemently.

'Bear with me . . .' I can hear tapping on a keyboard.

'I'm bearing,' I say back.

In a sing-song the voice continues, 'As I was saying, our first available appointment is for tomorrow. We can get a technician to you late-afternoon, estimated time of arrival approximately seventeen thirty-one.' Each word is enunciated slowly and clearly as if I were some kind of idiot.

'Tomorrow?' I whisper despairingly. 'Well, if that really is the soonest, I suppose . . .' Suddenly the receiver is whisked from my hand.

'I'm afraid I'm not satisfied with this level of service,' Clarky says firmly.

'Sorry? Who am I speaking to?'

'Her husband. I'm a journalist,' he adds. 'I've been listening in on your conversation and, I have to say, I'm seriously annoyed about this.'

I smile.

'It's unacceptable, I'm afraid. What are you going to do about it?'

Clarky is nodding as the voice tries to get a word in.

'My wife has just had twins and I will *not* let her be messed around like this.' He pauses to listen for a moment. I notice how much I like hearing him call me his wife.

'No, that won't do. Do you know what it's like having twins? No, I'm sure you don't. Are you a reputable company? No, I asked you if you were a reputable company?' He waits for an answer. 'Well, I can see I'm going to have to write an article for the *Daily Mail*, and then the whole nation will know that you weren't able to provide the swift service that my wife, who's just had twins, needs.'

I put a hand over my mouth, trying not to laugh.

'What's your name?' demands Clarky.

There's a pause. 'OK, Steve,' he repeats. 'Today, at five o'clock, Dean will be coming to the house. No, that will be fine, we can just about hang on till then. Number eight Rudolf Road, Shepherds Bush. Thank you, Steve.'

When he puts down the phone we both burst into laughter. I fling my arms around him and my big tummy hits his. 'Clarky, you are a genius! You should be on the stage.'

'Just one of my many hidden talents.'

'Thank you. You are my hero.' I stand back from him as if surveying a new person in front of me. 'How did you do it?'

'Actually,' he runs a hand through his hair, 'it's Aggie. A trick she's taught me.'

A thorn of jealousy pricks me. 'Clarky?' I ask tentatively.

'Yes?' he replies in the same tone.

'What are you doing for the rest of the day?'

'Well, I'm supposed to be looking for work.'

'I'm supposed to *be* working, but . . .' I laugh, playing with my wedding ring. 'I wondered if we could spend the day together? I know this sounds funny, but I've missed you.'

'Missed me? But I haven't gone anywhere.' He does a turn on the kitchen floor. He taps his shoe against the ground. 'I think I'm real.'

I push his arm playfully. 'Seriously, Clarky, I haven't seen much of you lately, understandably, so how about we go out today, do something fun? Like old times? What do you say?'

The phone rings and we both listen to it as if it's some strange noise from outer space. Eventually I remember it's my phone in my house. So I pick up.

'It's Aggie,' she says. 'Clarky's not with you, is he? I've been ringing his home and mobile but he's not answering.'

'Yes, he's here. Thank God!' I add with a laugh. 'Helping me mend my washing machine.'

'Don't you have instructions or can't you get someone out?'

'Well, he's a genius, he used one of your tricks to do just that. Someone's coming over to fix it later.'

I'm not sure she's listening. 'Can I talk to him?' she snaps.

Clarky and I go on a London tour bus. We sit on the top deck and watch the frantic world go by. We only half listen to the commentary on Madame Tussaud's, the Houses of Parliament, Westminster Cathedral, Harrods, the London Eye. 'Do you realise we have known each other virtually all our lives?' I tell him, linking an arm through his.

'And we're still talking. It's a miracle.' He smiles. 'How's George? How did the piano lessons go?'

'He was keener on making Jack the cat play than himself. His swimming is great, though, all thanks to Aggie for introducing us to the teacher.'

'Look over there, J.' He nudges me. 'At that old couple.' There's a frail woman in black trousers and a pale pink top pushing a man in a wheelchair. He has a thin rug over his knees. She places a flower behind his ear, he laughs as if the petals tickle, she kisses him gently on the cheek and then they continue walking down the busy London pavement.

There's something indescribably touching about what she has just done. Clarky and I watch silently until he finally says, 'I'm sorry I haven't been in touch for a while.'

'It's fine. I know what it's like when you first start going out with someone.'

'Aggie's great. I just wish she wasn't so insecure. Her last husband, "the sod", has a lot to answer for. When El was born he started drinking, lost his job, had an affair . . .'

I start to chew my thumbnail. 'Poor Aggie. She didn't tell me about that. What did he do?'

'He ran his own carpet-cleaning business. Aggie told me his chief claim to fame was that he'd cleaned Rod Stewart's carpet. "How was I supposed to get excited about that?" she said.'

I smile.

'Anyway, he used to just sit in the pub, all day long, drinking himself into a stupor, believing the whole world was against him because what on earth had he done wrong to deserve a child like El? When she found out he'd been unfaithful she filed for divorce. She told me she'd never been in love with him in the first place, so how could she be expected to love him when he was a drunk who gave her and El no support?'

'He makes Finn look like an angel.'

'Me too. It's easy to impress after him.'

'You *are* an angel, though.'

'Josie.' He blushes.

'But you're getting on great, aren't you?'

'Yes.' He shifts in his seat. 'She's a bit jealous about you and me, though. Didn't like the idea of us spending this afternoon together. She was really prickly on the phone and I can't be bothered with that.'

'What did she say?'

'Nothing. She didn't have to. She was abrupt, that's all.'

'Oh, God. She should get together with Finn. They'd bond over that one.'

'I nearly lied to her today, but then I thought, no, that's wrong. I should be able to see you and not feel guilty.'

I press my lips together, heat creeping into my face. 'I'd probably be jealous too. I'm even jealous of Alessia, the phantom medic. She's on this conference with Finn. But jealousy's a waste of time. We have to trust, don't we?'

'Exactly. I'm not going to start lying when we've nothing to hide, right?'

We look at one another. I see us as children again, on the school bus. I see him sticking up for me with that quiet self-assurance when I had to wear my head brace.

'When Aggie's not being insecure she's funny, genuine,

so unlike the girls I've dated in the past. It's about time I found someone . . . El's cute too. His language is appalling, though.'

'My God, he's a little terror! George called me a bitch the other day, and his father an arsehole. Guess who taught him those words? Finn was furious. It's not funny.'

'I know. I've got this system going. Each time she blasphemes in front of him Aggie has to put a pound in the jam jar. And each time El swears he has to forfeit watching *The Simpsons*.'

'And what about you?'

'I never fucking swear.'

I laugh.

'If I had called my mother a bitch or Dad a bastard, can you imagine the punishment?'

'He would have locked you in your room for a year!'

'Yeah, and thrown away the key.'

There's another short silence. 'You're one of the most important people in my life, Clarky,' I find myself saying.

'Aren't I *the* most important?' He smiles and then says, 'What's brought this on?'

'I don't think I say it enough, so I'm saying it today.'

'Well, I feel the same, J.'

'D'you remember that holiday we had in Spain?' I start. 'In the bank?'

'What made you think of that?' he asks, his voice warm with the memory.

'I don't know. I just had this image of you trying to cash your traveller's cheques when . . .'

'You'd told me the Spanish for buying a dozen eggs!'

We both laugh. 'I've always wanted to be a tourist and sit on an open-air bus,' I tell him. 'What have you always wanted to do?'

He thinks. 'Play my violin in front of the Queen.'

'You will one day. In fact, I'm sure of it. She'll invite you to tea.'

'With cucumber sandwiches?'

'Of course.'

'Actually, I always think there's something missing from a cucumber sandwich.'

'Like a piece of salami?'

'Exactly. What else would you like to do?'

I bite my lip as I think. 'Learn to sail.'

'You could go to Australia, the Whitsunday Islands. I'd like to drink champagne every day for lunch.'

'Throw out all my clothes and start again with an unlimited budget.'

'Date Michelle Pfeiffer.'

'Marry Colin Firth.' I laugh. 'Dance like Madonna.'

'Play like Yehudi Menuhin.'

'Draw like Leonardo da Vinci.'

'Talk like they do on *EastEnders*. Tell people I think they're "silly cows".'

'Who would you call a silly cow?'

'I don't know . . . people who don't give their seats to the elderly on the tube. Or nuisance callers telling me to switch phone companies, or mean traffic wardens.'

'I'd like to call Ms Miles a silly cow or some of the competitive mothers, like Mrs Heaven whose children are all so super-talented. Hang on, though, you put the washing-machine man in his place, that was good.'

'That was role-play. It wasn't face-to-face. It's difficult, isn't it, always speaking your mind?'

'It can be. What do you want to say?'

'Lots of things.'

'Like?' I encourage him.

He's about to say something when the bus abruptly jolts to a halt. The noise around us comes into focus. Passengers start to disembark. Clarky laughs as if he could have predicted this. He takes my hand as we climb down the steep steps. 'That's the story of my life,' he says. 'Something always stops me.'

Clarky and I wait at the school gates for George. He's arranged to meet Aggie here too. She told him she might be late because she had to deliver a dozen frozen lasagnes across London.

The school bell rings and lots of children start to file out. A girl with two blonde pigtails pushes Eliot across the playground. Aggie arrives just as he is delivered to the front gates. She kisses Clarky full on the lips. 'Hello, you.'

He kisses her back.

'Hi, Josie.'

'Hi. Thanks for letting me steal Clarky for the afternoon.'

'That's OK. But he's all mine now.' She kisses him again.

I turn away, unsure of where to look. Come on, George.

Everyone has gone except for Clarky, Aggie, Eliot and me. 'There he is,' Clarky finally says. 'Why have they gone over there?'

'Where?'

Clarky points to the outside loos, a small brick building to the left of the playing field.

'Who's he with? What are they doing?' I ask, panic rising to the surface.

Clarky tells Aggie to take Eliot to the van. Reluctantly she leaves us.

I wish I could move quicker. Clarky runs across the playground and I follow as quickly as I can. Two boys have George pinned up against the brick wall. 'Let him go!' I screech at Jason. 'Stop it!' But it's too late. Jason has punched him in the mouth. He starts to laugh. George's lip is bleeding. 'Spastic,' he tells him, giving him another punch, this time in the stomach. George doubles over.

'Hello, Daddog,' he murmurs painfully.

'How dare you hit my son! Fight back, George! Don't let him get away with it. Hit him!'

'He can't fight.' Jason spits on to George's shoe. 'He's a spasmo.'

George throws himself at Jason then, arms around his hips, pulling him to the ground. 'I'm not a spasmo!' He's thumping Jason's chest now and is surprisingly strong. Jason is laughing but I can see that George's thumps hurt.

I can't watch any longer. Clarky prises them apart. He pushes Jason against the wall. 'You should be ashamed of yourself.' Then he turns to the others. 'You too, for letting someone like *him* tell you what to do. Haven't you minds of your own?'

Jason claps his hands in derision. This boy is seven, how did he become so nasty so young? 'Who are you? You're not George's dad, are you?'

'Go home,' Clarky says. 'All of you. No one's interested in what you think. And don't ever lay a hand on George again.'

'Why aren't you doing anything?' I scream at the headmaster. 'I have told Ms Miles, I have told all the teachers, that Jason bullies my son, but what do you do? Nothing!'

Calmly, Clarky tells Mr Phipps what happened.

'I can't believe this is going on in my school,' is all he says.

'Well, believe it! Look at him.' I present George and his bleeding lip like an exhibit. 'Why wasn't there someone on gate duty tonight? If we hadn't been there, who would have stopped Jason? There needs to be a teacher supervising at all times.'

'Jason should be expelled for that kind of behaviour,' Clarky adds.

'If you're not going to step in and take action then George has my full permission, and his father's, to fight back.'

'Mrs Greenwood, Mr Greenwood . . .' The head looks at Clarky. 'I can't allow that. I'm a father, too, and between you and me, Jason deserved to be hit back. He is an aggressive boy. I understand why George did it, but I can't condone tit for tat. I have to show the children at my school that fighting is not acceptable.'

'Well, show them then!'

'I will ring Jason's mother, but it's difficult. His father died only last week.'

There's a painful silence, our own predicament put firmly into perspective.

'Jason's father's dead, Mr Phipps?' asks George, and he starts to cry.

Mr Phipps nods. 'It's all right, George. I'm not excusing his behaviour, but he is a troubled boy, taking his anger out on the easiest target.'

'That's not fair on George,' is all I can finally say.

'I agree. And I will do something about it, I promise.'

George is asleep, Baby and Mr Muki beside him, and Rocky curled up at the end of the bed. I brought him home and bathed his face and lips with warm salted water while Dean fixed the washing machine. His stomach was bruised so I rubbed some arnica into it.

'Ow, it hurts, Mum,' he said. 'Ow.'

'Try and be brave. There's a good boy.'

'I'm not a spasmo, am I?'

'*This is the hardest thing I find about ADHD,*' Emma once wrote to me. She had told me Nat had been called 'scum' and 'lowlife'. '*If no one else existed in this world my gorgeous boy would be the happiest he could be.*'

'Why won't Jason let me be in his football team then? I want to play.'

This is what I find so odd. Even after today, George still can't see how badly Jason has treated him. He will go back to him; he *still* wants to play on his team because at least Jason gives him some sort of attention, even if it is negative.

'Dad doesn't think I'm any good at football either. He never plays with me.'

'You're good at other things, like building your Lego, and you're a very good swimmer, and do you remember that model you made of the *Titanic*?' George spent three hours constructing it. I didn't understand his explanation of why it wouldn't sink, but I believed him when he described it so earnestly. 'No two people are the same, that's what you've always got to remember.'

'But I want to play football. I want Dad to play with me.'

I try Finn again. His mobile was switched off earlier.

'What's wrong?' he says when he hears the tone of my voice.

'Can you talk?'

A chair is scraped back and he says, 'Excuse me.' I can hear his footsteps against a marble floor.

'Are you eating?'

'Just dinner with one of the lecturers and Alessia.'

'It's George. He was hit at school today.'

'How badly?'

'His lip was cut, he's bruised.'

'Who did it to him?'

'Jason, the one we've been having trouble with for ages.'

I think Finn is almost in tears.

'Don't worry. Thankfully Clarky was there to break it up.'

'Clarky?'

'Yes.'

'How come?'

'He was just there. We spent the afternoon together.'

'Weren't you working?'

'Finn! Does it matter?'

'No.'

'Can you have a quick word with George? I'll take the phone up to him.'

'I'm sorry I wasn't there,' Finn says, so quietly that I can hardly hear him. 'I should have been there. Poor George. Oh, God, I should be with you.'

'How's the conference going?'

'Good,' he replies half-heartedly. 'Interesting.'

I hand the phone to George. 'I'm all right, Dad. I hurt my lip and he hit me in the stomach.' He listens to his dad. 'Are you going to die? Jason's father's dead. I think that's why he hit me. I hit him back, though. Am I bad, Dad? I don't want you to die. Batman's parents died, didn't they? You won't, will you?'

George listens again. Finally he's laughing. Finn always has this magical effect on him, as if sprinkling gold dust over his hurt. 'I love you too, Mrs Jammie Dodger. I'll be all right.' He hands me back the phone.

'Finn?'

'I'm so sorry.'

'It's OK. Look, you go back to your dinner. Call tomorrow.' I hang up.

'Dad said you had to switch my brain off tonight, Mum.'

I press the imaginary button.

George shuts his eyes and only minutes later he is asleep. I stroke his hair. The time when I love him most is when his face is calm. His arms are raised over his head and he seems at peace. I look at him and can't imagine my life any differently. I would defend him to my death.

33

The children start to file out, but there's no sign of George. Since the bullying incident he is even more determined not to go to school. All my physical energy is spent getting him there when secretly a part of me wants to keep him at home, protected. I envy Finn for being away and I envy him for not having to be the parent who drags their son to school, hearing, 'I HATE YOU,' over and over again.

Aggie parks her white van across the road. 'You did go out with Clarky, didn't you?' is the first thing she says to me and the question feels out of place, like a thistle in a bed of roses.

'Hi, Aggie! Nice to see you.'

'Sorry.' She laughs quickly, clearing her throat. 'I just wanted to know because . . .'

I stop her in her tracks. 'I didn't, OK.'

'So there was never a drunken snog, never a *fling*?'

'What is this? I haven't had a great time recently with George and I could do without the interrogation! Sorry,

Aggie,' I say afterwards. Why do we always feel the need to apologise after raising our voice? Clarky's right. They don't do that in *EastEnders*.

'I'm sorry about George, I really am, it's awful, but I need to know. I can't help thinking Clarky's hiding something.'

'He's not.'

'I've had one bad marriage, I don't need another.'

Why did I ever lie about our one night? One small lie multiplies and what was so unimportant suddenly becomes a major issue. I'm tempted to just tell her, get it over with. Who cares anymore? 'Uh-oh, here's Ms Miles.'

'Josie, you're changing the subject.' Aggie is still looking at me, as if under a magnifying glass, scrutinising my every expression and piece of body language.

'There's nothing between us and never has been. I understand your concern, but please stop going on about it, Aggie. There are bigger things in this world to worry about.'

For once I am pleased that Ms Miles is standing in front of us. The last time she came to the gates she told us that George had spun Eliot around in his wheelchair so fast that he had fallen head first into the badminton nets.

She clears her throat before announcing, 'George asked one of the other boys to close the window today because it was cold enough to . . . "freeze his balls off". I think was the vulgar expression he used.'

Eliot bursts out laughing.

'El made me do it, Mum,' George pipes up.

Ms Miles flinches. 'Of course he didn't.'

'Why not? Because he's in a wheelchair?' I blurt out, sick of him not being accused of anything, ever. From the corner of my eye I see Eliot sticking his finger up in my direction.

Aggie turns on me, affronted. 'Well, it's true,' I say. 'George's disability is invisible; Eliot's chair does him a lot of favours. He's just stuck his finger up at me now, for instance.'

'No, he didn't,' she answers back.

'Excuse me, but he did, and it's not the first time.'

'I didn't do anything, Mum.'

My mouth is wide open. Little horror!

'I'm sure you didn't, El,' Aggie says, staring at me frostily. 'Come on.' She leaves after a quick goodbye which I ignore.

I am *furious*.

Before Ms Miles can issue a punishment I tell her, 'Eliot's language is filthy and he does tell George to say things. So, in future, unless you have something positive to say about my son, I don't want to hear it, OK? Is that understood?'

On the walk home I ask George what he ate for lunch today.

'Sausages. I was so good going round the shop that day, wasn't I?' he asks again. George has talked constantly about how good he was at the supermarket.

'Yes, you were such a good boy.' Ruffle of the hair.

'Thank you. They like Eliot at lunchtime because if they push him in his chair they go to the top of the queue,' George explains to me, 'and they get chips and ketchup. They like Eliot in school, but they don't like him in the street. There they ignore him or poke him and call him "carrot head". El's my best friend. I like him wherever he is.'

A large part of me is proud to have a son who's different. As well as petrified. 'George, don't run on. Wait!' I pull him back but he's seen something and wriggles free.

It's in the middle of the road and looks like a squashed hedgehog. 'STOP, GEORGE!' I scream now. There's a car coming towards him and it isn't slowing down. I run out as fast as I can and grab him by his jumper. 'Let me go, Mum.' A car beeps its horn furiously at us as it does an emergency stop.

I raise my hand in apology. 'Poor hedgehog,' George says. 'Can we take him home, Mum? Bury him in the garden?'

The driver winds down the window. There is a build-up of traffic behind him now. 'For God's sake, can't you control your son?' I don't hear what he says next.

'George, come on.' I drag him away from the hedgehog and on to the pavement.

The driver sets off again. I can see him shaking his head.

I kneel down. Whatever I say today, whatever instruction I give, it won't make any difference tomorrow. Other children progress, they learn a routine and become more independent by the day. But for George there is no such pattern. He is about to see Dr Nichols to have his height and weight recorded, blood pressure taken, may have a blood test to check his glucose levels, and then we'll see Sandy the pharmacist who dispenses his Ritalin. But why are we even bothering to do all of this? Nothing makes him better. Oh, Finn! I need you. I can't do this anymore. I can't do it, can't do it, can't do it.

I grab George and force him to stand still. 'You NEVER run out on to a road. You could get killed. When will you understand what I'm saying to you? Do . . . you . . . understand?' I shake his shoulders, emphasising each word.

'But I'm not sure if he's dead or not, Mum. Someone will run over him again if we leave him on the road and then he'll really be dead,' George says anxiously.

I take a deep breath. 'I know it's sad that the hedgehog has suffered, but I'd rather have a "without doubt" dead hedgehog than a possibly dead George. Do you understand?'

'Yes.' But he's looking at a woman walking past us wearing a bright purple skirt.

I don't know how to get through to him. 'Take my hand and don't let go,' I tell him as we walk on. He turns round once more to look at the squashed hedgehog. 'Animals go to heaven, don't they?' he asks.

34

George and I are sitting in Dr Nichols's office. Finn is still away at his conference and I've barely spoken to Aggie since our spat at school. However, I'm taking George to the pool after this appointment so I'll talk to her there and clear the air.

He is quiet during the consultation. Normally he runs around the room, grabbing the stethoscope, listening to the doctor's heartbeat, pumping up the blood pressure cushion, pulling down the ruler that measures his height. Today he sits with his head bowed.

'How are you getting on at school, George?' the doctor asks.

'Don't know.' He swings his legs under the table. 'Don't know,' he repeats like a broken record.

I tell Dr Nichols about the bullying. 'The headmaster is nice, though. You like him, George, don't you?'

'Mr Phipps sees me as a true person. A proper human being. He's been helping me with my handwriting, trying to get me not to push so hard on my pencil. I can do it when he watches, but when he doesn't I start doing it hard again, I don't know why.' George is shaking his head frantically, still not looking up. 'I'm stupid. STUPID.'

Dr Nichols tells him this can't be the case because his school reports have improved. 'Mr Phipps gives George a table that faces the wall,' I explain, 'with just his own things on it, to avoid any distraction, and he also insists that teachers tap George on the shoulder if they want something rather than shouting at him.' Another technique Mr Phipps told me about was stating the obvious to George and how this should be applied at home too. We, i.e. the teacher, or Finn, or me, might think he understands what we want him to do, but because so many other distractions buzz around him like flies, he needs to hear it time and time again in order to bring him back to reality where he really *hears* the instruction.

Dr Nichols is visibly impressed. It's the first time we've talked about any kind of improvement in the classroom and George's grades. 'How about hobbies outside school, George?'

'I'm rubbish at everything.'

'That's not true . . .' But Dr Nichols stops me.

'Mum made me do piano,' George continues.

'What would *you* like to do?'

While George is being weighed and having his height measured, the doctor addresses me. 'If a child chooses their own hobby, they are taking responsibility. They can't blame the parent by saying, "It's your fault, you made me do it." '

'But George loves his swimming,' I tell him, 'I don't know why he didn't tell you about that. I'm taking him to his lesson now.'

'He could be nervous,' Dr Nichols suggests. 'If it's something he's good at, he might be scared he's going to muck it up, like everything else.'

'I didn't think you were coming,' Aggie says from the gallery above the swimming pool. It's hot and the smell of chlorine is overpowering.

'I had to take George to see Dr Nichols,' I tell her. 'He's been difficult lately, what with the bullying, and he hates school even more than usual.'

We look at each other awkwardly. Do I say something first? 'Well, he's a different boy in the water,' Aggie says. 'Look how much fun they have together.'

I run a hand through my hair. 'What am I going to do when I have the baby? I can't get him here then.'

'I'll bring him,' she offers.

'That sounded like a terrible hint.'

'I would have offered anyway.'

'Well, I'd love to take you up on it, thank you.'

'Good.' Aggie bites her lip. 'You've done a lot for me, Josie, so let me do something for you.'

'Thank you,' I say once more. 'That's really kind.'

We turn to watch them again, tension still hanging heavy in the air. One of us has to say something because we're both being too polite. I crave to hear Aggie swear. Frédéric is gliding El through the water, George following in his purple goggles. 'I feel I need to clear the air,' Aggie says, staring ahead.

'Me too.' I sigh with relief.

She smiles now. 'I do this, you know, have a self-destruct button I press when something too good's happening. I know there's nothing going on between you and Clarky, he assured me of that, and you're happily married, for Christ's sake. I still find it hard to believe you've never dated, but even if you have, what business is it of mine? It's in the past and it doesn't matter now. I trust you both. I'm sorry, Josie.'

'It's fine. I'm sorry too. I don't blame you, OK. You've been through enough, what with your ex-husband having an affair and . . .'

'He told you?'

Oh, God. It was going so well . . . 'Clarky mentioned it briefly. He didn't go into it at all.'

'Don't look so worried, Josie. I would have told you anyway.'

I breathe another sigh of relief. I'm not sure what's allowed anymore. I can tell there is another reason why she sounds happier. 'He wants me to go travelling with him. Wants El and me to join him over the Christmas and New Year break.'

'That's wonderful,' I say, trying not to breathe in the smell of chlorine.

'Isn't it!'

I look into her eyes. Her smile is full of hope and the anticipation of a new adventure. It was the smile I wore when I first met Finn.

'Just so you know,' says Granny's sharp voice, 'my grandchildren mean the world to me, especially the one you've picked.' I can hear the kettle whistling in the kitchen. It's about to boil. Or explode. 'If you have any intention of hurting Finn then you'd better stop what you're doing right now, do you hear me?' She looks firmly at my engagement ring, almost willing it off my finger. The tea trolley rattles into the sitting room, Finn pushing it across the white fluffy rug that looks like snow. Granny sits back in her chair with a sweet smile. 'Josie and I were having such a cosy chat, weren't we?'

I stare at her.

'Cat got your tongue? Do you have a credit card of your own? Do you? DO YOU?'

'That's none of your business, Granny.'

'IF YOU HURT MY BOY I WON'T EVER FORGIVE YOU.' She's laughing wildly, the tea trolley rattling an accompaniment.

I wake up in a sweat and look around frantically. Is she in the room? Am I going mad? I gulp hard and wipe my forehead. My breathing is unsteady. I wedge the pillow back under my bump. I can't stop thinking about Finn's granny. It's as if she knows my doubts. My thoughts. I don't dare shut my eyes. Relief pours through me when I realise I'm on my own, it was a dream, that's all. Finn still sleeps downstairs, as he says I disturb him with my fitful dreams and sleep talking. I wonder how his conference is going? He didn't call me today and his mobile was switched off when I tried. I close my eyes but hear her voice again. Leave me alone, Granny, I tell her.

I go downstairs and make myself a hot chocolate. I sit down on the deep red sofa and turn on the light on the table next to me.

I look at my watch. I pick up the phone and call Tiana.

'Have you heard Clarky's taking Aggie travelling?' I stir my hot chocolate.

'I know! Normally he can't even commit to a second date. This has got to be serious. I think they're good together.'

'Mmm.' I breathe heavily.

'You all right?' she asks.

'Sort of. It's stupid.'

'What?'

'I've had Clarky to myself for so long and I have to get used to the idea of sharing him now.'

'You're bound to feel like that. Everyone knows you're close.'

'Aggie has been through so much and deserves every bit of happiness with him . . . I didn't think I was the green-eyed monster kind. I should be unconditionally happy for them.'

'It's hard to let go of a friend.'

I feel a lump in my throat. She's right.

'I had to let go of you,' Tiana tells me. 'It was one of the happiest but hardest things, watching you get married.'

'But nothing changed between us.'

'Of course it did! Not in a bad way but you had George. You couldn't come out dancing with Christo and me. We saw each other but only for tea or coffee or Sunday lunch. I never told you this but I felt like I was being left behind, that I had no one to attach myself to instead. And you have Finn.'

'Do I? When I need him, he's not here.'

'What do you mean?'

'Seeing as you're so psychic, have I held on to the right person?'

She's silent. Finally, 'You're joking? Clarky?'

'I'm confused. Clarky supports me. He's always there for me.'

Tiana can't listen. 'That doesn't mean you love him, J.'

'It's probably nothing,' I say.

'Too right it's nothing. Honestly, Josie! You're just feeling lonely. Finn's away and you spent a lovely afternoon with Clarky and then he was the one who saved the day with George at school. It makes your mind play games. You start to think you'll have a better life with that person, you can skip off into the sunset with them and leave all your problems behind. You and Clarky have a huge amount of history, but that's all it is, isn't it? He's happy now, Josie. I've seen him with Aggie and they are perfect together, don't ruin it for him.'

'That's the last thing I want to do.'

'He's finally got you out of his system.'

'You've spoken to him about it?'

'Come on, you know you've always been his Achilles heel. Besides, can you honestly imagine your life without Finn?'

'No, but something's got to change.'

'Whatever Finn's faults,' she says, 'his heart is true to you. If I had a Finn in my life, believe me, I'd never let him go.'

'I wish you'd meet someone, Wise Owl.'

'I think I have,' she confesses quietly.

'What? Who?'

'Christo.'

'NO!'

Normally she would have laughed, but I think she's cross with me for even having these feelings for Clarky. I shouldn't have said anything.

'J, I'm glad you told me,' she says, as if she can read my mind, 'but this has got to stop. It's fatal thinking the grass is greener because it never is. Talk to Finn, tell him he needs to pamper you more, make you feel special.'

'I don't have time for pampering!' I say, exasperated. 'That's not what it's about. It's George. I need Finn to take more responsibility, take more of the load off me. I can't do it all on my own. I'm *unhappy*, Tiana.'

'I'm sorry,' she says more softly, 'but you need to talk to Finn about this, not start fantasising about someone else, especially not Clarky.'

'Why didn't you tell me? About Christo?' I need to change the subject.

'I was going to. We've been seeing each other for a few months . . .'

'A few months?' I exclaim incredulously.

For a moment her voice returns to its normal happy tone. 'I've been longing to tell you, but Christo made me promise not to. He didn't even want to tell Finn. We wanted to keep it quiet until we knew for sure. We were seeing each other at your dinner party.'

'I thought you left early! You are such a dark horse, but I'm so happy for you.'

'I'm happy for me too. It's weird falling for such a close friend,' she says without even thinking what she's saying. 'It could have been so wrong, but it feels *right*. All I ask myself is, why on earth didn't we do it before?'

35

I am in the bedroom trying to work out what I have to buy for the baby. She'll need a new cot mattress and car seat. The one we had for George is out of date and wouldn't pass today's safety standards. Finn returns home from his conference this evening, but I'm surprised when I hear him shout, 'Josie!'

I rush out on to the landing. 'Hello. What's going on? Why's George . . .'

'He could have been run over on that road! Or picked up by some nutter.'

'But George had a lesson with Mr Phipps.'

'That's tomorrow, Mum.' He appears and flings his Thomas the Tank Engine rucksack over the banisters.

'No, it isn't. It's today.'

'For Christ's sake, Josie, it was not today. What would have happened if I hadn't seen him on the road? It's lucky I was driving back from the airport.'

'It was today!' Then I am remembering flashes of a

conversation. Mr Phipps switching days around. He had called me at Ruby's office. 'Are you OK, George?' My stomach feels as if it's been wrenched upside down, I'm thinking of all the danger I could have put my son in.

'Yes, Mummy, I'm fine. Where's Rocky?'

'He's OK now, but he shot across the road when he saw me, nearly got run over.'

'All right!' I screech, like a car braking. 'I get it. I made a mistake. Stop shouting at me, please.'

'You can't afford to make a mistake like this. You can miss a deadline, you can miss a hair appointment or a Pilates class, but you do not . . .'

'Don't patronise me! I didn't do it on purpose.' I walk back into our bedroom and sit down. The bed is covered in old baby clothes and blankets and things I had packed away in a suitcase years ago, thinking I'd never see them again. Finn follows me. 'If you're so perfect, *you* can look after George. I'm sick of doing everything!'

'What do you mean?'

'Exactly how it sounds, Finn. I do *all* the day-to-day stuff with George. "I'll play football with you, darling. I'll take you shopping. I'll take you swimming. I'll take you to the doctor's. I'll go to parents' evening. I'll cook your supper." I do *everything*!'

I can't even look at my husband. 'When was the last time you bought me flowers? When was the last time you took me out to dinner? You're happy to go out with Alessia but not your own pregnant wife. Oh, NO!'

Finn looks like he has won now. He walks over to the window. 'If you're going to start being jealous of a work colleague then I'm not even going to listen to this rubbish.'

I wish he'd stop using that expression 'work colleague'.

'I don't feel like your wife, I feel like a donkey.'

Finn laughs. 'This is about George, not you and me.'

'George is about us,' I scream at him.

'Well, it was lucky I saved our son's life then.'

'You might be treated like a god in that hospital, but it ends there. Is this what it's going to be like when the baby's born? Am I going to do everything all over again? Give my own life up?'

'What do you mean?'

'I gave up that job in Paris for you, because I was pregnant.'

Finn looks tired of this argument.

'It was an amazing opportunity for me.' I need to deal with this resentment that's still lodged deep in my subconscious. 'I gave up work when George was born.'

'Isn't that what mothers do? Look after their children? Most people see it as a privilege.'

'You're just like your father. For once I see Gwen's point of view. She was miserable too, your dad working like a maniac, never around, stuck in that big lonely house.'

'No one's forcing you to stay.'

'I love you most of the time, Finn, but sometimes I hate you.'

He doesn't look up at me. 'What is it Granny says? Only very boring people look and behave the same way all the time.'

'She would know. I was desperately unhappy, Finn, day in, day out, with a screaming George and postnatal depression, but nothing changed in your life, did it?' I open a drawer and slam it shut again. 'What have you ever given up for me? I can't even get you to commit to an antenatal class!'

Finn sits on a corner of the bed. 'I couldn't miss the conference,' he tells me again. 'I never pushed you into having this baby. I have been nothing but patient.'

George runs into the room and out again, but Finn and I are too involved in each other to see how upset he is to hear us shouting.

'What are you doing?' Finn asks me.

I start to throw clothes into the case.

'Going someplace nice?'

'Anywhere would be an improvement on here.'

'How long are you going for?'

'Don't know.'

'You're not really going, are you?' He is beginning to sound nervous. The phone rings. 'I'll take it, shall I?' I say when Finn makes no attempt to pick it up.

It's Granny. 'You must be fat by now?'

'I'm pregnant, not fat.'

'Same thing,' she cackles. 'How's my lovely grandson?'

'Fine.'

'And my bird of paradise? Is my boy looking after you properly?'

'No, Granny, he's not. I have to go, something's in the oven.'

She starts to roar with laughter. 'Something in the oven, my foot! You never were a good liar, Josie Greenwood. What's wrong? Hand over Finn.'

I shove the phone his way.

'Granny, I can't talk now. And before you ask, I did buy you some twigs from duty-free.' He hangs up.

I start walking downstairs with the case.

'Look, can you stop this now?'

'Stop what?'

'Pretending you're going.'

'Who says I'm pretending?'

'Let's calm down, OK?'

'Too late for that. You've said quite enough, thanks. I'm a terrible mother who nearly had her son killed out there on the road, so over to you now, Finn. Good luck.'

'Oh, come on, J, you're eight months pregnant. You can't leave.'

I don't say anything.

'What am I going to do?'

'You'll work it out.'

'Let me guess. Off you run to Clarky when the going gets tough. I don't know why you didn't marry him instead.'

I laugh mockingly. 'That's the first sensible thing you've said all night.' I open the front door, moving Finn's suitcase out of the way.

He shuts it and stands in front of me. 'Please, Josie, don't do this. It was the shock of seeing George, that's all. It won't happen again.'

'But it will.'

'It won't,' he promises.

'You always do this! It's too late.'

'Josie, I love you, don't go.'

'Throw in "I love you" and everything's OK? You're only saying it to save your own skin.'

George comes downstairs clutching Baby and a Lego box under one arm, and pulling his Thomas the Tank Engine duvet behind him with the other hand. His Lego slips from his grasp and pieces start to fall downstairs. 'I'm ready, Mum, but I can't find my book on the planets.'

'George needs you. You can't leave.' Finn thinks this is his best chance of my staying. 'I am sorry.'

I can feel tears in my eyes.

George places his duvet and Lego in front of me. 'I'm just going to get my homework books and my PE stuff,' he says earnestly, before running upstairs and tripping up on the way. 'And my goggles,' he calls out. He is still holding Baby.

I can hear him turning his room upside down, looking for all the things that create a safe world around him.

If I don't go now, I never will. I push Finn's arm away and finally he allows me to open the door.

'Josie,' he says more gently, 'don't go.' He is watching me walk away. I can't turn around. I can't go through with it if I see George again. I'll have to take him with me, and I can't. Not tonight.

'Please, Josie.'

'Mum! Wait for me!' George cries out. Now that he has heard the door shut there is panic in his voice.

But I keep on walking.

36

'What's happened? Josie?' I had been banging on Clarky's door. When he opened it I rushed in, out of breath and talking so fast he couldn't keep up with me. 'I've left him . . . left him . . .' I was saying. I had to gasp for air. 'Didn't pick George up from school . . . got days mixed up . . . Finn went mad. I can't cope . . . can't cope.' I stop. 'Oh, God, I'm sorry.' The table is laid for supper. There are candles and the room is dark, lit by a couple of dimmer lights. I can smell curry coming from the kitchen.

'Is Aggie coming over? I'd better go,' I say, but make no attempt to move. I can't even feel my feet.

'Shh, it's OK.' He leads me to the sofa and I tell him again what happened. My mobile rings. It's Finn.

'Is George OK?'

'No, he wants his mum.'

'Tell him I'll see him tomorrow.'

'So, you're coming home then?'

'No. You'll have to take George to school.'

'I can't.'

'You have to.'

'This is ridiculous. I can't be late for the hospital. My ward round starts at eight-thirty.'

'I don't care.'

Finn is in shock. For once he has full responsibility for George. Good.

'When will you come home?'

'I'm not sure.'

'So you're staying with Clarky?'

'I don't know.'

'J, I deserve this, I understand that. I'm so, *so* sorry about tonight, you have to believe me, but please come home. We'll work this out . . . I'll . . .'

I'm about to cry again. 'Tell George I love him.'

'Josie, wait!'

I hang up. 'Honestly, it's such a mess.'

Clarky is holding me close when Aggie walks into the room wearing a bright pink coat that clashes with her hair. She's holding a stripy umbrella. 'It's so wet . . . oh, hello.'

We spring apart like an adulterous couple. Clarky walks over to her and they kiss quickly on the cheek. 'Hi, Josie. What's going on?' asks Aggie.

'She's had a bad argument with Finn. I said she could stay. You don't mind, do you?'

'Oh, right.'

I want to disappear. I shouldn't have come. She shakes

her hair loose from its ponytail. 'Shouldn't you be talking to Finn, not Clarky? You're eight months pregnant. This stress can't be doing you any good, and what if your waters break tonight? Hot spicy food brings on a baby, doesn't it?' She looks at my enormous bump.

'Aggie, can we talk?' Clarky pulls at her arm and leads her out into the hallway.

'I arranged a babysitter for El tonight, I thought we were going to talk about our plans?'

'I know, but look at her. She needs someone.'

'I understand that, but why does it always have to be you?' she asks in a hoarse whisper. 'What about Tiana, or someone else?'

'That's not fair. We're like family to each other, that's all.'

'Family! How long are you going to pull that one off? I really like Josie, she's my friend, but this is *exactly* why I get so funny about you two.'

'Why are you making me feel as if I'm betraying you? We're old friends, how many times do I have to tell you? I will not let her down,' Clarky says with finality.

'Well, then, I'm going,' Aggie states.

'Why can't we all have supper together?' he insists. 'I've made plenty of curry. I don't want you to go, but we have all the time in the world to talk about our future. She needs me right now. Don't make a scene, please.'

'*Me* not make a scene? What about Josie! She's eight

months pregnant, what the fuck's she playing at? Now's no time to be falling out with her husband or leaving herself with no roof over her head. She can't always rely on you. This was our night!'

'What are you doing?' they both snap at me as I walk past.

'You're right, Aggie. What am I doing? I can't always rely on Clarky. I'm sorry.' I'm struggling with my case and trying to unlock the door.

I feel a hand on mine. 'You're in no fit state to leave,' he says.

Aggie stands with her arms firmly crossed, still dressed in her long bright pink coat.

'I'm going,' I tell Clarky. 'I'm sorry I barged in, Aggie.'

'It's all right. You can stay if you want,' she adds reluctantly.

'I would never have come if I'd known you'd planned something.'

She's tapping one foot against the carpet. 'Sorry for getting so arsey.' Aggie's tone has finally softened, like rock-hard butter beginning to melt.

'Look, I'm going home, I'll be fine,' I assure Clarky. 'Aggie's right. I need to sort this out with Finn.'

'OK, but I'm calling you a cab,' he says.

I get into the taxi. Clarky kisses me goodbye. 'I'm sorry about Aggie.'

'Don't be. Go and make it up to her. She's only just met you, it's natural she wants to spend time with you.' I smile, holding back the tears. We look at one another. What do I want from him? Is it possible to love two people? Don't cross the friendship line. Yet the line is so blurred I can't even see it anymore.

'Go and enjoy your curry. Don't wait out here, it's raining.' He closes the cab door with a slam. I wave goodbye to him. I have to let him go. I have no right to be holding on so tightly.

'Where are you going, love?' The driver revs up the engine.

'Anywhere you want,' I say, looking out of the window, tears now flowing down my face. He gives me a strange look before I tell him to take me home.

37

'I can't leave, Mum. I could have the baby any day now. It could be a week, or three, or it could be tomorrow. Or today. All I want to do is come home, see you and Dad, but I can't. I'm stuck.'

'Have you got everything ready for the hospital?'

'Yes.'

'Well, you have to stay put. You can't take any risks at this stage.'

'I know.' I twist the telephone cord tightly. 'I wish I could leave Finn, but he has to work. He can't look after George, and if I did leave, I don't know what he'd do. I have to do what's best for my son and he can't take time off school anyhow. But Finn made me so cross, Mum.'

I tell her about our screaming match and she listens quietly, taking it all in. I don't tell her about the complication with Clarky. Am I in love with him? I can hardly look Aggie in the eye when we pick our children up from school. I told her how sorry I was about the other night and brought flowers as a peace offering; tulips which I know are her favourite. She's been quiet, pretending that she has to get home to finish her cooking. The last thing I want to do is hurt anyone, let alone Aggie who has already been let down in the past. I need to get a grip on my life. This has gone too far.

When I finish telling Mum about the argument she says boldly, 'He takes you for granted. He always has. I like Finn but he makes up his own rules, that boy.'

'I'm about to have a baby, Mum, and I'm terrified. This isn't how I imagined it would be.'

'Do you want me to come and stay? Would that help you?'

The offer is so tempting. All I want to do is see her. I yearn to go home and find a hot-water bottle in my bed and the smell of Dad's fresh coffee in the kitchen. 'Can I come and stay with you after the baby's born? It'll be George's summer holidays then. I know we talked about you coming to London, but I need some time away. Can I do that?'

'You don't have to ask. Your father and I set aside the month anyway. We've already bought a cot.'

It's George's Sports Day today. School term has nearly ended.

Finn and I are trying to build bridges. I'm glad I didn't race home. I can't run to Clarky; I shouldn't hide behind my parents. Finn and I need to sort this out. We're sleeping in separate rooms, mainly because I am so uncomfortable at night and can't sleep. However, if anything, our argument has made things better.

I was working late in my studio last night on David's project when Finn sat down on the stool next to my desk and looked at the screen, telling me in great detail why he liked the pink-and-white floral image. 'I can see that on a perfume bottle. It's eye-catching. I mean, I like the green one with the pretty leaves, but, no, it's not quite as effective. The pink one is more French, more sophisticated somehow. Show me how you do that?' he'd asked, leaning in closer. 'You're so clever.' I'd been playing around with the size and colour of the image.

'It's simple when you know how.'

'It's not. I couldn't do it.' From the corner of my eye I could see he had something in his hand that he'd wanted to show me, but I had to get my work finished. 'I'll leave you to it.'

'Finn,' I'd called out as he was walking out of the room.

'Yes?'

'What's that?'

'Just a boring medical journal, has pictures of the conference.'

'Show me. Is there a picture of Alessia?'

'Yes, think so.'

'Can I have a look?'

He'd smiled, handing it to me.

There was a group picture near the middle of the magazine. 'Is that her?' She was standing in the front row. Average height, neat figure, dark hair, a cute smile, but . . . 'She's not what I expected,' I'd said.

'Don't you think she's pretty?'

'Yes.'

'What did you expect?'

'I don't know. Someone beautiful, I guess. You know, one of those people who just are so good-looking they're another breed altogether. She's, I don't know, kind of like me. Normal.'

'But you're gorgeous, J.'

'Hey!' I'd called, touched by his comment and ridiculously relieved that at long last I'd seen a picture of her. If only I'd seen one a year ago. 'Don't go. Are you featured in there?'

'There might be something.'

'Let me see.'

'Middle section, page eighteen.'

I must have almost laughed. The photograph of Finn was terrible.

'I blinked when the flash went off,' he'd said, trying to snatch it back from me. Underneath it read, 'Finn Greenwood is a promising young doctor with an exciting future in medicine.' It went on to describe his department at the hospital. 'Finn, that's great.' I'd sighed with pride and our faces were so close; I wish I'd kissed him then instead of turning away.

The other day he came home with some supper; he had been to the fancy butcher and bought us some delicious steak. He's pledged that he will start cooking at least once a week and at the weekends, especially when the baby's born. He's also been bringing me tea in bed before he leaves for work. And George and he made me breakfast last Sunday. I had to move back into the main bedroom so George didn't notice the sleeping arrangements. The breakfast was pretty disgusting as usual – soggy toast and scrambled eggs – but Finn had bought some pink roses too. The only sad thing was he'd asked George to put them in a vase, but what he hadn't seen was his son cutting the stems off so short that the roses had looked beheaded, bobbing up and down in a cereal bowl. 'They're like Henry VIII's wives,' Finn said, smiling and putting the tray on my lap. During breakfast George had turned on the radio and Michael Jackson's 'Thriller' started to play. It's a house rule to dance to this song. If we don't, bad luck will follow. We hadn't heard it in months.

Finn had lifted the tray from my lap with an encouraging, 'Come on, we can't break with tradition, especially now. We need all the luck we can get.'

We'd stood in a line, me attempting to kick my legs to the music but looking like a fat baboon. I could hardly lift my feet off the floor. We'd all started to laugh so much that it hurt. I'd clutched my stomach and collapsed back down on the bed. I'd watched Finn and George as they pulled faces at me, George dancing manically on his thin little legs.

It is moments like these, of pure happiness, that I love; that make it all worthwhile.

Finn took George to the car-boot sale after that breakfast, telling me to rest and watch movies. They'd arrived home carrying a terrifying mask which came complete with a tube of fake blood to smear over it.

'How much for this?' George had quizzed his favourite car-boot lady.

'For you, Billy Whizz, one pound fifty,' she'd said.

'I'll give you ten pence.'

'Why did you let him buy it?' I'd cursed Finn when they returned home, watching him cover his face with it and make strange haunting noises. 'Stop it!' I'd quavered. 'When he's at school, I'm putting it straight into the dustbin.' Finn had laughed at that and I'd pulled the mask off him and held his face firmly in my hands. This time there was no looking away. I'd kissed him.

We also took George swimming last weekend. Uncle Ed had joined us. 'I can see such an improvement in his style,' Finn had said incredulously, all of us watching from the shallow end.

'It's Frédéric. He's able to see through George's condition and appreciate his talent because he bothers to look hard.'

'Watch, Mum! Dad! Uncle Ed!' George proceeded to do at least five metres backstroke. He'd kept his legs beautifully straight and kicked them in time with his arm action. We'd all clapped furiously.

It had been the first time Finn had seen George's lessons paying off, and just to see him look so happy and to act like we were a family felt good. No, it felt *great*.

Finn has promised George he will be at his Sports Day. Last year George came last in the 100 metre sprint because he was waiting for his dad to turn up. Everyone had laughed and pointed at him, still standing in front of the starting line. George's mood has brightened considerably because Finn will be watching him swimming again then. 'Don't let him down,' I'd warned. 'It's better to say no than to lead him on.'

'I will be there,' Finn had promised. 'What race is he in?'

'Front crawl and backstroke.'

I have every faith he will come this time. Something feels different. Like we're making a new start and I'm falling in love with him all over again.

I'm making the bed when the doorbell rings. Rocky starts to bark. I slowly walk downstairs, irritated that I have been disturbed. It's an effort to move at this stage. The baby's weight bears down on me. I feel like my unborn child is lumped between my knees, not in my stomach, just hanging there between my legs like a huge sack. Finn kindly likes to tell me it looks as if I have swallowed an extra-large basketball. I can't possibly get any bigger, can I? Where will the baby go, for God's sake? George can't believe it. 'It's got to come out soon,' he keeps on saying.

I unlock the door.

Clarky doesn't brush his shoes against the mat as he always does. 'What's wrong?' I ask.

'I'm going mad.' He walks into the sitting room and starts pacing, just as Finn does when he has something on his mind.

'Clarky?'

'No one else is here, are they?'

'No.'

'No one really understands our friendship, do they?'

'What's wrong?'

He scratches the back of his head and laughs. 'Aggie. After you'd left that night she was questioning me about us again.'

'God, I'm sorry. I shouldn't have come over, it was a mistake.'

'Well, she won't let it go now. Why was I always the one you ran to? Why, why, why? Can I be honest?' He doesn't wait for me to say anything. 'You're my best friend and I want you to be happy, but there's this tiny side of me that rejoices when you and Finn argue. It gives me hope. I've always believed that maybe, one day, you'll see that you can't live without me.'

'I can't,' I say simply. 'You'll always be a part of my life.'

He lets out a frustrated groan. 'But not in the way I mean. Why do you act so innocently when you . . . ?'

'I know what you mean,' I say quietly.

'I don't want to be someone who lives their life hoping a marriage breaks up, especially yours. What kind of person would that make me? But do you know what it's like, loving someone and knowing you can never have them?'

I bite my lip. I can't believe he is saying this and it's my fault. 'No.'

He laughs drily. 'I ought to run courses, at least make some money out of you. Come and subscribe to, "All you need to do to get that person out of your head".'

'Clarky, you've met Aggie. I'm having Finn's baby. I love him.'

'I know, and I love Aggie.'

'Good, so don't ruin it.'

'But . . .'

'But what?'

'She's not you.'

'Clarky, you've got to stop this, OK? You need to calm down, think about this properly. I love you . . .'

'But only as a friend,' he finishes impatiently. 'That's what you were going to say, isn't it?' He follows me into the kitchen. I lean against the table, tired and out of breath.

'It's George's Sports Day today. I have to go in a minute.'

'What time?'

'It starts at two, but George's races are later.'

He looks at his watch. It's midday. 'I'll come with you.'

'I don't think that's a good idea. Finn will be there. He's making a real effort, he promised to be there for George today.'

Clarky is looking at the blackboard. Finn has written on it, 'Remember, George's first race, three o'clock.'

'Is everything fine between you now?'

'Clarky, we can't do this! We have to let it go. I'm married; you're in a relationship. This is stupid, it's leading nowhere except to hurt people.'

'I can't let it go.'

'You have to. I shouldn't have come round that night,' I reiterate. 'And I'm hugely to blame. I shouldn't depend on you so much. It was hard seeing you with someone when I've always had your undivided attention. But that's me being selfish and childish. Coming round that night finally made me realise that. Aggie deserves a lot better than this.'

'Where are you going?' There's panic in his voice.

'To the bathroom. Jesus, Clarky!' The phone rings. 'Can you get that?' I call.

'I'm afraid she can't come to the phone. She's gone to the loo . . . I came over to see Josie . . . I'm just answering your question. Right.'

I open the door. 'What did Finn want?'

'The times of George's races.'

'I told him this morning. Do I need to call him back?'

'No, it's on the blackboard. He was only checking.'

'Oh. Good.'

'I want to come,' he says. 'I'd like to support my godson.'

'I'm calling Finn.' But before I even make it to the phone the doorbell rings. That will be Mrs B.

She walks in wearing a long red skirt with a tight frilly shirt, her long hair plaited and coiled into a bun. She stops when she sees Clarky. 'What's he doing here?'

'He's going to drive us to school, aren't you?'

'Yes.'

'Right. How are you, Justin?'

'Very good, thank you.'

'Not working today?'

'Clearly not. If I was I wouldn't be here, would I?'

'Right. Don't get your knickers in a twist.'

When his back is turned she nudges me. 'Why's he always hanging around here?' she huffs like Finn's granny. 'There's something about him I don't trust.'

38

Clarky, Mrs B and I walk into the steamy swimming pool area and take our seats in the audience. Rows of blue plastic chairs edge the pool. The seating area is filling up. I wave to Mr Phipps who is seated at the front. 'Is that the nice headmaster?' Mrs B asks.

Four children line up on their starting boxes. They're divided into 'houses' that are all named after fruits. George belongs to Prickly Pear house. They are one of the best. He said they'd chosen him because it didn't matter if they had one lame duck in the team. Currently they are in second position, following closely behind the Pink Grapefruits.

'Hi, Mum! Hi, Daddog! Mrs B!' George waves as he holds his nose tightly and dive-bombs into the turquoise pool.

Ms Miles has to get him out. It's odd seeing her in a tracksuit and sweater. She looks less severe, but I am reminded of her strictness when she says, 'It's not your race, George, you're a Prickly Pear, NOT a Wild Strawberry.'

I hear another whistle, this time even louder. George is running around the edge of the pool in his black trunks that slide halfway down his bottom. He's making his way over to us. 'Where's Dad?' he asks. 'He promised he'd come.'

'George, you have to behave otherwise you'll be disqualified, darling. Your father will be here any minute, all you need to do is think about your race.'

'That's right, George. Finn's a busy man, but he will be here,' Mrs B confirms adamantly.

Clarky laughs quietly with a shake of his head. He knows the loaded implication behind that remark.

'Concentrate now,' Mrs B instructs. 'Don't watch us.' George darts off.

Ms Miles drags him back to the other Prickly Pears who are sitting on the bench behind the diving boards.

The first breaststroke race starts. I hear a door open. It's not Finn. Come on. Why do you have to cut it so fine? The traffic can't be that bad at this time of day. 'Stop fidgeting,' Mrs B says, 'he'll be here.'

It's the backstroke race for the older boys now. A Cooking Apple swims wonkily into the other lane and hits a Prickly Pear by mistake. I can't sit still. I can see George constantly looking towards the door, waiting for Finn to walk through it. I can't bear it. Finn promised me he wouldn't let us down. Promised. I hate him.

Finally it's George's first race: the front crawl.

The whistle goes off and George is still standing on his box, waiting for his dad. I am beside myself. 'Go on, George!' Clarky shouts. But he's disqualified for delaying too long. The scores are updated. The Prickly Pears are still second, but if George hadn't been disqualified and lost them five points they would be in the lead.

The Prickly Pears huddle in a circle. 'Team talk,' Jason, their captain, says. George tries to enter the circle. I watch as he is pushed away. 'You're a loser. We never wanted you on our side. L-O-S-E-R,' Jason spells out. George sits on his own at the end of the bench. His team is understandably furious, but why do they have to be so mean with it? I wish George wasn't on Jason's team. I thought the school had a policy of keeping them apart?

I ring Finn again. There's no answer. Where are you? George has one more race. He won't swim unless his father is watching. Then I have an idea. 'What are you doing?' Clarky asks, as I struggle to push my way over to the Prickly Pears.

'Mrs Jammie Dodger says you've got to win it,' I tell George. 'She's so sorry not to see your race, but she's with you all the way. You just swim your heart out, that's what she said.'

'Dad's not coming?'

'No, darling. Will you swim for me, your old mum? And Mrs B?'

'And Daddog?'

372

'Yes, for Daddog too.'

It's the final race. Everything depends on it. It's still between the Prickly Pears and the Pink Grapefruits. The team are asking the teachers if they can swap Julian for George. 'NO!' Clarky and I shout out. 'Let George swim!'

The referee takes us through the scores for the final time. If George wins, the Prickly Pears win by a point.

'In lane one, the Wild Strawberries.' The parents clap. 'Come on, Steven, you can do it,' shouts his father. Steven waves. He's wearing red trunks. 'In lane two, the Cooking Apples!' There's a chubby boy with blond hair lifting up his chubby arms.

A door opens. Please let it be Finn.

'He's my best friend,' Eliot tells the dinner lady as he is manoeuvred to the front to watch. They sit on the other side of the pool, directly opposite us. I'm too flustered even to smile at Eliot. I wonder why Aggie isn't here? At least his arrival is delaying the start. HURRY UP, Finn.

The referee resumes his role. 'In lane three we have the Pink Grapefruits.' There's more shouting and cheering from each team. 'And finally, in lane four, the Prickly Pears.'

'Come on, George,' I shout. 'You can do it!'

'Go, George!' shouts Eliot who starts to clap.

'Come on, my boy!' Clarky shouts.

'Your boy?' Mrs B says, her tone as sharp as acid.

373

He rolls his eyes. 'You know what I mean.'

George is so nervous he falls into the water because he's waving too hard at Eliot. I put my head in my hands, hardly daring to look up again. The rest of the team shout and scream at him. The referee blows his whistle. I can hear Ms Miles saying he should be disqualified for fooling around. Dear God, please don't disqualify him. Don't give him penalty points either. The entire room is quiet as we wait for the decision. Mr Phipps stands up and says, 'Let George have another go! Ms Miles, sit down!' Everyone claps as George jumps out of the pool and stands on his box again.

He is the only boy wearing a swimming cap. It's the one with a frog on it that Mrs B gave him.

I am so nervous as I watch the referee putting the whistle closer to his lips. The boys look so serious, as if they are competing in the Olympics. 'On your marks, get set . . .'

BLAST OFF!

'GO, GEORGE!' Clarky, Mrs B, Eliot and I shout.

The children jump in holding their noses and then flip over to start their backstroke. We watch in silence. You could hear a pin drop.

'COME ON, GEORGE!' shout the Prickly Pears from the bench line. 'He's not bad,' says Jason.

'He's good,' Clarky says calmly, watching George's legs and arms moving effortlessly through the water. Where is Finn? Why can't I ever count on him?

George is currently in second place behind the Pink Grapefruits, but it's close. 'He's bloody good,' Clarky now says with amazement.

'Thought you didn't swear,' I mutter. 'That's a pound in the jam jar.'

'I'm feeling the pressure.'

I am muttering instructions under my breath. 'That's right . . . kick, kick. Go, George!' For the first time in her life Mrs B is quiet.

George is creeping up on the Pink Grapefruit as they reach the end of the first length. He flips over and kicks his feet against the edge of the pool, giving himself a head start on the last length. Clarky is jumping up and down now. 'COME ON, GEORGE.' He grabs my hand. The Pink Grapefruit is catching up and has overtaken.

'FASTER, GEORGE,' Eliot's shouting. 'He's my best friend,' he tells the dinner lady again.

They are level pegging. 'GO!' Clarky and I now screech. They both touch the end of the pool. It looks like it's a draw.

We wait to hear the results. 'In first position . . .'

Clarky and I stand poised, clutching each other's hand.

'George Greenwood, the Prickly Pears!'

Clarky and I scream. Mr Phipps claps and looks over to me. The Prickly Pears are thumping George on the back in triumph. Even Jason looks pleased and shakes his hand. The dinner lady pushes Eliot over to George and his team. I can see Eliot's round glasses are misted over with steam.

'He's a winner!' I'm crying at my son's Sports Day, I am so overwhelmed. Mrs B runs over to George to congratulate him. I turn to Clarky and kiss him on the lips. 'He did it!' We cling to each other. He holds my face between his hands and kisses me back. I throw my arms around him again.

'DAD! I did it!' George calls.

'You did it,' Finn repeats. 'I'm so proud of you, George.'

Finn's here? Clarky and I move apart quickly. Finn's sleeves are rolled up, his tie loose, dark jacket slung over his shoulder. He walks towards us. I'm watching him almost as if it were slow motion. He stands in front of us but before I can say anything, with one deft punch he hits Clarky in the middle of his face. 'I should have done that a long time ago,' Finn says, relief flooding his voice. Parents and children gasp in horror, as if on a movie set where something inexplicable has happened. Clarky staggers back into one of the plastic chairs, but manages not to fall over. His nose is bleeding.

'Finn, stop! What are you doing? You turn up late and then you have the nerve to attack Clarky?'

'I have the nerve to attack Clarky when you've both been having an affair? Give me a break!'

'An affair?' I shout.

There are more gasps.

'Don't be ridiculous. An affair?' I repeat.

'So you and Clarky were playing Scrabble just then?'

'George won the race. I was overexcited. I'd have kissed Kermit the Frog if he'd been next to me.'

'Thanks,' Clarky mutters.

'Why is Dad fighting?' I hear George whimper. 'Why is Dad hitting Daddog?' Mrs B shields his eyes. The referee blows his whistle. 'Everyone, outside,' he shouts. Ms Miles is ushering all the children towards the changing room area, flapping her hands wildly. Mr Phipps follows, keeping everyone calm. 'Out, now.' The parents walk out slowly, excited by the drama.

'Is that your dad?' one of the children asks. 'He's cool!'

Clarky straightens up but Finn pushes him back again and this time he falls heavily to the ground, knocking over more chairs. 'All I was doing was supporting George in the race.'

'And getting off with my wife!'

'It wasn't a proper kiss! Besides you should have been here, Finn.'

Parents stall at the exit. They suddenly have the shuffle syndrome: very painful feet that can't move at speed.

'I should have been. Are you going to tell her or shall I?' Finn asks Clarky.

'Tell her what? That you're unreliable, you only think about yourself?'

'You know, you little shit.' Finn stands over him. 'You've been lying to me.' He hits him again, hard in the jaw.

'Finn, leave him alone, please!'

'Do you think I'm a complete idiot? You two have been having an affair all this time, haven't you? All those late-night visits and phone calls and there's me still believing you're "just friends". Have you slept together?'

'Finn! Please can we sort this out at home?'

But he won't move. He looks around the empty pool. 'I'm not late.'

'But Clarky told you it was at three.'

Finn looks at him. 'Do you want to set her straight or shall I?'

Clarky wipes the blood from his nose. He shakes his head.

I turn to him. 'What? You lied?'

'I knew there was something about him I didn't trust!' Mrs B says with triumph.

'I don't know what I was doing, J, what I was thinking.'

Finn laughs scornfully. 'All you've ever wanted to do is to split us up. There always were three of us in this marriage.' He turns to me. 'You, me and him.'

'You don't deserve her.' Clarky stands up with renewed strength.

'Don't you dare tell me what I do or don't deserve.' Finn pushes him towards the pool edge.

'She's too good for you,' Clarky says, pressing Finn against the diving board and hitting him hard in the stomach.

'STOP IT!' I shout. 'BOTH OF YOU.' Clarky turns to leave, but Finn grabs him from behind, throws him forward, pushing with all his strength, and with one final heave Clarky is thrown into the water.

My husband walks over to me then. Tell me this is a horrible dream? 'Nothing happened, Finn.'

He shakes his head crossly. 'That's what you've said for years. The least you can do is give me some kind of explanation. You owe me that much. I've respected your friendship, but I won't have him hanging around us any longer, I can't do it. Have you slept with him?'

'No.'

'If you're lying to me . . .'

'I'm not lying.'

Clarky clambers out of the pool, dripping water in front of us. 'Josie, tell him the truth.'

The colour drains from Finn's face. 'What?'

'We slept together, Finn,' he says. 'It was years ago. Ask Josie about that night in Venice. We've never talked about it, but it's clearly time we all did.'

Everything stands still. I feel numb.

'Is that true?' There is this terrible hurt in Finn's eyes; I have ruined everything that is sacred to him. He looks like he did as a young boy watching his own parents' marriage dissolve in front of his eyes.

'We were only eighteen,' I call after him. 'It was one night, that's all. Don't go!'

He stops, but doesn't turn round to face us. 'I can't believe this. You've lied to me all this time. What else have you two lied about? You deserve each other. Good luck to you.'

'Finn!' I call out desperately.

He turns round and walks back to me. 'I wanted to see George win.' His eyes are watering now. 'He's our boy, not Clarky's. He's my son. It was my race to watch. It's *our* family.'

'I know.' I reach out to try and touch him, but he moves away from me again. 'I'm so sorry.'

'Have I been a fool all these years? Have you and Clarky been in love all this time, right under my nose? I'll never forgive you, I can't.'

'No, Finn . . .' I start to cry. 'It's just . . .'

'I am here, you know,' says a dark shamed voice.

'Go away, Clarky. Haven't you done enough damage?' He looks back at me, waiting.

The smell of chlorine is suffocating. 'Finn . . .' I stagger forward, clutching my stomach. I know it's happening. There's nothing I can do to stop it. This is it.

'Josie?' Finn rushes towards me.

'Are you all right, J?' Clarky asks, his voice heavy with guilt. Finn pushes him aside, condemning him to irrelevance.

'Finn. Finn . . .' I groan, grabbing his arm. The pain owns me; it has claimed my body. 'Get me to the hospital. NOW.'

39

Ten days later

I'm at my parents' home, sitting on the kitchen window seat that looks out over the fields. I had a baby girl, but you knew that. She's beautiful with dark hair like Finn's. We decided to call her Scarlett Emily. The last time Finn and I were here, we'd conceived our baby. Look at us now.

After Scarlett was born Finn had said he thought it best if I went to my mother's instead of her coming to London as originally planned. Of course we both knew that what he was really saying was he needed time away from me. I know he found it a hard decision, especially when I said I didn't want to leave him. In his eyes I could see how torn he was between not wanting to be parted from us, but at the same time wondering how he could pick up the pieces as if nothing had happened.

Finn is in contact, daily, but we keep it strictly to Scarlett and George news. When I tried to tell him that there's been no affair, that it was that one night long ago, he shut down instantly, like a light switching off. 'Why should I believe anything you say?' was the bleak reply.

Ed has sent flowers. Gwen sent me a card from her and Dicky, saying she was sorry she hadn't had time to see the baby yet and hoped the birth wasn't too hideous. I threw it in the bin. Even Ruby sent me flowers and a message. *'Gem Communications is not the same without you! Natalie and I rattle round the office. Come back as soon as you can. Love to the sprog. Ciao, Bella.'* I'd laughed at that.

Tiana calls me regularly. She's found a new job teaching Spanish to businessmen. 'So many handsome single men in hot suits – and now I'm engaged! The longer that ring is on my finger, the more desirable I become.' But all she really wants to know about is Finn.

'I'm not sure he wants me back,' I told her during one call.

'He does. Give him time.'

'Have you spoken to him?'

'Christo has. He says Finn looks awful. He misses you and Scarlett. Hates not seeing you.'

'It doesn't have to be like that. We're right here. He could take paternity leave.'

'He's not ready. You know Finn, he's proud.'

'Proud? He's as stubborn as hell.'

'He can't carry on as if nothing's happened. He's complicated like that.'

'You don't need to tell me. Tiana, we need to be together. We need to talk otherwise how are we going to work this out? Forget about me, he needs to see his daughter. How can he not want to hold her? And then there's George who can't understand it. He believes it's his fault. He doesn't say it, but I know that's what he thinks.'

'I know. You'll sort this out, Josie, because you have to. You and Finn are my foundation. Without you two, everything and everyone falls apart.'

Mum and Dad are looking after the baby and me. And Rocky. And George. Their house is a haven. They bought it when it was no more than a run-down barn, an ugly-looking building, large and grey with little charm, but I could see that the surrounding land and views were tempting. Initially I'd thought they were mad because it was so much work, but they love projects. They renovated it and turned it into a country house. The kitchen is my favourite room. It's huge with a large oak table running down the middle. Half the room is painted a clotted cream colour. The other half, the cooking area, is a rustic orange. It's full of pretty things that I'd like to take home. There's an Aga and copper saucepans, mugs with flowers on them, large goblets for wine and small coloured glasses for sherry. Now I look out on to the downs beyond the sweeping lawn which Mum and Dad keep immaculate. I can see the tree house which Dad made for George, and Rowan the pony chomping at the grass. This is my favourite place to sit with a drink as I listen to stories of village fairs and the wedding marquees Mum has decorated, and there are always a few bed and breakfast tales to tell as well.

'How's the B & B going?' I ask her. Mum's chopping some carrots and parsnips for soup. Scarlett is finally asleep in her Moses basket. Mum pushed her outside to let her get some fresh air. 'Busy. I'm glad to have this time off.'

'I wouldn't call George, Scarlett and me time off!' George and my father are playing in the tree house. 'Mum . . .'

'Do you remember that time we had a Japanese couple staying and you helped with the breakfast? We put a melon out, didn't we, thinking they'd have one slice each, plenty for us later, but they ate the entire thing, even the skin! Wasn't that extraordinary? I'm sure they got indigestion.'

'And I remember that young man who stank of after-shave; it was everywhere in the house.'

'Oh, yes, I remember too. I had to air the room for weeks.'

'Mum?'

She's stirring the soup. 'Yes?'

'Have you and Dad ever gone through a difficult time?'

She comes and sits with me. 'All marriages go through rocky patches and if people say they don't, then they're lying!' She flicks a hand through her hair. 'Every now and then I wonder what would have happened if I had married that German, Klaus, who taught me to fly an aeroplane. But we've always talked, your father and I, and I know he is the only person I'd really want to be with. He makes me happy.'

I am drawn to look at her gold wedding ring, out of shape now and looking battered by time, but still firmly on her finger, an old friend.

'Do you think Finn will trust me again? I mean, it's not as if I've committed a terrible crime. It wasn't adultery. Surely marriages go through a lot worse? You hear all kinds of horrible stories in the newspapers . . . wives poisoning their husbands . . .' Mum smiles at that. 'Or men going through mid-life crises and leaving their wives for women half their age,' I continue. 'My only fault was I didn't tell him about Clarky.'

'Well, actually, you lied,' Mum can't help adding.

'And you've never lied?'

'To your father?'

'Yes.'

'No, not really.'

'Oh, come on, Mum! Never?' I stammer incredulously.

'I might have told the odd fib, you know . . . that I didn't leave the iron on all night, or I didn't drop the lasagne on the floor and then scoop it back into the dish.'

'Ugh! Did you do that?'

She laughs. 'At the dinner party I gave when we were first married.' She hushes her voice. 'Don't tell him!'

'Dad would find it funny now. Finn's hardly the perfect husband either,' I say.

'I know,' she reiterates. 'Goodness, nobody's perfect.'

'Sometimes I feel I bring George up on my own. Like a single mum.'

'I understand that.'

'And I can't see how it will ever change.'

'He'll never completely change, darling. You knew the type of man Finn was before you married him. He's ambitious and I'm sure he'll be the most successful consultant, but that will demand more of his time too.'

'I know, but you can see it from my point of view, can't you?'

'Of course,' she answers reassuringly.

'Do you think he'll trust me again?' I ask once more.

'Yes, I'm sure he will.' She presses her lips together in thought. 'I'll always remember the sermon that was given at my wedding. The vicar said that when you love someone you create a secret garden with walls around it, and only you two have the key. You play; you have a lovely time in this garden. When you get married you have children, more responsibilities, and the garden is neglected. Unless you go back to nurture it, it will soon be overgrown with weeds. Start to look like a terrible jungle. Whatever goes on outside the wall, whether it's work or health, whatever it is, you need to go back to that garden from time to time and find each other again. Remember what it was first like to *be* with Finn. Remember why you fell in love with him.'

I remember that initial glimpse of him at Momo's. I had never seen anyone so beautiful. It was like a million lights going off in my head.

She returns to the soup which has started to boil. 'Finn needs to do the same too. And where does Clarky fit into all of this?' she says tentatively, taking the pan off the heat.

I still feel angry with him. He's the reason Finn and I aren't together now. If he hadn't lied none of this would have happened, I tell Mum.

'Josie, I don't think that's altogether right. If Justin hadn't said anything you and Finn would have soldiered on. Clarky's probably made you see what's missing from your marriage, that there are things you and Finn need to talk about. In a funny way, this probably needed to happen.'

Listening to Mum, I feel angry, but guilty too. Subconsciously I've held Clarky back from building his own life. Who doesn't want someone who is always there for them, like a security blanket? I have used him. 'I haven't spoken to him since George's Sports Day. I think we need some time apart,' I tell her.

'When you two were growing up you were inseparable, like twins. Your father and I wondered if you'd ever get together.'

'And?'

'The thing is, I take the old-fashioned view. If you know someone so well before you've even married, well, it's almost like starting the journey at the end. What do you have to discover about one another along the way? I only knew your dad for a couple of months before we got engaged. I like Clarky, but it can't be easy for Finn when another man is always around. It's time Justin found himself a good woman who's not you.'

'He has, I just hope I haven't wrecked it for him. You're right,' I tell her. 'My behaviour these last few months, well, it's left a lot to be desired. It's not only Finn who needs to change. It's me as well.'

' 'Night, George.'

'Where's Dad? Who's going to switch my brain off?'

'I can.'

He pushes my hand away from his head irritably. 'I want Mrs Jammie Dodger.'

'Your father's on call this weekend.'

'Are you and Dad fighting?'

'No.'

'Dad hates Clarky.'

'No. It's complicated, George, but I promise you there will be no more fights.'

I do an impersonation of Mrs Jammie Dodger. 'You can't do it,' he protests. 'It's Sunday tomorrow. Who's going to cook breakfast with me?'

'I'm sure Grandpa will help.'

'I WANT MRS JAMMIE DODGER!' He starts to cry, hitting his pillow hard. 'I want Dad. Why isn't he here?'

Downstairs, I ring Finn. 'He misses you. We all do,' I say, leaving a message on his voicemail.

I wake up early the following morning. I didn't sleep at all because I can't stop thinking about what Mum said to me. Sunlight streams through the bedroom window. The birds are singing. I can hear Harvey the parrot already squawking in his cage, and Rocky and Holly, Mum's rescue sheep dog, are barking for their breakfast. I can smell Dad's coffee and toast. He's an early riser. When Mum's not in the house he gets up at five. I pull back the curtains, lift Scarlett from her cot. Her eyes are closed; her little hands move slowly and gracefully in front of her as if she is trying to feel her way now she is in my arms. Her eyes flicker at the noise, shutting themselves even more tightly. It must be strange being cocooned in warm dark liquid for nine months, where all you can hear is a reassuring heartbeat, and then being exposed to an environment of noise and light where there's no liquid, just air.

She smells so perfect, the crown of her head soft and vulnerable. I can't believe this little person is mine.

I look out of the window and see George in the field with Mum. She's trying, in vain, to show him how to tack up Rowan. If we leave him to do it on his own, he hurls the saddle on to Rowan and takes off at a gallop, clinging on desperately. This is why Finn hates the idea of him jumping. 'It's an accident waiting to happen,' he says.

I watch Mum handing him the apples. They get on so well because they have Rowan in common. Mum gave him a grooming kit last Christmas with his name engraved on it. George isn't that hot at grooming Rowan, might do one side very well and then get bored and leave the other, but he treasures the present like a box of gold. Inside is a body brush, dandy brush, mane comb and hoof oil. Mum didn't let him have the hoof pick. It's the one thing he cleans and sorts out immaculately. Finn can't understand why he can tidy the box so well but not his bedroom.

After I've changed nappies, dressed and fed Scarlett, I join them outside with the pram. 'You look much better,' Mum says as I approach the fence and lean against it. I'm still in my maternity jeans and a bright red baggy jumper. I leave the pram in the shade of a tree. Tentatively I open the gate and walk up to them. I attempt to stroke Rowan but his nostrils flare and his ears prick back. The little shit looks like he wants to bite me, so I back off. I think of Finn. He would be laughing by now. It's funny the little things you miss about someone when they're not around.

George laughs instead. 'He doesn't like you, Mum,' he kindly points out.

'That's only because I don't feed him chocolates.'

Mum tells me horses respond to the tone of your voice and body language. 'They're intuitive,' she says. 'Rowan doesn't like you because he knows you don't like him.'

'Can I get on him now?' George is jumping up and down

on the spot, his long gangly legs in a pair of jodhpurs. He strokes Rowan impatiently, leans his head against his mane, kisses him and pats his coat. Rowan stands proudly as he digs one hoof into the ground. George lets go of his bridle and rushes over to me. 'Mum!' he wraps his arms around my back and clings on tightly. 'Can I jump now?'

I look at the small red-and-white jumps. 'OK, but Granny and I are going to watch.' He hugs me even more tightly. I kiss the top of his head. 'Love you! Now put on your hat.'

'No.'

'Yes!' I grab him affectionately. 'Or I'll put it on for you. There.' I tighten the strap underneath his chin. 'Be careful. No showing off. Just do one jump first and see how it goes.'

George squints. 'The jumps aren't very high.'

'They are,' Mum says as she joins me. 'I lowered them right down,' she murmurs. 'Thought it was better to put them up myself at a safe level.'

I smile. The jumps are so small Rowan barely needs to lift his legs off the ground.

Mum and I watch George mounting up and then trotting to the first jump. Rowan stops, thinks about it and then decides to attempt it. My son is still on the horse, but instead of holding the reins he is clutching the pony's mane. We clap our hands. 'Well done!' I call out. 'Take hold of the reins!'

'It'll be the Grand National next,' Mum calls out.

'Hi, Dad.'

'Morning, darling. Clarky is on the telephone,' he says somewhat tentatively. 'Oh, and you received a letter this morning.'

I take the envelope, redirected to Mum and Dad's address in Finn's handwriting. Even his writing in black ink makes me feel sad that he's not here. I put the letter in my pocket. 'Tell Clarky I'll call him back.'

'He says it's urgent.'

I look at Mum. 'You'd better go,' she tells me. 'Clear the air once and for all. I'll watch Scarlett.'

I walk into the house with Dad. 'Thanks,' I say, taking the phone.

'Josie?'

'Hi.' Clarky and I haven't spoken since the birth.

'Congratulations about the baby and . . .' His voice is unfamiliar to me. Nervous.

'You could have ruined everything,' I tell him. 'In fact, you might have done. Finn won't see me.'

'I wasn't thinking, that was the trouble. It was a terrible thing to do. It felt like my one last chance to make you see I was much more dependable than him. I wanted to hurt Finn, not you and certainly not Aggie.'

'Well, you did that.'

'I'm so sorry, J,' he mutters, sounding deeply ashamed.

'Clarky, we've been friends all our lives, supported each other through pretty much everything. If I'm honest I was jealous of you and Aggie, but us believing we were in love was based on all the wrong reasons. We've used each other as comfort blankets for too long.'

'I know. In a funny way that punch-up with Finn was what we needed. My nose is OK, by the way, thankfully not broken so it hasn't spoilt my pretty face.'

I nearly smile. 'I'm glad.'

'We should have had a scrap when we were at Cambridge. The thing is, I think Finn and I could have liked one another if it hadn't been for you.'

'Thanks!' But I know he's right.

'I'm sorry, J, I really am, for lying. Do you want me to talk to Finn?'

'No!' I respond too quickly. 'No, look, it's up to us from now on, we have to sort it out on our own.'

'Please forgive me.'

'It's OK. We've all made mistakes, especially me. Can you forgive me too?'

'What for?'

'For taking our friendship for granted for too long. You needed to tell me to stop bringing my problems to you all the time.'

'I liked it, that was half the trouble.'

'How's Aggie?'

'We're moving in together.'

'You're what?' My overwhelming emotion is relief that I haven't mucked things up for her. That out of the wreckage there comes something positive.

'I told her everything. She didn't speak to me for days, she swore even more than usual. I was a fucking this and a fucking that and she wasn't going to put any fucking money in the fucking tin.' He laughs helplessly. 'She told me I had made her feel second best, and I understand that was how it seemed.'

'I'm happy you've worked it out, but how did you?'

'I told her the truth. That I was so used to being in love with you, so busy chasing this ridiculous dream that you and I should be together against all the odds, I couldn't see what a fabulous person I had right in front of me. When she told me she didn't want anything more to do with me I felt like my heart had been crushed to pieces. If she'd taken me back without putting up a fight, though, I don't think I'd have realised it. But I don't want to lose her and . . .'

'What?'

'. . . we do have a future. Things can never go back to how they were, can they?'

He already knew the answer to that question. They never could and, more importantly, we couldn't let them.

After the telephone call I sit down at the table and just think, enjoying the rare quietness. Some time passes before finally I open the letter.

'I *didn't think you'd be on email there so I thought I'd write instead to say congratulations*,' Emma writes. '*You and Finn must be delighted. I hope you're both enjoying the late nights and lack of sleep again! Please send him my best love.*

Oh, I would, if he was here.

'*You won't believe this but Nat walked into the kitchen yesterday with the biggest smile on his face. "Guess how many boys I had in my car today?" he asked, followed by, "FIVE, MUM!"*' I can hear George running towards the house now, Mum close behind, shouting, 'Take your boots off before you go inside! GEORGE!' Quickly I finish reading the letter before the peace is shattered.

'*He only has a small clapped-out Ford Fiesta. Probably not at all safe, but all I could think of was how normal this felt! Eighteen years on and my son has friends, he's doing the things that other teenagers do. You should have seen him when he was on the phone to one of the other British Gas boys, Josie, talking about going to Alton Towers and booking into a fun hotel.*'

'Take your boots off! Do as Granny says,' I tell my son. Already he has left a couple of muddy footprints in the kitchen.

'But, Mum!'

'Now!'

He flings them off and runs past me, saying he's dying for the loo. 'Love you, Mum!' he shouts.

'Love you back,' I say. I decide to keep the letter. It gives me hope deep down that George is going to be OK too. We'll get through this.

I touch Finn's handwriting on the envelope; a few of the letters become smudged with my tears. The doorbell rings. Is it Finn? It could be. Each time there's a knock my heart lifts as I rush to the door. There's an Interflora van in our drive. I don't want more flowers. I want Finn! I'm handed a beautiful bouquet with a small yellow card. I only want flowers if they're from him.

I rip open the envelope. *'My boy misses you. Don't break each other's hearts. I miss you too. Fondest love, Granny.'*

We shouldn't be apart, Granny, I tell her, as if she were standing right in front of me. I'm going to do something. I have to show him how much I want him back. I'm going to make this work. I won't let you down, I promise her.

The car is crammed full with luggage, George's riding boots, Einstein the monkey, Lego and other rubbish, and then there is all the baby equipment, Scarlett in her new car seat and Rocky sitting on George's lap. Dad is behind the driver's wheel, tapping it impatiently.

I hug Mum. 'Thank you for everything.'

'Come and stay whenever you like. I'm always here for you.'

'I'm doing the right thing, aren't I?'

'You're following your heart.'

I wish she'd simply say yes.

I wave and wind down the window. ' 'Bye, Granny,' says George. ' 'Bye, Rowan. 'Bye, tree house.'

'Josie!' Mum shouts now. 'Stop!'

'Oh, what is it now?' Dad is weary. 'We're going to hit the rush hour. Have you left something behind?' Reluctantly he stops the car.

'What?' I call out.

'You are doing the right thing!'

I blow a happy kiss and lean back in my seat.

The thing is, I know I am too. He's not expecting me home, but all I want to do is see him. Make it up to him. Tell him that I'm never going to risk losing him again. I know he still loves me and we shall live happily ever after.

I am going to give Finn such a surprise.

40

Nervously, I unlock the front door. Now that I am finally here my earlier idea of a blissful reunion has completely deserted me. The house is dark and deathly quiet. It smells musty, of stale cigarettes. Dad starts unloading the car and putting our luggage at the foot of the stairs. 'Hello,' I call out. 'Finn?' He could be in the bedroom. The shower. But the house feels empty. I switch a light on. I feel a painful thud of disappointment. Finn isn't here.

'Where's Dad?' George asks loudly, running inside. 'Where is he?' he demands again as if I've hidden him in a cupboard.

'I'm sure he'll be back soon,' I say, trying hard not to show any fear. What if Finn is angry with me for just turning up like this? Should I have called? Maybe I'm the last person he wants to see. He said he'd need time. Is this too soon?

Despite George talking and singing all the way home and constantly asking, 'Are we nearly there?' Scarlett is fast asleep. I take her upstairs and put her into our bed-room. The shutters are closed. The bed is made; in fact it looks as if no one's been sleeping in it. Then I see a pillow and blanket on the floor, along with a glass of water and an empty sachet of headache tablets. It melts my heart. Oh, Finn. What have you been doing?

I walk back downstairs and Dad tells me he needs to get home. 'I don't want to drive in the dark,' really means, 'I don't want to interfere or see the fireworks when he comes home.'

'Yes, you go, Dad. Thanks so much for driving us.'

'You'll be all right,' he tells me, clutching my hand. 'Precious girl.'

I feel teary when Dad has gone, like a small child saying goodbye at the school gates. Being cocooned at home has helped me get through this stretch of time. But I can't hide away for ever. Finn has to see us.

George tells me he's hungry which is a great distraction. It's nearly eight o'clock and I realise we haven't eaten much at all today. I open the fridge, but there's nothing in it except for a few rubber cheese slices curling at the edges, some eggs, a couple of sprouting potatoes and some off milk. I make him a toasted cheese sandwich. Other than a couple of coffee mugs, a used cereal bowl and the most sad-looking baked bean tin with dry tomato sauce encrusted down one side and a plastic teaspoon in it, the kitchen is tidy. Finn hates baked beans. It's strange coming into the house after only a fortnight. Already it has a different smell, even a different feel. There's no mess due to the absence of George and Rocky. It hasn't been lived in. There's a vase of dead lilies that Finn hasn't bothered to throw out. How pathetic they look, drooping on to the table.

Then there are all the things that remind me of a once happy home like the passport pictures of Finn, George and me that are pinned to the fridge by a strawberry magnet. There's his familiar writing on the blackboard. An old message: 'I love you if you'll buy me some of that nice soda bread.'

Finn's record player sits in the corner of the room. Objects that once looked so familiar and now I hardly dare to touch them, frightened I'm an intruder.

'Is Dad here?' shouts George. He was exhausted and cross that I hadn't let him stay up. In the end we'd made a deal. If I gave him a mug of hot chocolate *and* a bourbon biscuit he would go upstairs. He opens his door and runs to the top of the stairs.

'No, I was on the phone, go back to sleep.' I'd just been talking to Christo who had said Finn could either be at the hospital or eating out because he hated coming back to an empty house. 'I'll let you know if I hear anything,' he'd assured me.

Where is he? I'm pacing up and down the room. The longer he makes me wait, the more agitated I become. I've fed

Scarlett and set up her cot and George is fast asleep, at last.
I call Mrs B. 'I didn't wake you, did I?'

'Josie, you're back!' she says happily. 'You and Finn have
sorted it all out. I knew you would. When Michael and
I . . .'

'Mrs B,' I interrupt, 'have you seen him at all in the last
week?'

'Not a word. I've been round but he's never at home! I
tried to give him a nice coronation chicken. Why?' She
eventually gets the gist. 'Does he know you're home?'

'No.'

'Oh,' she says thoughtfully, followed by a helpful, 'I hope
he's OK. I don't know where he could be.'

I hang up and look at my watch again, wanting it to lie,
tell me it's not this late after all. But it's nearly eleven
o'clock. Calm down. It's probably something completely
straightforward. If he's eaten out he has to be back soon,
they don't serve food now. But it's not like Finn to sit in a
pub all night. He could be at a club . . . I'm worried. What
if he's done something stupid? I open the curtains, desperate to see the reassuring lights of his car. All I want to hear
is his key in the lock. Hear him say, 'Hi, honey, I'm home,'
as he drops his briefcase on the floor and takes off his tie
and shoes. Why isn't he answering his mobile?

I sit down on the sofa and stare at the television. The
noise makes no sense. I shut my eyes, terrified he's been
involved in a car crash and it's too late to tell him I love

him. Should I be ringing Accident and Emergency to see if he's been admitted? Should I be sitting here doing nothing? What if he's in terrible trouble?

I feel a tug on my arm. 'George, back to bed,' I murmur. I wrap the blanket around me and rest my head against the pillow. I'm wearing Finn's old hooded top that I'd found tucked in the back of our wardrobe. It still smells of him.

He takes a strand of my hair and tucks it behind my ear. 'Who's been sleeping on *my* pillow and *my* blanket?' he says, as if he's one of the three bears scolding Goldilocks.

I open my eyes. 'Finn!' I fling my arms around him. 'I've been so worried. Where have you been?'

'Dorset.' He kneels down by the sofa.

'What?'

'I wanted to bring you home. The thing was, you weren't there.'

'I'm here.'

'I can see that,' he says with that smile that's about to happen. 'So I turned my car round and came back again, fast as I could, because I figured I've already lost enough time and I can't afford to lose anymore, not with my family. Not with you.'

I hug him again and this time I feel his arms wrap tightly around me. I tell him I shall never again run to Clarky when the going gets tough. I will never lie again. 'Except if

I've done something stupid like get another parking ticket,' I add.

'J, I'm sorry too. I've done a lot of thinking and know I haven't exactly been the model husband. I need to be more involved in George's life, not deny how difficult he can be. We have to face his problems head on, together, without me shouting my head off. But,' he says, 'most importantly, I don't want to let things slide between us, the way people drift apart without even realising and then find there's nothing left to salvage. This past fortnight, I've been miserable. I was so angry. I went over and over it again, imagining you and him together. Nothing but my own stupid pride got in the way of my seeing you and our baby and George. But then I got tired, J. So tired of dwelling on the past. I don't want to lose you and . . .'

'Finn, there's no chance of that.'

'I want to see Scarlett. I've got to see her.' Quickly he stands up and gives me his hand. I take it and lead him upstairs, into the quiet dark room. He picks her up and out of the cot. I can see he's crying as he holds her close, breathing in the smell of her skin. 'I'm such a proud stubborn idiot.'

I lean across to kiss him. 'Yes, but you're *my* proud stubborn idiot.'

41

'Hello, dear, Mrs Bourbon here. You've been gone ages and ages. Where've you been?'

'I took your mother away for the weekend,' Finn says. 'How was Mrs B?'

'She took me to the car-boot. I bought a pog set.'

'I'm not even going to ask what that is.'

'What have you been *doing* all this time?'

'Having fun with your mother. I need to spoil her more.' I smile widely. I've just put Scarlett to bed and am about to join them but decide it's more fun listening outside the door.

'What did you eat?' George asks.

'Pepperoni and cheese pizza. We went dancing.'

'Where?'

'In Cambridge.'

'Why?'

'Because that's where we first met. That's where we fell in love. We went to my old club.'

'Can I go?'

'I'll take you when you're old enough.'

'What's that in your hand, Dad?'

'A matchbox.'

'Why?'

He pushes it open. 'I love you,' I had written inside, just as Finn had done after we spent our first night together.

'I love you,' reads out George.

'That's right. I love you, Mrs Bourbon. Now, go to sleep. It's late. I didn't expect you still to be awake.'

'But no one's turned my brain off.'

Finn presses the imaginary button.

' 'Night, Mrs Jammie D.'

' 'Night, Mrs Bourbon.'

DISCOVER ALICE PETERSON

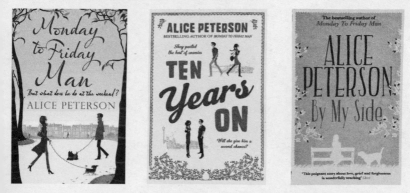

'This poignant story about love, grief and forgiveness is wonderfully touching.' *Closer* magazine on *By My Side*

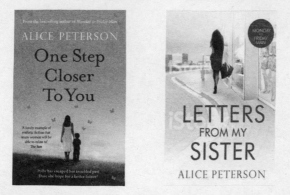

'A beautiful, uplifting, unconventional love story'
Paige Toon on *One Step Closer to You*